THE CHALK GIRL

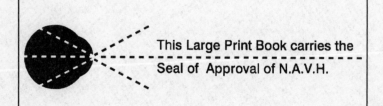

THE CHALK GIRL

CAROL O'CONNELL

THORNDIKE PRESS
A part of Gale, Cengage Learning

GALE
CENGAGE Learning

Detroit • New York • San Francisco • New Haven, Conn • Waterville, Maine • London

GALE
CENGAGE Learning·

LIBRARY OF CONGRESS CATALOGING-IN-PUBLICATION DATA

O'Connell, Carol, 1947–
  The chalk girl / by Carol O'Connell.
    pages ; cm. — (Thorndike Press large print core)
  ISBN 13: 978-1-4104-4594-0 (hardcover)
  ISBN 10: 1-4104-4594-1 (hardcover)
    1. Mallory, Kathleen (Fictitious character)—Fiction. 2. Police—New York (State)—New York—Fiction. 3. Policewomen—Fiction. 4. Murder—Investigation—Fiction. 5. New York (N.Y.)—Fiction. 6. Large type books. I. Title.
PS3565.C497C47 2012b
813'.54—dc23   2011050856

Published in 2012 by arrangement with G. P. Putnam's Sons, a member of Penguin Group (USA) Inc.

Printed in the United States of America
1 2 3 4 5 6 7 16 15 14 13 12

This book is dedicated to my cousin John, a vet from the Vietnam era, a laid-back soul with scuffed boots, a '63 Chevy and a dry sense of humor. He liked ballgames and cigarettes. A working man who rolled his own, he claimed no ambitions beyond the next Saturday night.

And he was a man of mystery.

My best memory of him is a warm summer day, sailing down the coast of Massachusetts in an old wooden boat full of cousins and cold beer. We dropped anchor in a harbor, where we were surrounded by boats a bit larger, but then a luxury craft pulled up alongside. It was *huge.* A crowd of well-dressed, smiling people — so many teeth and so white — leaned over the rail to wave at us, and that was confusing. We do not come down from yachting people, and we didn't know any of *them.* So . . . what the —

Then John, the most lax dresser among us, stood up in torn jeans and a not-quite-white tee. Cheers went up; they were waving at *him.* He crushed his beer can in one hand, waved back and then waved them the hell away. Apparently, John *knew* yachting people; he just didn't have much use for them. And the rest of us never got the backstory on that day. That was John Herland, man of mystery, and when he died, I'm sure he was missed by yachtsmen everywhere, but deeply missed by me.

ONE

On the day I was born, I ran screaming from the womb. That's what my father tells me when I bring home a story about the Driscol School.

— ERNEST NADLER

The first outcry of the morning was lost in a Manhattan mix of distant sirens, barking dogs and loud music from a car rolling by outside the park. The midsummer sky was the deep blue of tourist postcards.

No clouds. No portents of fear.

A parade of small children entered the meadow. They were led by a white-haired woman with a floppy straw hat and a purple dress that revealed blue-veined calves as she crossed the grass, moving slowly with the aid of a cane. Her entourage of small day campers showed great restraint in keeping pace with her. They wanted to run wild, hollering and cartwheeling through Central

7

Park, all but the one who waddled with an awkward gait of legs pressed close together — the early warning sign of a bladder about to explode.

Mrs. Lanyard read aloud from a guidebook. "The flock of grazing sheep was removed from Sheep Meadow in 1934." This was followed by a children's chorus of disappointed groans and one shy lament, "I have to pee."

"Of course you do." There was always one. It never failed. The sardonic Mrs. Lanyard raised one hand to shade her eyes as she gazed across the open expanse of fifteen acres spotted with people, their bikes and beach towels, baby strollers and flying Frisbees. She was looking for her assistant, who had gone off to scout the territory ahead for a public toilet. "Soon," she said to the child in distress, knowing all the while that a toilet would not be found in time. No field trip was complete without the stench of urine on the bus ride home.

After corralling her young charges into a tight cluster, she counted noses for the third time that morning. No children had been lost — but there was one too many. She spied an unfamiliar mop of curly red hair at the back of the ranks. That little girl was definitely not enrolled in the Lanyard Day

Camp for Gifted Children — not that Mrs. Lanyard regarded any of these brats as anything but ordinary. However, their parents had paid a goodly sum for a prestigious line on a six-year-old's résumé, and the extra child was poaching.

What an odd little face — both beautiful and comical, skin white as cream for the most part and otherwise dirty. The little girl's grin was uncommonly wide, and there was an exaggerated expanse between the upturned nose and full lips. Her chin came to a sharp point to complete the very picture of an elf. Elfin or human, she did not belong here.

"Little girl, what's your name." This was not phrased as a question, but as a demand.

"Coco," she said, "like hot chocolate."

How absurd. That would hardly fit a red-haired child, blue-eyed and so fair of face. "Where did you —" Mrs. Lanyard paused for a short scream when a rat ran close to the toes of her shoes. Impossible. *Inconceivable.* There was no mention of rats in her field guide — only birds and squirrels and banished sheep. She resolved to write the publishers immediately, and her criticism would be severe.

"Urban rats are nocturnal creatures," said Coco, the faux camper, as if reciting from a field guide of her own. "They rarely venture out in daylight."

Well, this was not the typical vocabulary of a child her age. The little poser might be the only gifted one in the lot. "So what about *that* rat?" Mrs. Lanyard pointed to the rodent slithering across the meadow. "I suppose he's *retarded?*"

"He's a Norway rat," said Coco. "They're also called brown rats, and they're brilliant. They won the rat wars a hundred years ago . . . when they *ate* all the black rats." This bit of trivia was punctuated by "ooohs" from the other children. Encouraged, the little girl went on. "They used to be boat rats. Now they live mostly on the ground. But some of them live in the sky, and sometimes it *rains* rats."

In perfect unison, the day campers looked skyward, but no rodents were coming from that quarter. However, another rat was running toward them. Twenty-three pairs of eyes rounded with surprise. And one little boy wet his pants — finally. It never failed.

Oh, and there — another rat — and *another* one. Vile creatures.

In a wide swathe across the far side of the meadow, sun worshippers abandoned their towels to lope away, and screams could be heard at that distance where people and their vocals were only ant size. Dogs barked, and parents on the run madly piloted baby strollers in all directions.

Mrs. Lanyard motioned for the children to gather around her. The little redheaded rat maven stepped out from behind the others and came forward, her thin arms outreaching, silently begging for hugs and comfort.

Oh, *Lord,* that child was filthy.

The girl's formerly white T-shirt was a mess of dirt smudges, grass-colored smears and food stains, some red as blood. And, of course, as was the case with the unwashed, the dreaded head-lice infestation was to be expected. "Stop!" Mrs. Lanyard stepped back and put up both hands to ward off the advance of this urchin.

The child's large blue eyes had a wounded look. Her arms slowly lowered to her sides. Coco turned to the other children, who took their cue from the old woman and also shrank away from her. The little girl's smile collapsed, and her hands folded over her stomach, as if this shunning had come with the pain of a punch.

A boy screamed, "Look! Look!" He jabbed the air with his pointing finger. "More rats!"

Oh, dear God, there were dozens of them.

Mrs. Lanyard raised her cane, prepared to

defend the little ones against this moving brown carpet of quivering, twitchy fur that was headed their way. However, the children — all wonderfully equipped to survive — promptly abandoned the old lady and ran off. The odd child followed after them, her hands fluttering like small white wings in a panic.

It was an inconvenient moment to suffer a massive stroke, but fortunately, mercifully, it would prove fatal for Mrs. Lanyard.

The rats were *so* close.

She sank to her knees. The wind took her straw hat to sail it far and wide. Now her pink scalp could be seen through thinning white strands of hair.

The rats were squealing, onrushing, almost here.

Her eyes rolled back, and there was no more fear, though vermin were all around her, dividing into columns to skirt the obstacle of her kneeling body, only wanting to get past her. Stone dead, she pitched forward to lay her head upon the grass, cutting her face on a jagged shard of glass from a broken bottle. There was just a trickle of blood from this wound, for her heart had ceased to beat and pump it.

Twitchy soldiers of the rat army, those closest to her, paused to look — to sniff —

to taste.

Mrs. Ortega could hear the sound of children's high-pitched squeals as she rolled her wire cart toward the park playground. Her short frame was deceptively thin, for she was strong — a side effect of hard labor. Her heritage was advertised by jet-black hair from the Latin side and her mother's Irish cream complexion. On a normal day during her travels down this path, she was sometimes accosted by women who were attracted by her cart of cleaning supplies. These strangers always approached with a needy, desperate look about them — a good cleaning lady was hard to find. And she would wave them off, saying, "Don't even ask. I'm booked solid."

Today, in a sharp departure from this routine, the cleaning lady was body-slammed by a stranger on the run, a young woman looking over her shoulder instead of watching where she was going.

A New Yorker, born and bred, Mrs. Ortega had a store of curses for moments like this, choice words that would chill the hearts of a motorcycle gang. She raised one fist in prelude, and then she saw fear in the other woman's eyes when pausing to scream a warning — "Rats!" — before running on.

Obviously an out-of-towner.

The cleaning lady's indignation subsided, and she lowered her fist. She gave handicap points to lame tourists; anyone frightened by the sight of a rat was surely feeble. New York City was the rat capital of the world. Her own neighborhood had once boasted more vermin than all of Manhattan, but her customer base, the Upper West Side, was becoming a major competitor for bragging rights.

Mrs. Ortega entered a noisy playground enclosed in the concentric circles of a long, round bench, a fence and an outer ring of tall trees. She shut the iron gate behind her and took her customary seat near the drinking fountain. Nodding to nannies and some of the children she knew by name, the cleaning lady settled a delicatessen bag on her lap. She planned to eat a leisurely morning snack before taking the subway to SoHo. Years ago, one of her customers had moved downtown, and that should have been the end of him, but Charles Butler had made it worth her while to spend an extra train fare. She looked down at her wristwatch.

Lots of time.

There was time enough to notice a man standing just outside the fence, and the cleaning lady recognized his kind. She had

14

a cop acquaintance, whose name for men like this was Short Eyes. The man was fixated on the jungle gym, a brightly colored structure with stairs full of climbing children and crossbeams for those who liked to dangle. And some whizzed down a metal slide, shrill, screaming happy kids — witless and fearless. But a few had good instincts, and they would survive to have progeny; native New Yorkers understood the darkest things about Darwinism. Short Eyes caught the attention of a small girl. He smiled — *so* creepy — and the child quickly turned away, her nose scrunched up, as if the sight of him could be a bad smell.

All the signs were there for even a child to see, but the children's guardians were blind, chatting into cell phones or gossiping with one another. There were no moms in the playground today, only the hired help. Moms were good at spotting predators. Mrs. Ortega was better. Her pervert radar was reinforced when Short Eyes used his camera phone to covertly take pictures of the youngsters.

Not wanting to alarm the nannies — brainless teenagers — the cleaning lady casually leaned forward, and one hand drifted toward the baseball bat nestled in her wire cart. This was an inheritance from

15

her father, a Yankees fan till the day he died. She carried it everywhere, but not for sentimental reasons. It made a fine weapon. She watched the man — who watched the children.

And then she was distracted by a dirty little face framed in curly red hair. The child peeked out from behind a tree that was rooted in the playground's cement floor. Her smile was too wide, too generous for any New Yorker's spawn. This little girl was a strange one, all right — and yet familiar.

The cleaning lady sucked in a breath. Though the child had no wings, she was otherwise the living incarnation of a statuette on the mantelpiece at home. Mrs. Ortega had a collection of fairy figurines, the legacy of a mother only one generation out of Ireland, a woman who knew the light and the dark side of the little folk: they sang and danced, smiling always, and they were mischief makers all. No good could come of seeing fairies in the flesh.

In the common-sense compartment of her brain, she knew this little girl was all too human and vulnerable, but the resemblance to the magical was uncanny and unsettling. Mrs. Ortega turned her head to catch Short Eyes staring at this same child as he prowled along the fence. The little redhead was a

16

likely victim, for she seemed to belong to no one. Easy prey. He was slowly rounding the perimeter, moving closer to the gate, stealthy, grinning; this was the way a cockroach would smile if it only could.

Mrs. Ortega's right hand wound around the handle of her baseball bat as the little girl approached one of the nannies, a fool teenager named Nancy, who suddenly took fright. And that was interesting because Nancy was built like a linebacker. The small child closed in on the older girl, arms outstretched, asking for a hug.

From a stranger? Well, *that* was scary.

The teenager left the bench at a dead run, so eager was Nancy to escape the threat of this tiny girl. The nanny collected her charges, twin boys, bundled them through the gate and swiftly walked them toward the park exit to West 68th Street. Thus abandoned, the fairy child's head bowed, and her arms folded to hug herself.

What was that on the kid's T-shirt? Oh, *damn.*

Mrs. Ortega had an eye for stains and an expertise. A cop might be fooled by ketchup, but not her. This was blood.

The child suddenly smiled, then danced on tiptoe to the edge of the playground, where the pervert was waiting by the gate

— the *open* gate. He was smiling, arms held out to receive her, and she ran to him, so happy, so anxious to give and get love.

Mrs. Ortega pulled the baseball bat from her cart.

Three men in uniform stood in the shade of an ancient oak tree and watched the rats swarm over the bloody mound that was the late Mrs. Lanyard.

One man broke ranks and walked toward the feeding frenzy in the meadow.

"No, you don't." Officer Maccaro, a twenty-year veteran of the police force, caught his young partner by the arm and restrained him. "Trust me, kid, she's dead — *really* dead." Ah, rookies — they were like toddlers. It wasn't safe to let them out of your sight for a minute. "Animal Control is on the way. We'll just wait." He turned to the other young man, who wore the uniform of the U.S. Forestry Service. "Jimmy, I've never seen so many rats in broad daylight."

"Well, Mac, the rodent population is zooming." But for the Midwest accent, the park ranger might be taken for a native city dweller — so blasé about vermin lunching on an old lady. "The poison bait wasn't working anymore. I think the rats acquired a taste for it. So the parks commissioner made a damn contest out of rodent control. And along comes the first contestant, this idiot, Dizzy Hollaren. He runs a small mom-and-pop outfit, mostly termites and roaches. So Dizzy's got a communal nest pinned down in that building over there." The ranger pointed to a brick structure at the edge of the meadow. "Before he plugs up the rat hole, he throws in a fumigation bomb. Works for roaches, right?"

Could this man be more sarcastic? Officer Maccaro thought not. "I'm guessing the rats had a back door?"

The ranger nodded. "They always do — and they swarmed." He turned back to the sight of rodents eating Mrs. Lanyard. "Normally, you'd never see a thing like that. Rats usually scatter when they spot people. I think these critters are jazzed on Dizzy's chemicals." He shrugged. "Sorry, guys. There won't be much left of that corpse."

"That's okay," said the younger policeman. "We got the victim's name from some little kids."

"Yeah," said Officer Maccaro. "Only twenty more kids to round up." He turned to the far side of Sheep Meadow, where police officers and park workers formed a line to comb the outlying parkland for runaway day campers from the neighboring state of New Jersey.

The ranger pointed skyward. Overhead, a large bird of prey circled the meadow. "Keep your eyes on the hawk. That bird's the reason why you *never* see rats on open ground like this."

Wings spread, the hawk streaked toward the earth. Only inches from the ground, talons extended, it swooped over the feeding frenzy and carried off a wriggling rat that cried out in a human way. The rest of the vermin continued their meal, unperturbed.

The park ranger nodded sagely. "They're definitely stoned." His head tilted back once more, and this time he was looking up into the thick leaves of the stately oak. "I hope none of the kids are hiding in the trees."

Officer Maccaro looked up to see a rat running along the lowest bough. "Oh, Christ, when did they learn to do *that?*"

Mrs. Ortega took some satisfaction in the sound of a bone breaking. The pervert sank to the ground and lay there screaming. She rested her baseball bat on one shoulder and looked around in all directions.

Where was that strange little girl?

There was no one to ask. The playground was empty now.

Two police officers were running toward her, and she waved to them with her free hand, yelling, "You gotta find a little girl!"

The youngest cop was the first to enter by the iron gate. He looked down at the man on the ground, who was curled up in a fetal position, not screaming anymore but crying softly. The officer turned on the cleaning lady. "*You* did this?"

Stupid question. Was she not holding a bloody baseball bat?

Mrs. Ortega nudged the weeping pervert with her foot. "Never mind this piece of garbage. He'll live. You gotta find the kid real fast. She's a magnet for creeps like him. You'll know her when you see her. She's got red hair, and she looks just like a little fairy."

"Oh, yeah," said an older policeman, smiling as he passed through the gate. "I think I saw her flying over the park."

"Don't humor me."

"Okay." The officer drew his gun and leveled it at her head. "Lady, drop that bat! *Now!*"

"I'm serious," said Mrs. Ortega.

"Yeah, I can see that." The man was staring at the bloody end of the bat.

Well, this was new.

The detective stood before a red prefabricated building, temporary housing for the Central Park Precinct. Next door, the older quarters, badly in need of renovation, were partially hidden by tarps, and the rooftops were crawling with workmen.

Damn town was always falling down.

He was far from his own station house down in SoHo, this man in a rumpled suit stained with week-old mustard, but Detective Sergeant Riker never had to show his badge. Uniformed cops stood in a cluster around the entrance, and then they parted in a wave, recognizing his rank by the air of entitlement that came with carrying a gun and a gold shield. Civilians only saw him as a middle-aged man with bad posture, an amiable, laid-back smile and hooded eyes that said to everyone he met, *I know you're lying, but I just don't care.*

Mrs. Ortega had used her telephone privilege to call in a favor. He anticipated spending his lunch hour to plead her case with the man in charge of this cop house, but after a few minutes' conversation, the commander handed him the key to the lockup, allowing Riker the honor of uncaging the Upper West Side's most dangerous cleaning lady.

Though the little woman scowled at him through the bars, the detective grinned as he worked the key in the lock. "I'm impressed." He opened the door and made a deep bow from the waist. "They tell me you broke the guy's right arm and three ribs."

Riker escorted her downstairs, where she was reunited with her wire cart. Mrs. Ortega carefully inspected her property, maybe suspecting the police of stealing her cleaning rags or the stiff brushes she favored for bathroom grout. "Where's my bat?"

"Don't push your luck," said Riker. "I'll get it back for you, okay? But not today."

"Took you long enough to bail me out."

"No bail," he said. "The charges were dropped. I'd like to take credit for that, but the call came from the mayor's office. He sent his limo to pick you up."

"What about the little girl? She's still out there."

"There's fifty cops in the park right now. They're hunting down kids from a New Jersey day camp. You told them the girl didn't belong in that playground, right? So she's probably one of the Jersey kids."

"No, that girl hasn't had a bath in days. She's lost or homeless. And I *told* them that!"

"If the park cops don't find her, I will. Okay?" And now that the cleaning lady seemed somewhat mollified, he asked,

"Don't you wanna know *why* the mayor sent his limo?"

She waved one hand in a shoo-fly way to tell him that she did not care.

Playing the gentleman, he held the door open as she steered her cart outside and into the smell of dust and the sounds of jackhammers and traffic along the busy road bisecting the park. He guided her to a wide strip of pavement where VIPs illegally parked. Beside the waiting limousine stood the mayor's personal chauffer, a man in a better suit than any cop could afford, and he was staring at his approaching passenger with disbelief. A nod from Riker confirmed that this little woman was indeed the mayor's new best buddy. "Hey, pal, open the trunk. The cart goes where she goes."

While the chauffer loaded her cleaning supplies, Mrs. Ortega settled into the backseat, taking everything in stride, as if this luxury ride might be routine in the average day of a cleaning lady. When the driver took his place behind the wheel and started the engine, she leaned forward and called out to him across the expanse of the stretch limousine. "Drop me off in Brooklyn!"

"City Hall!" yelled Riker, countermanding her order. And now he spoke to the cleaning lady in his let's-make-a-deal tone.

"The mayor just wants to shake your hand. Maybe you pose for a few pictures, talk to some reporters."

"Yeah, yeah." She turned her face to the passenger window, clearly bored by this idea.

"Listen," said Riker, "this is *big.* That bastard you busted up? He's a bail jumper from Florida. While he's been on the loose, the Miami cops found bodies under the floorboards of his house." And still the detective felt that he did not have her full attention. "Hey, you bagged a kid-killer. Good job."

"Riker, they gotta find that little girl. There's something wrong with her. Or maybe nobody raised her right. She just walks right up to strangers. And you know that creep wasn't the only pervert in the park. Where's *Mallory?* Why didn't she come?"

"Lieutenant Coffey nailed her little hands to a desk." For the duration of a probation period, his young partner was not allowed to leave the SoHo precinct during shift hours, not even to forage for food north of Houston, the demarcation line.

The tired child stood in a copse of sheltering trees and watched the frenzy in the meadow. A man in coveralls plugged one end of a thick hose into a hole in the ground and then entered the meadow, the heavy coil unrolling behind him. The nozzle end was pointed at the rats when he waved to another man. And now a strong blast of water from the hose scattered the vermin. Policemen in dark blue uniforms moved toward the bloody mess on the grass, and they knelt down beside it as more people ran toward them, bearing a stretcher.

Traveling in the wide circle of a lost child, Coco had come back to this place by an accident of wandering. She wandered on.

After minutes or hours — the concept of time eluded her — she came upon the lake again, though not by intention, for she had only the sketchiest idea of geography. She stood by a railing and peered through the thick foliage to see a familiar fat orange ribbon of fencing strung around the water's edge. Continuing on her aimless way, she kept close to a low stone wall that led her to another landmark. There were many drinking fountains in the park, and they all looked alike, but Coco recognized this one by the dead bird in the basin. The tiny brown carcass had attracted flies; their buzzing was loud and ugly. Hands pressed against her ears — *stop it stop it stop it* —

she left the pavement and ran down a path into the woods, her thin arms spread wide, aeroplaning, feet flying. Farther down the path, another marker for the place of red rain was found by chance born of panic.

Don't cry don't cry don't cry.

Coco slowed her steps to catch her breath. She walked over a trampled section of wire fence and into thick brush. Low branches reached out to make scratchy noises on her blue-jeaned legs. She stood on the thick root of a tree and hugged the rough bark of the trunk. Looking for love and comfort, she stared up into the dense leaves and called the tree by name.

The tree was silent. The child melted down to the ground and curled up in a ball.

Two

They're not monster size, but adults are afraid of them. Not Dad, of course. My father doesn't believe in monsters. And he doesn't believe in me.

— ERNEST NADLER

The detective closed the door to the lieutenant's private office, perhaps sensing that his boss's voice was about to rise a few octaves — a good instinct.

"Let Mallory out of her cage? Are you *nuts?*" The commander of Special Crimes Unit raked one hand through his light brown hair. A few years shy of forty, Lieutenant Coffey had a bald spot at the back of his head. It was his only outstanding feature and a reminder of what stress could do to a man. "It's not like it's the first time she's done this."

"And she's not the first cop to walk off the job with no goodbye," said Detective

Sergeant Riker.

However, this man's partner was the only one ever to fight her way back from desk duty, that graveyard of damaged cops.

But that was *last* time.

"This time is *different!*" Whoa. *Deep* breath. In a lower voice that would not slip under the doorsill, Jack Coffey said, "She was gone for three months, and I still don't know why."

Riker shrugged this off. "Since when does a cop have to explain lost time?"

Lost time? For most detectives that meant taking a walk around the block to clear their heads when the job got too crazy. But Mallory had taken a drive around the lower forty-eight states of the country, an area of six million square miles — not *quite* the same thing.

"The department shrink won't sign off on active duty." Lieutenant Coffey retrieved a psychologist's report from his wastebasket and handed it to Riker. "Cut to the top of page three — where Dr. Kane says she's dangerously unstable. I'll tell you why that got my attention. Your partner is so *good* at beating psych tests."

"And I'm sure she aced this one." Riker tossed the report on the desk. "Dr. Kane's afraid of women — especially women with

29

guns. That quack probably wets his pants every time he sees her."

"You knew what was in her psych report before I did. She *told* you, right?" Jack Coffey held up one hand to signal that a bullshit denial was unnecessary. Mallory could pick the locks to any data bank, and those computer skills had been sorely missed. In her absence, his detectives had been reduced to begging for warrants.

Closed venetian blinds covered a window that spanned one upper wall of his private office. The lieutenant lifted a long metal slat for a covert view of the squad room and his youngest gold shield. He was not the only one watching her. Other cops were stealing glances. Were they wondering if they could work with her again? These days, she could jack up the anxiety of any room just by walking in the door, and that had to stop.

Going by mere appearance, she was unchanged, still wearing silk T-shirts and custom-made blazers. Even her blue jeans were tailored, and her running shoes cost more than his car payment. Mallory would *wear* money if she could, flaunting the idea that she *might* be on the take, though he suspected her of being semi-honest. Her blond curls were styled the same old way, framing a porcelain mask with a cat's high *looked* like a fairy." She reached into a deep pocket of her dress and pulled out a figurine. "Like this one." The small ceramic creature had a wide smile, curly red hair and the wings of a giant housefly. "The mayor's limo driver took me home so I could get it for you." She walked into the office and set her fairy down on the corner of his desk. "Take a picture. It looks exactly like that little girl."

"So the kid had wings?" Coffey turned to his detective. "Riker, you left that out of your report. And what's this crap about the mayor's limousine?"

"No wings," said the cleaning lady. "She's just a little girl, and she's lost. Her T-shirt had blood on it. Was *that* in Riker's report?"

"Blood?" The lieutenant smiled. "Maybe a little backsplatter from your trusty baseball bat?"

"No!" Mrs. Ortega held her breath for a count of ten. Then she dropped her scowl and the New York bravado; this matter was that important to her. The little woman's tone was almost placating when she said, "There was blood on that kid *before* I creamed the pervert."

"Then she's probably one of the Jersey kids," said Coffey. "While you were in lockup, did the park cops tell you about the rat attack in Sheep Meadow?"

"The rats were on the ground. The blood was on the shoulders of her T-shirt — nowhere else." Mrs. Ortega folded her arms. "Good try, though."

The telephone rang, and Riker leaned forward to pick up the receiver, as if expecting a personal call on his lieutenant's private line. "Yeah? . . . Oh, *yeah.*" The detective listened for a moment and then held out the phone. "Boss, it's the mayor. He wants to talk to you."

A rat fell to earth, squealing all the way down, and landed with a thump at Coco's feet. She had seen this miracle before. The lifeless creature lay with its pale yellow underbelly exposed, and the shiny eyes stared at the sky from whence it came. Red droplets fell down to disappear in the dirt at the base of the tree. The rat twitched, and Coco felt icy. Fluttery.

She could hear her heart beating.

The rodent's body convulsed. Magically reanimated, it scrambled away in the underbrush, snapping twigs and making small mechanical squeaks and peeps. In a child's game of statue, she stood still as death, and her heart — *da dum, da dum, da dum* — was louder now and faster.

■ ■ ■ ■

Lieutenant Coffey settled into the chair behind his desk. He had concluded his telephone call from City Hall, and now he gave the cleaning lady his best political smile. "The mayor loves you, Mrs. Ortega."

The city's top politician was indeed her biggest fan, so happy that a civilian — not a cop — had broken the pedophile's bones in full view of a dozen witnesses, most of them under the age of six. The mayor also suffered from the delusion that Mrs. Ortega's heroism might balance out the bad press of rats eating a park visitor.

What a fool.

"The mayor tells me his limo driver was supposed to take you to City Hall — not Brooklyn. You're overdue for a photo op and a press conference."

"I *told* you," she said, "I had to go home and get my fairy."

"Of course, and thank you for that." Jack Coffey stared at the winged figurine perched on the corner of his desk, and he picked his next words with care, electing not to tell her that the missing pixie would have to murder three or more people before Special Crimes took an interest. With great diplomacy, he splayed his hands, a New Yorker's gesture to show that he held no animosity and no weapons. "The limousine is downstairs waiting for you . . . and the mayor's waiting . . . and the television cameras."

"No way," said Mrs. Ortega. "I'm not leaving here till you —"

"I'll tell the park precinct there's still one kid missing." Coffey picked up the figurine. "And I'll send them a picture of this thing, okay?"

"*Sure* you will." The little woman sat well back in her chair to let him know that she planned to stay awhile. *Screw the mayor.*

The lieutenant had only turned his head for a moment, and Detective Mallory appeared beside him, as if she had simply materialized from some other planet. Coffey knew that she did this trick to stop his heart, and he was about to point the way back to her desk when she smiled — never a good sign.

"I wonder," said Mallory, in the offhand manner of opining on the time of day, "how *bad* does the mayor want to see Mrs. Ortega?"

Jack Coffey could only stare at her, fascinated, though he knew what would happen next. The game was blackmail. The young detective wanted out of her cage. And she cheekbones. So pretty. So spooky. And what did that damn haircut cost?

And why didn't she fight back?

As a condition of reinstatement, he had humiliated Mallory by making her hand-maiden to the squad. For the past month of probation, she had done all their grunt work without complaint, filling out reports and filing them, making phone calls and track-ing down leads for other detectives, tethered all the while to a desktop computer. She daily took this punishment with no sign of reproach, not so much as the arch of an eyebrow.

So how did she plan to get even with him?

And when might that happen?

The lieutenant watched her sort paper-work — busywork — and he knew those neat stacks would line up precisely one inch from the edge of her desk. Her other name was Mallory the Machine, and this worked well with the unnatural color of her eyes — electric green. Sorting done, she just sat there. So still. So quiet. He could not shake the idea that she was spring-loaded.

Jack Coffey was a man in a perpetual state of waiting.

She turned his way to catch him staring at her like a common peeper.

The metal slat snapped shut as he backed

away from the window. "I don't make the rules." He turned around to face Mallory's partner. "No fieldwork till she gets a pass from a shrink."

"Got it covered." Detective Riker reached into his pocket and pulled out a twice-folded wad of papers. "Charles Butler signed off on her. She's officially sane."

As if that could make it so, simply because Butler had more Ph.D.s than God did. "Does Charles know why she walked off the job?"

"That might be in here somewhere." Riker unfolded the new psych report and scanned it — as if its contents might be a mystery to him.

Right.

Jack Coffey snatched the papers but never even glanced at them. He knew everything would be in order, and this new psych evaluation would trump Dr. Kane's bad review. Mallory's personal psychologist had better credentials than any department shrink, but the poor hapless bastard had one unfortunate weakness: Kathy Mallory. If she were barking at the moon, Charles Butler would just assume that she was having an off day. "Not good enough, Riker. She can't just waltz back in here like nothing happened."

Foolish words. He wished he could call them back — for that was exactly what she had done: Four weeks ago, Mallory had appeared in the squad room, hovering by the staircase door like a visiting wraith. And then, when all eyes were on her, she had taken up residence at her old desk by the window, a coveted spot that no one had encroached upon while she was away. During those months of lost time, other detectives had avoided going near her desk, as if it might be haunted, and some had even mentioned that the air was always colder there. The squad room had gone deadly quiet on that morning of her return; fifteen men with guns had sat helpless as hostages waiting for a bomb to go off. Riker, whose desk faced hers, had been the first to speak, saying, "The coffee sucks since you've been gone." Only Mallory had ever thought to wash out the pot.

Today, sanguine as ever, Riker said to his boss, "You want her to quit?"

"For now, she stays on desk duty." The lieutenant lifted one slat of the blinds and resumed his vigil on the squad room. Mrs. Ortega had arrived. He watched the cleaning lady pull up a chair close to Mallory's and sit down for a visit. Well, that was normal enough. The two of them shared a

33

mania for cleaning solvents. And now he glanced at the detective's neat desk. All her work was done. How many hours had he devoted to dreaming up new things for her to do? He had stopped short of handing Mallory a broom and dustpan. She might have liked that.

Riker flopped down in a chair. In the only concession this man ever made to his boss's rank, he had not lit the cigarette that dangled from his mouth. The dejected detective stared at the television set in the corner of the office and watched silent news clips of rats and running people. "Why not send Mallory to Central Park for the day? That's harmless enough. Worst-case scenario — she rounds up a missing kid."

Jack Coffey's smile said it all: *Not a shot in hell.* "I just got off the phone with the park cops. All the kids from the day camp are accounted for."

"And the one Mrs. Ortega reported?"

"No, not *that* one." Charles Butler's cleaning lady had filed today's only missing-person report on a damn pixie. "I figure Mrs. Ortega was going for a psycho defense after she beat the crap out of the pervert."

"I *heard* that!" The cleaning lady stood in the open doorway, her jaw jutting out, defiant and up for a fight. "I only said the kid

34

looked like a fairy." She reached into a deep pocket of her dress and pulled out a figurine. "Like this one." The small ceramic creature had a wide smile, curly red hair and the wings of a giant housefly. "The mayor's limo driver took me home so I could get it for you." She walked into the office and set her fairy down on the corner of his desk. "Take a picture. It looks exactly like that little girl."

"So the kid had wings?" Coffey turned to his detective. "Riker, you left that out of your report. And what's this crap about the mayor's limousine?"

"No wings," said the cleaning lady. "She's just a little girl, and she's lost. Her T-shirt had blood on it. Was *that* in Riker's report?"

"Blood?" The lieutenant smiled. "Maybe a little backsplatter from your trusty baseball bat?"

"No!" Mrs. Ortega held her breath for a count of ten. Then she dropped her scowl and the New York bravado; this matter was that important to her. The little woman's tone was almost placating when she said, "There was blood on that kid *before* I creamed the pervert."

"Then she's probably one of the Jersey kids," said Coffey. "While you were in lockup, did the park cops tell you about the rat attack in Sheep Meadow?"

"The rats were on the ground. The blood was on the shoulders of her T-shirt — nowhere else." Mrs. Ortega folded her arms. "Good try, though."

The telephone rang, and Riker leaned forward to pick up the receiver, as if expecting a personal call on his lieutenant's private line. "Yeah? . . . Oh, *yeah*." The detective listened for a moment and then held out the phone. "Boss, it's the mayor. He wants to talk to you."

A rat fell to earth, squealing all the way down, and landed with a thump at Coco's feet. She had seen this miracle before. The lifeless creature lay with its pale yellow underbelly exposed, and the shiny eyes stared at the sky from whence it came. Red droplets fell down to disappear in the dirt at the base of the tree. The rat twitched, and Coco felt icy. Fluttery.

She could hear her heart beating.

The rodent's body convulsed. Magically reanimated, it scrambled away in the underbrush, snapping twigs and making small mechanical squeaks and peeps. In a child's game of statue, she stood still as death, and her heart — *da dum, da dum, da dum* — was louder now and faster.

Lieutenant Coffey settled into the chair behind his desk. He had concluded his telephone call from City Hall, and now he gave the cleaning lady his best political smile. "The mayor loves you, Mrs. Ortega."

The city's top politician was indeed her biggest fan, so happy that a civilian — not a cop — had broken the pedophile's bones in full view of a dozen witnesses, most of them under the age of six. The mayor also suffered from the delusion that Mrs. Ortega's heroism might balance out the bad press of rats eating a park visitor.

What a fool.

"The mayor tells me his limo driver was supposed to take you to City Hall — not Brooklyn. You're overdue for a photo op and a press conference."

"I *told* you," she said, "I had to go home and get my fairy."

"Of course, and thank you for that." Jack Coffey stared at the winged figurine perched on the corner of his desk, and he picked his next words with care, electing not to tell her that the missing pixie would have to murder three or more people before Special Crimes took an interest. With great diplomacy, he

37

splayed his hands, a New Yorker's gesture to show that he held no animosity and no weapons. "The limousine is downstairs waiting for you . . . and the mayor's waiting . . . and the television cameras."

"No way," said Mrs. Ortega. "I'm not leaving here till you —"

"I'll tell the park precinct there's still one kid missing." Coffey picked up the figurine. "And I'll send them a picture of this thing, okay?"

"*Sure* you will." The little woman sat well back in her chair to let him know that she planned to stay awhile. *Screw the mayor.*

The lieutenant had only turned his head for a moment, and Detective Mallory appeared beside him, as if she had simply materialized from some other planet. Coffey knew that she did this trick to stop his heart, and he was about to point the way back to her desk when she smiled — never a good sign.

"I wonder," said Mallory, in the offhand manner of opining on the time of day, "how *bad* does the mayor want to see Mrs. Ortega?"

Jack Coffey could only stare at her, fascinated, though he knew what would happen next. The game was blackmail. The young detective wanted out of her cage. And she was entirely too confident of her second psych evaluation.

"The little girl is disabled," said Mallory. "She has Williams syndrome."

"That's right," said Mrs. Ortega. "Charles Butler says she'll never find her own way home. You can't let her wander around the —"

"Just a damn minute," said Coffey. "Charles saw her, too?"

"No," said Mrs. Ortega, "I called him on the way to Brooklyn. He diagnosed her over the phone — the *mayor's* car phone."

The lieutenant smelled collusion.

"You might want to find that little girl." Mallory was oh, so casual. "Pedophiles love Central Park. If the kid gets raped, it might wreck the mayor's whole day." It was unnecessary to mention that, via Mrs. Ortega, this detective now had the mayor's ear. And the word *payback* also remained unspoken.

In the darkest region of Jack Coffey's brain, a hobgoblin jumped up and down, screaming, "*Shoot* Mallory! Shoot her *now!*" But instead, the lieutenant turned back to the cleaning lady and forced a smile. "Okay, this is my best offer. I'll get the park precinct to spot you ten cops to find that lost kid. Deal?"

Mrs. Ortega rose to her feet and leaned

over his desk. One thumb gestured back toward the detectives behind her. "You throw in those two, and we got a deal."

Mallory sat down in the chair next to Riker's and stretched out her long legs. She opened her pocket watch, an antique handed down to her from the late, great cop Lou Markowitz. She usually trotted out this prop to advertise the generations of police in her foster father's lineage — and to call in favors owed to that good old man. On the day of her return, she had laid the watch on her desk as a plea and a dare to take her back. But today she held it up as an illustration of time passing. The mayor would be waiting, fuming, only moments from imploding.

Jack Coffey shrugged, and this was akin to waving a white flag of surrender. Sometimes losing was a good idea. Failure could be so restful. His tension headache was gone even before his two detectives had been dispatched uptown to Central Park. Mrs. Ortega was sent downtown to City Hall — a problem solved — and, by the scales of wins and losses, this might be a break-even day.

The lieutenant allowed half an hour before he turned on the volume of the television set. It was tuned to the cable channel for city coverage, and he expected to see the

40

cleaning lady and the mayor in a press conference. Instead, he saw a picture of Columbus Circle, and around it ran a river of vehicles flowing from the tributaries of broad avenues. The camera narrowed its field and shifted to the sun-washed plaza of Merchants' Gate, the southwest entrance to Central Park. The lens zoomed in on a monument, and atop this high pylon stood the golden statue of Columbia Triumphant riding her chariot drawn by three sea horses. The camera panned down to the tight shot of a little boy with many microphones framing his face.

And the lieutenant heard the second fairy sighting of the day.

The boy on camera invoked a celebrity pixie of storybook fame to describe a child who was still at large in the park. "But she wasn't blond like Tinker Bell. This girl had *red* hair." The boy's smile became sly. With special glee and a touch of the ghoul, saving the best for last, he announced, "She was covered with blood!"

Oh, great. Just great.

"I bet you're wondering how I know you're lying." Mallory did not say this unkindly, but her partner thought she *did* stare at the boy in the way a cat might gaze at its food

41

— no eye contact. Riker wondered if she saw the child as all of one piece, like a slab of meat that wore a little baseball cap.

The young day camper was slow to realize that he was no longer safe in the company of smiling, solicitous reporters. This tall blonde was an altogether different sort of creature — and he was in deep trouble. His mouth hung open when he looked up at her, as if she outsized the golden statue that was merely larger than life.

Mallory grabbed the little boy's hand and marched him around to the back of the monument that marked the entrance to Central Park. Riker followed close behind them to shield this kidnap from cameras on the other side of the plaza, where reporters interviewed the rest of the Jersey children, and where street musicians cranked up the music to compete with the honking horns of crazed drivers. Cars were frozen in a massive gridlock around Columbus Circle, and uniformed officers ran along the curb of the plaza, waving ticket pads at news vans insane enough to double-park. A civilian audience lined up to watch this circus, and food vendors appeared out of nowhere to cater the party.

No one noticed the child snatched by the detectives.

"That girl *did* have blood on her." The six-year-old's voice was whiny now, but he did not cry, and Riker gave him points for that. The little boy looked down at his shoes, a sure sign of guilt.

"Last chance," said Mallory, as if the authority to send him to hell was hers alone. "Tell me what —"

"He *lied*." A second tiny camper, a girl with a ponytail, stepped out of Riker's shadow and crept up to Mallory, saying, "That girl *wasn't* covered in blood." The child cupped her hands around her mouth and whispered confidentially, "It was just a *little* blood." She pointed to her own T-shirt and described the small red stains as they appeared on the missing girl's shoulder and one sleeve. "Here, and here, too. Oh, and her name is Coco."

Riker opened his notebook. "Coco, huh?" After jotting this down, his pen hovered over the page. "So . . . about this blood. Did you see a wound or a cut?"

"No, she was just spotty, and she looked like this." The little girl put two fingers into her mouth and stretched it into a wide Halloween grin with gaps of missing baby teeth.

"Well, that sort of fits." Riker held up a photograph of Mrs. Ortega's fairy figurine, and he showed it to this more reliable witness. "Did Coco look something like —"

"That's *her!*" The little girl squealed as she jumped up and down, so excited she could hardly stand it. "I forgot about the *wings!*"

Riker sighed.

And the little boy, the *confirmed liar,* nodded. "Yup, she had wings, all right." Small hands jammed into his pockets, he looked up at the sky with newfound nonchalance. "She's probably in Mexico by now."

Mallory hunkered down, her face a bare inch from the boy's. No escape, no mercy. And Riker winced.

"Tell me something," she said. "About those stains on Coco's T-shirt — did you see that blood *before* the rats *ate* Mrs. Lanyard?"

The little boy's body jerked to attention, eyes gone wide with the shock of a popped balloon. Evidently, this runaway camper had never looked back to see the rat attack. And the reporters — those *jackals* — had been too sensitive to tell him that the old lady was dead. All of this was apparent with the child's tears, big ones and so many of them.

The detectives had an answer of sorts, and they moved on to enter Central Park.

If asked, Coco would say she had walked

two hundred and eighty-three miles in the past hour to cross a span of parkland equal to four city blocks. In her reckoning, time and space were arbitrary things, though she did strive to be precise with her numbers.

The child followed four steps behind a woman whose face she had yet to see. Coco planned to ask if this stranger would please hold her hand. She badly needed to hold on to someone, *anyone*. It was a flyaway day with no anchors to a solid world, and tears were a near thing from moment to moment. But now her attention strayed to a man with a blue shirt and gray pants just like Uncle Red's clothing. But this could not be him.

Uncle Red had lately turned himself into a tree.

The lady ahead of her stopped and looked up. During Coco's travels through the park from nights into days, she had noticed that other visitors never looked up — only this woman. Maybe the stranger had heard a tree crying. Trees did that sometimes. But not this one. Oh, and now the red rain came down here, too, but only a few drops, and they landed on the back of the lady's dress.

"You're spotted," said Coco. "You've got red spots — like mine."

The woman whirled around, and a rat fell from the tree to land on her head. The lady screamed and batted at it, but the rat was tangled in her long hair, and now it was also screaming. Trembling, Coco rose up on her toes, poised for flight, and then she was off, feet touching lightly to ground as she ran, outrunning sound, chasing it out of her brain. Now there were footfalls behind her — too heavy for rodent steps, even if all the rats in the world stood on one another's backs. But she never looked over her shoulder to see what was behind her. After a long time, forever and ever, she found herself safe among the lions.

THREE

I'm two grades ahead of my age group. So I have classes with all three of them. In History, Aggy the Biter sits next to me, clicking her teeth. Every now and then, she reaches across the aisle to pinch me. Testing the meat?

— ERNEST NADLER

Riding shotgun with his partner would have been more exciting in a real car. Mallory rarely used a siren, preferring to frighten other motorists with close encounters that threatened their paint jobs and taillights. But today she was limited to the top speed of this small park vehicle, a glorified golf cart with a peanut-size engine.

Riker played navigator, consulting a map of narrow roads, meandering trails and the highways of Central Park. As they traveled north, he drew an *X* over a brand-new city landmark, the spot where the rats had eaten an out-of-towner. They were drawing close to the playground near 68th Street, where Mrs. Ortega had seen the missing child. He looked at his watch. Hours had passed since the rat attack in the meadow on the other side of West Drive. "We'll never find her around here. Kids make good time on the run." He despaired of locating one little girl in parkland that was miles long, half a mile wide and filled with a million trees to hide her. And yet his partner aimed the cart with confidence and sure direction. "So what do you know that I don't know?"

"Coco's not hiding," said Mallory. "She's trying to connect with people. She'll stick to this road."

His partner had the inside track on lost children. She used to be one — if it could be said that she was ever a *real* child. She had arrived at the Markowitz household with a full skill set for survival at the age of ten or eleven. Her foster parents, Lou and Helen, had never been certain of her age because the child-size Kathy Mallory had also shown a genius for deception. But stealing was where Riker thought the kid really shined in her puppy days.

Eliciting fear was a talent she had later grown into.

After passing the park exit for 77th Street,

Mallory pressed the gas pedal to the floor and jumped the curb to aim the cart at two boys with skateboards in hand. They wore kneepads and wrist guards and helmets, all the cushions that parents could provide to keep their young alive in New York City. True, these youngsters were teenagers, but *someone* loved them. When the cart braked to a sudden stop, the front wheels were inches from their kneecaps — and the boys laughed. No shock, no awe, for this was a *toy* car. And then the fun was over. They had locked eyes with Mallory.

Oh, *shit.*

Words were unnecessary. She only nodded to say, *Yes, I'm a cop. Yes, I carry a gun — a big one.* She tilted her head to one side and smiled, silently asking if they might have a bit of weed in their pockets that would interest her.

Teenagers were *so* easy.

Riker held up his badge and waved them over to his side of the cart. He reached into his pocket for the photograph of Mrs. Ortega's fairy figurine. "Okay, guys, this is how it works. One smartass remark and my partner shoots you. We're hunting for a lost kid. The girl looks something like this." He showed them the photo and read one boy's mind when he saw the smirk. "Forget you saw the *wings*." He nodded toward Mallory. "She *will* hurt you."

"Yeah, we saw the kid," said the taller boy.

"Well, you're headed in the right direction." He pointed back the way he had come with his friend. "Take the first path on the right. She was running east."

"She went into the Ramble?" Riker shaded his eyes to look toward that area of dense woods, once notorious as a haven for addicts and muggers with knives and guns, and for bob-and-drop rapists with rocks. In more recent times, the wildwood had been invaded by bird-watchers, joggers and grandmothers. "How long ago?"

"Maybe an hour — half an hour."

"Talk to me." Mallory zeroed in on the other boy's guilty face. "What else happened?"

This teenager looked down at the grass and then up to the sky. "She asked me for a hug."

"But she was dirty." Mallory stepped out of the cart. "Probably a homeless kid." Her voice was a monotone. "You thought you might catch something — bedbugs or lice." She circled around the boy, snatched his skateboard and tossed it under the wheels of the cart. And still, he would not look at her. "That little girl had blood on her

50

T-shirt, and she was scared, wasn't she? But you had plans for the day, places to go — no time to call the cops." Mallory held up her open hand and showed the boy his own pricey cell phone. He stared at it in disbelief as he patted the empty back pocket of his jeans.

"You think I can hit the water from here?" She glanced at the long finger of lake water bordered with an orange construction fence, and she hefted his phone as if weighing it. "Talk to me."

The teenager turned his worried eyes to Riker, who only shrugged to say *I warned you about her.*

It was the other boy who spoke first, maybe in fear for his own cell phone. "The girl was a little strange. . . . I thought she was gonna cry when —"

"When your friend blew her off?" With only the prompt of Mallory folding her arms, both of them were talking at once, and now they remembered — suddenly and conveniently — that Coco had run toward another park visitor.

"We figured *he'd* call the cops."

"Yeah," said Riker, "*sure* you did." *Pissant liar.*

The teenager gave him a snarky so-what smile — *no* respect.

Smug lies to cops should have conse-
quences, but rather than shake the little
bastard until his perfect teeth came loose,
Riker turned away and climbed into the
cart. Behind him, he heard a splash followed
by the boy's "Oh, shit! My *phone!*" Then
Mallory was back in the driver's seat, and
the cart lurched forward with the satisfying
crunch of a skateboard under one wheel.

The detectives traveled down a narrow
road and into the woods at the reckless top
speed of hardly any miles per hour. The
Ramble was a sprawl of thirty-eight acres,
thick with trees and lush foliage, beautiful
and disheartening. On Riker's map, this
area was a daunting maze of winding paths.
"We'll never find her in here."

"Sure we will. The kid's running scared.
She'll make all the easy choices." Mallory
passed every turnoff, staying on the widest
path and only slowing down for a closer
look at a low, flimsy, wire fence. And now a
full stop. One section of the fence had been
pulled down to the ground. Old lessons of
the late Lou Markowitz — she would always
stop to look at every odd thing. And then
she drove on.

As they rolled out of the Ramble and onto
open ground down near the Boathouse Café
on the east side of the lake, Riker answered

his cell phone. "Yeah?" He turned to his partner. "We're headed the right way. We got a fairy sighting on the mall."

Beyond the lake of rowboats and ducks, past Bethesda Terrace, they drove onto the park mall and into the mellow tones of a saxophone near the old band shell. Four people were coming toward them, frightened and running faster than the cart could go. The detectives traveled past them and down the wide pedestrian boulevard lined with giant trees, benches and street lamps from the gaslight era. High above them was a canopy of leafy branches, and up ahead was the sound of a Dixieland band, which seemed to orchestrate the civilian scramble for park exits. The music stopped when Riker flashed his badge.

"False alarm," said the banjo man, holding up his cell phone. "We thought the kid was lost, but then she hooked up with a tour group."

And the trumpet player said, "I gave them directions to the park zoo."

The cart rolled on, pedal to the floor.

"Hold it!" yelled Riker. They braked to a sudden stop as a gang of rats cut across the paving stones in front of them. "What the hell?" Downtown in his SoHo neighborhood, the rodents were all dilettantes who never turned out until ten o'clock at night, and they avoided people. They were rarely seen except as shining eyes reflecting streetlights and watching from the dark of alleys and trashcans. Sometimes he would see one scurrying close to a wall, but he had *never* seen *galloping* rats, backs arching and elongating. No doubt these were people-eating escapees from Sheep Meadow. Most of the vermin had cleared the path when one brazen animal stopped in front of their vehicle. The lone rat reared up on his hind legs and faced them down — absolutely fearless — almost admirable.

Mallory ran over him.

Upon entering the zoo on foot, the detectives decided not to show the fairy photograph. Instead they worked off the simple description of a small redhead in a bloody T-shirt. Here, where civilians were sheltered from hysterical screamers and marauding vermin, there were no signs of panic. A tranquil visitor pointed them toward the exhibit at the heart of a plaza, a raised cement pool where sea lions lazed atop slabs of rock, dozing and baking under the noonday sun. And there was the little girl, standing on the steps that surrounded the enclosure. A zoo employee kept his distance from her while making a long reach to hand over the traditional ice-cream cone for the lost child.

Mallory called out, "Coco!"

The tiny girl dropped her cone and ran toward them, laughing and crying, her puny arms outstretched to beg an embrace. The desperation on her dirty little face saddened Riker. A hug might well be oxygen to her, the stuff of life itself. She *needed* this. Mrs. Ortega was right — Coco had no survival instincts. The clueless child had picked his partner as a source of warmth and comfort.

Coco wrapped her arms around the tall blond detective, who not only tolerated the embrace but smiled down upon this poor bloodstained baby — Mallory's ticket to the street. No more desk duty. A lost child was found, and this had the makings of a great press release to lessen the damage to tourism done by bloodthirsty rats. The mayor would be so grateful.

Redbrick walls, trees and flowers enclosed the courtyard of the zoo's café. The luncheon crowd was terrorized by screaming gangs of toddlers and faster youngsters pursued by frazzled young women. Older women, veteran mommies, sat quietly, waiting for the children's batteries to run down.

And strolling pigeons were beggars at every outdoor table.

Coco, a born storyteller, alternately chomped a hotdog and gave the detectives more details of her odyssey through Central Park. No question could have a simple answer without the embroidery of fantasy. In respect to the spots on her T-shirt, she said, "The blood comes from the same place the rats do." She pointed upward. "There are rats who live in the sky." She looked from Riker's face to Mallory's, correctly suspecting skepticism in their eyes. "Some *do*," she said with great dignity and authority. "Sometimes it rains rats, and sometimes it rains blood." She shrugged one thin shoulder to tell them that this weather phenomenon was a bit of a crapshoot.

Mallory's indulgence was wearing off. "You saw the rats with the woman who —"

Riker put up one hand to forestall a grisly account of Mrs. Lanyard's demise. "So you saw all those rats in the meadow, huh?"

"Yes. Then everyone ran away. Me, too." In the child's version, a few dozen rats became a horde of thousands, and all of them were big as houses with teeth as long as her arms. "Rats are prolific breeders."

Riker wondered how many six-year-olds had *prolific* in their small store of words.

"Whose blood is that?" Mallory was not a great believer in sky rats and blood rain.

"It's God's blood," said Coco.

Riker stared at the red stains. The elongated shapes did suggest drops falling from above, but so much of the world was above the head of this child. "Where were you when the blood landed on your T-shirt?"

"In the park. There are lots of rats in the park. Most people never see them. They're usually nocturnal."

"Nocturnal? That's a long word for a little girl," said Riker. "How old are you?"

"I'm eight." She said this with pride. It might be true. She was smaller than other children that age, but her words were bigger.

Mallory placed her own hotdog on Coco's tray, and the child fell upon it as if she had not been fed for days. "You were in the park at night? That's how you know rats are nocturnal?"

"I read that in a book." The little girl demolished the second hotdog. "Granny used to give me book lessons every day. That was before I went to live with Uncle Red. But when it got dark, he had himself delivered to the park. I went to look for him, but he turned into a tree."

"So you were here all night?" *Now* Riker

was incredulous. "All by yourself?"

"Yes. I listened to the tree all night long — every night. You know the way trees cry. They don't have mouths, so it sounds like this." She covered her mouth with both hands and made a muffled plaintive sound.

Riker felt a sudden chill with this hint of something true. He stared at the blood on the child's T-shirt.

Whose blood?

Mallory used a napkin to gently wipe mustard from Coco's chin, rewarding her with this little act of kindness — training her — like a puppy. "Let's go find your Uncle Red."

It was the freelancer's day off from the despair of never landing a full-time job, and all he had with him was a damn camera phone. Though he had seen it happen with his own eyes, no photo editor would ever believe that rat had fallen from the sky. He had snapped the picture seconds too late, only able to capture an image of a rodent riding the back of a woman. He had followed the screaming lady on a chase of many twisty paths before losing her.

It was his first time in the Ramble, which had no helpful signs with cute names for these trails, and he had been traveling in circles for nearly an hour. As he walked, he looked down at the image displayed on his camera phone, looking for landmarks of the place where the rat-ridden woman had begun her mad dash. Finally he was on the right path again. Yes, this was where he had seen the rat come down from the sky. Looking upward at the overreaching branches, he conceded that the rodent had most likely fallen from a tree, though it was still a hell of a shot.

But when did rats start climbing trees?

He stared at the picture on the small screen of his cell phone, the photograph of a woman with a rat in her hair. In the background, there was a smaller figure — a red-haired child, her head tilted back — looking up at what? More tree rats? He stood on the exact spot where the curious little girl had been standing an hour ago. Staring up into the dense leaves, he detected something green but not leafy. A bulging bag was strung up on a high branch, and — *holy shit!* — it moved. A rat emerged from a tear in the bag, and now the creature was coming down through the leaves, dropping from one bough to land on a lower one. An acrobat rat? It paused on the lowest limb to have its picture taken. *Click.* Fat and ungainly, the rodent barely kept its balance

59

with tiny vermin hands. A drunken rat? Its fur was slicked down, and the rat shook itself like a wet dog, splattering the freelancer's white shirt — *oh, crap* — with drops of blood.

Mallory led a short parade of vehicles. Behind the detectives rode two patrolmen, and the third cart was driven by a park ranger. The little girl sat on Riker's lap, her head turning from side to side, looking for a dead bird, she said. They were traveling north, heading back toward the Ramble again, with only the child's cryptic clue of water tied with a fat orange ribbon; and that would be the maintenance crew's fence around a sliver of the lake, the same place where Mallory had tossed a teenager's phone into the water. As the three carts rolled along West Drive, the detectives learned that the formal name of Coco's granny was Grandmother. Uncle Red had no other designation.

And this child had survived more than one night in the park.

"Stop!" When the carts pulled over to the curb, Coco jumped out to inspect another drinking fountain, the third one along this route. "This is it," she said, pointing to the eyeless dead bird in the basin. She recoiled from the buzzing flies that covered the tiny corpse, and she ran to the end of a curved stone wall, holding both hands over her ears.

Mallory called the little girl back to the cart, and the search party headed into the Ramble, rolling on paths too narrow for larger vehicles. Coco could offer them no more guidance, but Mallory seemed to need no directions, and Riker had a fair idea of where she was going. She stopped the cart at the place where she had earlier paused for a closer look at something that passed for minor vandalism. Now she pointed to a small section of chicken-wire fence that had been forced down. "Coco, have you seen that before?"

"I didn't do it," said the little girl. And Riker had to smile, for this was his partner's trademark line. Coco climbed down from his lap to stand on the path. "We're here."

The park ranger left his own vehicle. "The kid should get back in the cart. We've got a rat swarm in the Ramble. That's why you don't see any people here. They swarmed, too."

"We're half a mile from Sheep Meadow," said Mallory. "Aren't rats territorial?"

"Yes, ma'am, but these aren't the same rats." The ranger pointed east. "Our new exterminator flushed another swarm out of a building on the other side of the Ramble. He was supposed to kill them, but he just got them stoned on chemicals."

"He fumigated *rats* . . . in a *park*."

"Yes, ma'am," said the ranger, his face deadpan, his voice without affect. "And now they're all so wonderfully uninhibited."

"Well, that explains a lot." Riker settled the child on the passenger seat of the park ranger's cart. "Okay, honey, you stay here and talk rats with the funny man."

When the detective had joined his partner by the downed section of fence, the ranger called to them, "Watch out! The rats are more aggressive now, and they bite. If you see one, don't run. That only encourages them. I think they *like* it when you run."

Mallory pointed to the ground where deep twin ruts were overlapped by shallow ones. "A tire-tread pattern for two wheels. That fits with something small, like a hand truck."

"A delivery guy's dolly. Coco said her uncle was delivered to the park." Riker's shoes left no footprints on the dry dirt. "So the dolly came through here after the rain, when the ground was soft."

"But it hasn't rained for days." Mallory bent low to examine the exposed earth and sparse weeds trampled by the wheels. "The dolly's load was heavy going in and a lot lighter coming back out."

Light by one body? And might that body belong to Coco's missing uncle?

Mallory, a born-again believer in sky rats and blood rain, was looking upward as she entered the thick of the trees. It was Riker who saw the patches of human flesh between the leaves of foliage on the ground — then the profile of a face — and now the fronds of a fern were pulled away to expose a naked man lying on his side. Wrists and ankles tied by rope, the body was bent backwards like an archer's bow. Riker reached down to touch the flesh. Cold and rigid. Late-stage rigor mortis? The one visible eye was sunk deep in its socket, and the bluish skin was mottled.

"Textbook dead." Riker called out to the ranger on babysitting detail. "Get the kid outta here!"

As the ranger's cart drove off with Coco, Mallory shouted at the two uniformed officers, "Nobody gets past you! Got that?"

The patrolmen stood guard by the fallen fence while the detectives made a closer inspection of the nude corpse. "Dark brown hair," said Riker. "I'm guessing this isn't the kid's Uncle Red. Maybe we still got another body to find."

He heard the rats before he saw them,

quick scrabbling through the underbrush, then twitching into view, dozens of them. The first one to jump the dead man sniffed out the soft delicacies of the eyes. Riker, a man with a fully loaded gun, not a shy or retiring type, was scared witless, but he would not run. Like Mallory, he stood his ground while rats ran around their shoes to get at the body. "Hey!" he yelled, waving his arms. That should have scattered them, but the critters seemed not to notice. All the rules of rodents were suspended today, and all that he could count on was the fact that vermin carried ticks and fleas and plagues from the Middle Ages. And their teeth were so terribly sharp.

His partner picked up a rock and nailed one rat with an all-star pitch. Oh, bless Lou Markowitz for teaching his kid the all-American game of baseball — and trust Mallory to pervert it this way. Calm and composed, she snapped on a Latex glove, then picked up the bloodied rat by the tail and dangled it. The rest of them lifted their snouts to sniff the air. She swung the limp rat wide of the corpse, and it sailed past the startled patrolmen to land on the path by the carts.

Setting an example for the other rats? No, not quite.

The vermin swarmed toward the smell of fresh, flowing blood and gnawed on their not-quite-dead brother rat. The carnage on the path was a frenzy of ripping teeth, blood fly and whipping tails. Mallory's early childhood on the streets had outfitted her with all the ugliest shortcuts for pest control.

One of the patrolmen called out, his voice young and hopeful, "Can we shoot 'em?"

Without a direct order from a superior, these patrolmen would be sent to NYPD Hell if they discharged their service weapons — even for the just cause of protecting a crime scene.

Riker gave them a thumbs-up, and the two officers whiled away their time picking off rats with bullets. *Bang!* went the guns, *Bang! Bang!* All around them, screaming birds took flight. The rats that were still alive remained. Still hungry.

The detectives knelt down beside the naked victim. Riker guessed that rigor mortis had set in hours ago. The bound corpse was frozen in his hog-tied pose.

Bang! Bang! Bang!

Ligature marks on wrists and ankles were crusted with old blood from a struggle to get free, and that had probably attracted the rats, though the abrasions showed signs of early healing. How long had this body been lying here? A piece of duct tape dangled from the dead man's chin. Another piece clung to the side of the face, and rough threads from a burlap weave were caught between the lips.

Bang! Bang! Bang! Bang!

Mallory looked up, and Riker followed the line of her gaze. His eyes were not so young, and he had to squint to make out the slack shape of green material hanging from a high bough of the tree, and there was a gaping hole at the bottom of this empty bag. Giving up the only vanity of his middle age, he donned a pair of bifocals to see twigs and branches bent and broken where they had slowed the progress of a falling body.

His partner leaned over the rigid corpse at their feet. With one gloved hand, she lightly touched straight lines of sticky residue where the tape had once covered the eyes and mouth. Here the skin was raw. "He rubbed his face against the burlap to get the tape off."

And patches of dried-out skin had come off with it. How long had this poor bastard gone without food and water?

"Okay, we got a real sick game here," said Riker. "Look at this." He pointed to a wad of wax that plugged an ear cavity. "Our freak's into sensory deprivation. No sight, no hearing, just starvation and slow death."

The detectives heard the buzz before they saw the insects that always came to lay their eggs in decomposing flesh. The first fly landed to crawl upon the dead man's eyeball.

The corpse blinked — and then it screamed.

FOUR

Before they can grab me, I warn them that I have superpowers. I can run like a rabbit, shiver like a whippet, and I can scream like a little girl. The three of them look at me like — what the hell? This buys me a few seconds, and I jump into the slipstream of a passing teacher. At lunchtime, they come along every few minutes like taxicabs.

— ERNEST NADLER

The victim had lost consciousness again as he lay at the foot of the hanging tree.

A tube connected the naked man to a bag of fluid held high by a paramedic, who used his free hand to swat bugs. His patient hovered between the status of a corpse and a live carry. "Starvation ain't the problem," he said to Detective Mallory, "and those rat bites won't kill him, but dehydration's a bitch."

"Best guess," she said. "How long has he gone without water?"

The paramedic shrugged. "I'd say three days at the outside. Any longer than that and he'd be dead."

Though the victim had been freed of bindings, his body was still frozen in the captive posture when he was lifted onto a stretcher and carried through the woods to a waiting ambulance.

Two patrolmen strung yellow crime-scene tape from tree to tree in a crude circle. One of them stopped to shout at a taxpayer, "We're not selling tickets! Get lost!"

And the civilian yelled, "I'm from the *Times!*" which made him a reporter and thus a legal kill in the codebook of the NYPD.

Mallory turned her eyes up to the high branches of the hanging tree and the remnants of the empty sack that had gone unnoticed by paramedics. She had no interest in what happened to the reporter as long as the carnage stayed on the other side of the yellow tape. Except for the *Times* interloper, panic had emptied the Ramble of people, and she still had hopes of keeping secret the detail of the burlap bag.

But then the man from the *Times* yelled, "You gotta come with me! There's a bag in a tree — rats running in and out of it — *bloody* rats!"

"Rats are climbing trees now?" The patrolmen laughed.

The detectives did not. Together they walked toward the path, and Riker said, "Check out the bloodstains on the guy's shirt."

The man with red spots on his shoulders yelled, "I'm a photographer! I got pictures!" He held out his cell phone to the approaching detectives and pointed to the image on the small screen. "See?" There was only time enough for him to blink before his phone disappeared.

The civilian was staring down at the empty palm of his hand — while Mallory, the best of thieves, clicked through his pictures, a portrait of Coco among them, and she transmitted them to her own cell. While the man she had robbed was trying to find his voice and a suitable tone of outrage, she said, "This is an *idiot*-proof camera. How could you screw up these shots?" Oh, and now they were all gone — erased. Well, accidents would happen. She saw a word forming on the man's lips.

Before the civilian could call her a bitch, her partner stepped forward to say, "Careful, pal." Riker held out his hand. "Okay,

70

let's see your press card."

"He doesn't have one." Mallory turned on the civilian. "You're not a photographer, at least not a pro. And I *know* you don't work for the *Times.*" He backed up with every step she took toward him. "So you're a reporter wannabe, right?" She had him up against a tree. "Just a lousy stringer with no steady paycheck." She smiled and lightly tapped his chest with one long red fingernail. "I can change that."

His grin was wide. All was forgiven.

He led them through the trees and across a small clearing, where a painter's easel lay abandoned on the grass. This might be Tupelo Meadow, but Mallory was uncertain. In her childhood, the Ramble had been a dangerous place, home to every form of lowlife, the detritus of human waste and cast-off needles with the dregs of heroin and blood. In the wake of a real-estate boom on the Upper West Side, the squats of petty criminals had been sold as condos and co-ops, thus pricing junkies out of the neighborhood. These days, on any *normal* summer day, there should be tourists and local people here, taking in the sun, feeding squirrels and birds. But now, all that remained were their possessions dropped in flight — soda cans and sunglasses, a sandal and a child's toy. This empty field supported the stringer's claim of rats swarming here, too — lots of them.

The aspiring reporter nodded all the while as Mallory explained the rules of journalism: Truth was overrated; information was currency; and he would take whatever she gave him, word for word, and nothing more.

They entered the woods on the far side of the clearing to stand beneath the tree that had rained blood on his shirt, and the newspaper stringer was promoted to Mallory's manservant. She inspected his hands to see if they were clean and then allowed him to hold her linen blazer. She jumped for a low bough and hoisted her body upward. Moving higher, limb by limb, she climbed close to the burlap bag. It hung at least twenty feet off the ground, held there by a rope tied off with a slipknot on a lower bough. The remainder of the rope was coiled in the fork of branch and tree. She unraveled it and let it drop to see the loose end form another coil on the ground below.

Long enough.

The stench from the bag told her that this second victim was not a fresh kill. The cloth had a hole chewed through it to give her a small ragged window on green-tinged flesh that had been gnawed. There was no blood in the wound. This had to be postmortem damage, though she could see fresh red splatters elsewhere on the skin. The rats must have chewed into some artery where blood still remained in a liquid state.

The detective called down to the patrolmen, "Grab the rope and pull!" And they did. With one yank from below, the slipknot on the lower branch came undone, and the bag dropped in a short fall of inches until the officers below held a taut line.

"Just hold the bag in place!" Mallory heard a squeak that was almost mechanical. Almost. She turned her head a bare inch, and now she was looking into shiny rodent eyes. The creature had no sense of fear. Its snout was inches from her face. *What long teeth you have.* It hissed. And then, balance lost, the rat dropped to the ground to land twitching and squealing at the feet of the two patrolmen, who seemed happy to see it.

Was it a sick rat, or just a clumsy one?

Bang!

A dead rat.

With better balance than vermin, Mallory dropped from the bough to land with cat's grace on a lower one, and so she made her way down through the tall tree and then swung from the lowest branch to stand beside the two officers. "Don't bring the bag down till I lose that guy." She nodded toward the newspaper stringer, who stood with Riker in the field, madly writing lines in a small notebook. Whatever her partner was feeding the man, she knew it would be nothing useful.

The second ambulance siren of the day could be heard in the distance as she approached the stringer. One hand with long red fingernails — call them claws — wound around the man's arm, and she led him farther away from her crime scene. As they walked, she dictated his copy.

Tomorrow morning, when the *Times* hit the newsstands, her status as lead detective would be a matter of public record — and not her lieutenant's call. The mayor tended to believe everything he read in the papers, even when half the lies came from his own office, and it was the police commissioner's job to kiss that fool's feet and make this news item come true.

"Nobody else has this story. I can keep it that way till tomorrow morning." Mallory took the pen and pad away from the civilian and jotted a brief note to this effect. It was addressed to the city desk editor, a man with debts in the favor bank that were owed to her foster father, and she signed it *Lou Markowitz's daughter.* Then she used the stringer's camera phone to take a photograph for the front page of tomorrow's edition. In perfect focus, she framed the hanging tree and the uniformed policemen. *Click.* "Okay, you're good to go." She returned his camera phone. "Go!" And he did. He ran.

Riker was doing damage control in the clearing. He waved off the ambulance crew twenty feet from the tree and then made a call to request transport for a corpse. Turning to the patrolmen, he said, "Lower the body. We gotta get it out of the bag and lose that rope before the meat wagon gets here."

Mallory nodded her approval. The worst leaks came from the lowest-paid employees of the Medical Examiner's Office. So now they had one body for the hospital, one for the morgue — two if she counted old Mrs. Lanyard — just a typical day in New York City, and there would be no mention of trees or burlap bags and ropes, no red flags that could be sold to the television networks.

When the bag was lowered to the ground and opened, what flesh remained on a female corpse would not help with identification. The body had been attended to by bugs and rats. And there was no chance of fingerprints; these extremities had been gnawed to the bone. There was silver duct tape on this face, too. It covered the eyes and mouth. And the dead woman had other things in common with the surviving victim: her bondage ropes, both ears sealed with wax, and her nudity.

Mallory loved money motives best. She looked for them where other detectives would see only evidence of insane cruelty. And so this corpse was a disappointment. The blond hair was high maintenance, but the untreated brown roots were years long. No upscale salon would miss this customer.

All around them was the bedlam of the emergency room, the babble of foreign languages and screams that needed no translation. Added to this background music were layers of odors: vomit and a whiff of bowel, medicinal smells and the cat-piss aroma of disinfectant from an orderly's mop and pail.

When crime-scene investigators arrived at the hospital, the male victim from the first hanging tree was comatose and awaiting a gurney ride to the intensive care unit. The pads of his fingers were quickly blackened with ink and rolled across the white cards that recorded his prints. A technician swabbed a Q-tip inside the man's open mouth for a DNA sample, and another CSI collected debris from fingernails. Then a man with a camera pulled back the sheet to expose more rat bites and flesh frayed by ropes.

The ER doctor had been ordered to stand aside — quietly — no more complaining, no whining, no yelling. He could only watch, head shaking in disbelief, and then he gasped when Detective Mallory plucked hairs from his patient's scalp.

The technicians stopped their work, and every face turned toward a late arrival. An angry bear of a man, the commander of Crime Scene Unit, stood at the foot of the gurney. Heller's slow-moving brown eyes had missed nothing, not the manhandling of the patient, not the petulant doctor who stood helpless with his back to the wall, nor the detective who had ordered his people to start without him — and obviously against medical advice.

Mallory backed away from the gurney, making a deliberate show of this submissive gesture. She knew how to pick her fights. Tomorrow, Heller would find out about the ropes and burlap bags stashed in the trunk of her car. She was saving herself for *that* battle.

Heller jabbed his thumb toward the doors of the emergency room. His technicians packed their gear and silently filed out. He nodded to the man with the stethoscope, and the doctor resumed his post by the patient's side. Turning on Mallory, Heller said, "That's *one.*" It was their custom to start a fresh count of her trespasses with each new case. He would reach the count of implosion when he discovered that his CSIs had not yet been invited to two crime scenes, but the young detective planned to be long gone by then.

Mallory handed him the bag of plucked hairs and left before he could order her out. She had what she came for. A close inspection of the roots had satisfied her suspicion of a bad drugstore dye job for a man in his twenties. And judging by the original hair color, the coma patient was most likely Coco's missing Uncle Red.

Books were neatly arranged on the shelves, and every scrap of paper knew its place, stacked in shallow boxes marked IN and OUT. It was the office of a very efficient man. The only clutter was on the back wall above his credenza, a cluster of plaques and framed awards that honored Dr. Edward Slope. His name also appeared on a roster more elite than the presidency. Over the past hundred years, only seven men had preceded him in the Office of the Chief

Medical Examiner. Though, without the clue of his white lab coat, he more closely resembled a military man in his bearing, always at attention, even while seated; his expression was stony, smiles were rare, and his wit was gunpowder dry. As a ground-breaking pathologist, his fame was international. At home, he was best known as a man who ate cops for breakfast.

Dr. Slope raised his eyes from the paper-work on his desk. "Hello, Riker." And now he acknowledged the second detective to enter his private domain. *"Kathy."* He so enjoyed needling her with the forbidden use of her first name.

"Mallory," she said, correcting him, as she always did.

She preferred the chilly formality of her surname, and the doctor's training in the use of it had begun upon her graduation from the police academy. But she had failed to distance him then — and now. As a charter member of the Louis Markowitz Floating Poker Game, he had first come to know her as Kathy the child, and she would be Kathy till one of them died.

"That woman's body just got here," he said. "What could you *possibly* want from me?" A tone of irritation conveyed that their business with him had better be mighty important.

A little girl stepped out from behind Detective Riker. Her blue eyes were enormous, and her smile was nearly as wide as her face. They had never met, but the doctor felt an instant sense of recognition. Children of this ilk bore a familial resemblance, though they were so rare that never were two of them born into the same family.

"I want you to do the kid first." Mallory lightly stroked the child's hair. "Before you do the corpse." And she had other demands as well. "Keep it off the books. I want bloodwork to see if she needs medication."

Riker, the peacemaker, stepped forward. "Coco remembers taking a pill every day, but it might've been a vitamin. Charles Butler says she's —"

"One of the Williams people." Though it cracked his face to do it, the medical examiner smiled, charmed to his toes. He left his chair to circle the desk and get down on bended knee. He wanted a closer look at the stellate pattern previously studied only on slides. "You have stars in your eyes," he said to the little girl. "That's very special and beautiful." She hugged him around the neck to complete his diagnosis of Williams syndrome, a condition that came with a longing for human contact and sometimes other ailments of the heart. Kidneys and liver might also pose problems. He looked up at the detectives. "Her blood tests should be run in a hospital with pediatric —"

"We can't do that," said Mallory. "Social Services will take her away. How well do you think she'd do in the system?"

Dr. Slope's nod conceded the point. Children did not thrive in that bureaucracy, and this little girl would wither faster than most. Mallory passed him a handwritten note, and he read her next demand in clear block letters that might have been printed by a machine: CHECK FOR RAPE.

And the doctor died a little.

There was no God.

The little girl and the chief medical examiner, a man who had cracked open the bodies of many a murdered child, went off in search of privacy for a more delicate violation. When an exam room had been secured and Coco was perched on the edge of a table, she reached out to touch his face — to console him. "Rats cry, too," she said. "Most people don't know that."

FIVE

As school traditions go, this one is kind of cool. Every year on the first day of spring and very early in the morning, somebody sneaks into the garden and draws the chalk outline of a girl on the flagstones. No one steps on it, and it lasts almost the whole day before the janitor is told to hose it away. My friend Phoebe calls the chalk girl Poor Allison. She jumped off the school's roof a few years ago. That was before my time. I ask why Poor Allison did it, and Phoebe says, "Well, why do any of them do it?" And I say, "What?"

— ERNEST NADLER

Coco held Riker's hand as they walked down the quiet hallway of a SoHo apartment house. The child was swaddled in a paper sheet of the type used to drape cadavers. She had been allowed to keep her shoes, but the rest of her clothes were in a plastic bag that swung from the detective's free hand.

"A friend of mine owns this whole building," said Riker.

"Is your friend the man or the lady?" she asked when they stood before the door of the only residence on the fourth floor. "I hear two people in there."

"Oh, yeah?" Riker could hear nothing. If anything, this place seemed empty to his ears. Mallory was still at the morgue, but the cleaning lady might have come by after the mayor's press conference. He wondered how the little girl would react if she was reunited with the bat-swinging, pervert-busting Mrs. Ortega.

The door opened. Coco looked up — and up — at a well-made man in a three-piece suit, who stood six-four in his stocking feet. His tie was undone, and this was Charles Butler's version of casual dress. Mallory had called ahead, and the tiny visitor was expected, yet he seemed surprised. And this was a trick of the eyes, heavy-lidded and closed by half with small blue irises floating in bulging egg-size whites. Charles went everywhere wrapped in the aspect of a startled frog with a large nose and a foolish smile. The way his face was made, this accident of birth, belied a giant brain and several Ph.D.s, one of them in psychology.

Coco rushed across the threshold to hug the tall man's legs in hello, and he knelt down before her, saying, "I understand you've had a busy day."

"Full of rats." She smiled. "Rats go to heaven. Did you know that? And sometimes they come back." The child went off down the foyer to inspect the large front room and its collection of antiques and contemporary art.

Riker loved this apartment. The architecture dated back to an era of tall, arched windows featured in the black-and-white film noir of the forties. He sat down on an ornate sofa reminiscent of other period movies, Jane Austen chick flicks, which he only attended under duress. The centuries-old furnishings should not have worked well with the modern splatter-paint artwork on the opposite wall — but they did.

There was no sign of the cleaning lady, though the smell of furniture polish hung in the air. "Mrs. Ortega told us you diagnosed the kid over the phone."

"No," said Charles. "I told her it *might* be Williams syndrome. That was based on the elfin features and the odd behavior — seeking physical contact from strangers." He turned to watch the child enter the adjoining room. "And then there's her shoes."

Shoes? Before Riker could say that aloud, he heard the opening bars of *Melancholy Baby,* note perfect. Coco had discovered the small piano of antebellum days. Charles had bought it for its provenance, he said, a documented tie to legendary riverboat gamblers of the 1800s. The man so loved poker, though he could not play worth a damn. He gave away every hand he held, good or bad, with a blush that would not allow him to bluff, and his tell-all face could not hide a thought.

The piano played on.

"They're musical people," said Charles. "Definitely Williams syndrome. It's all there — the facial features, that magnetic smile. And have you ever seen eyes quite that bright? There's a stellate pattern —"

"The stars in her eyes," said Riker. "Dr. Slope loved that."

"It might take a while to evaluate her. Given the emotional trauma, I'll have to go slowly." Charles, a reformed headhunter, had once been in the business of testing people for placement in projects that re-quired special gifts. And now, semi-retired at the age of forty-one, he only did consult-ing work for the police when a department shrink could not be trusted, which was most of the time. "But I can assure you right now that she's bright, very high functioning."

"That's great." The piano recital had ended, and Riker's voice dropped low, close to a whisper. "We couldn't tell if she was gifted or retarded."

The child came running out of the music room to stand before the detective and point an accusing finger. "That was so *rude*."

"Perhaps," said Charles, "I should've mentioned that most Williams people have remarkable hearing."

And that would explain why this child had been the only one to hear muffled crying from a burlap bag at the top of a tree.

The little girl looked down at the carpet, mortified, and this destroyed Riker, a sucker for every redhead ever born. He put up both hands in surrender. "Coco? You're right. I'm so sorry." He stabbed himself in the chest with one finger. "I'm an idiot. I wish I could play the piano like you. . . . You play just great, kid."

She smiled, eyes lit from within, her face lifting to his like a flower starved for light and warmth — and this exhausted the policeman's entire repertoire of poetic metaphor. "You tell great stories, too. Tell Charles about your Uncle Red."

"He turned himself into a tree." Coco had lost all interest in this topic. Riker could almost see a door closing in her mind. When she had returned to the piano in the next room, both men waited until her playing would safely mask their conversation. This time it was a classical piece, but Riker prided himself on not recognizing the titles of longhair music.

"A standard IQ test won't help you," said Charles. "Based on what Mallory tells me, I'd say Coco's both quicker and slower than average. She has the verbal skills of an older child, but the attention span of a much younger one. And I'm sure you noticed her Velcro straps. They're customized, added on to regular shoes. She obviously can't tie laces." He looked down at the plastic bag on the floor by the detective's chair. "You brought her clothes?"

Riker nodded. The clothing was more evidence that had not been turned over to the Crime Scene Unit. He was not looking forward to the inevitable showdown when Heller would claim the heads of two detectives for his trophy wall.

Charles opened the plastic bag and pulled out a small stained T-shirt, only glancing at it, and then he examined the tiny pair of blue jeans. "Another Velcro fastener. She has trouble with buttons, too. So . . . fine motor skills are a problem for Coco." He nodded toward the music room. "And yet she can play a complex piece by Mozart — from memory. However, if she were to walk out the door right now, I don't think she'd recall the way back. You see the problem? A Williams child is paradox incarnate."

"How would you rate her as witness material?"

"Well, she'll tend to ornament her sentences. She's a natural fabulist. For instance — her uncle turned himself into a tree?"

"But she believes that," said Riker. "The guy was inside a bag strung up in a tree. She heard him crying. That's how she found him in the Ramble. Hundreds of people walked under that tree, but she's the only one who heard him."

"Hyperacusis — sensitivity to sounds."

"We can't get one straight answer from that kid."

"Quite understandable. Another Williams quality is heightened empathy, and the victim was a relative. But she'd have problems with any change in her environment. She's probably been in a state of high anxiety all day."

"Longer. Coco won't say or can't say, but she had to be on the heels of the guy who kidnapped her uncle. Central Park is just too damn big for her to stumble on the right path, the right tree. The uncle was strung up maybe three days ago. So she's been loose in the park all that time, eating out of trashcans and running from rats." Riker covered his eyes with one hand, as if that would kill this picture in his head, for he was a man who loved children.

"Then it'll take quite a while to work through the emotional damage." Charles turned toward the music room to watch the tiny piano player. "She's very small for her age. What did Edward Slope say? Is she physically healthy?"

"The doc says she doesn't need meds. Her heart's in real good shape. And she wasn't molested. Can you evaluate Coco's disability — put something in writing for a judge? We need an order of custody." Riker handed him a folded paper. "And I need your signature on this."

Coco ceased her piano playing and reappeared in the front room. She pointed down the hallway. "That's a Eureka. It's the brand-new canister model."

Riker listened as if ears could squint, and now he made out the low hum of a vacuum cleaner behind a closed door on the other side of the large apartment. The cleaning lady *was* here; hers was the woman's voice Coco had heard from the hallway. He smiled. "A Eureka, huh? You saw the vacuum in the park playground, right? It was in that lady's wire cart?"

Coco giggled in the spirit of *guess again.*

Charles shook his head. "Mrs. Ortega doesn't carry a vacuum cleaner around with her. That one's mine, and Coco's right about the brand name. Excellent auditory memory skills." He turned to her. "So you recognized the sound of the motor."

She nodded. "Our upstairs neighbor had one. My granny's vacuum was an older one, louder — a scary Hoover." Coco faked a little shiver for them to illustrate that this was not her favorite noise. "That one could suck up the whole world. There were lots of vacuum cleaners in the house, and they all had different sounds and different names."

"So your granny lives in an apartment building," said Riker. "Well, that's something."

"She couldn't take care of me anymore. So I went to live with Uncle Red, and I never saw her again."

"That must've happened recently," said Charles. "Granny's neighbor had the new canister model, and it's only been on the market for a few weeks." He had finished reading Riker's paperwork. "Hold on. This document requests that custody be awarded to *me*."

Both men looked up to see Mrs. Ortega pass by with a feather duster in hand. The woman stopped, surprised and wide-eyed. If Riker had not known how tough she was, he would say she was frightened. Turning away from the little girl, the cleaning lady quickly made the sign of the cross. By Riker's lights, this was no sign of religion or relief. He had watched her make this gesture once before to ward off the evil of a three-legged cat encountered on a SoHo sidewalk. Apparently, in Mrs. Ortega's native land across the river, a square block of Brooklyn that housed her whole clan, those cats were trouble — and so was Coco.

Hours had passed since Riker's departure to join in the park search for more victims. And during this time, Charles Butler had filled a notebook with lines of childish fancy to decode. He had come to a few dark conclusions about the gaps in Coco's memory, places in her mind where she could not or would not go.

Such a fascinating mind.

Mrs. Ortega returned from Brooklyn in time for Coco's bath. She brought with her a collection of clothing culled from relatives with small children. The woman seemed agitated, but the little girl did not mind. The child clung to her when they emerged from the bathroom. Scrubbed pink and clean and dressed in secondhand pajamas, Coco sang for Mrs. Ortega, and then she did a little dance, smiling all the while. Growing tired as any child at the end of a long day, she curled up on the floor at the cleaning lady's feet and closed her eyes — and snored.

"Are they supposed to do that?" Charles could only wish that the child had come with a manual of operating instructions. "The snoring?"

Mrs. Ortega nodded. "The kid's getting over a cold. That's why I gave her the chicken soup." She wagged her finger at him. "Do *not* give her any crap from the drugstore."

"Of course not." It would not occur to him to second-guess this woman, who had many children in her extended family.

He scooped up the sleeping child and carried her to the guest room, where he put her to bed. Mrs. Ortega hung back on the threshold, clearly not wanting more contact with this little girl. It was Charles who covered Coco with a blanket and tucked her in. He closed the door softly, and whispered to his cleaning lady, whom he also counted among his friends, "Tell me what's bothering you."

She did not speak for a while, not until they were seated in the front room and she had finished her second round of sherry. Mrs. Ortega set the empty glass on the table, her eyes fixed upon the etched pattern of century-old crystal. "My mother, rest her soul — oh, her and her stories." She threw up her hands, exasperated, and then began again. "When I was a kid, I lost a lot of sleep 'cause Ma told me that fairies stole kids and replaced them with changelings." *What if* — that was the question in her eyes. She could never voice this thought, for she was a woman who prided herself on good horse sense.

"I can assure you," said Charles, "Williams children are blood relations to their parents. It's a problem of two missing chromosomes, not magic. She's merely a little girl, and they never would've found her if not for you. I hear you also saved Coco from a pedophile." He leaned forward to cover her hand with his. "You did a wonderful thing today."

This did nothing to brighten her mood. She turned in her chair to stare in the direction of the child's room down the hall, as if she could see what lay beyond walls and a wooden door. "You gotta wonder if fairy stories began with kids like that one."

"An interesting idea." And now Charles Butler was newly intrigued with all things regarding fairies — or that was the excuse he offered when he invited her to stay with him until she felt right with the world. And did she see through this ruse? Well, of course — yet she stayed. The hour was late when Mrs. Ortega told him the final fairy tale handed down through the Irish side of her family, and then a car service was summoned to take the lady home.

Charles never heard the door open and close. It was thirst that had awakened him in the small hours. He came to the end of the hallway and came fully awake, surprised to see that a wingback chair had been moved into the foyer, where it now faced the only entry to his apartment. By the dim light from the hall, he approached to find Mallory asleep in the chair.

Though he had known her for years, he could not set eyes on her without loosing a flock of crazed butterflies in his chest cavity. And this happiness of the moment coexisted with pain, the concomitant symptoms of a one-sided love affair. He was a realist on this matter. In the aftermath of Mrs. Ortega's night of fairy tales, he borrowed one from his own days in the nursery, and he substituted young Beauty's Beast with himself, a hapless man with the face of a clown.

He reached out to pull the chain of a nearby floor lamp. It came to light in bright-colored stains of Tiffany glass, and now he saw the revolver that lay across Mallory's lap. According to Riker, the rest of the force carried clip-loaded Glocks, and it was the detective's theory that his partner favored the old .357 Smith and Wesson because it was scary in a way that a semi-automatic never could be. It was a damn cannon of a gun, so Riker said, and Charles agreed.

Her fingers were loosely closed around it so that she might shoot the first person through the door. He listened to her steady breathing, the sound of deepest sleep, and he thought to gently lift the weapon from her hand — just as a safety precaution. Her grip tightened, and he promptly gave up on this idea, so startled was he to be looking down the barrel of the gun.

And *then* her eyes opened.

She lowered the revolver and fell back into sleep. And Charles thought to breathe once more.

Miles away, another woman was awakening, but she could not open her eyes. They were taped shut, as was her mouth. Wilhelmina Fallon could hear nothing, not the rumbling of her empty stomach or any sounds that might help to identify her place in the world. And how long had she slept? Was it day or night? She ceased to strain against the bonds of hands and feet. The only other tactile sensation was the feel of rough material against her naked skin. Her body's lack of hard support fueled an idea that she was suspended in space — that she might drop to earth at any moment, and this image chained back to an old memory of Ernest Nadler.

Oh, no. Oh, please no.

If she could have screamed, she would have.

This is the Ramble! The Ramble! The Ramble!

Six

On the way home from school, I quote Phoebe a line from a comic book. "If I can defeat my demons, I can be the hero of my own life."

And my father will love me again.

Phoebe thinks my comic-book philosophy will be the death of me. She says, "Remember Poor Allison."

"The jumper?"

And Phoebe says, "Maybe the girl thought she could fly."

— ERNEST NADLER

Privileged New Yorkers had high windows in the tallest buildings facing Central Park. Those who were still awake could see trees lighting up in a moving line, a glow worm slowly rolling across the Ramble as policemen in tight formation shined their flashlights up into the leaves. Cadaver dogs had proved useless for bodies in the sky. A sergeant called out to his officers, calling them back to the station house to wait for daylight.

High above a group of retreating searchers, Wilhelmina Fallon, not yet a cadaver, awakened stone blind. Thirsty, so thirsty. Hungry, too. And all the way crazy, she strained to hear.

Silence only.

Muscles weakened, she gave up the struggle against her bonds. The panic ebbed away, and so did the cramps in her belly. Dehydrated and disoriented, she made friends with delusion, and in her waking dream, she drank great tumblers of ice water. In the real world, her body was consuming itself in a ruthless effort to survive. Life was everything. Life was all.

It was morning in her mind, where an imagined table was laden with food, glorious food.

The aroma of fresh-brewed coffee was heady. An old-fashioned percolator bubbled on the front burner, and batter sizzled in the frying pan.

Mallory made an odd picture of domesticity, flipping pancakes while wearing a large gun in her shoulder holster. Cooking was a skill she had learned from her foster mother,

Helen Markowitz, and kitchens were her favorite rooms. This one was large, with warm ocher walls and a high ceiling. Charles Butler's appliances only looked a hundred years old; they were custom-made to blend with an era where the Luddite felt more at home. It was a peaceful place where even New Yorkers lost their cautious edge; and this was why Mallory favored kitchens over interrogation rooms.

The door in the hall closed. Charles Butler was gone. And now the detectives could begin.

Coco had finished breakfast, and she idly ran one finger around her empty plate. "Rats like fruit and vegetables, but pancakes — not so much." She went on to explain why hungry rats were attracted to the faces of sleeping infants. "Babies smell like milk, and the skin around their mouths *tastes* like milk. If you wash a baby before you put it in the crib, it won't get eaten."

"Good to know," said Riker, not even slightly put off his feed. Between bites, he smiled at the little girl. "Tell us about Uncle Red."

The child drew up her legs, hugged her knees and rocked herself. "He had red hair like mine. He said it ran in the family." She stood up to take a short walk around the table for the third time this morning.

If Charles Butler had been present, this would have been the signal to stop. He would not permit questions that agitated her. And so the psychologist had been sent outside on the errand of buying newspapers that Mallory could have easily retrieved from her laptop computer.

The detective filled the child's glass with more orange juice to lure her back to the table. When Coco returned to light on the chair, she perched there on the edge — a tentative visitor.

"So Uncle Red's hair turned from red to brown," said Mallory. "When did that happen?" She rephrased this for a child with a skewed sense of time. "After you got into Uncle Red's car, did you stop anywhere on the way to his place?"

"We stopped for food." Coco went on to describe the giant statue of a clown that greeted junk-food customers at a rest stop on the road. He was as tall as a mountain, she told them, and then she gave the statue lines of dialogue. But now she stopped mid-sentence, reading impatience in Mallory's face.

"So tell me," said Riker, whose patience with children was endless, "was that when Uncle Red dyed his hair? At the restaurant?

Maybe he did it in the men's room?"

"No, his hair was still red when we stopped at the drugstore. I fell asleep in the car. When I woke up, we were at Uncle Red's house. It was dark outside, and his hair was brown. Then he had himself delivered to the park." Coco excused herself to wash hands, her euphemism for a run to the toilet.

Down the hall, the bathroom door closed. The front door opened, and Charles Butler walked into his apartment, carrying three newspapers. He entered the kitchen in time to hear Mallory say to her partner, "That kid was snatched."

"How do you figure?" Riker laid down his fork. "Most perverts dye the *kid's* hair. This guy dyed his own. Sounds more like Uncle Red was on the run from somebody he knew. That fits with him getting strung up in the Ramble."

Mallory flipped a pancake onto Riker's plate, then traded the coffeepot to Charles in exchange for the newspapers, otherwise ignoring him as she spoke to her partner. "Two people with red hair, that's a problem — that's a detail for an Amber Alert. But he couldn't bring himself to dye Coco's hair. I say the creep had a thing for little redheads. *That's* why he took her." She pulled a bill from the pocket of her jeans and showed it to him. "This twenty says Uncle Red's no relation to Coco."

"You're on." Riker turned a broad smile on their host. "What about you?"

"No bet. I already know the answer." Charles filled three cups from the percolator, which he prized above a computerized coffeemaker that Mallory had given him one Christmas. That gift had been yet another of her failed efforts to introduce this man to a new century.

Riker sipped the brew and pronounced it wonderful. He glanced at the headlines as Mallory laid the newspapers down on the table next to his plate. One by one, he summarized the front-page stories: "Flesh-eating rats for the *Post,* more rats for the *Daily,*" and "Oh, shit!" for the *Times,* which carried a picture of the second hanging tree and two uniformed officers.

"It's all there," said Mallory, "the bodies, the bags, ropes — everything except Coco." She glanced at the clock on the wall. The man in charge of CSU would be reading his own newspaper right about now, and so would their boss, Lieutenant Coffey.

Riker attacked the remainder of his pancakes, his final meal before the war over *misplaced* evidence. Chewing and swallowing, he continued his argument for Uncle Red as a blood relation instead of a child snatcher. "Dr. Slope didn't find any sign of molestation when he examined Coco."

"The pervert and the kid were still in the getting-to-know-you stage." Mallory sat down to a cup of coffee. "I bet Uncle Red didn't have a clue about the Williams syndrome."

"But neither did Coco," said Charles. "She told me she was home-schooled by her grandmother. So the old lady — Coco says she's a hundred and ninety-one — she evidently realized there was something odd about her granddaughter, but she didn't have a diagnosis. I'll tell you how I know that."

At this point on any other day, one of the detectives would be bearing down on Charles, all but telling him at gunpoint to cut it short; but Mallory was sipping coffee, and Riker was still in the thrall of pancake rapture.

"Coco's never heard of the syndrome," said Charles. "If her grandmother had gotten the right diagnosis, there would've been special educational materials in the house. And the child would've noticed that. Her reading level is very advanced. She's read Dickens. Isn't that marvelous? And Coco tells me there were lots of pamphlets and books about rats. Her grandmother must've had a strong interest —"

"Okay." Riker's fork clattered to the plate. His last morsel was eaten, and now he rolled one hand to speed up the lecture. "Get to the part where the kid meets up with Uncle Red."

And a childish voice said, "That was the day I couldn't wake my granny." Coco stood in the doorway. "Granny was all stiff and cold." The little girl was wearing the button-up pants of Mrs. Ortega's youngest niece. She held them up with both hands. Buttons were a problem.

Mallory rose from the table to help her with this. "And then what happened?"

"I went outside. I wasn't supposed to, but I was scared. . . . Don't tell."

"You went outside to get help. That was very smart." How easy it was to manipulate a child starved for approval. Any praise would do. "And what happened then?"

"I ran down a million stairs before I got outside. And then Uncle Red stopped in his car."

"Did you recognize him?"

She paused to think about this. "He had red hair like mine. I told him about Granny. He said she couldn't take care of me anymore, and I was going to live with him."

When the pants were securely buttoned, Mallory tucked in the child's T-shirt. "Did he take you back to Granny's to pack your suitcase?"

"No, I just got into his car, and we drove and drove and drove."

Riker, the sorry man who loved children, was slow to set down his coffee cup.

"Tell them how you got your name," said Charles.

"Uncle Red said we had to change my name. It had to be something I could remember. He asked me what I liked best in the whole world, and I said flannel pajamas and hot cocoa."

Mallory reached out to snatch a twenty-dollar bill from Riker's hand. "And what was your name before that?"

Coco pursed her lips and then ran out of the kitchen. Moments later, they heard a ragtime riff on the piano in the music room.

"Baby Doll is what her grandmother called her," said Charles. "I'm sure she has another name, but she won't say what it is, and I'm not about to interrogate her. So I suggest you stick with Coco. She likes that one."

Mallory gathered up the dirty plates from the table. "Did you figure out *when* she was snatched?"

"No more than four days ago." Charles nodded toward the kitchen counter and the evidence bag that Riker had left here last night. "That was Mrs. Ortega's best guess based on the last time the child's clothes were clean. I believe it was early morning when Coco went outside to get help for her grandmother."

"Her *dead* grandmother," said Mallory. "Figure one day for the road trip with Uncle Red. It was dark when they got into the city. And he died his hair on the road. So he didn't stalk this kid. It wasn't a planned snatch."

"Crime of opportunity," said Riker. "The pervert saw her walking down the sidewalk . . . all alone." He pushed back from the table. "So . . . a day's ride from here, Granny's rotting away in her apartment. She hasn't begun to stink yet, not enough for the neighbors to call the cops."

"And nobody knows this kid is missing," said Mallory. "That's a bonus."

Seven

On the way to the dining hall, we have to pass through the creepy gallery of alumni portraits, and the eyes of the paintings follow us. I know some of the family names on the plaques below the picture frames. They come down from the robber barons of Wall Street — honored psychos of yesteryear. One of them is Phoebe's ancestor. He has a cruel mouth that says, "Come here, little boy."

— ERNEST NADLER

Jack Coffey wadded up his copy of the morning *Times* and bounced it off the rim of his wastebasket. That grand old lady of New York newspapers was behaving like a tabloid slut. After beating every other rag to the story of a double homicide in Central Park, the *Times* had won the right to name a killer with the town's first literary moniker: *the Hunger Artist* — shades of Kafka.

107

Riker slumped against the back wall of the lieutenant's office. This was the detective's firing-squad posture. Mallory had not yet clocked in, leaving her partner to explain why the front-page story mentioned information that their boss did not have.

And the head of Crime Scene Unit had not been privy to these details, either. Heller sat in a chair beside the desk, holding his own mangled copy of the newspaper. "I can bring your detectives up on charges — or you can tell me why I don't have this crime-scene evidence." He looked down to consult the small print of the *Times*. "I'm missing a few burlap bags and some ropes. Oh, yeah . . . and a couple of trees."

Jack Coffey was inspired now, *on* his feet and feigning his own bad attitude. "Your guys were at both of those scenes yesterday."

"Yeah," said Heller, "*eventually.* Mallory sent them to the hospital first. Two hours later, she remembers the location of the crime scenes. *Then* they go to the park, but nobody told them about any trees or —"

"That's when one of them heard about the bags and the ropes . . . and that *bastard* leaked the details to the press." Coffey looked up at his slouching detective, a cue that it was this man's turn to jump in.

Riker stepped forward. "I know the park

cops didn't leak anything. They wouldn't give up shit for a reporter. When I threaten uniforms, they *stay* threatened." He leaned down to tap Heller's newspaper. "Their own sergeant didn't get those details. But they would've answered questions from one of your guys."

"No way." Heller was never rattled. His demeanor was always dead calm. And so the man's slow rise from the chair was tantamount to a psychotic break. He held up his crumpled newspaper. "Nobody in my department did this."

"Yeah, *right,*" said Riker, possibly overplaying his role. "It wasn't the boys with the meat wagon. They only saw the body — nothing else. I suppose you're gonna blame Mallory for the leak? Give me a break. It's *her* case." He turned to his boss to see if this last part might be true.

"Damn straight," said the lieutenant. "So that leaves your team, Heller. And I don't wanna hear one more threat against my people." More magnanimous now, the commander of Special Crimes smiled. "Or, if you like, we can have a department hearing — a hanging party. And I'll have Detective Mallory explain why she didn't trust *your* people with evidence." He leaned forward, palms flat on his desk, still smiling. "Because you know someone's gonna ask. And you're wondering about that yourself, aren't you?"

The point was won, but not the game.

Without another word said, the head of CSU managed to convey that this was not over yet. He left the private office and ambled down the aisle between the desks in the squad room, turning heads with the sound of heavy footsteps. When the staircase door had closed behind Heller, the lieutenant retrieved his newspaper from the floor. He sat down to read it — *slowly* — while Detective Riker hovered, uncertain, somewhere between a clean getaway and a beat down.

Jack Coffey set the paper to one side, put his feet up on the desk and clasped his hands behind his head. "You better hope Heller never calls the desk sergeant at Central Park." The lieutenant's smile was genuine. It gladdened his heart to see the worried look on Riker's face. "Those park cops gossip like crazy. That's how I know there was a reporter on both of those crime scenes. I hear he was Mallory's pet."

Riker shook his head. "That guy was just a stringer, a freelance photographer."

"And today he's the newest hire at the *Times* — a *reporter*." The lieutenant wadded up his newspaper again, and this time his shot hit the wastebasket. He looked up at his detective. "Anything else you forgot to mention?"

Riker appeared to be searching for just the right words, not the truth of course, but something that might work.

"Never mind." Coffey waved him toward the door. "I don't wanna know."

Detective Riker turned a corner onto a narrow street paved with cobblestones from SoHo's first incarnation as a factory district. In more recent times, this neighborhood had been the haunt of boys and girls eking out a minimal existence in paint-stained jeans. They had decamped for cheaper quarters when money moved in with the Wall Street kids and the trust-fund babies. But now that crowd's antiques stores and trendy boutiques were closing doors. New York City was a quick-change artist, and the good old days were always six minutes ago.

At the middle of the block was the apartment house owned by Charles Butler. Keys in hand, the man stood beside his Mercedes and waved to the detective moseying down the sidewalk.

"Hey," said Riker. "Going somewhere?"

"I'm driving Robin back to Brooklyn."

Charles turned around at the sound of his front door opening behind him.

Coco stepped out on the sidewalk, holding Mallory's hand. They were followed by gray-haired Robin Duffy, a semi-retired attorney and a player in the Louis Markowitz Floating Poker Game. Riker truly liked this short, bandy-legged man. Duffy always had a bright smile that gathered up his bulldog jowls and crinkled his eyes to tell everyone how happy he was to be here, wherever that might be.

When hellos and goodbyes had been said, the old man embraced Mallory, holding her close, as if afraid that he might never see her again. And this was not because she had dropped off the planet for three months of lost time; he *always* did this.

As the Mercedes rolled off down the street, Coco announced that Mr. Duffy was her lawyer. Riker, long accustomed to hearing this news from felons, gave her a rueful smile and then turned to his partner. "Seriously? The kid lawyered up?"

"Robin's handling her custody issues." Mallory led the child down the sidewalk to an unmarked Crown Victoria parked at the curb.

When Coco had been strapped into a backseat safety belt, Riker climbed in on the passenger side, and he braced himself, though it was unnecessary this morning. His partner's driving was oddly law-abiding on the trip uptown, perhaps in deference to their young passenger.

Mallory adjusted the rearview mirror to catch the little girl's eye. "Coco, tell Riker what Granny did for a living."

"She killed rats!"

Riker smiled. That would explain a preoccupation with vermin trivia. "So Granny was in the pest-control business. Do we know where?"

Mallory nodded. "The company had a real catchy name — Chicago Killers."

All the way uptown, Coco entertained them with a monologue on rodents. And so the detectives learned that rats were ticklish, they sneezed and they dreamed.

The Mercedes traveled south, heading for the Brooklyn Bridge, and Charles's passenger said, "Kathy looks well." Robin Duffy was still allowed to call her Kathy, regarding her as the hand-me-down child of his best friend. He had lived across the street from her for all the years that she was growing up with the Markowitzes.

Robin stared at his friend for a while,

finally prompting him. "Kathy looks *very* well."

"Yes, she does." Charles would only commit himself to a comment on mere appearance. He would not invite any speculation on her state of mind or her lost time. And Robin would ask no direct questions. The old lawyer also had a confidence to keep and constraints of professional ethics; he had represented the young detective in the matter of getting her job back.

On one absence from the NYPD, her destination had been deep in the Southland, and on another trip, she had followed Route 66, but this time was different. It worried Charles, and he was honor bound to worry all alone. Upon her return to New York City, information from Mallory had been couched in bare compass points, though she had agreed that Mount Rushmore was big, and the Mississippi River was indeed mighty. Only one thing was certain: She had been on a very long road trip to nowhere. Whenever he recalled her meandering route, the wide circles and ever-changing directions, he formed a picture of Mallory spiraling, tumbling — falling through America.

On the other side of the bridge, the car rolled through a Brooklyn neighborhood of single-family houses with driveways and dogs in the yards. And the silence had become awkward.

"I thought Coco was absolutely charming," said Robin, in a safe change of topic. "She doesn't have a little girl's conversations."

"No, she has what's called a cocktail-party personality," said Charles. "That kind of patter is a skill that Williams children develop to form relationships with people." The sad irony was in the superficial quality of Coco's best trick — the very thing that prevented her from forming a meaningful relationship with anyone.

"What will become of her if I can't locate any family to take her in?"

"Coco will go into foster care," said Charles. "If she survives that, she'll grow up, get a job . . . and live alone." Did that sound like anyone else they both knew?

His passenger fell silent again, perhaps considering the commonalities of one broken child and another. Though, unlike Coco, Mallory never sought love or warmth from human contact; she only liked to *hunt* humans, and all her conversation revolved around death.

Charles glanced at the dashboard clock. By now the detectives would have found the runaway moon that, according to Coco, had gone to live in a box.

EIGHT

The rule is clear. No running in the halls.
But no teacher ever reprimands me. I think
they all know that I'm running from a beating, a biting or a toilet-bowl drowning,
whatever the day will bring.
— ERNEST NADLER

Summer-school children poured out of yellow buses, their screams and laughter chim-
ing in with the babble of other tourists waiting for the doors to open.

Coco's shoulders hunched. Both hands
covered her ears, and her eyes shut tight,
shutting out the noise and the bustle of the
crowd. The two detectives and the little girl
retreated to the high ground above the fray.
The path sloped upward to a bench in the
small park of flowers and trees that surrounded the Museum of Natural History.
The trio sat down and faced a gigantic
square box of glass and steel that was home

to an entire solar system. The majestic structure rose seven stories above the ground floor of the museum's planetarium.

"I know it looks different in daylight," said Mallory. The child beside her had seen this landmark only once, just a fleeting glance on a scary night, and her memory of it was somewhat flawed. "Is that what you saw from Uncle Red's window?"

The little girl nodded. Upon closer inspection in the morning light, Coco had been crushed to learn that it was not the moon that filled out this immense glass box, but only a pale white replica of the sun. In perfect scale, it dwarfed planets that were made of smaller balls suspended by wires to hang in frozen orbits. And that monster-size sun did not even float; it was securely anchored to the floor.

Riker patted Coco's hand. "What a gyp, huh?"

Mallory rose from the bench and turned around to face West 81st Street and a lineup of boxes on a grander scale, enormous buildings made of gray stones, brown bricks and, farther down, red ones, some with elaborate façades. This was Money Country, a land of liveried doormen and awnings to shelter the tenants on short walks to the curb and waiting limousines. Hundreds of windows faced the planetarium, and one of those apartments belonged to her comatose crime victim from the Ramble.

Evidently Charles Butler had not yet returned from Brooklyn to find a note slipped under his door by a SoHo patrolman, a polite request to report for shrink duty uptown. Riker turned to his partner. "We should get him a cell phone."

Mallory's mouth dipped down on one side. "Yeah, *right.*"

Riker envied the technologically retarded psychologist, who had an answering machine — a gift from Mallory — but never turned it on. The man strolled through an average day with no disturbing messages or any urgent summons. As an alien in a television nation, he was never made anxious by manic broadcasters with red alerts and terrorist forecasts, for he preferred to read newspapers, which told him only what had actually happened. Nor was he troubled by the jarring street noise of the hustling millions; it rarely penetrated the rolled-up windows of his Mercedes. And so Charles Butler smoothly navigated the most nerve-jangling town on earth.

"Here they come." Mallory pointed toward the patrol car double-parking near the corner of 81st Street and Central Park West. The uniforms stepped out of the vehicle. "There's only three of them."

"That's all the West Side could spare," said Riker. "They're helping the park precinct comb the trees for more victims."

And now the assembled officers were told to conduct a block-long search of sixteen-story buildings to find the apartment of a man with no name. "And these pictures won't help," said Mallory, as she handed each of them a photograph of the comatose crime victim. "None of the doormen knew who he was. His hair color's different." Starvation and dehydration had also worked changes on Uncle Red. "So the neighbors might not recognize him, either."

"You gotta be kidding." The senior patrolman folded his arms. "How the hell are we supposed to know when we got the right place? Half these apartments are empty — people out to lunch, off to work."

"Not a problem," said Riker. He was counting on the likelihood that Coco had been the last one to leave Uncle Red's place. "You're looking for the only unlocked front door in New York City."

Bless the rampant paranoia of a three-dead-bolt town.

■ ■ ■ ■

Except for the monkey, all the appointments were white — the couch, the rugs and curtains. The victim's clothing lay in a loose pile on the floor near the entrance. According to wallet ID pulled from a pants pocket, this was the home of Humphrey Bledsoe, a.k.a. Uncle Red, and Coco confirmed it by the only lamp in the sparsely furnished living room. Its base was a ceramic blue monkey. "This light was on." She ran one small hand over the animal's face. "I remember this."

Mallory looked up at the ceiling fixture, only a bare socket, and the bulb in the table lamp was low-wattage. So the room had been dimly lit when the stranger had come to take away Uncle Red bound and naked.

The child never ventured more than a few feet from Mallory's side, dogging the detective down an interior hallway of seven doors in a cursory search of the apartment, a palace by New York standards. "Which room was yours?"

"The dark one." Coco would not elaborate, and Mallory did not press for more detail.

Charles Butler had warned her not to

121

challenge any responses, but only to take what was offered. The child was very fragile; he had mentioned that *three* times. And yet this damaged little girl had survived for days in Central Park. By the lack of a sunburn on such fair skin, Charles had deduced that Coco had most likely suffered a meltdown, and then curled up in a ball in the safest place she could find. Mallory concurred, informed by the feral years of her own childhood — and days like that.

The detective and her redheaded shadow joined Riker in the front room.

"Smells like redecorating," he said.

Scents of plaster, paint and sawdust hung in the air. The couch and chair were new, still bearing plastic covers and store tags, and the hardwood floor had the look of a recent sanding. The large space was divided in half by two levels. A short flight of stairs led up to the raised section by the back wall.

"The guy moved his furniture in a week ago." The officer who had found the apartment stood in the generous foyer, one hand on the doorknob. "Before that, there were contractors in here every day for months. Sawing, banging, tracking sawdust and crap everywhere. The neighbors on this floor never met the new owner, but they all hate his guts."

When the officer had departed, Mallory looked down at the pile of clothes on the floor. "So Uncle Red and the other man were standing here." According to the child, the stranger who took her uncle away had worn coveralls; she called him the delivery man because he had brought a two-wheeler dolly — just like the one used by men who had delivered heavy boxes to her grandmother. "Coco, where were you standing when the delivery man tied up Uncle Red?"

"I told you. I was behind the door. Uncle Red said I couldn't come out. He said I shouldn't make a sound."

Mallory pointed to the arch that opened onto a hall's blank wall — a doorway with no doors. "Were you standing here? Maybe hiding behind a wall?"

The child shook her head, mystified, for she had already answered this question.

Riker turned to face the foyer. "The front door's the only one you can see from here. You know the kid wasn't hiding behind that one."

Mallory stared at the child. "Tell me the truth."

Coco spun her hands as she shifted from one foot to the other in her little dance of stress. Then she wrapped her thin arms around the detective and held on tight. Her

123

face lifted to show Mallory a smile forced wide. Her eyes were desperate, silently imploring *love me, love me, love me . . . please, oh, please.*

"No more stories," said Mallory. "I need the truth."

The child shook her head, uncomprehending, her eyes full of hurt, a prelude to tears.

"I need to know where you were hiding," said Mallory. "This is important."

"That's *enough!*" said the voice of authority from the foyer. "Not one more word!"

Both detectives turned toward the front door, not recognizing this tone, not from the very civil Charles Butler, who was bearing down on them, crossing the room in long strides. He picked up the little girl and rocked her in his arms, the gentlest of giants now. He smiled with his clown's face. And Coco smiled. All was well. She rested her head on Charles's shoulder and never saw his eyes turn hard when he looked at Mallory.

He handed the child off to Riker and said, "Take her downstairs. I'll collect her when I'm done here."

And Riker, who took orders from no one, did as he was told — siding against his own partner, and Mallory planned to make him pay for that.

Charles sank his hands deep into his pockets, where they balled into fists, so politely hiding that single display of anger. And his voice dropped into the calm range of an offhand remark. "So what's next for Coco? Waterboarding? Thumbscrews?"

NINE

On the way home from school, we stop off for a slice of pizza — Phoebe's treat. She says there's an upside to what they did to me today. I've marked my place in the annals of school history. She says, "They'll never get that bloodstain out."

— ERNEST NADLER

It had been the small joke of a desk sergeant to assign a flaming hypochondriac to the Upper West Side hospital, where a crime victim was under twenty-four-hour guard.

The young, germ-phobic Officer Wycoff sat in a metal chair on the intensive care ward, a large room of pale green walls and medicinal smells. A hub of technology — lights blinking, screens blipping — was manned by doctors in green scrubs and nurses in white, who monitored equipment when they were not hurrying to and fro; and all around them, beds were sectioned

126

off by privacy curtains in pastel colors. The pink curtain behind the police officer's chair concealed the comatose man from the Ramble.

Officer Wycoff had come prepared with reading material, a thick pile of computer printouts, to pass the time. And now, on the second day of his tour of duty, he was an Internet expert on all things regarding comas and dehydration. He was also vigilant in the extreme; he knew all the websites for hospital horror stories, all the ways that medical personnel could kill the patients, both deliberately and stupidly. *No one* got past him; not one doctor or nurse was allowed to touch the privacy curtain without first producing identification to back up the names on their hospital badges. And he took *notes,* by God. He knew *all* their names and addresses.

After the caregivers passed scrutiny, the policeman personally supervised every treatment, each change of IV bag and the catheter, too. He kept watch on monitors for machines that tracked vital signs of faint heart and failing kidneys. The staff found it unnerving to have medical decisions questioned by a man with a gun. However, to the officer's credit, he had caught a conflict of medication during one of his many perusals of the coma victim's chart.

So . . . if this civilian in street clothes, standing before him, thought she had a chance in hell of just waltzing past that curtain to see *his* patient, she had been cruelly misinformed.

"What's your name?"

An easy enough question, but apparently she was stumped.

Detective Mallory opened all the drapes to light up the front room of the apartment owned by Humphrey Bledsoe, alias Uncle Red. "That kid can tell me what happened here, but she *won't.* And I *know* she's not retarded."

"Right you are," said Charles. "Coco is *very* smart . . . and creative. She doesn't believe Uncle Red was turned into a tree. But a nice story is so much better than a frightening reality that she *cannot* deal with. She's only eight years old."

Oh, *huge* mistake. Mallory so disliked having obvious things pointed out to her.

"You don't want to get between me and a case! I need —"

"Mallory, shut up! Just *listen.*"

And she did shut up, but only because she was surprised to hear these words from him of all people. And so he had bought a moment to compose himself. Charles walked to a window that overlooked the planetarium across the street. He understood the child's limitations *and* Mallory's. "When you were her age, I know you went through worse things. But Coco isn't *like* you." He turned around to see a hint of anger in her eyes. Perhaps Mallory had inferred that this spoke well of the little girl — this lack of likeness to herself. To put her straight, he said, "That child doesn't have your coping skills. I wish she did."

And now he risked that other crime against Mallory, a repetition of facts already in evidence, but he was past caring what might offend her. "Coco was kidnapped, ripped out of the only world she knew. She also witnessed the violence of a man stripped and bound and carried off. *Then* she dared to go outside in the dark and confront a strange city, where she had nothing and no one. And she followed a sadistic killer into the Ramble — this little girl who has trouble with shoelaces and buttons. She was coming undone, breaking down, *shutting* down. And then you came along, Mallory. And *finally* Coco had somebody. That child only lives to please you." He waved one hand toward the window and its view of the planetarium. "She gave you the damn moon in a box." Never mind the small technicality that it was really the sun. "What a gift. What an ingrate you are."

Was Mallory paying attention? No, she was looking down at the floor, finding a pile of discarded clothing miles more interesting.

"This is where the perp assaulted Humphrey Bledsoe and bagged him," she said. "I need to know where Coco was hiding when this went down. If she saw the perp, maybe he saw her, too. A sadist could be looking for that kid." Mallory smiled, and he wished she would not, for this was hardly a happy smile, not at all friendly. "But you're right to take her away from me, Charles. You're so right." And her sarcasm said he was *so* wrong. "I only wanted to keep that kid alive. What was I thinking? I must be a *sociopath.*"

This last word was put out there to hang in the air between them like a dare. This was the way she had been characterized in Dr. Kane's psych evaluation for the NYPD. But Charles had been her champion in this matter, and he was her defender to this day, this moment. "I would never believe that of you." He would not — even if he knew it to be true.

She stepped closer to study his face. Was

she waiting for the red bloom in his cheeks that killed all possibility of deception and every chance of winning at cards? Well, she would not see him blush, not today. He was telling the truth. He would stake his own heart on the hope that she might also have one.

Lieutenant Coffey listened as an uptown desk sergeant told him on the telephone, "The coma guy's got a visitor." That young woman was being detained by the officer on hospital guard duty. "And you got *another* leak in your case."

After the lieutenant thanked the man for this brand-new wound to his stomach lining, he ended the call with a slammed-down receiver. Without opening the door of his office, he yelled loud enough to be heard by the entire squad, "Who's got a copy of the *Daily!*" He turned to his window on the outer room to see more than a few hands go up; this was not a *Wall Street Journal* crowd.

Janos rose from his desk with a newspaper in hand. The man was built like a refrigerator that could walk and talk; the five o'clock shadow of his beard appeared at nine every morning; and he had the most brutal face that God ever gave a detective — all of which made him invaluable during interrogations. He entered the private office on cat's feet and delicately placed his copy of the *Daily News* on his boss's desk.

Jack Coffey turned to page nine, as directed by the desk sergeant of the Upper West Side precinct, and there he found a picture of the surviving victim from Central Park, eyes closed and posed in a hospital bed beneath the headline: *Do You Know This Man?*

"And none of you guys caught this?" Coffey looked up at his detective. "Does anybody on this squad read *anything* but the sports pages?"

Janos always politely considered his responses and delivered them softly. "I like the movie reviews."

Though the *Times* had scooped the big story of the day, there was a reference to Central Park in this newspaper, too. But it was only a passing mention of the place where a dehydrated, naked man had been found. At least the photograph had been buried on the inside pages by an editor who favored rat-eaten little old ladies like Mrs. Lanyard over unidentified coma patients.

"Now our perp knows the guy's alive," said Coffey.

Oh, and the article had thoughtfully

provided the name and address of the hospital — so a killer would know where to go if he felt inclined to clean up this sloppy loose end of a living witness.

"So Coco was hiding behind a door." Charles Butler had been restored to his rightful place in the universe. Mallory ruled. She always won.

"No," she said. "The kid lied about the door."

"I doubt that. Her stories are for entertainment, not deception. Coco has no guile." Charles was staring at the raised section of floor on the other side of this spacious room. "Hel*lo*." He walked toward a short flight of steps leading up to that next level. "I knew something was off about this place. My parents had friends in this building. That's a chimney wall. So you have to wonder . . . why would anyone wipe out a fireplace?" That would be a real-estate sin in Manhattan. He climbed the stairs to stand on the higher floor, and Mallory joined him.

"Coco was hiding here," he said, so confident of what he would find when he lifted the area rug to expose a handle set into the woodwork. "And she *was* behind a door — a door in the floor."

Mallory leaned down to pull on the handle, lifting a square of wood to look into a dark hole. "This is where the bastard kept her." She ran one hand over the rough texture on the underside of the trapdoor. "He soundproofed it."

"It's a pedophile's dream house," said Charles. There would be no fear of a child's rescue, not by the accidental discovery of a building handyman letting himself in to fix a broken pipe. "You couldn't do this sort of renovation in any of the smaller rooms. And not over there by the windows. The raised floor would've overshot the sills. That's why he had to take out the fireplace."

He descended a short ladder into the secret room beneath the floor, where he had to hunch down to look around. "No light switch. At Coco's age, lots of children are afraid of the dark, and fear makes a good control device. So you'll excuse her if she left this frightening place out of her little narrative about a man who turned himself into a tree." By the light from the opening above, he could see stuffed toys and a bed that appeared to be unslept in. *Thank you, God.* Something crunched beneath his feet as the trapdoor was slowly closing.

"Give me a minute," said Mallory, "then open it — just a crack."

When Charles had finished his count-down, he lifted the square of wood by a few inches, and he was looking through the fringe of the area rug that once again covered this hiding place. The detective had closed the drapes and lit the only lamp. His side of the room was deep in shadow.

Mallory walked to the pile of clothes on the floor and stood in the place of a sadist, her eyes on the trapdoor. "Too dark. The perp didn't see Coco."

"She probably didn't see him, either, at least not in any detail." Charles climbed out and walked to the window, carrying a tiny pair of eyeglasses with one broken lens. "I found these on the floor — after I stepped on them." He pulled back a curtain for a few inches of light, the better to read the small print of the prescription on one stem. "If the glasses belong to Coco, she's near-sighted."

Through the slit in the drapes, he stared at the planetarium across the street. Poor eyesight explained why the child had mis-taken the mock sun for the moon. She had not seen the orbiting planets — nor could she distinguish a green burlap bag from the leaves of trees. He looked down at the spectacles in his hand, regarding them as yet another wound to a little girl. "This is why Coco could only tell you about the coveralls and the dolly, nothing about the Hunger Artist's face."

"But we're the only ones who know that."

And now the only evidence was gone. The broken eyeglasses had disappeared from his hand and entered the pocket of Mallory's blazer. The late Louis Markowitz had once described his foster child as a world-class thief, *born* to steal, and the policeman had said this with some degree of pride, adding, "What a kid."

Mallory perused the shadow side of the room, where the crack of a door in the floor had certainly gone unnoticed. "So the perp doesn't know I have a witness."

"Actually . . . you don't." Charles smiled.

"*I* do. Custodial guardianship, remember? That's why your man in Missing Persons called *me.* The Chicago police found the grandmother's body an hour ago. Dead of natural causes. Coco has no other family. But she has me."

He allowed a moment for the import to settle in. And now, with all the leverage he was ever likely to have, he laid down new rules for dealing with his young ward.

Mallory did not like them. Charles did not care.

The commander of Special Crimes Unit stood behind the pink curtain surrounding the coma patient's bed. In a face-off with Dr. Kemper, the hospital administrator, he held up a newspaper open to the page with the crime victim's photograph. "Somebody sold this picture to a reporter."

Kemper, a thin weasel of a man, took on an attitude of personal offense, one hand pressed to his breast, when he said, "It wasn't one of *my* people."

The lieutenant pointed to the patient. "This guy's wearing a hospital gown in the photo — so we can rule out the ambulance crew. They only saw him naked."

"I'll look into it."

What Jack Coffey hated most about this man was the smooth way he lied with a smile. The lieutenant turned to a nurse, who stood close to the administrator's side like a lady-in-waiting. "Go out in the hall and tell Officer Wycoff to bring in that woman."

When she had left on this errand, Jack Coffey only glanced at the prince of pricks who aggravated him so much. "I don't need you anymore. Take a hike."

The hospital administrator's smile widened as he made his hasty getaway. On the other side of the pulled-back curtain, Officer Wycoff stood beside the visitor he had found so suspicious. The woman was young, still in her twenties, and tall. No wedding ring. Though she had the unlined face and sexless body of a plump child, the quaint word *spinster* came to mind, perhaps because her mouse-brown hair was pulled back in a schoolmarm's bun. And the next word he thought of was *wallflower.* She wore a simple gray dress, the better to blend into a concrete city and disappear. There was only one standout feature, lush eyelashes that looked fake, but he knew they were real. This woman wore no makeup at all.

She twisted to one side, trying to see around him for a peek at the mystery patient. Coffey stepped aside, and she stared at the man on the bed. Her hand tightened around the shoulder strap of her purse as she shook her head. "I don't know him."

And did he believe that? Well, *no.*

She was turning round, ready to leave, and quickly. Coffey nodded to the officer, who caught the woman by one arm and restrained her. Eyes wary, she turned back to face the lieutenant. "I have to go."

Jack Coffey consulted Officer Wycoff's small notebook. "You gave your name as

Mary Harper?" He held it up so she could read the open page. "And this is your address?"

"Yes, I live on the Lower East Side."

"No, you don't. That address puts your apartment in the middle of the East River." Coffey reached out and slipped the purse strap off her shoulder. "So you made a false statement to the police. And now I get to search this bag for weapons before we take you in."

A nurse came through the curtain as the purse's contents were dumped out on the bed. "Can you do that somewhere else?"

"Oh, Coma Boy won't mind." The lieutenant looked down at the items spilled across the white bedsheet. No smokes, but there was a cigarette lighter, and he picked it up. Nothing else gleamed like real gold, and it was heavy — solid, not plated. This elegant bauble would not square with the lady's ugly walking shoes. In this town, rich women wore ankle-breaker stilettos. There were deep scratches on the gold surface. Maybe this lighter was a souvenir of better days. Or maybe not. And now he discovered another lie.

"Miss Harper, I believe you told Officer Wycoff you weren't carrying any identification." He picked up a snakeskin wallet. It

139

was beautiful. He held it close to his nose, and it even smelled like money; he wanted to marry it. The lady's driver's license was displayed in a clear plastic window, and she was not Mary Harper. *What a surprise.* "My detectives just identified our victim here." He waved toward the unconscious patient. "Phoebe Bledsoe, meet Humphrey Bledsoe."

TEN

They only mess with Phoebe when she's with me, and they don't hurt her much. Sometimes she gets bounced off a locker in the hall. A little violence in passing. It seems almost accidental.

I don't think they even see her.

Phoebe doesn't appreciate her superpower of invisibility. Maybe that's because Toby Wilder can't see her, either. Toby is entirely too cool to know that either one of us exists.

— ERNEST NADLER

Lieutenant Coffey sat down on the dark side of the one-way glass for a peepshow view of the lighted interrogation room. In other cop shops, covert watchers made do with bare rooms and maybe a folding chair or two. This one was decked out like a tiny movie theater with raised rows of cushioned seats

141

to accommodate the backsides of visiting VIPs.

The lieutenant was the only watcher in the dark room, and Phoebe Bledsoe was the sole occupant of the lighted one. Above the woman's head, long fluorescent tubes leached the color out of her face, and her feet tapped the floor while she chewed her lower lip. She chewed her fingernails, too; they were bitten to the quick after an hour of sitting there alone.

The door opened. Two detectives entered the interrogation room and sat down.

Showtime.

While amiable Riker made the introductions, his partner placed her hands flat on the table, the red arrows of ten long fingernails pointing at Miss Bledsoe. And then Mallory leaned in to stare at the woman up close. Such a hungry look. So intense. Some said she could do this for an hour without blinking, but that was only the cophouse mythology of Mallory the Machine.

Jack Coffey smiled. His detectives were running an interesting twist on the old game of good cop and bad cop.

Sane cop. Crazy cop.

The lieutenant had no trouble reading Phoebe Bledsoe's mind as she stared at Mallory: *What fascinating green eyes. Are they real?*

The woman quickly looked away. Every New Yorker was taught in the womb to never make eye contact with the lunatic. She turned to the *sane* detective. "Am I under arrest?"

"No," said Riker. "We just need some information." He scanned a sheet of paper and then flashed her a friendly smile. "I see you're a nurse at the Driscol School. So you're on summer vacation?"

Miss Bledsoe leaned forward. "Lieutenant Coffey said he'd charge me for making a false statement to the police officer. And obstruction — that was another charge."

"Don't worry about that." Riker dismissed this idea with a wave of one hand. "We're not here to give you a hard time." He turned to his partner. "Are we?"

Mallory continued to stare at Phoebe Bledsoe as if the woman might be lunch. She licked her lips.

On the other side of the glass, Jack Coffey's smile was wry. *Nice try.* He had no doubts about why his detective was playing crazy cop today; she knew he was watching her, wondering: *How crazy are you?*

Riker pulled a photograph from a manila envelope. "We found another homicide victim in the Ramble. She was bagged and strung up — just like your brother. But we didn't get to her in time. She's dead. We figure there's gotta be a connection to Humphrey. If you could just take a look at the picture? Tell us if you recognize this woman." He laid down the photo of a naked female with a rat-chewed nose and cheeks, tape covering the eyes and mouth, and only bare bones for fingertips. The picture had no ID potential — only shock value.

Phoebe Bledsoe rolled her eyes up to the ceiling. "I've got no idea who that is."

"That's what you said about your brother in the hospital." Riker raised his hands as if to say, *But hey, no hard feelings.* "And then you gave a phony name to the —"

"My mother told me not to call attention to myself."

"Your mother sent you to the hospital?"

"The picture in the paper wasn't very good. She couldn't be sure it was my brother. Humphrey was only sixteen years old the last time we saw him. He had chubby cheeks then — and his hair was red, not black. The man in that bed —" Her eyes lowered. Her hands clenched.

Jack Coffey could finish that thought for her: Humphrey Bledsoe's grainy newspaper portrait was black and white. His sunken eyes and cheeks had lost their definition to

144

a bright flashbulb. The better photo on a new driver's license bore even less resemblance to the coma patient, who was clearly not himself today.

"I wanna tell my lieutenant that you cooperated," said Riker. "Then we can make those charges go away." Once again, he held out the photograph of the female corpse. "I know this body's in real bad shape, but the woman was around the same age as your brother. He was twenty-eight, right? If you could give us a list of his friends —"

"I don't know his friends." She looked down at her chewed fingernails and then hid them in her lap beneath the table. "I *told* you — I haven't seen Humphrey in years."

Riker reached into the envelope and pulled out a clear plastic bag containing a blond strand of hair with long, dark roots. "This might help. Take a look at the dead woman's hair. . . . Miss Bledsoe? Could you please open your eyes?"

Mallory curled her fingers into a fist and banged the table with the force of a hammer.

Phoebe Bledsoe's eyes were wide open now as she edged her chair back a few inches. Prompted into a more helpful frame of mind, she studied the hair sample. "I still don't know who she is."

Mallory hit the table again, beating out the rhythm of a drummer — or a shooter — *bang, bang, bang,* staring all the while at her suspect. Under the table, the Bledsoe woman's fingers intertwined in a death-grip prayer.

Well, insanity made everybody nervous. It was an interesting moment for the watcher in the darkened room. His detective, the one recently voted the most unstable, was pretending to be unstable.

Riker leaned toward Phoebe Bledsoe. His was the reassuring face of reason. "You really need to cooperate. My partner here wants to charge you as an accessory to kidnapping."

"*I* kidnapped Humphrey? That's crazy!" The woman paused to steal a glance at Mallory, probably worried that she had offended the insane detective with the slur word *crazy.*

"No," said Riker, "not your brother. I mean that little kid he snatched."

Her mouth opened to mime the words, *Oh, no.* The shock was real. She shook her head. "I want a lawyer!"

Riker slumped low in his chair. "Like I said, Miss Bledsoe, you're only here for questioning. If we have to charge you with a crime, *then* you get a lawyer." While he packed up his envelope, preparing to leave, the suspect was rising from the table.

Mallory's hand flashed out to close around the woman's wrist, and she said, "Sit down." Her words had no rising or falling notes, no human qualities. "You're not going anywhere."

"I think I know what my partner is trying to say here." Riker stood up. "She wants to spend some quality time with you."

The frightened woman turned her head to stare at an empty chair on her own side of the table, as if intently listening to someone who was not there. Miss Bledsoe smiled, taking some comfort from her invisible companion. And Lieutenant Coffey had to work on a relative scale of insanity for the occupants of the other room.

Oh, please, not another nut who hears voices.

Schizophrenics were next to useless in court.

Riker sat down at the table. *Slowly.* No sudden movements. "So . . . Phoebe, who's your friend?" He casually gestured toward the empty space that commanded all of her attention.

Crazy was a game of musical chairs, for now the woman stared at Riker as if he might be crazy.

■ ■ ■ ■

A stretch limousine was a common sight at the Driscol School, though not in the summer months of vacation. In the backseat of this one, an attorney cautioned his client. "Miss Bledsoe, if anyone shows you another badge, just hand the bastard my card." It was the second business card he had given her in the past half hour. Perhaps this young man sensed that Phoebe had already forgotten his name. In another few minutes, she would not recall any distinction to set him apart from the law firm's other errand boys, all Yalies and Harvard graduates.

The rear door was opened by a chauffeur. She stepped out onto the pavement in front of the school, and the car rolled away. Phoebe looked up at the large building that dated back to an era when stone filigree was in fashion — and gargoyles. Two such monsters sat above the lintel, set to spring on anyone entering by the massive front door. The less grandiose neighbors, all brownstones, were also unchanged since the 1800s. The Landmark Society was rabid in the matter of external renovations, and with only the flaw of fluorescent street lamps replacing gaslight, they had managed to stop time on this Upper West Side street.

The school's founder had been a man with a penchant for carving his family name in stone all around the town. This mad quest to keep the Driscols in the public eye had been defeated elsewhere by urban planners who had torn his monuments down. But here on the façade of this building, the name remained in letters etched so deep that centuries of wind and rain could not obliterate them.

A narrow space between the Driscol School and the building next door was closed off by a tall wrought-iron gate. Phoebe fished through her purse for the key and unlocked it. On the other side of the iron bars, she made her way down an alley that opened onto a generous back garden. Chairs and tables were set in conversational groupings, and there were small benches here and there for the solitary teacher or student when classes were in session. Lush green ivy covered the rear wall, and flowers of many colors filled the wide wells of ancient trees.

A flagstone path led to a tiny cottage that had been a carriage house in the horse-and-buggy days. An anomaly in a city of skyscrapers, it sat on an adjoining plot of land not entailed to the school. Before the age of soaring real-estate prices, this had been a way station for family members who had depleted their trust funds or fallen into some other disgrace.

It was a hiding place.

Phoebe occupied the cottage with the grudging consent of her mother, the last of the Driscol line. By terms of the family trust fund, Phoebe did not count because she carried her father's name. She was merely a Bledsoe, declared so on her birth certificate.

A small boy walked beside her on the path. He was fair of hair and spindle-legged. For the entire eleven years of his life, he had been called Ernie. In later years, Phoebe had renamed him Dead Ernest, a pale joke, a poor play on words; being dead earnest had gotten him killed. In this incarnation that walked beside her, the child was much thinner. His T-shirt and jeans were dirty, and there were dead leaves in his hair. He had lost one shoe and a sock — and his life.

The little boy's feet made no sound on the flagstones. She had never mastered footsteps for her old classmate — never tried — for no one knew better than she that he was not there. And so the policeman's remark — "Who's your friend?" — had been somewhat unnerving.

"I thought they'd never let us go home,"

said Dead Ernest. He never said anything to elicit a response from her. They held no two-way conversations. Only crazy people spoke to the dead.

The boy who was not there had sprung from sessions with a child psychiatrist after the — *incident.* Dr. Fyfe, a believer in confrontational therapy, had said to her then, "Imagine the anxiety that troubles you. Picture it as a person. Talk to it, yell if you like, but get it all out." One snag — Phoebe had never been a confrontational child. And so she had constructed a facsimile of angst — Dead Ernest — but never railed against him. She had only listened to him, hour upon hour. After a succession of silent sessions, the young listener's therapy had been terminated.

Dead Ernest lived on.

Phoebe opened the cottage door to a large room with a high ceiling and a sleeping alcove. Apart from the kitchenette, every bit of wall space was lined with books. These volumes had been accumulated by generations of Driscols in hiding. They were all works of fiction — escape hatches.

She removed her gray dress — Dead Ernest called it her cloth of invisibility — and draped it over the back of a chair. The armoire's door was opened to a lineup of cotton frocks in bright colors and bold prints.

"You're running late," said the dead boy with one shoe.

Quite right. She had only twenty minutes to get downtown to the café on Bleecker Street. Phoebe undid her bun, and brown tresses fell in waves to her shoulders. After donning her dress and slipping on sandals, she ran a comb through her hair. Next came the perfume and a bright swatch of lipstick. *Done.*

She walked out the door, down the alley and into the street to flag down a taxi. Dead Ernest's legs were shorter; he ran to keep up and followed her into the backseat of the yellow car. And now they were off on a wild ride with a cabbie from the school of Oh-was-that-a-red-light? The first blown traffic signal was followed by the driver's diatribe on the thieving city of New York. "They speed up the yellow lights. Maybe you noticed, lady? If you're walking, you can start across an intersection on the green, watch it go from yellow to red, and die before you get to the other side. I *love* this town." After three court stories about the tickets he had beaten, the car stopped on the corner of Bleecker Street and MacDougal.

"You made it," said Dead Ernest.

With minutes to spare.

Phoebe Bledsoe was always the first to arrive at the Mexican restaurant. Over the years, she had known this place as a coffeehouse and café under different ownership, décor and menus. Only the location was unchanged — and the time of her rendezvous. She sat down at a table far from the sunshine of the front window. The old gold cigarette lighter was pulled from her purse, and she rubbed it between her fingers. As if by magic, the door opened, and a young man with long, dark hair walked in. He had always been slender, and now he was thin but still handsome — and probably stoned. It was hard to tell. He moved with an animal grace so deep, so innate, that he could not stumble or falter or fall even by an accident of overdose. He took his customary seat on the other side of the room. It must be one o'clock. He was never late.

"He's two years older than you," said Dead Ernest, as if this still mattered outside the society of children. "You never had a chance."

True, Toby Wilder had been beyond her then, as he was now. Yet this was the high point of every day, having lunch with Toby

153

at separate tables. She put away the gold cigarette lighter. One day, she should return it to him, though she was loathe to part with this memento — and he might remember that he had dropped it in the Ramble all those years ago.

"He looks like a sleepwalker," said the dead boy.

She stared at the real and solid young man. Were Toby Wilder's eyes less blue, less bright? No, but they lacked focus. When he looked out the window, he was blind to the jumpy foot traffic of tourists jamming the sidewalk — blind even to the waitress who handed him a menu — deaf to the girl when she asked what he wanted for lunch. And there was one other difference between Toby the child and his grown-up self: He had found a way to be still. His feet did not tap, and there was no tabletop drumming of the fingertips.

He had lost his music.

ELEVEN

Phoebe thinks Willy Fallon's body looks like the exoskeleton of an ant. And Willy is quick like a bug, but I say no. I see her as Spider Girl. I see Willy in my dreams, a pinhead atop eight long legs, scuttling across my bedroom floor in the dark of night. And this image of her stays with me all through the day. Every day.

— ERNEST NADLER

CSU investigators worked in the deep green shade of the Ramble, policing the ground around one of the hanging trees. They placed small yellow cones to mark the sites of found gum wrappers and cigarette butts. They had already removed a slew of rats shot dead by police officers. Every bullet spent had required a ballistics test and paperwork.

"Damn cops," said a CSI, who concentrated on the holes in the bark of a tree, the only holes not made by gun-happy rat killers.

They all looked up from their work when a park ranger called out to them, "We found another one!" The team of men and women followed him across Tupelo Meadow and into the woods. The ranger stopped and pointed upward. "Wait till the wind comes up." And now a mass of leaves waved aside to expose a green sack hanging from a high tree branch, well hidden from the flashlights of last night's searchers. It was a rare thing to arrive ahead of police and rescue workers, who contaminated every crime scene.

All eyes were on the team's newest member, CSI John Pollard, a small, well-muscled young man, who spent his free time mountain climbing. A tree should be easy. It was. Within a few minutes, he had made his way up through the leafy boughs and clouds of gnats to reach the burlap sack and its bulging load. On the ground, other CSIs gathered round the trunk, waiting for him to release the victim into their hands. But first, a nature photograph — *click* — a pristine shot of the branch untouched by ham-handed detectives. His fingers explored the outside of the sack. Its contents were stiff, unyielding.

No sign of life. No need to hurry.

He used a screwdriver to leverage the rope along the bough by a bare inch for one more shot. *Click.* There were no ruts or burns in the bark. The bagged victim had not been hauled up here by this rope. He found the loose end of it neatly coiled in a fork of the tree. Before he let the coil fall down to unravel into waiting hands — *click* — a picture of the slipknot that held the sack in place.

The rope dropped, and two CSIs pulled on it. The slipknot came loose, and the sack was quickly lowered through the tree limbs. As John Pollard climbed down, his eyes turned toward the ground, where his teammates were cutting into the burlap to preserve the rope's closing knot, and he had a glimpse of jet-black hair and naked flesh — a woman.

Wilhelmina Fallon stirred after she felt the hands probing her. She came awake to pain in every joint of her body. Then came the elevator sensation of going down and down. Finally, she lay on solid ground and felt a breeze blow across her bare body as the rough material was pulled away. Pairs of hands worked on the ropes at her wrists and ankles, then wadding was plucked from her ears, and a stranger's voice said, "It looks

157

like wax." Another voice said, "Bag it."

Ah, now she could *hear* — but she could not see, nor could she speak.

A lone hand touched her throat, and fingers pressed down hard. A woman called out, "I got a pulse!"

"No, don't touch that tape," said a man. "If she's dehydrated like the others, you'll peel the skin off her face."

Others?

"Wait for the paramedics!"

"Here they come!"

Sirens. She heard sirens, running feet, and a new voice said, "Oh, sweet Jesus."

One arm was pricked with a needle.

"Nod if you can hear me," said a woman close by.

And Willy Fallon nodded.

"Lady, I'm gonna cut a small hole in that tape across your mouth. Then I can insert a tube with water, okay?"

Willy nodded again. Oh, yes. *Yes!* Her mouth was flooded with a thin stream of cool water, and she swallowed, greedy for it, choking on it. She was *alive.*

Heller had always resented his promotion to commander of Crime Scene Unit — a damn desk job — and so he was a common sight in the field, observing his people at work. He stood beneath the newly discovered hanging tree, and he was pleased, but not because the latest victim had survived. This was the only pristine crime scene for the Hunger Artist. He turned to the man beside him. "Did you notify Mallory and Riker?"

"Yeah," said the park ranger. "They didn't even ask where the tree was. They just wanted the name of the hospital."

"Good." His technicians would have ample time to work the scene without those two underfoot, though the detectives could have done nothing to ruin his good mood. On the contrary, he planned to dampen *their* day. When he explained the mechanics of the crime, it was going to drive them both nuts. This thought put Heller in such rare high spirits he nearly smiled.

Like the other hanging trees, this one also had two screw holes drilled into the trunk just above the roots. He looked up into the thick leaves as he spoke to a veteran CSI. "What about marks on the branch?"

"No rope burns on this one," said the woman. "John got pictures."

"Okay," said Heller, "cut out the screw holes."

An appalled park ranger watched the CSU team cut a circular core sample from the tree trunk. "Why such a big chunk? That's a *lot* of damage."

Heller could have explained that he needed both screw holes in one piece of wood for tests and court evidence. Instead, he brushed his face, as if a bug had landed there, and the ranger took his meaning. There were no more protests from the tree lover when the team decided to saw off a branch as well.

Over the next hour, more equipment arrived. With a nod to the techs combing the ground around the tree, Heller made his way across a clearing to the site of an experiment. There he found his new CSI, John Pollard, a corn-fed boy from Ohio, experienced and solid on science. The only flaw in the youngster's résumé was the civilian status; he was a tourist in cop culture. Pollard had finished the last of three test runs, and now he loaded his equipment onto a hand truck outfitted with two oddball tires, a brand of inflatables to match tread marks found yesterday — one of the few bits of evidence they had not read about in the *Times*.

"How'd it go, John?"

"Very smooth, sir. But God knows there's gotta be easier ways to kill people."

■ ■ ■ ■

One eyelid was pulled back, and Wilhelmina Fallon stared into a brilliant white light. She heard a small mechanical click, and darkness followed. As she drifted in and out of sleep, words were caught in snatches at first, and now whole sentences floated back and forth across her bed. She recognized the doctor's voice when he said, "The sedative's wearing off. Don't expect much. She was hit on the back of the skull. The concussion wiped ten or fifteen minutes of memory."

"That's three for three," said the voice of a woman.

And the doctor said, "Pardon?"

Another stranger, this one a man, said, "Three bop-and-drops. Blows to the back of the head."

"Gotta go. Don't stay long, okay?" A door closed on the departing doctor.

The strangers' voices remained in the room. The door opened again, and feet walked in. There was no need to open her eyes. By their conversation, Willy knew all three of them were cops. She could even sort out the ranks by the deference the new voice paid to the other two. She ignored them, slowly waking to an inventory of soreness and pain from shoulders to ankles.

Now she recognized the new voice. After the tape had been removed from her eyes and mouth, this policeman had taken her statement in the emergency room. He was answering a question for the other two cops, saying, "Naw, she's fine. That tube in her arm isn't feeding her meds. It's for vitamins."

"Christ," said the other man. "It looks like she's been starved for a week."

And this one must be a detective.

"No, sir," said the man with lower rank. "More like twenty-four hours, give or take. She could remember a TV show from yesterday. Must've been on the skinny side before she got strung up in the Ramble. *Starvation chic.* That's what the ER doc called it. Your vic was naked when they cut her down. No ID yet."

And the female detective said, "You didn't get a name while she was conscious?"

"No, ma'am. She started screaming. That went on for a while before they sedated her."

"So the lady was in a lot of pain?" asked the other detective.

"No, sir. I think the doc knocked her out for being a bitch. It was *that* kind of screaming."

Willy repressed a smile. Just above her,

162

she could smell stale tobacco trapped in clothing when the male detective leaned over her and said, "Hey, Mallory, didn't this woman used to be somebody?"

Bastard.

"Society pages," said the one called Mallory, moving closer. On the other side of the bed, a discreet trace of very good perfume warred with the tobacco smell of the man. "But mostly tabloids."

"Oh, yeah," said the other detective. "Willy Fallon, party girl and queen of drug rehab. Doesn't look so good now, does she?"

Oh, really? Willy's eyes opened by slits, and one hand snaked out from beneath the sheet to grab the man's crotch. With his soft parts firmly in hand, she administered a light, threatening squeeze, a warning not to move — not to breathe. Her voice was hoarse when she asked, "What's your *name?*"

He looked so surprised. They always did. This one had the classic frozen stance for hostage testicles. "Lady, don't do it."

"He's a cop," said the woman. "Let go of him. *Now!*"

Willy turned her head on the pillow to see a tall green-eyed blonde. She glared at the woman's linen blazer. "Either you stole that from my closet . . . or we have the same tailor." *Oh, shit.* It looked better on the cop.

And now — another surprise.

The blonde snatched up Willy's free hand and bent back the fingers to bring on sudden pain, the kind that came with bright points of light, with shock and awe and the patient's agonized scream of "You fucking *bitch!*" The man's testicles were freed as the blonde's silently implied condition of ending the torture. But Willy was still yelling obscenities after her wounded hand had been released.

The cop called Mallory pulled a notebook from the back pocket of her superb designer jeans. Pen to the open page, her words were frosty when she said, "So, Miss Fallon, now that you're *awake* —"

"You *bitch!* You *cunt!*"

"— can you think of anyone who might want you dead?"

"I can make you wish you were never born!"

The man pulled back Mallory's blazer to expose a gun in a shoulder holster. "My partner can *shoot* you," he said. "She wins. Now answer the damn question."

The blonde seemed almost bored when she asked again, "Who wants you dead?"

"Tough one, huh?" The man smiled. "Just give us your top ten."

164

The patient recited an automatic response, a phrase oft repeated on the occasions of drunk driving and possession of recreational drugs. When she was done, the detectives could only stare at her, and the uniformed officer said, "Huh?" This was the first time these words had elicited any surprise from the police.

Willy raised herself up on one elbow. "Didn't you hear me, you *morons?* I'm invoking my right to remain silent. No more questions till my lawyer shows up."

The male detective answered his cell phone, said "Yeah?" and then turned to his partner. "Heller's got something."

The detectives quit the room, trailed out the door by the cop in uniform.

Well, that was easy.

Willy reached for the device that hung from her bedstead. So familiar from her days in drug-rehab facilities, this was a remote control for running nurses until they dropped. Oh, but first she must call a lawyer. Yes, that was rule one, impressed upon her when she was child — when her parents still cared if she lived or died.

What the hell was the name of that stupid assistant district attorney? Had she ever called him by his right name? No. When she was thirteen years old, she had alternated between Bowtie Boy and You Jerk.

TWELVE

Phoebe and I are always the first ones into the dining hall. When the doors open, we run like crazy so we can grab chairs at the end of a corner table, a safe place with two walls at our backs. We call it the Fox Hole. Everyone else calls it the Losers' Table. Even losers new to the school know to come here. They see kids in glasses or braces, the lumpy, shapeless ones and the pencil-shaped uncool, and every loser says to himself — These are my people.

Toby Wilder walks in. Phoebe's eyes shine. And there are other girls with shiny eyes, here and there, all around the room. He definitely has power over women — but he doesn't care. Toby sits down to lunch in his Fortress of Silence. Everyone wants to hang with this kid, but no one bothers him. Phoebe and I watch him from the Fox Hole. We all know our places.

— ERNEST NADLER

The private office of the man who ran Crime Scene Unit was a cluttered repository of weird dead things in glass jars and catalogues of arcane knowledge. Riker and Mallory had been kept waiting — and wondering how much trouble they were in — and how were they going to dig their way out?

Heller lumbered into his office and glared at each detective in turn. Sizing their necks for nooses? No hellos were offered. He opened a desk drawer and pulled out a photograph of two holes in tree bark. "This is what we started out with. Screw holes in trees . . . after we read about the trees in the newspaper."

Apparently all was not forgiven. Riker turned his head toward the sound of squeaky wheels. The new hire, CSI John Pollard, entered the room, pushing a hand truck that fit Coco's loose description of a delivery man's dolly. The long struts of the handle extended up from a square of metal between two wheels. A large cardboard carton sat on this low platform, held in place by buckled straps.

"That box holds a simulation of the murder kit," said Heller. "My guy's the same weight as the heaviest victim. John, sit on the box." The CSI perched tailor-fashion on top of the carton, and his boss secured him to the dolly with straps. "Now you got a rolling weight of just under two hundred pounds."

Riker eyed the hand truck with its load of box and man. "Could a woman move that thing?"

"One way to find out." Heller turned to Mallory. "Give it a shot." And then he walked out the door, unconcerned that this might give her a hernia.

She tipped back the hand truck and wheeled the carton with the ride-along CSI out of the office and down the hall. If this caused her any strain, Riker saw no sign of it. They entered a room of bare walls and a clean, steel table. This was a thinking-man's lab with no visual distractions — and no noise. Heller could gut detectives in here all day long, and no one would hear the screams.

John Pollard, freed from his bindings, began to unload the carton, and Riker shook his head — *no, no, no!* — as a jumble of equipment accumulated on the long table: a bag of screws, a cordless drill, a metal plate, a socket wrench, a pulley — and a *winch?* Attached to the winch cable was a heavy-duty hook used for towing cars and trailers. Two battery leads extended from its back end, and now — *Christ Almighty* — a car battery was set on the table. "What's with all this crap? Our perp used a *rope* to hang the sacks. We *gave* it to you. We even saved you the knots."

CSI Pollard leaned down to retrieve a bagged coil from the carton. "This is one of the ropes from the crime scenes. But the Hunger Artist used a winch cable to lift those bodies into the trees."

Heller laid a photograph on the table. It was a close-up shot of a branch. "You see those marks? Those are imprints from a chain used to hang this." He picked up an open-sided pulley. "Your perp threaded one of these with a winch cable."

John Pollard rested one hand on the winch. "This model can pull a rolling weight of five thousand pounds — cars, boats. It wasn't designed to *lift* anything, but we tested this one in the park." He touched the two red battery leads. "These hook up to any twelve-volt." He nodded to the car battery at the other end of the table. "I'm guessing the Hunger Artist would pick the lightest brand. That one weighs thirty-five pounds."

Mallory folded her arms, clearly not buying any of this. "There's no good reason

why a perp would make this so compli-
cated."

"I don't care about *why*," said Heller.
"We're telling you *how* he did it." He bent
down to the carton, pulled out a six-inch
length of branch in a clear plastic bag.
"Here's the damn *tree*, Mallory. *Look* at it.
Chain-link impressions — just what you'd
expect from holding dead weight. No sign
of burn or drag. The rope only held the sack
in place. It didn't pull anything over this
branch. A pulley and a winch lifted the body
straight up. That's the only scenario the
evidence can support."

"The Hunger Artist put a lot of thought
into this," said CSI Pollard. "In fact, he *over*
thought everything, every possible problem.
In all three trees, the sacks were tied off on
a high branch. If this guy hauled the victims
up with a rope and used his own body as a
counterweight, he couldn't even climb the
—"

"So that's where the winch comes in," said
Riker. A second rope would have neatly
solved the problem, but he only wanted to
end the windy lecture — before Mallory did.

"That's *right*," said Pollard in a tone
reserved for rewarding small children and
pissing off homicide detectives.

"No," said Mallory. "Doing it this way,

the perp would be out in the woods all night."

"Wrong." Smiling and smug, Pollard held up the cordless drill and clipped in the socket wrench. "I bolted a winch mount to a tree in ten seconds. Then I connected the battery to the winch, lifted a weighted sack, climbed up and tied it off with the rope." Pollard picked up the remote control. "I loosened the cable with this. Then I unlocked the chain, and the pulley dropped to the ground. I climbed down in one minute flat — removed the winch's mount plate — another ten seconds. Start to finish, seven minutes was my best time. It only looks like the Hunger Artist did it the hard way. This is actually the fastest, *easiest* way."

Mallory stared at the jumble of tools laid out on the table. "You got all this from screw holes in trees? That was the only *real* evidence, right?"

Heller was way too calm when he turned his face to hers.

And CSI Pollard prattled on. "The holes match a standard mount plate." He picked up a small plastic bag containing long screws with hexagonal heads. "These lag bolts fit the holes. One bolt would've worked, but he used two for every tree. Very clean holes, not what you'd find with a manual screwdriver. That's how I know your guy used a socket wrench attached to a cordless drill."

Who knew murder could be so tedious? Riker turned to his partner for support with this idea, but Mallory seemed almost too lethargic to pistol-whip John Pollard.

She stared at the two-wheeler dolly. "At least that makes sense."

Riker agreed. The police on patrol would have stopped anyone found in the park after curfew. A footrace through dark woods offered better odds of escape than a car chase, and an abandoned dolly would be harder to trace than a vehicle with a license plate. And it moved silently — no noisy motor. It was actually the safest way to transport an unconscious victim through Central Park.

CSI Pollard removed the empty carton from the dolly's platform. "Check out the tires. This brand matches tread marks from the first crime scene. Rubber inflatables — made to carry a heavy load over unpaved ground." And now, with a special smile for the *pretty* detective, he said, "I *told* you — this guy thought of *everything*." He popped off the balls of his feet — as if that would make him tall enough to appear on Mallory's radar.

Oh, but now she *did* notice him. How

unfortunate.

Mallory looked over the top of Pollard's head to see Riker's worried face, his silent plea — *Don't gut the little guy.* They could not afford one more feud with Heller's people. She nodded, and both detectives turned their backs on John Pollard to follow his boss down the hall to the private office, where another carton had been left on the desk.

"You can take this with you." Heller opened the box to show them reams of paper, enough to make a dozen telephone directories. "This is from our database — lists of every product brand to fit the murder kit. You got model numbers for the past ten years, manufacturers, outlets. Some of these places went out of business, so we threw in global liquidators. No index. Sorry. I guess you'll have to go through it page by page. I figure that'll take you guys a few thousand hours." He smiled, perhaps for the first time in years. "Have a nice day, Detectives."

Mallory and Riker exchanged looks that conveyed the same thoughts: Heller really knew how to hold a grudge — and they were totally screwed.

After dropping off the useless carton at

Special Crimes, the detectives traveled north into Midtown, home to the Hunger Artist's latest victim.

Despite a do-not-disturb sign hanging from the doorknob, the manager of the hotel unlocked the door to Willy Fallon's room. "She's been with us a little over six weeks. Her previous address was a hotel in Los Angeles." There was little more that he could tell the detectives about this guest. The description of a demanding bitch was couched in polite terms of "She can be difficult at times." And phone records showed no outgoing calls. "Not so unusual. Everyone has a cell phone these days."

Or maybe yesterday's party girl had no friends.

Mallory opened the door by a crack to see a cell phone lying on the floor next to a small pile of clothing. The manager was dismissed, and the detectives entered a clean and serviceable room, not a palace, but the kind of place where middle-management executives might stay on extended business trips — hardly the accommodations of an heiress to the Fallon Industries fortune. "Looks like the family put Willy on a budget."

"Well," said Riker, "the recession hit millionaires, too."

"The Fallons are *billionaires*." Mallory checked the bathroom to find towels draped over the side of the tub and an unwrapped bar of soap that agreed with the rumpled sheets on the bed. There had been no maid service since the kidnapping. Next, she opened the door to the closet. The clothes hanging on the rod were very expensive — and very last year. She emptied a purse on the dresser. No vials, joints or pill bottles, but there was a light dusting of white powder at the bottom of the bag. She wet one finger and dragged it across the satin material for a taste. "Cheap stuff. Willy's cocaine is laced with cornflower."

"That fits the budget theory." Riker stood over the small pile of cast-off clothes and shoes. "So this is where the perp dropped her and stripped her. Willy felt safe turning her back on the guy. And then —" He made a swing motion with one hand. "Bam, down she goes. You could kill somebody that way. The other woman, the dead one — she was pretty ripe. Had to be the first victim — the practice run. Maybe the Jane Doe was dead before she went into the sack."

"No," said Mallory. "Slope says our killer didn't even use enough force to knock that one out — just enough to stun her and knock her off balance. I showed him Humphrey's hospital X-rays. Same thing. I think our guy just got carried away with Willy Fallon. He hit her too hard. That's why she can't remember anything."

Riker leaned back against the door and stared at wall decorations, cheap reproductions in plastic frames. "What's our girl doing here? *I* could afford this place."

Mallory retrieved the cell phone from the pile of clothing on the floor, and she flicked through the list of stored numbers. "I've got one for her parents. It's a Connecticut prefix."

However, Mr. and Mrs. Fallon were not at home to the police at this time. And concerning any future date, according to the secretary who made all their social appointments, the detective had a better chance of being thrice struck by lightning on a cloudless day. "But one can always hope," he said. And the line went dead.

Wilhelmina Fallon was pain-free and flying high on medication as she multitasked from her hospital bed, clicking through TV channels and flipping the pages of newspapers until she came to the photograph of a coma patient found naked in Central Park. It took a long time to make a telephone connection to the reporter on that story. Twice she had to suffer insults of "Willy who?" from underlings, a reminder that her party-girl days were old news.

But not anymore.

After identifying the coma patient as Humphrey Bledsoe, Willy placed another call, this one to a TV news station. She was too impatient to wait for tomorrow's newspaper to restore her to fame.

On the other end of a third phone conversation, a hotel bellman assured her that, yes, he had removed her drugs from the room in advance of the police dropping by. And, yes, the bellman would be happy to take a small cut of her stash in lieu of a cash tip.

Willy had no cash.

The last call was made to her parents, also known as the Bank of Mom and Dad, but Mr. and Mrs. Fallon were not at home to their daughter. This time the snippy social secretary fobbed off her call on old Birdy, the downstairs maid.

A maid!

Willy had just suffered a kind of demotion. "Birdy, tell my parents I want to come home." And now she learned from the lowliest employee in the Fallon household that a trip to the family compound would not be advisable at this time. It was almost like a recorded message. Willy imagined the woman reading lines from a list of stock responses to cover every occasion.

"Birdy, I'm in the hospital. I nearly *died*. Do they know someone tried to murder me?"

Apparently there was nothing on the maid's list that might pertain to that question, and the older woman stammered, "I — I have to go now, Miss Willy."

Oh, of course — furniture to dust and floors to mop. This minimum-wage earner was a *very* busy person — no time for idle gossip with socialites.

Willy wondered if she should teach the old bat a screaming lesson in class etiquette, a shouted stream of four-letter words guaranteed to wither the tender soul at the other end of the line. She clutched the telephone receiver a little tighter, and her voice dropped to a begging whisper. "Birdy, *please* don't hang up on me."

Too late. Her connection to home and family was a dial tone.

After the telephone had been ripped from the wall and the pillows had flown across the room, a nurse walked in to find Willy crying and shredding newspapers into tiny pieces. Help was summoned. The words *Mommy, Daddy, Mommy, Daddy,* followed by a rant of obscenities were taken for a seizure, though the doctor hardly seemed worried or sympathetic as he put a needle into Willy's arm.

From the other side of the room, she heard the television set call her by name. And the anchorman went on to name Humphrey Bledsoe as another victim of the Hunger Artist. "A third victim remains unidentified."

A *third* victim?

"Oh," said Willy, "I know who that —"

"Problem solved," said the doctor, pulling the needle from her arm. These were the last words she heard as the room began to spin, and her eyes closed on the whirlwind of walls and furniture and newspaper confetti.

Thirteen

I can't use the school toilets anymore.
Humphrey and the girls might be hiding in
one of the stalls. But sometimes I have to
pee or die, and I do it in the garden out
behind the school. Now and then, teachers see me zipping my pants up or down,
but they never say a word. And this is
proof that they know what's going on. Not
ratting me out for peeing on a wall, that's
how they show support. Piss on them.

— ERNEST NADLER

The dissection room was a chilly place of
bright lights, stainless steel, and white tiles.
The medical instruments were best described as cruel. And the term *remains* had
a different meaning here. Yesterday's rat-
chewed corpse from the Ramble was today's
collection of body parts, organs weighed,
tagged and bagged, and tissue samples gone
for lab tests. A section of the dead woman's

181

jaw was also missing, and so was the brain and the sawed-off crown of the head. What remained on the table was a hollowed-out torso with putrefied limbs and a face obscured by a loose arrangement of surgical gauze above the bloody hole where the chin had been.

"If you want me to check for chloroform, a broad-base scan will take at least five days." The chief medical examiner stood beside the table and looked down at the body, the source of the stink in this room.

Detective Riker retreated to the wall of sinks and cabinets; he was not keen on the blood-and-guts side of his trade.

Mallory stood at the foot of the table, clicked on her recorder and said, "Jane Doe. Bag number two from the Ramble."

"She might be the second one found," said Dr. Slope, "but this woman is the Hunger Artist's first victim. I drew blood that was still in liquid form. That puts time of death within seven days. She was three, maybe four days dead when she got here. Heller can narrow that for you. He does wonderful things with fly larva."

Mallory stepped closer to the doctor. "I can't wait around for Heller to hatch flies. I need that little detail *now.*"

"Always in a hurry." The doctor picked up

a clipboard from the small tray table and flipped through handwritten notes. "Her ordeal did a lot of damage to the organs. It was a *slow* death." He scanned the lines and flipped more pages, sometimes glancing Mallory's way to see if she was sufficiently irritated yet. Apparently not. More page flipping followed. "As you might have expected — no stomach contents. That might've helped."

He smiled. She glared.

He held up an X-ray. "There's a hairline fracture at the back of the skull." Dr. Slope waited a beat, and then, before Mallory could remind him that she had *already* seen that X-ray, he said, "Well, you know *that* didn't kill her. Off the cuff, I'd say cause of death was dehydration. But then I found something else that was much more interesting."

Riker rolled his eyes. All he wanted right now was one standout detail that would marry up to a missing-person file. And Slope *knew* that. The stack of reports from the tristate area posed a huge expenditure of man-hours. But now the detectives would have to listen to a lecture. And this was his partner's fault. Mallory and the doctor had a game to play. It had gone on for years. It would never end.

"All right, let's start over," she said. "Give us the basics. Age, height, weight —"

"Mid to late twenties. Height, five feet six. Weight, one hundred ten pounds. Does that help?"

No. That would fit a great many missing women from New York, New Jersey and Connecticut, but Mallory never answered obvious questions. "What about tattoos?" she said. "Injection sites? Birthmarks? Anything *useful?*"

"There's one truly rare feature." Slope's pause was long and maddening, but Mallory was cool. Somewhat disappointed, the doctor walked to the counter and picked up a specimen bottle. "This is it."

Riker saw something white and wormy floating in liquid. "Our vic had an alien baby?"

"Oh, no," said Slope. "The woman's most remarkable feature was in her brain."

And Mallory did not shoot him.

"I found this tumor on the pituitary gland. It's not cancerous, but it would've caused other problems. It's been there for a few years. The symptoms would've been obvious to her general practitioner. It's situated in a tricky location for surgery, but doable. And it's odd that she never had it removed."

"Bad healthcare plan," said Riker.

"I don't think so, but I'll get to that later. A tumor in this specific location presents with a variety of symptoms, and not always, but *sometimes,* a drastic change in personality. I know that was the case with our Jane Doe."

"Wait." Mallory clicked off her recorder and folded her arms against the doctor. She was not buying this. "You diagnosed a change of personality . . . in a dead woman."

"You're skeptical. I can always tell." Dr. Slope gave her an evil smile as he lifted a strand of the corpse's hair, half its length brown, half blond. "I can date that tumor back to her last salon appointment. My wife is a blonde. I know the cost of hair coloring. There are three different shades for these highlights to make them look natural . . . like your hair, *Kathy.*"

"Mallory," said the natural blonde, correcting him — again.

"It cost Jane Doe a lot of money to maintain this process. And she had another expensive habit — cocaine. I found old surgical scars from repairs to the damage in her nasal cavity."

Riker's chin dropped to his chest. Scars inside the nose so rarely turned up in the details collected by Missing Persons.

"So she had money to burn before the

185

tumor showed up," said Mallory. "So?"

"Well, two years ago, she not only stopped dying her hair — she also stopped brushing her teeth. She has dental caries in the age of fluoride. I had a forensic dentist consult on the damage, and his opinion nicely fits my timetable for the tumor. Also — and this goes back to your question on injection sites — there are none, and no additional scaring in the nasal cavity. The standard tox screen shows no recent drug abuse. So that's *another* change in behavior."

"Okay," said Riker. "So far, we're working off the description of a blonde with brown roots and cavities. *Thanks.* You got a photo of her face *before* you messed her up?" He was hoping for something that might actually help. Right now they had nothing, not even her eye color. The last time the detectives had seen this corpse, strips of duct tape had covered the eyes and mouth.

Dr. Slope pointed to the counter. "There's a set of photos in that envelope. But you won't need them. I'll have her name by this time tomorrow."

Riker's head lolled back, and he stared at the ceiling. Was Mallory drawing her gun on the doctor? Did he care?

"And that brings us to the plastic surgery,"

186

said Slope. "The woman had a chin implant."

That would neatly explain a gaping wound where the chin used to be. Any serial numbers on the prosthesis would lead them to the surgeon who did that operation. Riker looked at his watch. A search like that could be done in an hour or less. Why wait till tomorrow?

"She also had breast augmentation." Dr. Slope held up a bag with two implants that looked like small white pillows. Riker knew they would be soft to the touch; their perfect shape was the only memorable thing about the first teenage girl he had groped in the backseat of his father's car. Ah, nostalgia.

The doctor mistook his smile for interest, and the lecture continued. "The prosthetics were traced to a European company. Unfortunately, with the time differential, I won't get a call back until tomorrow morning. Then we use the codes to find the surgeon, and *voilà*."

They were going to lose a day in the identification. Well, even with the damage of a rat-chewed face, maybe they could rule out some of the missing-persons reports that had come with pictures. Riker opened the medical examiner's envelope and stared at the first photograph of the victim's face.

"What the hell is *this!*" It was not a question but an accusation.

"Oh, the *mole,*" said Dr. Slope. "Didn't I mention that?"

Sarcastic bastard.

Forgetting for the moment that autopsy damage made him puke, Riker walked to the head of the table and used his pen to dislodge the gauze from the dead woman's face, what was left of it. The duct tape was gone, and now he could see the exposed upper lip — and a mole with two incredibly long, thick hairs that resembled cat's whiskers.

Riker was heading for the door, and Mallory was right behind him, when Slope called out the final punch line. "So . . . you think the mole might be helpful?"

Riker stared at the autopsy photographs laid out on his desk, and then he looked up at his partner. "With Heller, we had it coming, but what did you do to Slope? I mean *recently.*"

Unannounced visitors to the squad room interrupted his grousing. Charles Butler came through the stairwell door with Coco, and behind them was Robin Duffy, Mallory's biggest fan. And so it was difficult to say who was happiest to see her. Coco won

188

for the widest grin as she ran down the aisle of desks, her arms spread wide, and she handily beat the old lawyer in this footrace to hug their favorite detective. Then Duffy's arms reached out in heavy-duty-embrace mode, and he squeezed her tight. Across the room, two detectives raised their heads to watch the spectacle of people who liked Mallory well enough to risk this.

Charles took Coco's hand and led her toward the lunchroom, the home of a giant, twelve-tier candy machine. "This will be fun," he said, jingling the change in his pockets. "We're going to practice your motor skills with coin slots." And when the child hung back, reluctant to leave Mallory's side, he said, "Just for a few minutes."

As they disappeared down the hall, Robin Duffy laid his briefcase on a desk and opened it. "Kathy, I need you to sign some paperwork." He glanced at his watch. "I have to catch a plane to Chicago. The executor for the grandmother's estate wants Coco returned to Illinois."

"Sure he does," said Riker. "Easier to rob the kid if he's got custody."

"Coco isn't going anywhere," said Mallory.

"That's what Charles said." Robin held up an affidavit with the psychologist's signature. "This says she can't be relocated until he finds her a permanent home. I've got a hearing before a Chicago judge." The old man handed her another sheet of paper. "I took the liberty of drawing up your statement, Kathy. In effect, it says Coco isn't going anywhere. Just sign it, give me a copy of the material witness warrant, and I'm off to the airport."

When the paperwork was done, Charles Butler reappeared with a chocolate-covered child. Mallory knelt down with a tissue to clean the little girl's face and hands. This was pure reflex; she cleaned *everything*. Coco gifted the detective with a candy bar and another hug that smeared Mallory's silk T-shirt, normally a hanging offense. But Coco got clean away with this, and down the stairs she went, hand in hand with Charles, the elf and the giant.

Riker answered his phone on the first ring, saying, "Yeah?" He listened to the desk sergeant for a moment and then said to his partner, "The mole man's downstairs."

The middle-aged visitor to the SoHo station house had a sweet smile and an odor of homelessness about him, though he was clean-shaven and wearing freshly laundered clothes. For many years, Mr. Alpert had managed a soup kitchen to feed the poorest of the poor, and now he smelled like them. A man of faith, he handed Detective Mallory a religious pamphlet, having determined, almost immediately, that she had not yet found the Lord.

He followed her up the stairs to the squad room, saying, "I thought I'd have to make the identification at the morgue."

"That won't be necessary," said Mallory. Only one missing-person report had mentioned the giveaway detail of a mole with cat's whiskers.

They passed through the staircase door and into the squad room of tall windows, empty desks and one man standing. "Hey, there." Detective Riker extended his hand. "Thanks for coming in. We'll have you outta here real soon."

"I'd appreciate that," said Mr. Albert. "We're shorthanded at the mission." He sat down in a chair beside Mallory's desk. "How did Aggy die? Was it an accident?"

"We won't have the autopsy report till next week," said Mallory — and not to spare this gentle soul the details of a death with drawn-out suffering, but to forestall the questions that always followed a finding of murder.

Riker opened his notebook. "You don't

have any idea what Aggy's last name was? She never mentioned any relatives?"

"No, sorry. She didn't talk very much. I can tell you she had mental problems. Poor woman. Some sort of compulsive disorder. There was this thing she did with her teeth." Mr. Alpert turned his head from side to side as he clicked his teeth, biting the air like a dog snapping at flies. "Like that."

Riker broke off the tip of his pencil. "Okay, a mental case. You were helping her."

"Oh, no. Aggy was helping *me.* She worked in the mission kitchen six days a week. Never late, not once in almost two years. When she didn't show up one day, I got worried. The next day, I filed a report with the police."

"So she's been missing for a week," said Mallory. "Did you go to her apartment? You didn't give her address in your report."

"I had no idea where she lived, but I know she wasn't homeless. Her clothes were always clean, and she had spending money." He pulled a snapshot from his back pocket. "This was taken at our last Christmas party. She's the one in the middle."

Riker studied the image of Aggy, so busty before Dr. Slope deflated her by removing the breast implants. "Do you know who her friends are?"

"*I'm* her friend." Mr. Albert shrugged to say he couldn't name another one. "She's a bit off-putting — incessant praying and that odd thing she does with her teeth. But she knows a lot of homeless people. When she's not working in the soup kitchen, she carries around baskets of sandwiches and gives them out to panhandlers. Some of the street people call her Saint Aggy."

The two partners were late to join the rest of the squad assembled in the incident room, where every wall was lined with cork from baseboard to ceiling molding. The front wall was covered with Riker's messy mosaic of autopsy pictures and crime-scene shots. On the floor was the carton of lists to track down items of the murder kit, but this CSU box remained sealed, and now it was kicked into a far corner by the angry commander of Special Crimes, who called it "Useless crap!"

The energy in the room was climbing. Detectives filled half the folding chairs, notebooks out, pencils ready, waiting for the boss to get on with the show. Other men milled around, and some gathered by the pinned-up array of maps and diagrams for the Ramble. That patch of the cork wall was Mallory's work. Each paper was equidistant from the ones surrounding it; her thumbtack style had machine precision. She sat at the back of the room, alone.

Jack Coffey took his place behind the lectern. "Listen up!"

Most of the men took seats, but some remained standing, and Mallory was still alone, flanked by empty chairs — as if she had picked up some contagious disease on the road during her lost time.

"This wasn't a spree attack," said the lieutenant. "We got space between each one of the Ramble hangings — three to four days." He pointed to the carton at the back wall. "Don't waste time chasing down Heller's crappy leads. If we get a suspect who keeps pulleys and winches around the house — great. Otherwise, screw it. CSU's a dead end. We concentrate on the victims."

And now it was Riker's turn to address the squad. His back was still turned to them as he pinned up pictures of the Hunger Artist's surviving victims, Humphrey Bledsoe and Wilhelmina Fallon. Last, he added the mission photo of the dead woman, known only as Aggy. "Okay, guys." Every head turned his way. "This is what we got so far. A comatose pedophile, a bitch socialite, and a dead saint with a boob job. Theories? Any?"

FOURTEEN

Twice a week, when Humphrey's in therapy, I go over to Phoebe's house after school. If her mother's not there, we bounce off beds and couch cushions, flying high — like freaking superheroes.

When Phoebe's mother is home, we tiptoe everywhere. We are mice.

— ERNEST NADLER

Comatose Humphrey Bledsoe's organs were failing, one by one.

The patient was in a delicate limbo, tubes running in and out of him, machinery breathing for him, and the next twenty-four hours would be a critical period. This was the medical opinion of the young policeman in charge. Officer Wycoff continued to screen everyone approaching the pink privacy curtain around the hospital bed. Three people stood before him now, seeking an audience.

They had come to the intensive care ward with the blessing of the mayor, or so said the mayor's aide, a slight, nervous man who did not figure into the police chain of command. And so the young officer was unimpressed. One member of the visiting trio was a sour-faced woman with sturdy, ugly shoes and a severe black suit to match her close-cropped hair.

The mayor's aide gestured toward the other woman, the tall redhead who reeked of money with her pearls and silk and very high heels. She appeared to be only ten years older than his patient, but the man from the mayor's office insisted, "This *is* Mr. Bledsoe's mother."

Hands on hips, the young policeman barred her way, saying, "Prove it, lady."

She seemed to find this amusing and cheerfully handed over her wallet, hardly the picture of an anxious family member. Wycoff narrowed his eyes. Could this woman be more suspicious? According to her driver's license, she was fifty-two years old, and only half her surname matched the patient's.

Mrs. Grace Driscol-Bledsoe was allowed beyond the privacy curtain on a limited passport: Officer Wycoff would only permit a half-hour visit. She patted his arm as she

196

passed him by, saying, "This won't take a minute, my dear." True to her word, it took only seconds for her to bend over the hospital bed and speak a single word in the ear of her comatose son.

"Die," she said.

And, obediently, he did.

As the society matron sailed off beyond the curtain, the monitors sounded alarms, and the officer yelled, "Code blue!" A crew of nurses rushed a crash cart to the bedside, and there were charged paddles held high with repeated shouts of "Clear!" before each electrical shock was administered, but the dead man could not be brought back.

Moments later, the bad mother was arrested near the elevator and handcuffed by the young policeman. Nobody screwed with *his* patient. And why was she laughing? The officer reached into his shirt pocket and withdrew the card with a case detective's cell-phone number.

"Wycoff is my new favorite cop," said Riker.

The detectives stepped off the elevator and strolled down the hall. Outside the door to the intensive care ward, a young policeman awaited them with his prisoner. The smiling redhead in pearls and handcuffs fit Officer Wycoff's description of the grieving mother. And the mayor's aide had been aptly described as a yappy lapdog in a suit. But Mallory focused on the dark-haired woman, who would not stand out in any company — if not for the small, black-leather bag hanging from a shoulder strap. It was a miniature version of a doctor's Gladstone.

Officer Wycoff read Mallory's mind and said, "That one never got *near* my patient." He consulted his notebook stats gleaned from driver's licenses. "Alice Hoffman, forty-five years old — same address as my prisoner." He turned from the drab brunette to the elegant redhead. "And this is Grace Driscol-Bledsoe, age fifty-two."

The mother of their late crime victim was close to Riker's age, but his skin was creased, and hers had been ironed by a first-rate plastic surgeon. And there were other indicators that she had buckets of money. Her eyebrows were perfectly defined arches that seemed to ask, *If I knew who you were, would I care?* And Riker flashed her a smile to say, *You bet your ass, lady.*

"She's not a suspect," said the mayor's aide, scrunching up his face. "Oh, this is too much!" He listed the lady's good works as the director of the Driscol Institute, a charitable foundation, and then he de-

198

manded that her restraints be removed. "This *instant!*" And when that failed, he went on to make the pompous determination that death by suggestion was not murder. "Hardly the crime of the century."

Though the aide was annoying, both detectives concurred with the amateur legal opinion, and the cuffs were removed. Grace Driscol-Bledsoe flicked one hand at the mayor's man, and he backed up to the wall to stand beside the other minion, Miss Hoffman.

Mallory stepped up to the mother to do the honors. It was her turn to say the customary words for moments like this. "We're sorry for your loss."

The lady laughed, and Riker found that weirdly refreshing.

"Your son kidnapped a little girl." Mallory waited a beat and then added, "But that doesn't surprise you, does it?"

"Actually . . . no." Mrs. Driscol-Bledsoe opened her purse and pulled out a business card. "Just tell my lawyer where to send the money — whatever the child needs." Her tone was dismissive, and she held out the card with an air of *Just take it and be on your way.*

Mallory did not accept the card. She never even glanced at it. The young detective's left hand went to her hip, a move that drew back her blazer for a glimpse of the gun — just a subtle reminder of who was in charge of whom. "Is that how you usually handle your son's victims? You just pay them off?"

"Guilt doesn't work on me, Detective." The door to the ICU opened, giving the woman a glimpse of the pink curtain around the bed of her dead son. "Monsters are begot by monsters." Her smile was gone when she turned her face to Mallory's. "You might do well to remember that."

The mayor's aide crept up behind the society matron, and he covertly nodded to the detectives, silently urging them to believe this.

Charles Butler puffed out his cheeks to make a great show of holding his breath while Coco slowly buttoned her cotton shirt. This bright pink garment was no hand-me-down apparel. It was brand-new, a gift and a bribe from Mrs. Ortega, the sworn enemy of Velcro fasteners. The cleaning lady stood behind the child and anxiously worked invisible buttons in the air with her own hands, as if to offer encouragement via black magic.

The last button on Coco's shirt was done, much applause followed, and the child looked up from her labors, quizzical. "Is this going to take forever *every* day?"

"No," said Charles. "But fine motor skills will always be a *bit* of a problem."

"Because of my Williams syndrome." She had read all the literature that he could find on the subject, and he had answered her many questions, but the child's conversations always ran back to rats, the staple of her interactions with everyone.

"Your progress with buttons is amazing." He gave her his most foolish smile, a guarantee of a smile in return. Children loved clowns.

"Next," said Mrs. Ortega, "we do shoelaces."

Or maybe not.

Coco fled to the music room. Apparently tying shoes was akin to a far mountain that could not be scaled today. *Things to do. Songs to play. Sorry.* A moment later, a delicate sonata wafted out to them.

"I watch her little fingers flying over those piano keys," said Mrs. Ortega, "and I just don't get it." Tired and defeated, the cleaning lady flopped down in an armchair and turned her eyes to the adjoining room. "How can the kid do that — when she can't tie shoelaces?"

"Her brain is wired differently. It's a

mystery. Ask any neurologist. But I think you can blame her grandmother for the lack of bow-tying skills. I'm told the woman knew she was terminally ill. So the problems of buttons and laces were resolved with Velcro, and all the time she had left was invested in Coco's strengths — music and reading." In Charles's opinion, the grandmother had made an excellent choice.

However, his cleaning lady was not so impressed.

"Laces are important, too," she said, "when you're eight years old."

"Right you are. But that's a job for a physical therapist." Based on his evaluation of Coco's motor skills, the problem of tying shoelaces could not be resolved in a few dedicated hours. It might take weeks or months to work through it. Or she might never learn.

Charles failed to hear his front door open, and Mallory's hello from the hall was all but lost below the ripple of piano keys. But Coco heard it. She came flying out of the music room, aiming her little body like a cannonball, and now the young woman was prisoner to the child as tiny arms locked tightly around her. The detective absently stroked the little girl's hair in the manner of petting a dog.

Mallory's brain was also wired differently, also a mystery. And she always confounded him, as she did now when she lifted Coco high in the air and said, "Buttons! Did you do them all by yourself?"

"Yes!" Grinning widely, the child sailed over the moon with joy; so happy was she to be with the one she loved best.

Charles Butler could hear warning bells in Mallory's gentled voice. Another thing that would cost him sleep was the way she smiled at this child. The homicide detective had a limited repertoire of such expressions: one smile said, *I'll get you for that,* but this one was worse; it was the smile that said, *I've got you now.*

Phoebe Bledsoe hurried through the school's back garden and down the flagstone path to enter her cottage on the last ring of the telephone. She set her grocery bags on the desk as the answering machine picked up the message.

And a woman's voice said, "It's Willy Fallon. Your mother won't take my phone calls. You tell her I'll be paying a visit real soon."

Phoebe reached out to the machine and erased the call. Her hand trembled with a shiver from the sudden exchange in her veins of ice water for blood. Willy had always had that effect on her as a child. In some respects, school days had never ended. Dead Ernest appeared — a companion to stress — but he could not speak; if she was sliding into shock, then so was he.

Before both legs could fail her, Phoebe sat down in a chair facing the window that looked out across the garden. Had the shade trees grown taller? No. Those great oaks and elms were old when she was very young. Even the flowers remained unchanged, the same colors from one planting season to the next. Without the play of children or a wind to move the leaves and blooms, her view of the school and its garden had the frozen quality of a snapshot taken fifteen years ago.

Of course, today there was no sign of Ernie Nadler's blood on the wall. That was different.

FIFTEEN

Phoebe wants to be a teacher when she grows up. I can't believe it when she tells me this. Teachers don't see bruises or blood. They don't hear the screams. Why, Phoebe, why? And her answer? She says, "That's why."

— ERNEST NADLER

The muggy air was thick, and the sky was still light in this evening hour. Detective Mallory cut the engine on the small park vehicle, saying, "This is the best spot. Lots of bugs here."

Coco wore new eyeglasses, and she was looking upward, grinning. "I can see the leaves on the trees!" Previously all the greenery had melded into a solid color for the nearsighted child. She climbed off Charles Butler's lap to step out on the path. At the sight of tiny flying lights, the little girl ran off down the trail to chase the lightning bugs. She grabbed the air and missed and reached out again.

"I don't think she'll catch one." Charles smiled as he unfolded his tall body to stand by the cart. "She's never done this before. But it was a wonderful idea for refining motor skills." Though he knew that Mallory had suggested it only to lure the child back to the scene of three hideous crimes, claiming that the Ramble was the best place in the world to hunt these insects. On the predictable upside, the child did not know one wooded area from another.

Mallory rounded the cart to stand beside him and watch Coco's failed attempts to snatch bugs from the air. "I say the kid catches one. She's stubborn."

"Indeed." And so was his cleaning lady, the taskmaster of buttons. One day Coco would also learn to tie shoelaces, but probably not anytime soon. And bug-catching might also be a bit beyond her abilities just now.

Charles and Mallory followed the child down a path of lush green shadows. Here and there were lamps reminiscent of the gaslight age, but they had not yet been turned on. The way was lit only by insects with magical taillights that blinked on and off. Coco ran ahead of them, hands outstretched to reach a firefly on the wing. Failing in this, she veered off in pursuit of another one lower to the ground. A slow-flying lightning bug hung in the air, and she clapped her hands together.

Oh. A *dead* bug.

Undaunted, she wiped her hands on her jeans and went on to the next one.

Mindful of the little girl's remarkable hearing, Charles spoke softly. "I met with a colleague of mine, a psychologist who treats children with special needs. He has connections in Coco's home state, and he's going to help me locate a family for —"

"Foster care? No way," said Mallory. "She won't survive in the system."

He put up both hands in surrender. She was absolutely right on that score, though her own foster parents had been stellar exceptions. Most children would be passed from home to home like mythical small birds of paradise, forever in flight for lack of feet to land on any solid ground. And, no, Coco would not survive that.

"I have something more permanent in mind," said Charles. "I finished her evaluation. Apart from the blind spots of Williams syndrome, she's gifted — intellectually as well as musically. That's a huge attraction for adoptive parents. And there are lists of people pre-qualified to adopt special-needs children. Oh, and there's one more thing in her favor — Coco's grandmother left an estate that will pay for a very good education."

"And the adoptive parents inherit if anything happens to Coco. No kid should be worth more dead than alive. I'll have to think about it for a while."

"Mallory, it's *not* your call. She's my responsibility."

"She's *my* material witness, and I've got all the paperwork that says it damn well is my call. She's not going anywhere."

Charles's eyes were on the child as she crept up on a blinking insect. "I picture her in a little house on a road with lots of shade trees . . . two loving parents . . . a backyard chock-full of bugs. You see, *my* standards are very high. Coco's are not. She thinks if she can make you love her, you'll make her breakfast every morning. And if she wakes up in the dark after a nightmare, you'll always be there. That's her little dream. She doesn't know your interest ends when the case is solved." He fell silent as the tiny girl came running toward them, hands cupped, so happy — more than that — *triumphant*.

Coco held her prize up to Mallory. "Will

you hold my bug? I want to get another one."

"Sure." Mallory took the insect from her hands, and now the pulsing light leaked through her own closed fingers. When the child was safely out of earshot, she said, "Coco stays in New York till I get a lineup of suspects."

"You know she can't identify the Hunger Artist."

"But my killer doesn't know that. And Coco knows more than you think. It's just a matter of asking the right questions."

"There won't be any interrogation. Mallory, you agreed to the rules. You can only take what she gives you."

"I know she followed a killer into the Ramble the night Humphrey Bledsoe was strung up." Her eyes were on the child, who had stopped on the path to talk with a small family. "Look at that. She'll walk right up to strangers, anyone at all. But you know she never tried to make contact with the Hunger Artist. She had him in sight, but she *knew* he was dangerous."

"I'm sure she was terrified."

"You're missing the point, Charles. She knew exactly what was going on that night."

"And then she filtered the violence through a fairy tale. That was the only way

209

she could deal with the emotional trauma." He turned to face Mallory. "I won't let you expose her to a lineup with a murderer. Let's be very clear about that."

The detective studied his naked tell-all face, looking there for fault lines, and, judging by a telling flash of disappointment in her eyes, she had found none. Mallory looked down at the closed hand that held a fragile bug. "Without glasses, Coco's vision is good for what? Eight or ten feet? Suppose she got a close-up look at this guy?"

"But would she have seen him clearly . . . in the dark?"

"The moon was full."

Charles waved his hand upward toward the thick canopy of leafy branches that blocked out the sky. "So much for moonlight."

Mallory countered his gesture by touching the pole of a lamp at the very moment when all the path lights were turned on — as if she had timed it. And now he realized that she had done exactly that — leading his conversation, anticipating his every response and stunning him with a magic act, this staging of a child's nightmare timed to an increment of a second by some infernal clockwork in her brain.

It could have been worse. He was merely

speechless for the moment and a bit off balance. She could truly cripple him when she wanted to.

"So . . . let's say the kid got a good look at the killer," said Mallory. "Coco could describe him for a sketch artist."

"No, she couldn't," said Charles. "The artist would have to ask leading questions. In Coco's description, your killer might be three feet tall or as big as a house. Other characteristics would be just as unreliable. The man may have three eyes. She's already given him two red tails."

Mallory smiled. "Those were battery cables. The perp was probably carrying his winch in a knapsack. The cables must have been trailing."

"And voilà — a monster with two red tails."

"So Coco's remembering more details about that night."

"In fact, she is." Charles pulled a sheet of paper from his pocket. "She drew this today. It's her concept of the delivery man's dolly." He unfolded a cryptic drawing of disconnected elements. In one corner was a circle within a circle, and a wheel was an easy call for that image. Isolated on the opposite edge of the page was an elongated *U* shape. "That has to be the handle." And in the center of the child's drawing was a free-floating square solidly filled in with black pencil. "I'm guessing that's the dolly's platform for carrying things." Was it necessary to add that Coco had difficulty with spatial relationships? "So here you have free-floating pieces of the dolly, but if you didn't know what it was — Oh, my."

The young huntress had returned with another lightning bug in hand. Charles accepted this one for safekeeping. Mallory pointed to the drawing in his free hand. "Coco, can I have that?"

"Yes! Do you *really* like it?"

"Very much. This is my favorite part." Mallory pointed to the solidly filled-in square.

"That's the black box." And now Coco was off again, on the run, with only a backwards glance that said, *Bye. Sorry. Bugs to catch.*

When it was time to go, Charles and Mallory had run out of fists to hold the trophy fireflies. In a deft sleight of hand, without losing a single insect, he confined them all to a knotted handkerchief, which now glowed like a linen lightbulb. Charles asked how many bugs she had caught tonight, and the five fireflies in the handkerchief became a legion of a hundred and six.

Coco always strived to be exact about the wrong number.

The cart's two passengers were dropped off near the 81st Street exit, where a police cruiser was waiting to escort Charles and Coco back home to SoHo. Then Mallory turned the small vehicle down a paved path winding south to The Yard, a park maintenance depot, where she had left her own car. As she drove around the perimeter of the depot's woodsy acre, every shape of stored hose and pipe was visible from the road. And blades for snowplows were lined up alongside a small tractor and a midget steamroller. This equipment was only partially hidden by trees and shrubs, and it was protected by a short fence that a four-year-old could scale.

Zero security.

The detective rolled through the gate and into a parking lot in front of the maintenance building. Here she spotted the man who had loaned her the cart. He had since changed his T-shirt and jeans for dark brown coveralls that would fit Coco's description of the Hunger Artist. A full trash bag in hand, he strolled over to meet her.

"You're working late," said Mallory.

"I'm a volunteer. I make my own hours."

He set the trash bag down beside the cart. "And I favor cooler evenings for heavy work."

"Those coveralls don't look like park issue."

"They're not," he said. "A few years back, I got these from one of the plumbing contractors. I helped him with a bad leak in the park zoo. I wear 'em when I got a real dirty job, like today." He removed one of his gloves to take the vehicle's keys from her hand.

Mallory looked toward the trees that sheltered machine parts and heavy equipment. "You have a dolly around here for moving light loads — something you'd keep outside at night?"

"Smaller stuff like that gets locked up. If you'd asked me yesterday, I would've said no." He led her away from the building and up a path to higher ground, passing a forklift that was missing some of its parts. A pole light illuminated a small machine graveyard, a place where motors and rusted metal parts littered the ground.

A dolly leaned against a birch tree. It looked like Heller's demonstration model, buckled straps and all, but with one additional feature. A bracket was welded to the metal struts of the long handle, and it held a car battery — Coco's black box.

"It's not one of ours," said the park worker. "No idea how long it's been here. I found it when I was cleaning up today." He pointed to an area of thick undergrowth and shrubs. "It was lying under those ferns over there." He kicked one of the two wheels. "These tires got some wear on 'em, but they're still good."

"They're inflatables," said Mallory.

"Right you are."

They looked like the tires on Heller's dolly. And she knew the treads on this one would match impressions found at the first crime scene. She stared at the park worker's heavy gloves. "Were you wearing those when you moved this thing?"

"Oh, yeah." He looked down at the discarded machine parts at his feet, some of them with ragged, rusty edges. "This is tetanus country back here. I'd be a fool not to wear gloves."

When Mallory called Crime Scene Unit to come and pick up the dolly, it was no surprise to find that Heller was also working late tonight. "I don't think you'll find any fingerprints," she said to him. "The metal's too clean." Unlike everything else in this part of the depot. And then she took some pleasure in needling him with the news that she could also identify the manufacturer of the car battery — without touching his useless carton of lists. "Child's play," she said.

"No, she didn't trip over it in the park," said Heller to the rising young star of his department. "Now go get that fucking dolly."

CSI John Pollard was halfway to the office door when Heller thought it only fair to give the man a warning, but only one — because he favored trial by fire. "Develop *all* the evidence, John."

"Did I miss something, sir?" Pollard was smug, entirely too confident that he had missed nothing.

However, there was a flaw in this young man's work. He had fallen in love with a theory of the crime, departing from the science to play detective. And, yes, he had missed something. "If you screw up, Mallory will eat you alive."

John Pollard laughed on his way out the door. Evidently he also had his own theories about long-legged blondes with guns. He probably thought Mallory was . . . *cute.*

SIXTEEN

This morning, my parents go totally nuts, running through the rooms, screaming my name. Then my father finds me waking up on the floor of my bedroom closet. I don't remember how I got there. Maybe I was hiding from dreams of Aggy the Biter or Spider Girl. Humphrey is never the stuff of my nightmares. That creep giggles and hits like a little girl.

But there I am in my pajamas and not quite awake — 'in the closet.

My father shakes his head and says, "What the hell is wrong with you?"

Well, I've already lost his respect, so I say, "I have a scary life."

And Dad walks away.

— ERNEST NADLER

After putting Coco to bed, Charles Butler spent the remainder of his evening restoring the broken spine of a rare volume. He sat at a cluttered table in the workshop adjoining his library. It was a small space crammed with glue pots, spools of thread, all the tools a bibliophile could want — and perfect peace. The solitary window was triple-pane glass to block out the noise of the street, and the walls were quite thick. Though, as a concession to his tiny houseguest, he had left the door ajar.

This was where he came to work out the knotty dilemmas of life — like Coco forming a bond that would damage her when it broke. For his own part, he had managed a professional distance; the child well understood the relationship of doctors, dentists and the like with their patients. That was not the attachment he worried about. Hours into his bindery project, the book was mended, but he had no solution to the problem of severing the tie between Coco and Mallory.

And then he heard the scream.

Heart in his throat, he ran out of the workshop, passed through the library and down the hall to his guest room. One outstretched hand preceded him through the door. A flick of the wall switch lit a bedside lamp that shared the nightstand with a large jar and its captive fireflies from the Ramble.

The child was frightened, and her thin arms raised up to him for a hug.

"So you had a bad dream." He held Coco close and rocked her. "Do you remember what scared you?"

"Yes!" She wormed free of his arms and reached under her pillow to pull out a small device that looked rather like a cell phone.

But Charles had never seen one quite like it.

There was no pad of tiny numbers that would have posed some difficulty for Coco. Instead, there was a single large button that glowed when the child pressed it. The button plate was a lighter shade than the surrounding plastic, though, on the whole, this alteration had the seamless look of something manufactured by a machine — and Mallory might as well have signed the contraption. In fact, she *had* signed it. The big glowing button bore a capital *M* in the exact shade of the detective's red nail polish.

Coco smiled, connected now to the one she loved best. "I had a bad dream," she said to the phone, and then she listened for a moment. "It was about rats and wheels. . . . They both squeak. . . . Yes, the delivery man's wheels. . . . Yes, all the way to the tree."

Charles nodded, though these words had not been addressed to him. Sounds were a problem for Williams people. Lightning storms could terrify, while vacuum cleaners only caused anxiety. And what of the delivery man and his sounds — the noise of nightmares. Whatever Mallory was saying to the child, it had a calming effect. Coco lay back, smiling, eyes closing to tired slits.

Charles held out his hand, saying, "May I?" She handed him the customized cell phone and then burrowed deep into her pillow. He put the phone to his ear. "Mallory? This isn't what we agreed upon." His rules had stipulated no unsupervised visits by police, *any* police. "Covert phone calls are not exactly in the spirit of the —"

"Put the phone back under her pillow," said Mallory. This was an order. "If you don't, she'll cry." And on that note of emotional blackmail, the connection was broken.

The child held out her hands to take the phone, and Charles gave it back to her, unable to cut this new tether to Mallory without causing more trauma — and tears.

The damage just went on and on.

And when — exactly *when* — had Coco received the one-button cell phone?

He had not taken his eyes off the detective from the moment of her arrival until their departure from the Ramble. Later — long after dark — had Mallory been watching from the street below? Had she seen the light come on in his workshop window? Yes. That would have been her opportunity to break into his apartment for a visit with the little girl.

There was not a lock in the world that could keep her out.

Charles walked to the bedroom door, reached out for the wall switch and turned off the lamp — but not the light. *What?* He stared at the jar of winged insects on the bedside table. Did it glow more brightly now? Oh, yes. Since he had put the child to bed, her small handful of fireflies had increased their numbers tenfold and then some — with a little help from Mallory, the stealthiest of burglars, a champion snatcher of bugs.

It was childhood's perfect nightlight.

The squad room was dimly lit, but the lights burned bright down the hall in the geek room, Mallory's domain. During her three-month absence, other cops, who only knew their way around laptops, had been lost in this small space packed with electronics, nests of wiring and computer elements stacked in alien configurations. And now Riker noticed that more toys had been added since his partner's homecoming four weeks ago.

Once upon a time, this had been her after-school playground. In those days, when she was shorter, only twelve or thirteen years old, the computers allocated to Special Crimes had been antiquated castoffs from other departments, always crashing, totally useless. But Lou Markowitz's foster child had shown a natural affinity for these machines, and Lou had set her loose in this electronic playpen one afternoon.

As Riker recalled, only an hour or so had passed before the little runt had come stealing into Lou's office, saying, "With the right parts, I can fix the computers like new."

The former commander of the unit had been preoccupied with a murder at the time. And so Lou had missed this moment as the beginning of a brand-new crime wave — even as he was abetting it, giving her the forms she needed to requisition her parts. And then the boxes had begun to arrive in the squad room — not *small* boxes of spare parts, but great *big* boxes, *new* computers. Lou had been baffled by the first delivery. What the hell? There had been no paperwork to backtrack a requisition, and no one had even asked him to sign for the packages. Then he had noticed little Kathy dragging her loot down the hall to the geek room, and he had averted his eyes — for *years*. Perhaps the old man had seen this as a kind of progress: His baby felon was stealing for a higher purpose.

As the grown-up Kathy Mallory would say — yeah, *right*.

On some level, the child had always been all about getting even with Lou for ending her childhood career as a feral street thief. But once Kathy's stolen hardware needs were met, she had found a whole new world of things to steal on the Information Superhighway. The child would lay her stolen goods on Lou's desk, pages of purloined intelligence from data banks in the federal and private sectors. How many times had she stopped the old man's heart this way? Kathy had always worn her *Gotcha* smile each time she crept into Lou's office to hand him one of her — gifts.

Enigmatic brat. That had been Riker's thought on those curious occasions, though he would never say a four-syllable word out loud. That little half smile of hers had driven him nuts. And then one rainy night after three rounds had been poured in a cop bar down the street, Lou Markowitz had clarified this small mystery, saying, "Kathy thinks she's stealing my soul . . . and it's true." And then the old man had lifted his glass in a toast. "That's my baby."

Tonight Riker cleared a small table and laid it out with deli napkins and sandwiches. The aroma of hot pastrami filled the geek room. "The park worker's clean, no rap sheet. When the CSU guy picked up the dolly, he collected the coveralls, too. Pollard says you can buy 'em anywhere." Was Mallory even listening to him? No, she was communing with her computers, turning from one monitor to another.

He put a cold can of beer in her hand — ladies first — and then popped the metal tab on his own. "Coffey never called Tech Support while you were gone." Riker settled into the chair beside hers. "He wasn't sure how much of this equipment was legal."

Mallory tapped her keyboard, her eyes on the screen that displayed the ViCAP logo. Days ago, Detective Janos had used the Violent Criminal Apprehension Program to run a national search of old crimes that would match up with the Hunger Artist. Janos had followed every FBI protocol, answering a tedious hundred and ten questions, writing up addendums, and filing separately for each victim. And after all that work, he had come up dry.

Tonight Mallory was visiting the same federal computers, making no polite knock on the door with a password, no badge number and no tracks left behind. *Backdoor access* was the phrase she used for robbing the feds blind. "There were better places to string up those bodies," she said. "It's not like the old days when you could hide an elephant in the Ramble."

"Yeah," said Riker. "The way it is now, any bird-watcher could've spotted those sacks." Though sacks in trees were not likely to wind up on a police report. "Maybe we're just looking at a high-risk perp."

"No," said Mallory. "I think he's got some history with that place."

Riker watched as his partner neatly by-passed the long FBI questionnaire; she wanted no helpful interference from a federal crime analyst. And now an inserted disk released her pet, a virus named Good Dog, a computer canine that could run wild, leaping security fences to roam every file and bring home a bone. Mallory made no mention of winches, sacks and pulleys, batteries or drills. Instead, she typed in a narrow field of description for her dog's bone: Central Park, NYC, abduction, hanging.

Simple. Elegant. Riker liked it. These few words guaranteed a short list. Swinging by the neck or strung up in a sack, any form of hanging was a rare crime.

"I've got one hit." Mallory tapped a key to print out the pages on her screen. "Not a match — just a questionnaire from somebody else's search."

"And it wasn't Janos." Riker scanned the pages as they came from the mouth of the printer. "This is a real old one — a hundred and eighty-four questions." This prior search dated back to a time before the ViCAP forms had been streamlined. Fifteen years ago, some NYPD detective had typed in this description to search the data bank for a similar crime. Back then, the FBI had come up with no matches.

An hour later, when both detectives had finished their late dinner and read all the pages, Mallory said, "You *know* there's something wrong here."

Riker nodded. This old case should have been front-page news in its day. "It's the kind of crime you don't forget, not ever." Yet he had never heard of a young child strung up and left to die in the Ramble. How was that possible?

Mallory used one long red fingernail to call her partner's attention to the line that named the author of this early search.

"Oh, Christ," said Riker. "The detective was Rocket Mann?"

The moniker had no good connotation. Also known as Rolland Mann, this former detective, a mediocre cop in every way, had risen quickly through the ranks for no clear reason beyond that catchall term *dirty.* And today he was only one rung below Police Commissioner Beale.

"This is bad." Riker picked up his copy of the *Post* and turned to an inside page to show her a news item. "Check this out." Rhyming lines of bold type above the story read: TOP COP'S HEART STOPS. Old man Beale was in the hospital awaiting bypass surgery.

"And that makes Rocket Mann the acting commissioner." Mallory tapped keys until she was inside an NYPD archive. Slowly she scrolled down the items on the screen. "Mann never opened a case file on that boy. No one did. That year, there were only routine assaults and homicides in the Ramble."

Over her shoulder, Riker read the site-specific list of dead junkies, winos, one tourist shot and two stabbed.

"*No* kids," said Mallory. "Nothing to fit Rocket Mann's questionnaire. That case got buried . . . and now we get to ask him why."

The acting police commissioner could not legally refuse an interview, but Rolland Mann could make life hell for the cop who demanded it. Following protocols and ascending hierarchy, one rank reaching up to the next — the first man in the line of fire would be their boss, the commander of the Special Crimes Unit.

Riker lifted his beer to salute his partner. "Well, kid, this is the ultimate payback for a month of desk duty. When you tell Coffey we have to interview Rocket Mann, the lieutenant's head will explode."

Mallory clinked her beer can with his in a toast. "Good times."

SEVENTEEN

This time the skin's broken, and I bleed through my sock.

At lunchtime, Phoebe looks at my bloody ankle and says it's too bad Aggy's a legacy student. Otherwise, they'd put her down for biting humans.

— ERNEST NADLER

Elderly Mrs. Buford paced the floor in her fuzzy pink slippers, awaiting the newspaper delivery. Yesterday's *Times* had been stolen, and she had her suspects. Chief among them was the man across the hall, the one least likely to care about the terrible importance she placed on her morning paper. The crossword puzzle helped her to chart the inroads of Alzheimer's by the boxes she could not fill with her diminishing inventory of words and names. Getting old was *such* a pain in the ass.

She consulted the clock on the wall.

Where was that damn paperboy?

Her pacing stopped. She held her breath. Ah, there it was, the soft ploff of the *Times* hitting the carpet in the outer hallway. Mrs. Buford opened the door to the sound of more ploffs as newspapers were dropped at other doors. She waited for the woman across the way to retrieve her own paper. Their neighborly exchange of good mornings was another high point of the day's routine.

Oh, no. This time the door was opened by the husband, a most unsettling person. Rolland Mann made her feel like bugs crawled beneath her skin. He was a civil servant, if she remembered correctly, though this hardly squared with an apartment in a luxury high-rise building. Well, he must be far up the ladder of city politicians, but he was certainly not an elected official, not with that weak chin, that pasty flesh. And his hair was rather sparse in places. This put her in mind of a nervous cousin who pulled it out by the roots. When he bent down to collect his *Times,* she focused on the long, spidery fingers. And now for an uncomfortable shift in metaphor, he glanced up at her with reptilian eyes.

Cold-blooded *snake.*

No, wait — nothing so grand as that.

Cold-blooded *worm.*

She called out to him, "Good morning!" Always cordial, Mrs. Buford refrained from asking if he had yet murdered his wife. It had long been her impression that the poor woman only stayed with her husband under duress, and such marriages could only end badly.

He took no notice of her.

Rude bastard.

Rolland Mann was fixated on the front page, wholly engrossed in a story, his fingers curling tight around the edges of the newspaper. His face was even paler than the usual cadaver countenance.

The elderly woman looked down at her own copy of the *Times* to see a familiar title in bold headline type. It was something she had read in her school days. The earliest memories were strongest now. Yes, this was the title of a short story by one of the Russians — or maybe a German. In any case, it was a classic. She read on to learn that this was a sequel to a story in yesterday's stolen newspaper, and the police had identified one of the Hunger Artist's victims as Humphrey Bledsoe.

Across the hall, the neighbor crept backwards into his apartment, softly closing the door behind him — quiet as a thief.

■ ■ ■ ■

Though pathologists were not in short supply today, neither were dead bodies. And so the chief medical examiner donned a plastic visor and a pair of latex gloves.

Detective Mallory looked down at the corpse on the dissection table. The dead man was naked and washed, all prepped for the first cut of the morning. "This one can wait."

Dr. Edward Slope nodded in perfect understanding. Of course. This middle-aged victim of a bullet wound was not *her* corpse, was he? No, this one belonged to a completely different precinct. "Go away, Kathy."

She had been on best behavior today, allowing his use of her given name to slide, but now both hands were on her hips, a prelude to bringing out all the knives and guns. "Cut Humphrey Bledsoe first."

"This is *my* shop. I get to pick the — Hey!" The doctor managed to grab a scalpel before she rolled aside the table holding his instruments. "There's no rush on the Bledsoe autopsy. I'm waiting for identification by a family member."

"It's done," she said. "Mrs. Driscol-Bledsoe identified her son at the hospital."

"That's not *quite* the story I heard from Grace. She relied on the police ID when she —"

"*Grace?* You *know* that woman?"

"Yes." And what new crime had he committed now? "Of course I know her. The Driscol Institute funds half the costs of running my rehab clinic — thanks to Grace."

Many doctors had country homes; Edward Slope had a country clinic for drug addicts. Kathy Mallory had never understood his penchant for working on live patients after hours — and worse — free of charge. In her world, the only good junkie was a dead one.

"Next time you come up to my clinic, read the patron plaque in the lobby. You'll find Grace Driscol-Bledsoe's name engraved at the top. Very generous woman. She presides over the board of trustees for the —"

"How much money does she control?"

"At least a billion dollars, probably more." He laid his scalpel down on the dissection table — too tempting. "Please tell me you're not looking for a money motive in the Ramble murders."

"That woman recognized her son at the hospital — *no* hesitation. That's a *fact.* So I have to wonder why she'd come all the way down here for another ID." The young detective folded her arms, regarding him

233

with grave suspicion. "And how many *other* city officials does she own?"

"That was hardly subtle, Kathy. Here's a thought. Why don't you ask her?"

"We can't get past her lawyers — and the mayor." She glared at the corpse on the table, the one in line ahead of *her* corpse. "So you're giving a friend special privileges."

And did he rise to this bait? He did not. "Grace is only getting what she's entitled to. She said she'd drop by sometime today. I'll personally do her son's autopsy, all right? *Tomorrow.*"

"I need it done right now." She stood, firmly planted between the doctor and his table of instruments. "I arranged for the funeral home to pick up the body in three hours. That's all the time you've got."

"*You* arranged it?" Edward Slope removed his plastic face guard. Was he getting too old for these sparing matches? *Hell, no.* "You don't give a damn about that autopsy. It won't tell you anything you don't already know." Did he sound sufficiently indignant? He hoped so. "It's all about the funeral, right? I understand the interest in victim funerals, but since when do the police *schedule* them? Did you even *tell* the family about your arrangements?"

"No, Edward, she did not." The voice of

Grace Driscol-Bledsoe echoed off the tiled walls. In the company of a morgue attendant, the elegant redhead strode across the wide room with the tap of high heels. Another woman, drab and dressed in black, lagged a few steps behind on rubber-soled shoes, and this person was not introduced.

The socialite took both the doctor's hands in hers, drew close to him and kissed the air between them so as not to smudge her lipstick. "The funeral director gave me the news twenty minutes ago. His people have been burying my people for a very long time. My son's funeral was arranged on the day he was born." She turned a disingenuous smile on Kathy Mallory. "But the *family* usually sets the date. So imagine my surprise when the director called — out of the blue — to ask my preferences for music and flowers . . . for *tomorrow's* services."

When the detective approached her, Grace Driscol-Bledsoe handed over a business card, saying, "Call my lawyer."

Translation? *Kiss off.*

The chief medical examiner so enjoyed that. He extended one arm to the lady and personally escorted her to the viewing room where Humphrey Bledsoe's remains awaited her formal identification. And the young detective was left behind to reflect on what she had done wrong.

Right.

When the chief medical examiner and his most generous patron stood before the viewer's window, the blinds were opened to display a corpse laid out on the other side of the glass. "That's my son," said Grace. *No* hesitation. And that brought on the doctor's first vague feeling of something a bit — *off.*

"Not surprising that my daughter didn't recognize him. Edward, dear, please try not to mess him up too badly. I'm told that Detective Mallory ordered an open-casket ceremony."

The woman handed him a small, square envelope engraved with her name and return address. His own name was penned in an elegant script — like a party invitation. He opened it. Yes — a party, a purely social occasion. His eyes traveled from smiling mother to murdered son. Evidently, the rich *were* different.

The cork walls of the incident room were newly bloodied with more cadaver photographs recently delivered by the Medical Examiner's Office. Dr. Slope, in an unexplained change of heart, had put a rush on the autopsy of Humphrey Bledsoe.

Sixteen detectives sat on metal folding chairs arranged in audience formation. In advance of today's briefing, a long table had been moved to the front of the room, where a crime-scene investigator laid out evidence and props to simulate the Hunger Artist's murder kit. Lieutenant Coffey stared at the array of duct tape, a rope and a sack followed by a pulley, a drill, long screws and a metal plate. *Make it stop.* Next came a winch and a remote control — every damn thing but the trees. *Oh, crap.* The CSI had brought the trees, too. A circular chunk of barked wood was laid down alongside a section of branch.

The lecture had not yet begun and the squad was already bored witless. Jack Coffey leaned against the door, cutting off their only avenue of escape.

"I'm guessing you guys never went through our carton." CSI John Pollard smiled at his own lame joke about the box of useless leads.

None of the detectives laughed, but neither did they draw weapons. They were all game to end the war with Crime Scene Unit.

"Your perp's been stockpiling his murder kit for a long time." John Pollard held up an evidence bag containing a coil of rope.

"This brand was discontinued five years ago. It was sold in hundred-and-twenty-foot lengths. Forty feet of rope was found at each crime scene." And now, as if cops could not do simple math, he said, "The perp used up the whole coil." He moved on down the table to pick up a burlap sack. "The bags were made in only one batch and field-tested all over the city — docks, warehouses. That was four years ago. They were never sold to the public. So the Hunger Artist found them or stole them." Pollard looked down at the more common paraphernalia spread across the table. "Nothing here would cost more than a few hundred bucks. The perp paid cash. Count on it," he said, assuming that a roomful of seasoned detectives might need his help with this deduction.

They all looked at him with eyes that said, *Drop dead.*

The CSI rolled out the dolly that Mallory had found in the park. "No prints. It was wiped clean, but I traced the serial number. It was sold to a landscaper out in Queens. The guy died a few years back. I interviewed his widow. She says her husband got these inflatable tires from their kid's go-cart."

All around the room, heads lifted. *Now* Pollard had their attention. This CSI had crossed a line when he interviewed that woman. Unlike some of Heller's staff, this one was a civilian — not a cop — not one of them.

Pollard slapped the black car battery attached to the dolly's long handle. "This powered a joist for lifting heavy loads up to roofs and terraces. Cheaper than hiring a crane. The landscaper worked off the books — no payroll names, no client list. This dolly was stolen off a jobsite seven years ago. The widow doesn't know which one. She only remembers her husband was working in Manhattan that day."

And what might the widow have remembered if a real detective had done that interview? Jack Coffey bit back the first obscenity that came to mind.

Pollard returned to the table, and the wave of his hand encompassed everything on it. "We figured out every detail." And now, item by item, he told them the mind-numbing story of working up all of his evidence from screw holes in the bark of trees. And finally — *finally* — the little guy raised both hands to say his magic act was over — and maybe he was expecting applause.

Fat chance.

"You missed a few things," said Mallory

239

from the back row of chairs. And CSI Pollard pretended not to hear this.

Jack Coffey shook his head to warn her off — as if that ever worked. Mallory left her seat and moved toward the front of the room. *Damn it!* Just when things were going so well — when they were having all this nice make-up sex with CSU — she had to mess with this man.

Mallory set a small bottle on the table. "That's chloroform. It belongs in the murder kit."

"No, I don't think so." John Pollard gave her a patronizing smile. "I can show you the ME's X-rays of skull fractures. The victims were subdued by a blow to —"

"Two of them were *stunned*," said Mallory. "Only Willy Fallon was hit hard enough to knock her out. The perp needed to keep his victims quiet." She picked up the duct tape. "And this won't do the job." She ripped off a piece and covered the CSI's mouth. "If you want to make noise, you can still be heard. Try it."

And now he *was* heard. The sound he made resembled the amplified buzz of a startled mosquito. When he raised his hands to pull off the tape, she slapped his wrists. "No, that's cheating." She used more tape to bind his hands behind his back.

The lieutenant knew this was the time to step in, but one glance around the room told him that his whole squad was solidly behind Mallory's bad behavior. They *loved* this. She was one of them again, and all for the minor price of a twit's dignity.

Jack Coffey smiled. He could live with that.

Mallory owned the room. "We have a witness who puts our perp in coveralls, posing as a delivery guy. That's how he gets them to open the door. Then he drops the victim with a blow to the back of the head." She glanced at the cluttered table and then turned to the CSI. "You got so carried away with your little screw holes, you never developed evidence for the assaults."

Now Pollard was making quite a lot of noise — despite the tape on his mouth. He might be the best show-and-tell exhibit ever presented for a briefing.

"Even if the perp *had* knocked out all three victims — would he count on them staying that way? No," said Mallory. "Not his style. He *over* thinks everything — mark of an amateur. No injection sites on the bodies — so I know he sedated them with this." She lifted her bottle in one hand and a small cloth in the other as she continued the education of the CSI. "You can buy chloroform on the Internet. You can even make it at home. This is what he used to keep them quiet while he wheeled them through the streets and the park — because *that's* the risky part. And this bottle is the only item on the table that can break our case." She turned to face her happy audience. "The ME's broad scan for chloroform will take another three days to confirm. Pollard didn't even request it. *I* did. And he didn't use a mass spectrometer on the sacks to check them for chemicals. That's two mistakes. Three . . . if we count his interview with the landscaper's widow."

There were get-even smiles throughout the room.

"And then the perp does this." It was definitely in the spirit of payback when Mallory, with a trip and a shove, laid out CSI Pollard on the floor and hog-tied him. After covering his body with the sack, she rolled him over to close the opening with rope. Next, she dipped the dolly's wide step underneath him. Braced against a wall, the squirming man was neatly loaded onto the metal platform, ready for transport.

At this point, someone might have said that *even* a *woman* could have done it. But no one did.

EIGHTEEN

The mad Driscol lives in the old carriage house behind the school. Phoebe says her great-aunt lost most of her brain cells to a stroke. Years ago, the old lady ditched her nurse and ran naked into the garden when it was packed with students. All the girls were weirded out by the saggy breasts and belly of old age, says Phoebe. But from the boys' point of view, a naked woman was a naked woman.

And now I understand one more school tradition.

In every classroom that overlooks the garden, the boys begin and end the hour lined up at the windows, hoping to catch sight of a naked mad Driscol.

— ERNEST NADLER

"Bagging the man was going a tad too far." It was Jack Coffey's policy to discipline detectives in the privacy of his office.

Mallory opened her pocket watch, a silent reminder that she had more important business.

The lieutenant bypassed his line about the crucial importance of a good working relationship with CSU. Perhaps it was best to begin this lecture at gunpoint. "You only *think* I won't suspend you."

"I found an old case of a hanging in the Ramble." She laid a ViCAP questionnaire on his desk.

Coffey scanned the lines of standard FBI questions, page after page of them. The filled-in responses told the story of a little boy strung up in a tree for three days. "When did this happen?" He flipped back to the dated cover sheet. The incident had occurred fifteen years ago, back in his younger days as a rookie cop. "How come I've never heard about this case?"

"There never was a case — no investigation, no paperwork." She reached out to tap the line for the petitioner's name and rank. "He buried it."

"Shit!" The former detective listed here was now in charge of the NYPD during Police Commissioner Beale's hospital stay. Rolland Mann might be only hours away from absolute power. "So, Mallory . . . got any more bombs in your pocket?"

"I know why they call him Rocket Mann. Fifteen years ago, he should've made his bones on a case like this, but that didn't happen. Well, it did, but not in the usual way." One long, red fingernail pointed to the date. "Ten days after that, Mann got his gold shield. There's nothing in his job jacket to explain it. Before the promotion, he was a brand-new white shield."

"A baby dick with training wheels." Coffey stared at the old questionnaire. "There had to be a case file. Maybe it was sealed or expunged. That works if the assailant was a juvenile." He looked to her for a nod of confirmation on this theory, or — even better — a shrug to say that she had not yet illegally unlocked every juvenile file for that year.

She shook her head. "Rocket Mann's ViCAP search is the only proof that it ever happened."

The date placed this mess in the early, dirty days of a decentralized NYPD, when no cop was allowed to know the crime rate in the precinct next door. Reporters had learned to get their new-and-*improved* crime stats from the mayor's office. Despite the sensational aspects, it would have been easy to keep this old case out of the media — low risk of leaks, fewer cops to silence.

Central Park was the only uninhabited precinct in Manhattan.

Mallory laid down a map of the Ramble. It was marked with the Hunger Artist's crime scenes, all three of them clustered in one small patch of the acreage. The epicenter, Tupelo Meadow, was marked with an *X*. "That has to be the clearing in Mann's ViCAP description. So that's where the boy was found hanging. We want an interview with Rocket Mann."

Did he feel a tension headache coming on? Jack Coffey gave himself up for dead and placed a call to One Police Plaza. Mallory's request would go first to Chief of Detectives Joe Goddard. The chief would then carry her message up the chain of command — or wad it into a ball — his call. But payback was a certainty. Rocket Mann was next in line for the job of police commissioner, and he would not want a light shone on this old case — not after he had gone to the trouble of burying it.

His head was shaped like a bullet with a crew cut. All the detectives stared at the man whose shoulders nearly filled out the frame of the staircase door. As the chief of detectives crossed the squad room, every believer in his legend listened for the sound of knuckles dragging on the floor.

Joe Goddard, alias God, had come down from his aerie at One Police Plaza to pay them a personal visit, and this could never be a good thing. The man wore a silk suit, but he was no one's idea of a politician. The chief of D's was brutally straightforward, and every word out of his mouth gave him the pedigree of an education on city streets. He never smiled, never tried to hide the fact that he was dangerous. The chief walked by the desks of Mallory and Riker, saying to them in passing, "You're with me."

The detectives rose and followed him to the front of the room, where Jack Coffey emerged from his office to shake hands with the boss of bosses.

"I need some privacy for a meeting," said the chief. And it was clear that the lieutenant's company was not wanted when he said, "Jack, I've got no problem with you." He turned to glance at Mallory and Riker. "And these two aren't in trouble . . . yet."

Lieutenant Coffey nodded and stood to one side as the three of them passed him by. Then he closed the office door behind them and walked away.

Chief Goddard sat down at the desk. The detectives remained standing in the unwritten protocol for dealing with this man:

Show respect or be pounded into the ground.

The big man held a fax sheet in his hand and waved it like a flag. "I bypassed the chief of the department and *personally* delivered your request to Rolland Mann. And I showed him your copy of his old ViCAP search. He'll see you this afternoon in Commissioner Beale's office. He moved all his stuff in there the other day — five minutes after they carted the old man off to the hospital. If Beale dies in surgery, then his first deputy won't be just the *acting* commissioner. That's what I hear from City Hall. A permanent appointment is in the bag. . . . I can't have that."

He turned from one detective to the other, silently asking if he had made himself clear.

Oh, yes. Very clear. There was a war on in the Puzzle Palace. Riker and Mallory had just been drafted as foot soldiers.

"When I said you guys wanted a meeting, that made him nervous. And the bastard agreed to it way too fast. It was like he knew you were coming for him. Your lieutenant isn't invited to sit in on that meeting. Me neither. That's how I know you guys have something on that little prick. He's going down — with or without your help. The acting commissioner can't promise you squat. . . . I want you to *remember* that."

So lines were being drawn and every soldier on Rocket Mann's side was dead meat.

"That bastard can't make you guys bulletproof . . . but I can." Unsaid were all the other things that the chief of detectives could do to them.

Joe Goddard was not in line for Commissioner Beale's job. He would first have to kill the chief of the department and maybe a few of the fourteen deputies serving one notch below Rolland Mann. And so Riker believed the chief of D's when the man sat well back in the chair and said, "I like a nice clean house."

Riker stole a quick look at his partner. If Goddard asked them for dirt on the deputy, they were both dead. The detectives had none to give him — not yet — but they would not be believed. No, they would be gutted. Any minute now.

Mallory wore the poker face of a world-class player when she said, "We need Rolland Mann to close our case. *Then* you can have him . . . and everything we've got on him."

It was a good bluff and a worthy gamble, but her delivery showed no respect; it lacked a groveling tone. That much was easy to read in Goddard's face. Could this man be more pissed off? Riker thought not.

"You don't set the terms. I do," said the chief. "I liked your old man, Mallory, but I never owed Lou Markowitz any favors. So now your partner's wondering why you're still standing." His angry eyes fixed on Riker, and there was ugly menace in his voice when he said, "I'm in a real good mood this morning. So the kid skates on insubordination." Turning back to Mallory, the offender, he said, "Detective, you're young, and maybe you need this spelled out." He pounded the desk for punctuation. "Don't *ever* fuck with me! First, you close out your case. If that takes more than seventy-two hours, you're overpaid. *Then* you bring me Rolland Mann's head."

Outwardly, Riker was deadpan, though inwardly grinning. The chief had phrased this as his own idea, and now it was an order: They were going to do it Mallory's way.

Chief Goddard pulled a wad of papers from his breast pocket. "You'll need this." He handed Riker the fistful of small, yellowed pages filled with handwritten lines. "Those are personal notes from a retired cop. Officer Kayhill was on park patrol fifteen years ago."

Riker scanned the sheets, straining to read them without his glasses. Damned if he would wear his bifocals in front of this man. After two pages, he turned to Mallory. "This backs up the ViCAP questionnaire. Kayhill was there when the kid was found hanging in a tree."

"Yeah," said the chief of D's. "And I'm sure he filed an incident report, but that seems to have disappeared. If Rolland Mann should ask — tell him you got those notes at Kayhill's nursing home this morning. The old guy's senile. No worries about him backing you up. Kayhill's notes say the victim was alive when he was cut down. But the boy couldn't talk — no ID."

And Riker, still squinting at the notebook pages, had just gotten to the part that explained why the boy was mute. "And then the kid was shipped off in an ambulance." He looked down at the desk blotter as Goddard laid out a document with a raised seal. The words *Death Certificate* were writ large.

"This boy's a good fit," said the chief. "He's from the Upper West Side, and his parents reported him missing three days before the hanging in the Ramble. *Has* to be the same kid."

For one scary moment, Riker thought his partner was going to challenge Goddard on this point; they had been through the Missing Persons reports for that period and come up dry. But Mallory only picked up the document. "This boy died a month *after* the hanging." She handed the death certificate to Riker. "Check out the date."

He held it out at arm's length and nodded. "The same day Rolland Mann made the ViCAP search." If this death had resulted from the park assault, then the acting police commissioner had buried a child's murder.

The little boy who was not there waved both hands in wild protest and silently formed the words, *No!* and *Don't!*

Against the good advice of Dead Ernest, Phoebe Bledsoe answered the telephone.

"My condolences on Humphrey," said the voice of Willy Fallon. "I just heard the funeral announcement on TV. Very tacky. Most people place obituaries in the —"

"I gave my mother your message." Phoebe turned to Dead Ernest, who mouthed the words, *Hang up, hang up.*

"She still won't take my calls," said Willy. "So try again. Try harder! Tell her the third victim is Aggy Sutton. That's not on the news — not in the papers. But you already figured that out, right? . . . And when you

252

talk to your mother, tell her you're next."

Phoebe shook her head.

And Willy laughed, as if she could see this gesture of denial through the telephone line. "You were there that day. Does your mother know that, Phoebe? Do you think that might get her attention? Will there be cops at the funeral tomorrow? I could talk to *them*."

NINETEEN

It's four blocks in the wrong direction, but
sometimes Phoebe and I follow Toby
Wilder home after school. He's a traveling
safety zone. Nothing bad happens when
he's around.

Phoebe wants to marry him. I want to be
him. Toby is contagiously cool. He walks
to a rhythm of music in his mind, head
bobbing, fingers snapping. So cool. And
that music — I can almost hear it when it
rises to a crescendo in his brain, when he
can no longer help himself, and he has to
stop and dance on the sidewalk. Pass-
ersby smile at the dancing boy, and their
heads bob, as if they can hear the music,
too.

— ERNEST NADLER

They had been kept waiting in the anteroom
for thirty minutes. Mallory and Riker had
used the time to chat up Rolland Mann's

bodyguard, a detective who had once worked the SoHo precinct and owed a favor to their lieutenant. And so they learned that Detective Monahan hated his new boss, and the acting commissioner had ditched his bodyguard at least once on the day he took over Beale's office. But Monahan was a savvy cop, and today he had resolved that problem by posting a white shield downstairs to follow the man if he should leave the building unescorted.

Mallory handed Monahan her cell phone. "Not today. Call him off."

"Detectives?" On the other side of the room, the secretary cupped a telephone's mouthpiece. "It won't be long now. They're almost done."

The door opened, and two civilians emerged from the private office. The men crossed the reception room with toolboxes in hand and Tech Support IDs pinned to their shirt pockets.

"He'll see you now," said Miss Scott.

The secretary buzzed Mallory and Riker through the door to the inner sanctum, a large office that had always been a Spartan place. Police Commissioner Beale was a man with the soul of a cost accountant, and frugality was his religion. Apparently his deputy, Rolland Mann, had inside information on the old codger's heart surgery. One side of the desk was piled with decorator swatches of material for drapes and upholstery — just in case the commissioner died on the operating table. A wide-screen plasma television explained the need for Tech Support. If Beale should survive and return to work, the sheer expense of this TV set would kill him. It hung on the wall with the appearance of a hasty job. Dangling wires bypassed the modern equipment on the shelf below, connecting instead to a videocassette player, a piece of outdated technology.

The man behind the desk struck Mallory as odd — because he was so ordinary. She could understand why the commissioner had chosen him as second in command: Rolland Mann was a younger version of Beale, a bloodless clone of bureaucrats everywhere. It was hard to believe that he had ever been a cop. He was too . . . *soft.* His face was doughy, and the long, white fingers seemed to have no bones. She sized up the acting commissioner as a worm with attitude. He pretended not to notice that minions from the lower ranks had entered the room during his leisurely perusal of a newspaper.

In the spirit of career suicide, Riker followed his partner's lead and sat down in a chair with no invitation to do so. Mallory stretched out her long legs and said, "Hey." Deputy Commissioner Mann looked up, displeased — then confused. She dangled a pocket watch to let him know that she did not have all damn day for his nonsense. Her insolence was just short of a warning shot, the preamble of a bullet being chambered in her gun — taking aim — and then she looked down at the papers in her lap, scanning the lines — keeping him waiting.

Call it an experiment. This was the moment for fireworks, a sharp reprimand at the very least. Insubordination at this level was a major offense. But Rolland Mann only cleared his throat — and that was telling. He folded his newspaper and laid it down. "I'm told you're looking at old cases from the Ramble."

"No," said Mallory, without looking up from her copy of the ViCAP questionnaire. "Just yours."

And now they had a game.

"You wasted a trip, Detective." He held up his newspaper to display the Hunger Artist headline. "There's no connection between this case and —"

"*Your* case," said Mallory, leaving off the mandatory *sir*. "You were the only detective

257

on that one. No partner." This was only a guess, but she was right. Mann was startled, and now he must be wondering how she had acquired that information — since there was no case file to consult. She held up the yellowed pages supplied by the chief of detectives. "These are Officer Kayhill's personal notes. You remember him. He was the cop who found that kid strung up in the Ramble." She shuffled the small, loose papers like playing cards. "He mentions your name." Mallory looked up. "You were there that night."

Did he seem relieved? Yes. And now he smiled. "That led to my first bust as a probie detective."

Rolland Mann's old ViCAP questionnaire listed no name or age for the victim, only describing a prepubescent male. Mallory leafed through the rest of her papers to find Chief Goddard's copy of the death certificate, and she read the dates that began and ended the short life of a child. "How old was the boy you found in the Ramble?"

"I don't recall. A skinny little kid. I remember that. He weighed maybe seventy pounds soaking wet. Oh, and he was fully clothed." The deputy commissioner looked down at the front page of the *Times*. "Your three vics were naked adults. And mine wasn't found in a sack. The kid was strung up by the wrists. No duct tape, either."

"According to your ViCAP questionnaire," said Riker, "there *was* sensory deprivation."

"Right," said Mallory, in the manner of being helpful. "Your perp sealed the victim's eyes and his mouth — the ears, too — just like *our* case. Maybe that was a detail you held back from the press?"

As if to correct his partner, Riker leaned toward her to say his line on cue. "The reporters never got *any* details. There was no story."

"You're kidding." Aiming for mock surprise, Mallory turned back to Rolland Mann. "How could you keep a thing like that away from the media? Oh, and one more thing. Your ViCAP entry doesn't say what the perp used to seal the kid's —"

"Hold on." Riker took the patrolman's notes from her hand. "I think there's a line in here about that," he said, as if this might be news to her. "Yeah, here it is." He held up one page and addressed the acting commissioner. "Your perp used *glue*."

That startled Rolland Mann, but now he lifted one shoulder in a shrug, as if that detail meant very little to him. "Yeah, it was glue. Heavy-duty stuff — you could use it to bond metal. But the glue never made it into the record. When my perp pled out in court, it didn't even come up."

The detectives were left to wonder how there could have been a trial for a homicide case that had been buried.

"No one's ever gonna hear about the glue," said Mann. "Is that clear, Detectives?"

"Clear this up," Mallory said to him, *dared* him. "Why would anybody in the DA's office pass up a detail like that one?"

"Overkill. An assistant DA traded a confession for a plea bargain."

"And who was that ADA?" Riker smiled. His pencil hovered over an open notebook page. When ten seconds had passed in stone silence, he raised his eyebrows as a prompt.

"Cedrick Carlyle. . . . No point in talking to him. He can't tell you anything. My perp was a juvenile — *sealed* records." Rolland Mann dropped his copy of the *Times* in the trash basket by his desk. "So I don't expect to read about that case in tomorrow's paper." He pushed an old-fashioned videocassette across his desk. "That's the kid's interview. The tape doesn't leave my office." He handed Riker a single sheet of paper. "And that's the written statement. You don't get to keep that, either."

"This confession isn't signed." Riker

handed it off to Mallory.

"The signed version is in the sealed record," said Mann. "Officially, my copy doesn't exist, and you never saw it. Clear enough?" His hand rested on the telephone, an elaborate affair of blinking lights and long rows of names on labels for easy-access calls. "I push one button on my speed dial, and you're both gone — that fast." It made him angry to see Mallory smile. The anger dissipated as he watched Riker silently writing a line in a notebook.

There could be no doubt that the detective was jotting down that threat, that clear act of obstruction. And then there was the lesser offense of exposing juvenile records without a court order. But the notebook line was only for show, to put Rolland Mann's mind at ease about the possibility that Riker was wired for sound — and he was. Even without the protection of Joe Goddard, the two detectives were bulletproof today — all day.

Eyes cast down, Mallory read the unsigned confession of the accused, a boy named Toby Wilder, age thirteen. "A kid didn't write this. I'm guessing you helped him with the wording?"

Rolland Mann's silence lasted too long. "The boy brought flowers into the Ramble.

I told him that would go over good with the judge. It showed remorse . . . and it made Toby look guilty as hell. So *yeah* . . . I helped him."

Mallory rose from her chair and crossed the room to the plasma television on the far wall. She fed the videotape into the mouth of the old cassette player on the shelf below. The screen came to life, and there was Rolland Mann, fifteen years younger, with all his hair. In shirtsleeves, tie undone, he sat across the table from a schoolboy. Tears streamed down Toby Wilder's face. Detective Mann was smiling, speaking softly, to bond with his child suspect.

Mallory picked up the remote control and clicked it to pause the film. "What about Toby's parents? Why aren't they in the room?"

"The kid's father ran out on him when he was eight or nine, and the mother waived parental rights. After the interrogation, a lawyer was called in." Mann's chair swiveled from side to side as he stared at the image on the wide screen. "Then we had to give the kid a plea bargain. And that was pure charity."

Mallory nodded, though not in agreement. She knew they had missed the fun part, the hours of questioning that had led up to a child's taped confession. There would be no coercion in this segment of the interview, probably the only part that had been safe to film.

"It was a good deal for Toby," said the acting commissioner. "The kid got four years in juvenile detention. Not bad for a charge of felony assault. You know he didn't find that glue in the park. He had to bring it with him. The assault was premeditated. Real cold."

Mallory clicked the play button.

On-screen, a young Rolland Mann was saying to the boy, "Okay, Toby, let's say you and this other kid had a fight. He was a fag, right? He made a pass at you, and you hit him." The detective splayed his hands. "Hey, who wouldn't? But then you got scared — thought you'd killed him. It ain't so easy to tell if a guy's dead or alive. I've heard of people waking up in the morgue. So I think a judge is gonna understand that part. When you strung the kid up in that tree — that wasn't torture. You just wanted to hide what you *thought* was a dead body. Okay so far?"

The boy made no response. By the soft focus of his eyes, Mallory knew Toby Wilder had shut down. He saw nothing, heard nothing. The boy was barely there. She froze the picture again. "How high off the ground was the victim hanging?"

"At least fifteen feet, maybe twenty."

Riker removed his bifocals after reading the unsigned confession. "Nothing in here about the glue. What did Toby say about that — off the record?"

Rolland Mann threw up his hands, frustrated now. How many times did he have to explain this? Testy, he said, "I never *asked* Toby about the glue. And that was more charity. With the glue in evidence, he would've been tried as an adult. You see — the victim wasn't dead when we cut him down. Now that was the lawyer's selling point to make Toby go along with a guilty plea. The DA's office agreed not to press murder charges if the victim died."

"So the victim was in bad shape," said Mallory. And that would explain the date on the death certificate supplied by the chief of detectives. "And it took him a month to die." There was no denial from the acting commissioner, and now she knew for certain that the boy had died from his injuries.

Rolland Mann's younger self on the screen was saying to the boy, "So this is how it went down, Toby. You brought flowers into the Ramble 'cause you thought that little kid was dead . . . and you were sorry. And then you called the cops and led us to the body. You felt bad. You couldn't stand the idea of leaving him there, all alone, strung up in that tree. Those flowers — that was like saying you were sorry. That looks good to a judge."

Mallory had yet to hear the sound of the child's voice, and now the taped interview was over. "Toby never admitted to anything." She rewound the tape. "Maybe I missed it." She clicked the rewind button and played it again. "His lips are cracked. Did you give him any water? Did you remember to feed the kid?"

Mann slapped the flat of his hand on the desk. "I didn't torture him!" He took a time-out for a count of ten seconds. Calmer now, he said, "If Toby wasn't guilty, what was he doing in the Ramble? This was fifteen years ago — before your time, Detective." He turned to her partner. "Riker, you remember those days — the kind of scum who hung out there. Damn junkies even robbed each other, *killed* each other. So what would an innocent kid be doing in the Ramble — with a bouquet of flowers? And Toby led that park cop right to the crime scene." The deputy commissioner left his desk to stand beside Mallory. He took the remote control from her hand and froze the picture on the screen. "I agreed to meet with you so you wouldn't waste time on Toby Wilder. It's a solved crime. No link between my case and yours."

Mallory faced the screen and its frozen image of a thirteen-year-old boy. "Any cop can make a kid cry. It's almost too easy. If this was a solid bust, it should've been high profile. But it never made any headlines."

"And we have to wonder why," said Riker. "Maybe there was something hinky about your evidence. And what does it take to keep a thing like that quiet? How much influence —"

"Careful, Detective."

Mallory's turn. "How long did the kid hold up before a lawyer got to him? Maybe eight hours? Ten? Any kid that age, innocent or guilty, should've broken, but not him. Before you started taping, he told you he didn't do it, right? And you *believed* him. That's why you kept your own personal copy of the interview. You knew this case could come back on you one day."

"That's *enough,* Detective Mallory."

Riker was on his feet, coming up behind Mann's back. "I know why there's nothing about the glue on that tape. The victim was hanging twenty feet in the air — an hour after sundown. Toby couldn't see that detail from the ground. All he saw was a kid's body hanging in a tree."

Mann whirled around to face Riker, and now it was Mallory who stole up behind him, saying, "Toby didn't even know about the glue. How could he?"

Mann turned full circle to gape at her, and Riker's next words made him turn again.

"Toby never saw the glue . . . so you never mentioned it. That's the kind of detail you'd hold back to rule out crackpot confessors. But you didn't want to rule out Toby Wilder."

"No," said Mallory, working the man's blind side again. "You couldn't risk him telling a story that wouldn't match up with the evidence — the *glue.* What a good career move."

They had worked him like a spinning ballerina, and now he shouted, "Stop!"

Stop the music.

Rolland Mann returned to his desk and sat down. He took a deep breath.

And break time was over.

"The boy didn't do it." Mallory stepped up to one side of his chair.

"And you *knew* that," said Riker, from the other side. "Now you wanna kill the connection between your case and ours. You don't want us digging around in your old business."

Rolland Mann's fingers curled around the telephone receiver. "Remember what I said about the speed dial? One phone call and you're —"

"You make that call, and we'll have to return the favor," said Mallory. "It all comes back to the glue." She waved the patrolman's personal notes. "And then there's your ViCAP questionnaire. Fifteen years ago, you ran a search for a killer with a similar MO. That would've been a *month* after Toby confessed. You *knew* he was innocent."

"Here's what I don't understand," said Riker. "How did you get that kid in front of a judge when there was no investigation? We can't even find an incident report."

"It's like the assault on that little boy never happened," said Mallory. "What'll we find when we run Toby Wilder's name?"

"A record of four years in juvenile detention," said Rolland Mann. "But you'd have to break the law to get that much. Juvie records are *sealed.*"

"But not police reports on assaults. So how did you get that case on a court docket — a case that didn't exist?" And then she knew. Mallory stepped back from the desk. "You never got a signed confession, did you?

Not for the Ramble assault. No, you got Toby to plead out on some *other* crime, right?" Yes, she was right. His eyes were so much wider now.

"And then," said Riker, "a *month* later, you ran that ViCAP search."

Mallory held up the death certificate. "That was the same day Ernest Nadler died."

Rolland Mann confirmed all of this by withdrawing his hand from the telephone. The mention of the child victim's name had unnerved him.

Mallory pocketed the written confession as she crossed the room to stand before the old videocassette player. She pressed the eject button and pulled out the tape. "We're taking this. I think you can trust us to be discreet."

The detectives strolled out the door with their purloined goods.

TWENTY

Today I discover the terrible importance of surviving till class picture day.

They keep the yearbooks at the back of the school library. I take down the one for the year a girl jumped off the roof, and I look through the pages of students posed for headshots, looking for Poor Allison. No one remembers the family name. The only lasting impression of her is the yearly chalk outline on the garden flagstones.

Phoebe says I won't find the chalk girl in that section. "It was her first year, and she didn't live long enough for class picture day — so they tried to erase her." Turning ahead to the section of sporting events and other group pictures taken throughout the year, she stops near the end. "Here she is. They missed this one." Phoebe points to a photograph of a little red-haired girl standing with other kids. She's the shortest member of the chess club. "Count

them," says Phoebe. "Ten kids in the picture, only nine names in the caption."
— ERNEST NADLER

Riker sat in the passenger seat, staring at the rearview mirror, averting his gaze from the traffic violations of his tailgating partner. He could feel the shift of hard lane changes, but preferred not to meet the eyes of terrified motorists sharing this crowded patch of road with Mallory. Every car up ahead was threatened with a rear-end collision. He touched his seat-belt clasp to be sure it was fastened. *Oh, what the hell.* The air bag would save him. He checked the side mirror one more time. "You were right. Goddard's got nobody tailing us."

"This was always a closed game," said Mallory, "just the chief of D's and Rocket Mann — and us."

The car stopped for a red light, and Riker loosened his death grip on the rolled-up ViCAP questionnaire. "So the guy wipes out every trace of the kid's assault — and *then* he makes a permanent record of the whole damn thing in the FBI database."

"It's original," said Mallory. "Not your garden-variety blackmailer. And Rocket Mann was patient. He waited a solid month for the victim to die. Murder's worth a lot

271

more than an assault charge."

"Yeah," said Riker. If not for Mallory's raid on ViCAP, the old FBI questionnaire would have stayed buried in the system. Mann's blackmail victim only needed to know that it was there, and that it could be retrieved at will. Better than a bank vault. "So that poor kid who got sent to Juvie — he was just a scapegoat."

"He had other uses," said Mallory. "If the dead boy's family asked for their pound of flesh, Mann only had to show them the interview tape — and maybe a booking sheet for Toby Wilder."

The sealed records of Family Court resolved the problem of convicting Toby for a different crime. And Ernest Nadler's parents would never know their son's murder had been covered up for profit — the meteoric rise of a mediocre man, Rocket Mann.

Calling up CSI Pollard's line on the Hunger Artist, Riker said, "The guy thought of everything." He removed the small microphone that passed for a tie clip. "Almost everything." Reaching into his breast pocket, he pulled out the recorder, the damning voice record of Mann's interview.

"We're not sharing that with the chief of D's," said his partner. "Not till our case is wrapped."

"If we hold out on him —" The car lurched forward. Then it stopped short, foiled by gridlock, and Riker blessed his seat belt, else he would have lost his teeth on the dashboard.

"Joe Goddard's a fool for chess," said Mallory to the man who had taught her that game when she was eleven years old. "He's a regular player in Washington Square Park. And he's not bad."

"Good to know. So the chief looks six moves ahead. So?" *Oh, Christ!* Now he understood why she wanted to hold something back — a bargaining chip. Joe Goddard had already made a move that gave two detectives power over him; he had bluntly spelled out a plan of conspiracy, a career ender for the chief of D's if things went sour.

Mallory finished his thought. "You have to wonder how Goddard plans to keep us in line — and quiet." The car moved forward, but her head was turned to one side, facing her partner and not the windshield, a little act of terror that she saved for special occasions. "Here's the problem. If the chief had some dirt on me, he would've spelled it out before our meeting with Rocket Mann. He'd never risk us changing sides. So I have to figure he's got something on *you*."

"Well, he doesn't." Riker had the cleanest badge in the NYPD, and the brat *knew* that.

Still driving blind, Mallory rounded a corner and *then* decided that she believed him. She turned her eyes back to the road and what lay ahead of them — two pedestrians in the crosswalk.

The hairy roundabout in traffic was over; they had come full circle and pulled to the curb. On foot, they entered a giant archway that tunneled through a Centre Street building, and they emerged on the next street to stand at the foot of a public promenade paved with brick and lined with trees, lamp posts and benches. At the far end of One Police Plaza was a small gatehouse for the courtyard of NYPD Headquarters, a fourteen-story fortress built to withstand a siege of nonexistent enemies. Riker's other name for this place was Paranoia in Spades, and so he knew they would not have to wait long.

Mallory checked her cell phone to read a text message. "It's the gatehouse cop." He was their spy, their eye on the revolving door.

The detectives took cover behind a large sculpture, a frozen collision of gigantic red disks fused at odd angles. A few minutes later, Rolland Mann walked past them without his bodyguard, heading for the arch.

"Nice timing, kid." Riker kept his position behind the sculpture — against his better judgment — waiting for another high-ranking official to walk by.

"He's coming," said Mallory. "Pay me."

The man with the bullet-shaped head, Chief of Detectives Joe Goddard, was moving fast on the promenade, and then he slowed his steps to maintain a covert distance behind the acting police commissioner.

Riker handed his partner a twenty-dollar bill for a lost bet. He had not believed that Goddard would risk doing a shadow detail. And now they had solid proof that there was no official investigation into police corruption; the chief of D's was running an under-the-table game.

The two detectives strolled through the arch and along the sidewalk of Centre Street. Riker insisted that his partner walk behind him. She had the strange idea that she could become invisible with only a pair of sunglasses to hide her, deluded that men would not stare at her.

Mallory really believed she was good at this.

But today she deferred to her partner. On shadow detail, Riker was the best of the

275

best, though he would admit that Goddard was not all that bad. Fortunately, the chief had not anticipated being tailed, and there was never a backwards glance; the man was so focussed on his own quarry. And so they traveled, turning corners and walking down side streets, four ducks in a row.

The parade came to a halt when Rolland Mann stopped at the spread blanket of a sidewalk hawker and paid cash for a slightly used, certainly stolen, cell phone — a convoluted precaution in an age of anonymous calling cards and disposable phones.

How paranoid could he be?

Transaction done, onward they marched. Riker saw the action of a number punched into the cell phone that was then held to Rolland Mann's ear to hear the rings. The time between this call and the next one suggested that no connections were made, but the third number resulted in a conversation of several minutes.

Calling concluded, Mann stopped by a vendor's cart and purchased a bagel in a white sack. He looked around in all directions. His three followers had already stepped into shop doorways and out of sight. While Mann pulled out his bagel, Riker looked down at his side to see Mallory using the camera function of her phone. *Click* — a picture of Mann unfurling a handkerchief and wiping his prints from the cell phone — *click* — slipping the phone into the paper sack and — *click* — after crumpling the sack, he tossed it into a city trash container. Now, bagel in hand, he strolled back toward One Police Plaza.

A moment later, Chief Goddard stepped out on the sidewalk to retrieve the thrown-away phone from the rubbish. Riker followed Mallory's cue and used his camera phone to snap a picture of the chief of detectives rutting around in the trash. Why not? In addition to proving chain of evidence for the ditched cell phone, this snapshot would make a great Christmas card.

Goddard never saw the two detectives, side by side, melding into foot traffic and turning a corner.

Coffey looked up when his senior detective broke with tradition to make a courtesy knock on the door to his private office. "Where's your partner?"

"She's badgering another TV station to announce Humphrey Bledsoe's funeral." Riker flopped down in the chair before the desk. "I might need to do some damage control."

"Something to do with God?" And by that, the lieutenant could only mean Chief of Detectives Joe Goddard, every squad's higher power. Coffey threw up his hands. "You're too late. I just talked to him on the phone. He asked me if I told Mallory she failed her psych evaluation. When he talked to you guys, he had the impression that she didn't know yet. I guess he's sending a message . . . maybe a threat?"

"But you submitted Charles Butler's psych rebuttal, right?"

"No, Riker, you really don't want me to do that."

"She's got a right to challenge Dr. Kane's evaluation. I know her lawyer gave you the —"

"You mean this?" The lieutenant held up the wadded ball of a legal document and tossed it over his shoulder. "All gone. Mallory's still in limbo."

"What the —" Riker was silenced when the lieutenant raised the flat of his hand.

"I went to see Charles Butler today." Jack Coffey unlocked the top drawer of his desk. "I had a problem with his rebuttal. Small detail — thought it might be a typo. So he showed me his calendar dates for Mallory's sessions and a draft of his report — a damn carbon copy from a *typewriter*. Will somebody please get that man a computer?" The lieutenant pulled two sheaves of paper from the drawer and laid them on the blotter, side by side. "Here's Dr. Kane's original evaluation, the one she *failed.* And this is Charles Butler's rebuttal. Read the dates." He sat back and laced his fingers behind his head.

When the detective looked up from his reading and said, "Shit," the lieutenant smiled.

Charles Butler's four-page defense of Mallory's sanity mentioned the department psychologist's evaluation, but Charles's rebuttal had been written — and *dated* — a full week before Dr. Kane's findings were submitted to the NYPD. Riker stared at one document and then the other, uncomprehending. "How could this —"

"You *know* what happened. She couldn't wait for the official psych report. It was taking too long. So she hacked into the shrink's personal computer. She knew what was in Dr. Kane's report long before it landed on the chief's desk — and mine."

Riker shook his head. "Mallory doesn't make mistakes like this."

"Kane's evaluation might've had a different date on it — when Mallory broke into his computer. His report should've gone out weeks ago. Your partner probably thought I was sitting on it all this time — just to torture her with more desk duty. Computer hacking couldn't tell her that Dr. Kane had the flu. I got that from his secretary. And that's why his report was delayed." The lieutenant slipped the two evaluations back into his drawer — and slammed it. "It's like Mallory took out a billboard ad to say she broke the law."

"What're you gonna do?"

"Me? Nothing. She doesn't need my help to crash and burn. But it's gonna take her a while to shop for another shrink . . . so she can make a *legal* challenge." The lieutenant's meaning was clear. Charles Butler was officially out of the loop; the man could not simply alter the date of his rebuttal. "So, Riker . . . here's your other problem. I think Chief Goddard *likes* Dr. Kane's report. He didn't even reprimand me for putting a psycho cop on the street. He *wants* Mallory on this case. The chief might sit on that lousy psych report for years — or take her badge tomorrow if she gets out of line. That's his style."

Riker nodded his understanding of *style.* Joe Goddard's motives were pure — and delusional. The chief of D's wanted to reshape the NYPD in his own image. Toward that end, he collected dirt on people from ranks above and below his own. If they could not be remolded to his liking, he *removed* them. If Mallory failed to bring in the goods on Rolland Mann, she was gone. That was the message in Goddard's phone call to the lieutenant.

"Give the chief what he wants," said Coffey. "And for God's sake — don't give Mallory a heads-up. That's your only real shot at damage control."

By the time she saw Goddard coming for her, it would be way too late. But Jack Coffey was right. Riker knew his partner would never go quietly. And if she had advance warning? He summoned up the biblical passage of the Pale Rider, placing Mallory in the saddle of Death's horse — *and hell followed after.* "I won't tell her."

Coco reached under her pillow to pull out the one-button cell phone so she could say good night to Mallory. The connection was made, and now she covered the mouthpiece and looked up at Charles Butler. "She wants to know if you got the package."

"Yes, tell her it just arrived."

This was conveyed to the detective on the cell phone. And then, in response to some question of Mallory's, Coco said, "I don't remember." The little girl's eyes shut tight, and her head turtled into her pajama top. "I don't think he said any —"

And, on this note of stress, the interrogation was ended. Charles took the phone and said, "Good *night,* Mallory."

He remained with the little girl, distracting her from anxiety with a chapter from Dickens's *The Old Curiosity Shop,* evidently not a thriller among youngsters. After only a few pages, Coco drifted off to sleep.

On his way down the hall, he rehearsed his next conversation with Mallory, a hard lecture on rules for dealing with fragile children. Stopping by the glove table, he picked up the box from the NYPD and opened it to find a videocassette. This would explain the earlier delivery of an old-model television set with a slot below the screen that would neatly fit this tape. The mechanism was so simple that this gift failed to include Mallory's standard operating instructions for Luddites.

He sat down with a glass of red wine and played the fifteen-year-old film of schoolboy Toby Wilder and former detective Rolland Mann. He saw all the signs of trauma in the bone-weary child, whose head moved slowly, side to side — not in a gesture of defiance but one of bafflement. The boy never spoke, never voiced his only question, but asked with glassy eyes, *How could this be happening?*

A heightened sense of empathy had kept Charles Butler out of private practice, working one-on-one with patients. There were limits to what he could endure via other people's pain, and now he felt helpless and hopeless, free-floating in a child's angst. The psychologist had no trouble lip-reading Toby's silent punctuation to every utterance by the detective in the final minutes of the tape. Over and over, Charles, in perfect unison with the boy, mouthed the word *Mom.*

And then the tape ended — too soon.

The telephone rang, and that would be Mallory. He picked up the receiver. There were no salutations. Before she could utter a single word to startle and amaze him with her prescient timing, he said, "You're right, and you're wrong. The tape wasn't edited, but the interview did end abruptly . . . at a very odd moment. Rolland Mann was taking his cue from someone off-camera. You can see it in the lift of his head, a sudden break in eye contact with the boy. And you're right about the time factor. The interrogation probably went on for hours before they started taping. The boy shows signs of fatigue to the point of exhaustion. But this is the odd part." Charles had no doubt that the child, heart and mind, was at the point of giving up and giving in. "Toby was broken. He was about to confess."

TWENTY-ONE

Toby doesn't always go straight home after school. Some days we follow him into Central Park. Phoebe and I always stop at the entrance to the Ramble. It's dangerous in there, and we know that without being told. Even in the daylight, every rock and tree is a hiding place for trouble and pain, for the down-and-outs, the scary wigged-out people with nothing to lose. "They'll cut you as soon as look at you." That's what a cop says when he chases us away. But I've seen Toby Wilder dance into the Ramble.

— ERNEST NADLER

If the city had a heart, and Riker doubted that, it would not be in this neighborhood of river views and promenades, where dogs were walked by handlers so that the wealthiest residents could live their whole lives up in the clouds of Penthouse Land.

Riker strolled down the sidewalk with Charles Butler, the only rich man he ever liked. Behind them, Mallory walked hand in hand with Coco, who was followed by the uniformed officer assigned to guard the material witness. The little girl sported a brand-new pair of designer eyeglasses with nifty red frames — a present from Mallory to replace the less stylish ones that Charles had bought. Coco scrutinized each face in the long procession that slowly moved toward the funeral home. In this single-file line that extended around the block, there were politicians that even Riker, an impolitic cop, could recognize.

Charles identified other important faces, those from the social register of New York bluebloods. "These people came because Grace was born a Driscol. Her late husband, John Bledsoe, wasn't well regarded. I understand he walked out on his family, and then he drank himself to death."

Smiling, Riker looked back at the long line behind them. He wondered how many of these high-minded people knew they had turned out to pay their respects to a dead child molester. "How did Coco take it when you told her Uncle Red died?"

"Very well. I think she was relieved."

"Did you tell her about Granny yet?"

"No," said Charles. "Maybe we'll talk about that tomorrow. Mallory's right. This funeral is good preparation. Coco's never been to one before. We'll just sit in the back row. I don't want her to view an open casket. She has no real experience with death."

"You're kidding me." Riker jabbed a thumb back over one shoulder. "That little girl knows fifty ways to kill a rat."

The small party stopped in front of Harrow and Sons Funeral Home, a building that might pass for a century-old bank. Coco shook her head and told Mallory that she had not recognized anyone. And Charles wore a wobbly smile that asked, *What? What just happened?*

"Oh, bloody hell!" The man now realized that this procession of upscale mourners was actually a lineup of potential murderers. Child by the hand, the angry psychologist stalked off without another word. Coco waved back at the detectives until she and her guardian were around the corner and out of sight.

Mallory entered the building, and Riker stayed behind on the sidewalk to check out the early shots taken by a police photographer. Assured that they would have a complete record of every visitor, he climbed the stairs to be met by a young man in funereal black, who led him down a hallway of dark-paneled wood and velvet couches, one of them occupied by Mrs. Driscol-Bledsoe's companion, Hoffman. Seated beside this woman were two men in expensive suits. Riker recognized one of the suits as the lawyer who had collected Phoebe Bledsoe at the station house.

The detective followed his guide into a large room that could hold a hundred people, but only two chairs had been set out, one for Humphrey Bledsoe's mother and one for his sister. Phoebe was on good behavior today, no nail-biting and no conversations with invisible people.

Riker's escort confided that the rest of the chairs had been removed to discourage people from remaining for long. "The mother declined a religious service." Mr. Harrow seemed very young to be scandalized by this, but it made sense to Riker. Sending up prayers for a pedophile was like begging for seven plagues upon your house.

The air was thick with the perfume of floral offerings. They were extravagant, as if each sender of a basket or a wreath feared being outdone by another. Central Park did not have so many flowers. At their center was the coffin, a grand affair of ornately carved wood. Humphrey Bledsoe's hair had been restored to its natural red color, and there was no sign of the autopsy damage. The face had a creepy lifelike quality — and it smiled. On Coco's behalf, Riker was inclined to spend a bullet to mess up that smile. Instead, he took up a post behind the chairs of Mrs. Driscol-Bledsoe and her daughter. And now he watched his partner moving from one flower arrangement to another, admiring the blooms — while stealing cards of sympathy, acquiring a list of those most anxious to curry favor with the pedophile's mother.

For the next hour, the mourners entered the room single file and walked to the casket for the obligatory view of the dead pervert, and this was followed by condolences to the family. One by one, they were dispatched in polite society's version of the bum's rush. Riker admired the matriarch's ability to keep the crowd in motion, quickly withdrawing her hand from one person to offer it to the next in line. Even the mayor was given short shrift. And then it was Rolland Mann's turn. The acting police commissioner had an anxious look about him. He leaned close to Humphrey's mother, but he had not gotten out three whispered words before he was dismissed.

The last of the mourners were three stragglers in the clothes of workaday people, a man, a woman and a teenage girl with red hair the same shade as Coco's.

Phoebe leaned toward her mother, and Riker heard her whisper, "Who are those people?"

"I think those are the Coles," said Mrs. Driscol-Bledsoe. "I only met them once or twice, and the girl was much younger then."

The three Coles queued up at the coffin and took turns spitting on the corpse.

"That's different," said Riker.

The pop-eyed funeral director was obviously another Harrow of Harrow and Sons, an older version of Riker's escort. This distinguished gentleman sucked in his breath, and then, wits recovered, moved toward the desecrators. Mallory snagged him by one arm and pulled him back to the coffin, commanding the man as if he were a dog, saying, "Stay." Now she followed close behind the little family of vandals. Their leader was angry as he approached the dead man's mother.

"Mr. Cole, thank you for coming." Grace Driscol-Bledsoe said this with surprisingly little sarcasm. The man expelled a huge glob of mucus, and it rolled down the front of the lady's silk blouse. Without missing a beat, she said, "Always a pleasure."

Mallory and Riker followed the Cole family outside, and there on the sidewalk they learned that these people were residents of a small Connecticut town where Humphrey had attended prep school. The father then held his tongue until his wife and daughter were safely ensconced in a taxi. "He raped my child when she was six years old, but the town wouldn't prosecute. They wouldn't even *arrest* him. The parents and the politicians, they did this dirty backroom deal, and that little bastard was sent to a mental institution — more like a spa for rich people. So we sued the parents."

Riker looked up from his notebook to ask, "What grounds?"

"Negligence. They neglected to warn the town that their son was a monster." Mr. Cole's anger and pain seemed brand-new, as if the assault had happened only this morning and not years ago. "They *knew* what their kid was. They *always* knew. That's why they settled out of court." The man climbed into the waiting taxi, and the damaged little family rolled away.

"The settlement almost put a small dent in my husband's stock portfolio."

The detectives turned around to see Grace Driscol-Bledsoe standing behind them atop the steps of the funeral home.

"Of course, the lawsuit was ridiculous. It would've been dismissed for lack of merit, but my late husband actually gave the Coles more than they asked for." She descended the stairs, stopping short of the final step, no doubt liking the advantage of looking down on them. "He wanted to spare the little girl a painful court appearance. My John was a sentimental man."

"You mean, he knew his kid was a cockroach," said Riker. "So how did Humphrey wind up with all that money?"

"When John sold his company, the proceeds went into a trust for our son's psychiatric care. One condition — the boy would be institutionalized until he was cured." She bestowed a patronizing smile on Riker. "I know what you're thinking, Detective. Pedophiles are only cured when they run out of money to pay their therapists. And we did our best to make sure that wouldn't happen. But after my husband's death, Humphrey hired lawyers to break the trust fund and get him out of the asylum. The court case dragged on for years. Even after taxes and legal fees, my son had more than a hundred million dollars . . . but only three months to enjoy it."

"And now all that money comes back to

you," said Mallory.

"So I'm told."

"My partner loves money motives," said Riker. "But I guess we're looking at an insanity defense, right? Maybe it runs in the family?"

"Oh, my son wasn't insane — just a pedestrian little pervert."

"He's talking about Phoebe," said Mallory. "Your crazy daughter is on our short list."

"There's nothing wrong with her."

"What?" Riker tilted his head to one side. "She talks to people who aren't there."

"No, she doesn't. She only *listens*." Mrs. Driscol-Bledsoe's tone implied that this was a perfectly rational thing to say.

"Okay," said Riker. "Phoebe only *hears* invisible people. That's still —"

"That's a symptom of incompetent therapy, *not* mental illness. And I can name six people who visit cemeteries and converse with gravestones."

"So Phoebe has a psychiatric history," said Mallory, "and her invisible friend is dead."

"Dead and real short," said Riker. "Kid size. She always looks down when he talks to her." And now for a long shot. "This invisible, dead kid — what's his name — *Ernest?*"

Bonanza.

Riker caught the startled look in the woman's eye, only a flicker, gone in a second. Then he looked past her to see three men in suits walking down the stairs of the funeral home. Such beautiful suits. They gathered around Mrs. Driscol-Bledsoe as she stepped down to the sidewalk. Mallory was focused on the action down the street, where yet another suit was opening the door to a waiting limo, and Phoebe Bledsoe ducked inside of it, escaping.

Riker smiled. "Nicely done." So the lady had only spoken to them to draw fire from her daughter. "But now we have to wonder why Phoebe needs your protection."

Mallory stepped close to the society matron. Closer — threatening distance. "You just moved your own kid to the top of our suspect list."

Both women were tall, meeting eye to eye, and this had all the makings of a showdown, three hired guns and a diva against Mallory. One of the lawyers whispered in Grace Driscol-Bledsoe's ear. Evidently, she was that rare client who heeded her legal advisers, and the attorneys walked off with her in the lockstep of a marching band. Another limo door was opened, and the lady vanished.

■ ■ ■ ■

There was no funeral for the other murder victim from the Ramble. And this was due to lack of interest by the parents of Agatha Sutton. So said the victim's younger brother when he met the detectives at the door to his sister's apartment. The boy looked to be in his early twenties, and his teeth were perfect, a hallmark of expensive orthodontia in his childhood. Now the score was three for three; all of the Hunger Artist's victims had come down from money.

Barry Sutton wore a long-sleeved shirt in the heat of summer, a sure sign that he was covering the needle marks of drug addiction.

"We're sorry for your loss," said Riker.

"Save it for someone who cares. My sister was an animal." The youngster jangled a ring of keys. "Mom and Dad are in Italy for the summer." He tried one key in the lock and then another. "They won't be back anytime soon, not on Aggy's account."

"Okay," said Riker. "How did *you* get along with your sister?"

"I didn't." He tried the third key. No luck. "Sorry. This is my father's set. I've only been here once before to look at the place with a real-estate agent. My parents bought this condo for Aggy."

"Odd they didn't pony up for her surgery," said Mallory. "The medical examiner told us your sister had an operable tumor . . . and her symptoms were hard to miss."

"Our family doctor warned them that removing the tumor might cure Aggy. They liked her better when she was insane. They could cope with insanity."

The fourth key turned in the lock, and Barry Sutton led the detectives inside. A simple dress lay on the floor in a pile with a pair of sandals and underwear — the same way they had found Humphrey's clothing and Willy's. The killer had also bopped and dropped Aggy a short distance from the door.

The front room was bare of any furnishings. "I should've expected this," said the victim's brother. "My parents bought the place fully furnished, but Aggy gives everything away. A lawyer managed her trust-fund allotments so she couldn't give away all her money, too."

The space was generous in size, but even so, the word *squalor* came to mind with the smells of body odor and windows never opened. A stink of garbage led them to the kitchen, where a peanut butter jar stood open and roaches scaled its glass sides. A loaf of bread was moving, breathing with the activity of feasting bugs inside the wrapper. Barry Sutton recoiled and fled to the bedroom, and there a bare mattress lay on the floor. The open closet contained four simple dresses, all exactly like the one in the pathetic pile in the living room. This was a basic Mother Teresa wardrobe — not even a spare pair of shoes.

"Okay, she's nuts," said Riker. "We got that. How long has this been going on?"

"A couple of years. I call it the brain tumor from heaven. Before the tumor, my sister was just mean. Then she went crazy." He turned to Mallory. "Crazy is good."

Her slight nod was an almost imperceptible agreement. "What did Aggy *do* to you?"

"Aggy the Biter?" Barry Sutton rolled up one sleeve to show them that he was not concealing any needle marks, only an ugly scar. The wound was healed, but the missing chunk of flesh made an indent in his arm. "She did that when I was ten and she was seventeen. That was the year my parents sent her to Europe. The bribe to stay there was plastic surgery and support money. Aggy was butt-ugly and flat-chested when she left. When she came back, she had breasts and a chin — but she'd lost her mind. My parents got a competency hearing so they could make all her medical decisions."

"And they decided to keep the brain tumor," said Riker.

"You think that's cold? I call it self-defense." Aggy's brother rolled down his sleeve and then handed over the keys. "Lock up when you leave, okay? *Mail* me the keys. I don't want to talk about my sister anymore."

TWENTY-TWO

The gym teacher lines us up between basketball hoops, wall-to-wall boys and girls in school ties and blazers. It's class picture day. Everyone takes a turn in the chair in front of a background screen that looks like a curdled sky.

It's my turn. The man behind the camera is stalled for a minute. He's staring at my neck. My hair is slicked back with a comb I wet in the drinking fountain, and now half a bite mark shows above my collar. The photographer asks if he can see the whole thing. So I undo my tie and shirt buttons. He's impressed. He whistles. Now he can see some of my bruises, too, the ones that only show in gym class. And the gym teacher says to him, "You can airbrush the picture, right?"

"Oh, yeah," says the photographer, "and for a little extra, I can drop by once a week and airbrush the actual kid. Then it won't matter who's beating the crap out of him, right?"

So the gym teacher walks away real fast, and I know he's going to rat this guy out to the headmaster. But the photographer isn't worried. He winks and says, "Well, kid, as Christ on the cross once said of the Romans — fuck 'em if they can't take a joke."

I laugh. He snaps the picture.

— ERNEST NADLER

By the terms of an agreement forged in the mayor's office, lawyers would be in attendance for the police interview at the Driscol-Bledsoe residence on the Upper West Side. When Hoffman, the drab employee, opened the door to the detectives, she was still carrying her small Gladstone bag on a shoulder strap. The woman ignored Riker when he asked, "What's in the bag? Is your boss shooting up or snorting it?"

Hoffman left them alone in an entry hall larger than the average New Yorker's apartment. The floor was a circular chessboard of black-and-white marble tiles, and a polished table at its center was decked out with a profusion of flowers. They strolled past the grand staircase, through an archway and into a space of ballroom proportions

300

and a cathedral ceiling that spoke to Mallory, saying, *Money lives here.*

These environs were familiar in a way. This was a grander version of Charles Butler's taste — modern art on the walls and antiques on the floor. An education at Barnard allowed her to recognize the style of Frank Stella in a gigantic wall sculpture of curving shapes and primary colors. She was accustomed to artwork on this scale, having viewed it by slides projected on a classroom wall. Mallory could also name Motherwell as the artist of a large work on canvas. And the furniture was an elegant mix of pieces named for the reigns of long-dead kings and queens.

All of this she saw with a cost accountant's eye.

This was the showroom, the gathering place for cocktail parties, for independent conversations upon a loveseat here and couches over there, and circles of armchairs on the far side. Though visitors clearly came here not to be entertained, but to be cowed by extreme opulence, to stand in awe beneath the largest crystal chandelier that money could buy.

Mallory slowly revolved, finally turning her gaze on Grace Driscol-Bledsoe. The lady of the house was enthroned in a high-back chair by the fireplace — the *only* chair in that part of the room. She was surrounded by an honor guard of three lawyers, who stood tense and watchful. Their employer tapped one foot, annoyed to be kept waiting.

Well, *damn.*

As the detectives crossed the wide floor, Mallory deflated the props of the room with a dismissive wave of the hand, saying, "All of this belongs to the Driscol Institute, right? The antiques, the art. You don't even own the house."

Grace Driscol-Bledsoe barely suppressed a smile of touché and inclined her head to say that this was so.

Approaching the woman, Mallory looked down to see indents on an area rug, impressions left there by chairs recently removed, forcing the detectives to stand in attendance, less like a police interview, more like an audience with royalty. The furniture was telling them to state their business, make it quick and *get out.*

Mallory held up a bulky envelope. "I've had a look at your personal finances."

One of the lawyers stepped forward from the chorus. "You're out of line, Detective."

"I don't think so," said Riker. "Her family trust fund is managed by the Driscol Institute. A charity's books are public record. Why do we need to explain that to a lawyer?"

"After taxes," said Mallory, "you're barely middle class." And now she engaged the socialite in a contest of who would blink first. "But then you've got the kickback potential that comes with control of a multibillion-dollar charity."

"Yeah," said Riker. "So we're curious about —"

The attorneys were all talking at once, jockeying for position as the most indignant, the most outraged, until Riker waved his arms and yelled, "Hold it! I got an easier question. Okay, guys?" He turned to the woman in the throne chair. "You got any photos of Humphrey? We need a shot of him as a kid."

"A picture taken at least *fifteen* years ago," said Mallory.

Grace Driscol-Bledsoe made her first error. Or was it an insult? Perhaps she thought so little of the police that she could not be bothered to feign surprise — to ask why they would need such an old picture of a recent crime victim. "Sorry." She only smiled at this lost leader of a long-ago murder. "I threw away his photographs, but I can show you a portrait of Humphrey and his father." She led the detectives and lawyers down a hallway to open the door to a small bathroom off the kitchen. A large, gilt-framed oil painting hung on the narrow wall above the toilet. Her husband, the late John Bledsoe, was posed with one hand on his son's shoulder, conveying a sense of possession. "Humphrey was ten years old when that was painted."

Mallory pulled out her camera phone to snap a picture.

"Oh, my dear. I can do better than that." The woman disappeared into the kitchen for a moment, and then she reappeared at Mallory's side, knife in hand — a *long* knife — and so sharp. The attorneys took one step back in the unison of a startled Girl Scout troop. The detectives were more blasé about a potential stabbing.

Grace Driscol-Bledsoe smiled. "You don't think I'm dangerous? I can assure you . . . I *am*." She kicked off her stiletto heels, climbed up on the toilet seat and cut out Humphrey's head. After handing it down to Riker, she carved out her husband's head and gave him that piece, too. "Shame to break up the set."

Mallory's eyes remained on the ruined canvas, the portrait of headless father and son. "So Humphrey was your husband's favorite?"

"Oh, yes. John had visions of building a dynasty, and Humphrey was his heir apparent." She climbed down and turned back to admire her handiwork with the knife. "I think I like it better this way. My husband gave me a diamond necklace when I delivered a son. For Phoebe I got nothing. And when the bastard died, he didn't leave one dime to his daughter."

When they had all reconvened beneath the crystal chandelier of the larger room, Mallory moved on to her favorite subject. "Let's talk money. The income from your family trust fund has no cost-of-living increase. It wouldn't support you in a shoebox apartment."

"My family has always been dedicated to public service. We are not about money."

"And then there's your token salary," said Mallory. "As director of the Institute's board of trustees, you don't make enough to buy your clothes." The detective clicked through a gallery of pictures on her cell phone. The small screen displayed an archive of society pages that featured this diva of the New York charity scene. "I'm looking at designer originals. Not one outfit off the rack. And the shoes you're wearing now are a thousand dollars . . . apiece."

"I've never had to pay for my wardrobe, Detective. I'm sure you can understand why. I could charge the designers to advertise their wares on my back, but I settle for clothes, handbags . . . and shoes."

"Internal Revenue might have a problem with the gift tax," said Riker.

A lawyer stepped forward. "The clothing is regarded as a donation to the Driscol Institute. It's worn to charitable events, then recycled at auctions to benefit worthy causes."

This man could now be identified as the tax attorney in the gang of suits. Mallory turned from one man to the other. "Who can tell me how many politicians the lady has in her pocket? What do they cost on average, and how do you recycle them? Another auction? Influence to the highest bidder?" By their looks of surprise, by their lack of howling, she confirmed that there was not one criminal lawyer in the pack.

The detective turned her attention back to Grace Driscol-Bledsoe. "You directed the Institute to fund charities in the names of city council members. They must love that. Good deeds get them votes. Five of them sit on the Contracts Committee. That gives you a majority voting block. How many of your friends benefit from city contracts?"

Before the first lawyer could raise an objection, she looked down at her cell-phone screen. "Oh, here's one." She held up the phone to display the society-page photograph. "The guy with his arm around your shoulder?"

"Oh, yeah," said Riker, squinting at the small image. "He was awarded a bridge-maintenance contract. *Big* bucks. And doesn't he look happy?"

"If I follow the money," said Mallory, "and I do — you haven't deposited your kickbacks in any personal bank accounts. Every large transfer of funds sets off federal alarms. . . . So they had to be cash payoffs."

Riker leaned into the conversation with his punch line. "Do you mind if we search your house for a safe?"

All three lawyers were talking, then shouting to be heard over one another's threats. The words *warrant* and *slander* figured in all their comments until their client silenced them by raising one hand. Addressing Mallory, she said, "The Driscol Institute always has glowing reports from the auditors. In this world, it's not what you know, my dear. It's what you can prove."

In sidelong vision, Mallory saw the woman's companion hovering near the entryway. "Your personal income might support a cleaning lady, but not a full-time employee like Hoffman, not if you like to eat regular meals." The detective bent down to make a show of examining a silver pendant resting on the socialite's bosom. The engraving was fine work, but the jeweler had not been able to disguise the function of the tricked-out button at its center. The older woman's hand quickly covered it.

This was the soft spot.

"It's a medical-alert medallion, right? You press that button and an ambulance shows up?" Without waiting for an answer, Mallory glanced at the companion standing on the other side of the room, still carrying her small Gladstone bag. "Hoffman's a nurse? That would make her a very *expensive* employee."

Riker cleared his throat. "I think you get the point, ma'am. You don't want us to *prove* anything. That's the last thing you want." He turned to the lineup of suits. "Right, guys?" This time, the suits were quiet, and they seemed a little tense. "Relax," said the smiling detective. "We only want access to Phoebe."

"That's out of the question," said Grace Driscol-Bledsoe.

"Because she's guilty," said Riker, "or because she can hang you?"

"Phoebe doesn't make a dime off of Humphrey's death," said Mallory. "No motive. That's all on you."

The doorbell rang. Hoffman had disappeared, and one of the lawyers volunteered to play butler, leaving the room to answer the door. He returned a moment later. "Miss Wilhelmina Fallon is here. Should I show her in?"

"I'd rather you gutted her on the doorstep," said Mrs. Driscol-Bledsoe. "But that's not in your job description, is it?" She leaned toward Mallory. "Dear, may I borrow your gun?"

"What's the tie between Humphrey and Willy Fallon?"

"And Agatha Sutton," said Riker. "What's her connection?"

"And we're still wondering," said Mallory, "how crazy Phoebe figures in."

"For the last time, Detectives — my daughter is not insane — not delusional. When she was a child, a therapist had her personalize — humanize — her anxiety. You could say she's listening to her inner critic."

"Right," said Mallory. "Can you prove that?"

"*I* can." Willy Fallon sat in a wheelchair beneath the arched entryway. A brown paper bag was clutched in her hands like a

309

vagrant's idea of a purse. Behind her stood a woman in a nurse's cap and white uniform. The nurse guided the chair across the floor toward the gathering by the fireplace. And as she rolled, Willy said, "We had the same psychiatrist when we were kids. Phoebe was a moron for going along with his crap." She held up one hand to stay the nurse and then sharply turned the wheels of her chair to face Mallory. "I could sue you for what you did to me."

Grace Driscol-Bledsoe took a long look at the wheelchair, the only visible evidence of injury, and then turned to Mallory. "I'm guessing you broke her legs? My dear, you have my deepest respect and admiration."

Willy turned her head to sneer at her escort, the woman in the nurse's uniform. "Did I hear you giggle, you stupid cow?"

The nurse removed her hands from the chair and addressed Mallory, correctly identifying the center of power in this room. "There's an ambulette parked outside. When you're done with Miss Fallon, just kick her to the curb. They'll take her away." Willy's escort left the room. Moments later came the distant slam of the front door.

Mallory smiled, happy in the way a cat is happy to see its living lunch, this meal on wheels. She walked up to Willy Fallon and leaned down to grasp the arms of the chair and slowly roll it back and forth. "So what's the connection between you and Phoebe — apart from the psychiatrist? Was she a good friend of yours?"

"That dweeb? No way. We went to the same school. That's *it*."

"The Driscol School? How long ago was that? Maybe fifteen years?"

Hoffman had reappeared to stand at Mrs. Driscol-Bledsoe's side. Following whispered instructions from her employer, she took command of Willy's chair and steered it toward the entry hall.

While Riker and Hoffman negotiated the wheelchair down the stone stairs to the sidewalk, Mallory handed the ambulette driver a twenty-dollar bill for his goodwill and affection.

When the patient had been loaded into a vehicle slightly larger than a station wagon, Hoffman retreated out of earshot, and the driver answered the detective's question. "No, ma'am, she doesn't need the chair. She walks just fine." According to his boss, the owner of the private service, Miss Fallon had only wanted to avoid the paparazzi.

"Since when?" Riker stepped into the end of this conversation. "Back in her party-girl

311

days, she loved those bastards."

And now they learned from the driver that Miss Fallon's credit cards were maxed out. He had been paid in cash from a brown paper bag full of money.

As the ambulette pulled away from the curb, Riker placed a call to the desk sergeant who had arranged for the crime victim's security at the hospital. After a short conversation, he folded the cell phone into his pocket. "The cop on guard duty never saw anybody go into Willy's room with a paper bag. But that guard left hours ago — when Willy declined police protection." He handed a law firm's business card to his partner. "She says any questions have to go through the family lawyers."

Mallory called the number on the card and was told that the firm no longer represented Miss Fallon; the rest of the family, yes, of course — but not her. And why not, the detective might ask? The lawyer continued without troubling her to actually pose the question. "Well, you've met this woman, right?" The Brahman voice on the phone now restated his position. "I would prefer to be eviscerated and forced to watch dogs eat my entrails. But I *am* discreet. I can only allow you to ponder all the things that might be worse than that."

On that final word, the call was concluded, and Mallory turned to her partner. "I'm guessing that Willy neutered a lawyer."

Wearing paper hospital slippers, Willy Fallon shushed across the lobby of the residential hotel. The manager blocked her way to the elevator. Before he could broach the subject of her overdue bill, she reached into her brown bag, pulled out two banded bundles of money and pressed them into his hands. "That should cover it."

The hotelier, too long accustomed to credit cards and traveler's checks, stared at the cash in surprise — then suspicion. He raised his eyes to hers, as if to ask, *What is this?*

Willy rode the elevator up to her hotel room. Yellow tape had been used to seal the door, and now it hung from the frame in loose strands, a sign that the room had been visited following the search by police. She opened the door with caution, but the place had an empty feel to it. The walls and furniture were filmed with black dust, and the drawers had been turned out on the floor. Damn cops never put anything back where it belonged. The hotel maid must have run away screaming. Willy entered the bathroom to see that her meager store of drugs was back in its plastic bag inside the toilet tank, many thanks to the hotel bellman.

She changed her hospital garb for real clothes and found her cell phone, not for one moment finding it odd that the police would leave it behind. *Stupid cops.* She called all the Wilders in the telephone directory, and finally she was down to one, a Susan Wilder. Was that the name of Toby's mother?

No one answered when Willy called.

The storefront window on Columbus Avenue was decorated with full-length portraits of brides and headshots of actors who were almost famous. In the front room of the shop, a selection of wedding albums had been pushed to one side of a display table, and chairs had been provided for the two detectives. They flipped through pictures of children posed against the ersatz blue background of school photographs.

The proprietor was soft-spoken, soft-stepping. His faded blue eyes were crinkled and kind. "Hey, if one of those brats turned up dead, I'd like to take the credit, but I'm not a violent man." He laid a leather-bound volume on top of the stack of yearbooks. "This is the one you want. It's my only copy, so I'd rather you didn't take it." He handed Riker a stack of Post-its. "Just mark the ones you like, and I'll scare up some enlargements."

Mallory rapidly turned the yearbook pages, scanning faces, reading names. "They're *all* here — even the Nadler kid. This is where it started." She flipped back to the beginning and used a Post-it to mark the portrait of eleven-year-old Phoebe Bledsoe. This photograph was taken when she was Ernest Nadler's age, but the murder victim was not among these children. She had found him two grades ahead of his age group, posed with the thirteen-year-olds.

"So he was a smart little kid," said Riker.

Ernest Nadler smiled at the homicide detectives, as if someone had just told him a fine joke. After marking his picture, Mallory turned back to the page with Humphrey Bledsoe's headshot. This face was unstructured and flabby.

And Riker said, "Creepy smile, huh?"

Yes, the picture was a predictor of Humphrey's pervert future. On the next page, Willy Fallon was skinnier at thirteen, almost insectile. And toward the end of this section, Aggy Sutton was no surprise, baring *all* her teeth, but not to smile. Toby Wilder's was the last photograph in this group of thirteen-year-olds, and Mallory lingered over this one.

"Oh, I remember *that* face," said the photographer. "*Great*-looking kid — and nice enough, but he couldn't sit still — feet tapping, fingers snapping all the time. I know I've got more shots of him. What's the name?" The man leaned closer to read the caption. "Okay." He disappeared into a back room and then returned with more pictures in hand. "My private stash. I like these better." He laid them out on the table. "They cover the three years he went to the Driscol School."

This was not the still and somber boy of Rolland Mann's interview tape. Every one of these photographs was blurred. This was Toby in motion, Toby when he was hyper-aware and juiced on the batteries of child-hood — so *alive.*

When the proprietor had given them a complete set of pictures, one for each student they had marked, Mallory stared at the enlarged portrait of Ernest Nadler. The line of the child's shirt collar was slightly — minutely — *off.* "You airbrushed this one." She glared at the photographer, as if this might be a felony. "We'll wait while you make a new print from the negative."

"Oh, I don't have that neg anymore. When

I was making up prints for the kid's parents, I had a chemical spill in the darkroom."

"And you remembered which negative got wrecked," said Riker, "fifteen years later. Must've been a hell of a shot . . . before you cleaned it up."

"A memorable shot," said Mallory. "So you kept an original print . . . for your private stash. Now I want to see what you airbrushed out."

"My partner really likes kids," said Riker in one of his more imaginative lies. "Trust me, pal, you don't wanna piss her off."

And that part was true.

She rose from the table, and the man moved away from her, back stepping all the way into the next room of filing cabinets, where the original print was found — very quickly.

And now they could see what had been airbrushed from the yearbook shot.

"Teeth marks," said Riker. "*Damn.* It's like Aggy the Biter signed his neck."

It was a very small school reunion at the Mexican restaurant on Bleecker Street: Phoebe Bledsoe and a dead child on one side of the room, Toby Wilder on the other.

"I hate to see him like this," said Dead Ernest. He glanced at his companion. "And what about you, Phoebe? You wanted to teach the classics. Now you spend the whole school year locked up in the nurse's office."

And no one ever came to visit the spooky nurse. Driscol students were remarkable for soldiering on with the scraped knees and stomachaches that plagued every other school in America.

"You have a degree in English lit, and what did they offer you?"

Custody of a box of Band-Aids. She should thank her mother for insisting on the nursing credential tacked onto the end of her education, else she would be jobless.

"You were robbed," said Dead Ernest.

Perhaps. She had spent her lonely workdays reading great literature. At night, she read comic books aloud for penance . . . for Ernie. Not much of a life, not what she had planned.

Toby's meal was done. He rose from his chair and moved toward the door. Phoebe's fingers worried over the surface of the gold cigarette lighter, the only piece of him that she could keep with her.

Dead Ernest also left her. Phoebe had no energy to sustain him or restrain him. She watched her old playmate approach the door. As the next customer came in, he slipped out. The child was always at the

318

mercy of flesh-and-blood people to open doors for him. But even if a phantom could manage solid gateways, Phoebe would never allow him to take his hands from his pockets.

She traveled home alone.

When she stepped out of the taxi in front of the Driscol School, the key to the alley passage was in her hand — but the iron gate was unlocked and ajar. Could she have forgotten to close it? No, that was unthinkable.

She passed down the narrow walkway between the Driscol School and the neighboring building, traveling halfway across the back garden before she saw him standing by the door to her cottage. Rolland Mann was losing his hair. It was gone to the pinfeathers of a chick newly hatched or a chicken prepped for slaughter. The deputy police commissioner's name always topped the guest list for her mother's charity galas, and he was a regular visitor to the weekly salons at the mansion. But Phoebe had first come to know him when she was a child and he was Detective Mann.

"The gate was wide open," he said. "That was careless, Phoebe. Especially now." He held up a folded copy of today's *Times*. "The third Ramble victim hasn't made the papers yet, but they've all been identified. It looks like someone's cleaning up loose ends." He paused. Waiting for her reaction? "You need police protection. I could post a guard on the —"

"No! . . . No more police." One hand of chewed fingernails rose to her mouth. Self-conscious now, she hid both ruined hands behind her back.

At least she did not have to face this unwanted visitor alone. Stress had summoned up Dead Ernest. He stood behind Rolland Mann and stuck out his tongue.

The deputy police commissioner, following the track of her eyes, turned around to see that there was no one there. Then he looked at the door. "Oh, your phone's ringing. Don't you want to answer that?"

No. She had no plans to unlock her door while he was still here.

"You need protection." And now the man measured his words very carefully, giving each syllable equal weight. "You do see the problem, don't you, Phoebe?"

Why did he always talk to her as if she might be only half bright? She inclined her head to listen to the dead boy, who clarified this mystery. "He thinks you're nuts."

Rolland Mann smiled, as if in agreement with a voice he could not possibly hear.

"There were *five* children in the Ramble when the incident happened." He held up five fingers in case she could not grasp such a high number. Adding insult, he counted them off, folding his long fingers one by one. "Ernie's dead, Humphrey — Aggy. And Willy Fallon *nearly* died."

All that remained was the worm-white thumb — herself.

"It's simple math, Phoebe." He turned his back on her and walked down the flagstone path, saying, "Call me if you change your mind about protection."

TWENTY-THREE

My guidance counselor tells me that school days are the best times of my life, and I should relish every second. When she tells me this, I want to scream, "You silly old fuck! It's hell every day, five days a week! It's war!"

— ERNEST NADLER

By all appearances, Charles Butler had recovered from Mallory's funeral scam to expose a little girl to a lineup of murder suspects. He was smiling broadly, happy to see the two detectives at his door, and he ushered them into his apartment.

This extended babysitting detail would be wearing on anyone. Maybe Charles was starved for adult company. That was Riker's thought as he bent down to receive a hug from Coco. "Hey, kid. Can you play something for us? Know any good rock groups?"

She clapped her hands together, eyes lit

brightly, *big* grin. "Echo and the Bunny-men!"

Charles smiled. "Sounds charming."

"Excellent choice," said Riker, "post–punk rock."

And Charles stopped smiling, somewhat less charmed.

Coco took Mallory's hand and led her into the adjoining room. Moments later, the two men in the parlor were listening to a piano duet.

Riker slapped his worried host on the back. "It'll be okay. As long as you can hear the music, you know Mallory isn't beating the kid." And now the detective recognized the opening bars to an old song from a garage band that almost made it. "Oh, this is vintage. It's called 'Crazytown Breakdown' — a hit single back in the early nineties."

The man who loved classical music had a baffled look about him. Charles Butler's golden oldies predated rock music by centuries.

In the next room, two voices rose in song, high, pure notes running up and down the scale of the melody. When they came to the refrain, they both banged out the music and belted out the lyrics. Great fun — so said the child's giggles accompanied by a softer ripple of piano keys.

Charles was entranced. "I've never heard Mallory sing."

Riker had, but only once and long ago. That was the day of her little rock 'n' roll rebellion at Special Crimes. A child-size Kathy Mallory had been suspended for some playground transgression before her school day had ended, and Lou Markowitz was on midget duty until his wife could arrive to pick up their foster child. He sat at his desk, facing Kathy's chair. Her legs were shorter then, and her sneakers dangled above the floor. Maybe the kid was only bored when she began the staring contest with Lou, but then she had escalated with lyrics, putting their little war of nerves to music. The child had sung the old man this same refrain — *Crazy is a place I know. I come and go. I come and go* — over and over, all the while fixing him with her weird green eyes. And, with his best poker face, Lou had, one by one, snapped six lead pencils in two before saying, "You win."

Today this old song had the same unnerving effect on Charles Butler — and not by accident. What had this poor man done to Mallory?

On the next note of "— *cra-a-a-zy* —" Riker described the invisible dead boy who spoke to Phoebe Bledsoe. "Her mother blames it on a child psychiatrist." The detective consulted his notebook for a name. "Dr. Martin Fyfe. This guy had Phoebe *personalize* her anxiety." He squinted at his shorthand, isolated words standing for sentences and whole paragraphs. Most of his notes had been written on the fly while being shown to the door. "Well, that backfired. The kid was supposed to confront her problem — *talk* to it — but she only listened." He looked up. "Is this nuts, or what? So then the shrink tells the mother that Phoebe's delusional, and the kid needs *years* on the couch." He closed his notebook. "The mother fired the shrink."

"A good maternal instinct." Charles looked into the music room to watch the piano players during a lull in the song. "Dr. Fyfe was a fraud — not actually a psychiatrist." Assured that Mallory was not browbeating Coco, he turned back to Riker. "Fyfe *did* have a Ph.D. in psychology. Unfortunately for his patients, his education was the next best thing to a correspondence course in cartooning. But you don't need any credentials for psychodrama, and that's what you described."

Charles rose from his chair, and Riker followed him down the hall and into the library, where every wall was thick with books, and shelves soared to a high ceiling. The music of the piano was thin and tinny here. Coco's guardian had one ear cocked toward the open door, monitoring the piano duet, as he walked toward shelves filled with magazines. Their wooden holders were labeled by dates and titles of *Psychiatric* this and *Psychology* that.

"So Phoebe Bledsoe started her therapy about fifteen years ago?"

"Give or take." Riker watched him pull out holders for the nineties.

"Fyfe would've been in a rush to publish a case like hers. I can almost guarantee that Phoebe Bledsoe made it into print. There won't be a real name mentioned, but he wouldn't change the patient's gender or her age. This might take me a while."

"Hey, you've got a photographic memory."

"Sorry. I've only read one of that idiot's papers."

Riker glanced down at his wristwatch. "Me and Mallory got plans to ambush an assistant DA. We gotta corner the weasel before five." The detective stared at the stack of professional journals still piling up on the table. "This is gonna take all day, huh?"

"Not that long." Charles picked up a large

stack as if it weighed only ounces, and he carried it down the hall to the front room, unwilling to leave Coco and Mallory unchaperoned. He set the journals on the coffee table and sat down in line of sight with the piano.

Riker's load was lighter by half, but he felt the strain of seldom-used muscle when he placed his stack beside the taller one.

The psychologist's eyes scanned the printed word as fast as he could turn the pages, faster than anything passing for speed-reading. His face had the deep red flush of embarrassment, and that was understandable. This man was shy about any evidence of freakishness — his giant brain and even his tall stature. He always seemed apologetic when looking down at someone of average height. Being closely observed while reading at the speed of light — that must be humiliating.

Gallant Riker turned away to watch the singing piano players, and his feet tapped to the beat. Without turning his head, he said, "So you know this Dr. Fyfe pretty well."

"No, only by name and a bad reputation." Charles held up one of the publications. "Years ago, this journal sent one of Fyfe's papers for peer review. It was a case study on an eight-year-old boy. The idiot fed a child unwarranted drugs. Then the reviewer — a *real* psychiatrist — looked into his background and discovered that Fyfe wasn't licensed to prescribe an aspirin. The article was evidence of illegal traffic in drugs — he bought them on the street. But it was a charge of child endangerment that got him suspended the first time."

"The first time? How many — ?"

"Three suspensions."

"What does it take to get your license pulled?"

"You'd have to kill someone on the ethics committee. That would get their attention. As a provision of reinstatement, Fyfe wasn't allowed to work with children anymore. But that would've been too late for Phoebe Bledsoe. Would you like a tutorial on psychodrama?"

Riker rolled his eyes.

Charles smiled. "It'll only take a minute. It's that simplistic." He pointed to the empty armchair beside Riker's. "Imagine, if you will, that the source of your anxiety sits there. Now you speak to it. You pour out your heart, all your angst and fear. It's a game anyone can play. There's a drama school on the Lower East Side that uses it for a class exercise." Charles picked up another journal and resumed his page turning, stopping suddenly. "Here we go." He slowed down to read at a speed close to that of a human being.

And Riker listened to the music from the other room, the never-ending song of crazy. What was Mallory playing at?

When Charles was done with the article, he closed the journal. "The child mentioned here was eleven years old. Her therapy began a month after the death of a class-mate."

"That's our girl," said Riker.

Charles turned his eyes to the music room, distracted by the song begun again. "Fyfe's patient was suffering from night-mares and a fear of being left alone for any length of time. She was unresponsive to a standard talking cure. So Fyfe introduced her to psychodrama, and he helped it along with twice-weekly doses of a psychotropic drug. Now that'll really mess up a child's brain. Then, as if the little girl didn't have enough problems, she became delusional. Did I mention that Fyfe is an idiot? He could've confused delusion with a coping mechanism or a rich fantasy life."

"You mean the invisible playmate?"

Charles nodded as one finger ran along a line on the open page. "Here, Fyfe says her delusion took the form of the dead classmate, but the girl wouldn't say any more than that. No feedback at all. She only listened to an empty chair."

"The mother says Phoebe's listening to her *inner critic.*"

"That's pop-psychology, but there might be a kernel of truth . . . if this little girl felt some responsibility for the boy's death. That also fits with her silence during therapy sessions. Children are geniuses at keeping the secrets that eat them alive."

"You think she's nuts? Could Phoebe have killed the invisible kid?"

If that had not come out quite right, the psychologist was too polite to say.

"No idea." Charles laid the journal down. "If this is a portrait of Phoebe . . . if the behavior is ongoing, I can only confirm that Dr. Fyfe sent her to live in a private hell, locked up with a dead child — and she's still there."

In the next room, the song of crazy ended.

Twenty-Four

Phoebe's brother isn't in school today. She says he can't come back till Mr. Carlyle fixes his last mess. Girl trouble, she says. Humphrey's got a thing for little girls.

And all this time, I thought her brother wanted to be a girl. But who is Mr. Carlyle? Maybe he's Humphrey's therapist?

"No, he's only a toady," says Phoebe. One night a week, her house is full of toads, her mother's pets.

You can't make this stuff up.

— ERNEST NADLER

One day, years ago, while Mallory was being fitted for a cashmere blazer, Riker had wandered into the tailor shop — and the tailor had asked him to leave, concerned, and perhaps rightly so, that stains on the policeman's crummy suit might be infectious to Mallory's fine new threads.

Her partner was not a stylish man.

331

But she knew Riker held strong opinions on bowties — like this bright yellow one around the scrawny neck of Cedrick Carlyle, one of many assistant district attorneys, and perhaps the one with the smallest office. Prior to the last renovation, this cramped space might have been a storage room with a copy machine where the desk was now. The little man behind that desk was the joke candidate of election years, best remembered for his trademark yellow bowtie. In Riker's fashion philosophy, bows should be reserved to the pigtails of little girls or the collars of tiny dogs hatched from peanut shells.

ADA Carlyle was pouting, eyes fixed on the keyboard of his laptop computer. He had yet to acknowledge that there were two detectives in this room that was too small for one visitor. So Riker, perhaps realizing that he had been way too polite, rephrased their inquiry on the old Ramble case of fifteen years ago. "We're here about the railroad job you did on Toby Wilder."

The lawyer stopped typing for a moment, puzzled, maybe undecided as to whether he should bark or roll over. But then the little man continued his two-finger keystrokes.

This was not the response Mallory had hoped for. She wanted his watery gray eyes to spin around in their sockets.

Carlyle never looked up from the laptop screen when he said, "You'll have to come back later." He waved one hand toward the door, as if they might have some trouble finding their way out of this closet. "Next time, make an appointment." In the hierarchy of the justice system, an assistant district attorney should trump a cop.

But not today.

"This is a homicide investigation." Mallory leaned over the desk and slammed down the lid of his laptop. "We outrank everybody today." There was only one extra chair, and it was piled with papers. She swept them to the floor and sat down.

Following suit with the swipe of one hand, Riker cleared a seat for himself on one corner of the desk, sending books and pens crashing to the floor — just a touch of violence to set the proper tone. "We don't *like* the way Toby Wilder's case was handled."

This got the little man's rapt attention. Mallory liked that. She liked it a lot. There was no protest, no righteous indignation. Carlyle had probably lived his whole life avoiding confrontation — until now. She leaned forward to lie to him. "Rolland

Mann said the bogus confession was your idea."

The prosecutor wiped his palms on his sleeves. A sweaty act of guilt? And now he whined, "You can't blame me. The kid's own lawyer pled him out on the wino murder."

The detectives exchanged glances. The *wino* murder? What wino?

"I could've taken the kid to trial," said Carlyle, "and I would've won a conviction — no problem."

"No, I don't think so," said Riker, playing it casual, as if the wino's murder was not news to him. "You've *never* won a trial."

"Your cases never get that far," said Mallory. "You plead everybody out. That's your specialty, right?"

The lawyer assumed a prosecutorial smile, the one they all used for talking down to stupid cops. "In a plea bargain, the criminals get less jail time, but the taxpayers save the cost of a trial. Everybody's happy."

"Easier to keep the details quiet, huh?" Riker leaned forward.

The smaller man leaned back.

"Right," said Mallory. "That's why you sent Toby to Family Court. Sealed records. So . . . was it your idea to substitute victims — trading the Nadler kid for a dead wino?

How bad did you need to bury a felony assault on a little boy?"

The little man had found his spine, and he straightened up in his chair. "You're right about one thing, Detective — those records *are* sealed. You know I can't discuss the case with you. I *can* tell you it was a clean plea bargain. Toby Wilder got off light."

"Because he confessed to killing a wino instead of torturing a little kid?"

"Pleading out to a lesser charge is done all the time," said Carlyle, as if the murder of a drunken bum might be on the scale of petty crime. "I always get good results."

"Oh, yeah?" Riker laid a copy of a child's death certificate on the desk. "You conspired to bury a murder. That's a felony."

Carlyle looked down at this solid piece of evidence, and his back curved into a slump.

Oh . . . crushed again?

Mallory opened her notebook and pretended to consult the pages. "Fifteen years ago — the first time you ran for district attorney — you outspent your opponent two dollars to one . . . and you *still* lost." She looked up to catch the man's wince. "How did somebody like *you* raise that kind of money?"

Riker unfolded a sheet of financials, the fruit of Mallory's love for money motives.

"You got a lot of street-name cash donations to your election fund."

"Most people use credit cards or checks," said Mallory, liking the effect of Carlyle's head swiveling back and forth from cop to cop. She left her chair, walked around to the back of the lawyer's desk and bent down close to his ear. "That kind of cash spike on one deposit slip sends up red flags."

Riker leaned into the little man's personal space. "Even cash leaves tracks, pal. Suppose we backtrack donation names to payroll lists — and the people who own those companies? Now suppose just one of them got a sweet deal on a plea bargain." He smiled. It was unnecessary to finish this line of thought for the lawyer.

Mallory placed one hand on Carlyle's shoulder — just to make him jump. "Who told you to nail Toby Wilder for the wino's murder?"

The ADA was stalled, weighing his options, but neither detective had expected an answer to that one. The statute of limitations would not save him from a charge of conspiracy in a homicide case. Murder never went away.

And now, on cue, Riker made an easier demand. "Get us a warrant to search Toby Wilder's apartment."

Carlyle bowed his head. "I need probable cause for that."

"Find one," said Riker. "If a judge gives you any grief, call the acting police commissioner. You and him go way back, right? Rolland Mann was the detective on the old murder case — and I don't mean the wino."

Mallory slapped her hand down on the death certificate. "He means this little *boy!*" She swiveled the lawyer's chair from side to side. She was not done playing with him. "The warrant should also give us access to common areas in his building — and the basement, too. We're looking for tools from a murder kit. You railroaded Toby fifteen years ago — so it shouldn't be hard to screw him over for a few more killings in the Ramble."

The building superintendent had only glanced at the warrant. He was sullen and slow to find the right key among the many attached to his belt loop. Finally the door was opened, and the detectives entered Toby Wilder's dark front room.

Riker so loved owning the soul of an assistant DA; it guaranteed that warrants would be plentiful from now on, and the lack of probable cause would never present a problem.

He opened the curtains to windowpanes that had not been cleaned in a decade. The diffused sunlight of an air shaft illuminated a couch and chair with threadbare, grimy arms and burn holes in the upholstery. The screen of an early-model television was smashed. Maybe their boy had a temper. Yes, he did. There was an empty wine bottle visible on the other side of the set's broken glass.

This place had the smell of a loser, a whiff of morning-after vomit in the air.

In Mallory's book of scores and records, Riker ranked high as an extreme slob, and so he looked around Toby Wilder's apartment with a competitor's eye. Discarded clothes strewn on the floor — check; takeout cartons with days-old, crusted food — check. Dead flies on the windowsill — just like home. But now, upon closer inspection, he realized that he and the boy had something else in common: too many empty beer cans and bottles to pass for a social drinker.

And there was another nasty habit, one they did not share, though the detective could not readily say what Toby was sniffing, popping or smoking. Drug use was evidenced only in the turned-out pockets of pants and jeans, and by recent swipes in the dust on the floor in front of the couch, signs of the morning hunt for dropped grains of cocaine or stray pills to take away the raw ugliness of a brand-new sunny day. Upon awakening, Riker might look around for a bottle that was not quite empty. But this boy had scraped the floor for something, *anything,* to jump-start his heart. And in the far corner, Mallory was bending down to retrieve two empty pharmacy bottles.

"These aren't cheap on the street." She handed them to Riker, and he read the labels, variations on the theme of oxycodone — more addictive than heroin, and neither one had been prescribed for Toby Wilder.

"He favors painkillers," said Rolland Mann from the open doorway, and the detectives turned on him in unison. "Vicodin, Oxycontin. He also needs sleeping pills. That's why we got you a warrant for suspicion of drug possession."

"You *knew* the kid was an addict," said Riker. "So, all this time, you kept tabs on him."

"I admit to an ongoing interest in the boy." Rolland Mann walked into the room, turned his back on them and addressed the faded wallpaper. "This place is rent-controlled. Toby inherited the lease from his mother. She sold her condo and moved in here when her kid was sent to Spofford."

Spofford. Before the children's jail was closed down, that was the name New York parents invoked when they told their wayward offspring that they were going straight to hell. Toby's drug habit was hardly surprising — given where he had been caged.

The detectives walked down the short hallway, passing the kitchen and its stink. Mallory opened a door to a room of chintz curtains and an unmade bed. And this had to be the dead mother's room. A pair of lavender slippers were neatly paired on a scatter rug, still waiting for her to step into them. And a book lay on the quilt, pages down, perhaps open to the last passage read by the lady before she died. A thick layer of dust lay on every surface, undisturbed for years. Preserved as a shrine? *Yeah.*

The junkie had loved his mother.

Riker opened the next door. *Jesus Christ.* He stepped inside for a closer look. *Not* wallpaper. "Hey, you gotta see this!"

Rolland Mann and Mallory followed him inside the second bedroom, bare as a monk's cell, with only a small chest of drawers and a narrow bed. The floor was swept clean. Toby had carved out a niche of order surrounded by the chaos of four walls covered with music: lines of scales, time signatures and thousands of notes filled in all the space from ceiling to floor. Riker's instrument was guitar, and he could read sheet music, but here he was out of his depth. "These are some seriously scary chords."

Mallory pulled the narrow bed away from one wall, and the music was there, too. And behind the dresser — more music.

Only Rolland Mann showed no surprise. "The kid was on a fast track for Juilliard, but he could've had his pick of full scholarships anywhere in the country." The acting commissioner consulted the screen on his ringing cell phone. "Colleges were courting Toby when he was only thirteen years old. Some kind of musical genius."

Rolland Mann could have used the ground-level entrance for high-ranking politicians and other criminals visiting the Supreme Court on Centre Street. Instead, he elected to climb the many steps to this grand Grecian temple. Once inside, he passed through a checkpoint with the jostling crowd of ordinary people. None of them took any notice of him, and his rise to the rank of acting police commissioner was too recent for his face to make any impression on officers manning the metal detector. They simply waved him on, and he was free to enter a rotunda ringed by tall pillars. The vast space was brightly lit by a great iron chandelier and by sunlight from the center of the dome. The art and architecture were scaled for giants, and every living thing therein was reduced to bug size — so many bugs — lawyers and uniformed officers, jurists and jurors. It was a place where a rising star could be seen with a loser without arousing suspicion.

He saw the loser's yellow bowtie bobbing in a throng of jurors being herded toward elevators.

Though that little man had campaigned in every election for two decades, no voter could remember his name, but if the silly tie was mentioned, people would say, "Oh, yeah, *that* guy." A political consultant, the late John Bledsoe, had recommended the bright yellow bow for its recognition factor. And Cedrick Carlyle — fool that he was — had no idea that his adviser's more common name was Satirical Bastard.

As the assistant district attorney hurried toward him, Rolland Mann did not return the wave. He was distracted by other concerns. He wondered if his wife would manage the courage to leave him today. He was hardly listening as he strolled across the rotunda.

Cedrick Carlyle pranced at his side, whining, "I might need to produce witness statements for the wino murder. Please tell me you kept copies."

"From juvenile records? *Sealed* records?" Rolland Mann's eyes were fixed on some distant point above the smaller man's head. "Why do you need copies? You can't even discuss those witnesses with Mallory and Riker — not without losing your job *and* your license to practice law."

ADA Carlyle clenched his teeth, his hands and no doubt his buttocks, too. *What to do? What to do?* "Right after they left, Willy Fallon called me. She asked how much those detectives know about the old Ernest Nadler case."

"*New* case. There never was an *old* case for the Nadler boy. That was your idea, wasn't it? Something you cooked up with Toby Wilder's attorney?" Well, that shut his mouth. And now they were done. The acting police commissioner walked away with a plan of catching a cab to take him home.

Would his apartment be empty, or would Annie still be there? This had been guesswork every day since the Hunger Artist's murders had come to light.

TWENTY-FIVE

We follow Toby Wilder inside the Ramble
now. It was Phoebe's dare. But we never
get far before we lose sight of him. We get
lost in there sometimes, and when that
happens, we run, hearts a banging,
screaming up and down the paths, looking
for a way out. Everyone we see might be
a crazed killer, or at least more dangerous
than what trolls the halls at Driscol.
Phoebe says this is good training. This is
Monster School.

— ERNEST NADLER

The ambulette was not Wilhelmina Fallon's
idea of luxury transport, and the driver was
getting surly. She ordered him to pull over
in front of what might be Toby Wilder's
apartment house, a redbrick building on a
shady Greenwich Village street. This phonebook listing for Susan Wilder was the only
lead she had not exhausted, but no one ever

answered the phone.

The driver opened the vehicle's rear door to engage the hydraulic platform for his wheelchair passenger. "Don't bother," said Willy. She abandoned the chair and every pretense of a handicap. Stepping out on the sidewalk, she donned her sunglasses and reached into her purse for the brown sack of money. Her tip was lavish. The man's eyes lit up at the sight of so much cash. And now he had surely forgotten how badly she had abused him and berated him for talking to those two cops.

"Wait for me." Willy turned toward the apartment building. Behind her, wheels burned rubber as they peeled away from the curb, and she thought she heard the driver laughing as he sped off down the street.

Prick.

The vacated parking space was quickly filled by a police car. Willy retreated to the other side of the street, forgetting for a moment that the pills in her purse were legal prescription drugs from the hospital. She turned back to see a uniformed officer open the vehicle's rear door. A man unfolded from the backseat, and, as he left the car, he was preceded by his large nose. A tall man, a *rich* man — nice suit. Nice body, too. A small red-haired girl scrambled out behind him. Strange pair — a giant with the eyes of a frog and a kid with a cartoon smile.

Willy foraged in her handbag and pulled out her cell phone. Playing the tourist, she snapped their picture. The police car rolled away, and she drifted back toward Toby's apartment house, stopping in the middle of the street.

A great hulking thug in a bad suit emerged from the building to greet the other two freaks. This one had a menacing face even as he smiled and bowed down to delicately shake the child's tiny hand. He was everybody's idea of a mob hit man, not a typical babysitter even by New York standards — and yet the girl was left in his company as the tall frogman entered the building alone. Willy stepped onto the curb and heard the little girl call her new minder by name, Detective Janos.

Another damn cop.

Forgoing her plan to go inside the apartment house, she looked up to catch sight of uniformed officers framed in a third-floor window. What was going on up there? Was Toby Wilder under arrest? And why would a little girl —

Oh, no.

Willy had attracted the attention of the

detective on the sidewalk. She looked down at the small screen on her phone to observe more discreetly. The mystery child tugged on the man's sleeve, and when his eyes turned down to hers, she informed him that a rat could be flushed down a toilet three times before it drowned. "Four times is the charm."

Lowering her dark glasses, Willy stepped onto the sidewalk, bowed down to a child's eye level and said, "*I* like rats."

And now the thuggish cop was rabidly suspicious, perhaps because rats were the enemy of every sane New Yorker. Behind the child's back, he held up his badge and mouthed the words, *Move on.*

Willy crossed the street and sat down on the stoop of a facing building. In a duel of sorts, she took another picture with her camera phone, and Detective Janos shot her with his.

Satisfied that Janos and Coco were getting on well, Charles Butler climbed the steps to the third-floor apartment, where he was admitted by a policeman in uniform. Once inside, he could see the two detectives standing in a room at the end of a short hallway.

"Hey, Charles." Riker beckoned him to

join them.

The psychologist walked in on an argument in progress.

Mallory stared down a badly dressed man, whose jangle of keys gave him away as the building superintendent, and he was angry when he said to her, "Your guys took the winch off my car. *My* car. Toby doesn't drive. I need that winch to tow a trailer of furniture out to Jersey. That's my sideline, short hauls. When do I get it back?"

While Charles gaped at the music notations on every inch of wall space, a police officer entered the room, holding up a cordless drill. "We found it in the basement."

And the angry super shouted, "That's my personal property! I *need* that drill!"

"We'll give you a receipt." Mallory turned in a half circle, waving one hand to encompass the stunning display of notes that covered the walls. "Now what about *this?*"

"It's been there forever. The kid did that when he got out of Juvie — oh, maybe ten years ago."

With a nod from Mallory, the man left the room. A small woman with a giant camera entered next, and Riker instructed her to record every square foot of the musical walls. And now both detectives turned to their expert on the subject of gifted people.

"It's jazz," said Charles. "You can see that much in the tall chords." He reached out to touch a single stack of vertical notes. "Chords taller than triads. . . . Not help-ful?"

No, apparently not. Riker only shrugged, and Mallory, of course, was annoyed.

"That's a G-thirteen, an *extended* chord," said Charles. "Extended intervals are an-other clue."

Riker smiled. "I bet you can't hum a few bars."

"Not really. There *is* an underlying melody, but this is a complex orchestra-tion."

"Like the old big-band sound?"

"Bigger — a full symphony orchestra." Charles pointed to different areas as he rattled off instruments. "Woodwinds, brass and strings. And there — percussion sec-tion. Here, a full complement of saxo-phones. Did you find any sheet music — more notations like these?"

"Nothing like that," said Mallory. "No music at all. The guy doesn't even have a stereo. He probably hocked it for drugs."

"And the only radio is busted," said Riker. "Looks like it hit a wall on a bad day."

It was difficult for Charles to believe that the boy only had one song in him. "If I transcribe it to music paper, I can get an expert opinion on the derivative influence. Jazz is not my forte."

"Actually," said Riker, "we're just wondering how nuts this kid might be."

"Oh. . . . Well, I'd hardly call this evidence of insanity." Charles pointed to areas here and there where notes had been whited out and written over. *Pentimento,* the artist's change of heart, went to the bones of the melody, and these changes were carefully drawn — done last. "The boy began with a rush in the physical act of the initial notation. You can see the hurried hand in the lean of flags and time signatures. Periods are almost dashes — as if he couldn't wait to set it all down. For the most part, it has the seamless quality of a single continuous act. And yet . . . I'd say he'd been working on this for a very long time. Before he ever went to these walls, he had already integrated dozens of instruments and the change of octaves to make them blend. Most people don't realize that you can't use the same notes for different instruments, even when —"

He turned to his audience of two bored detectives. "Sorry." Back to the wall. "This boy could hear his orchestration as a full-blown work of art before he made the first stroke. Now the absence of music in this apartment — not even a radio to play a song — that's very telling. It's like, years ago, the boy let all his music out in one frantic act. And then . . . silence."

"He's a junkie," said Mallory. "His habit probably started in Spofford. The cop who put him there said Toby was beaten by other inmates, and he wouldn't defend himself. So he was kept away from the general population."

"That happened off and on," said Riker, "starting when he was thirteen."

"A *child* in solitary confinement? That's obscene." But now everything was clear to Charles, here on these walls in a stream of music, and he saw the final note as a kind of death. The best of the boy had bled out.

Spacey was his state of mind, and Toby Wilder floated through his days in the lighter gravity of Mars. Silent days. Airless. Sounds of the city were filtered through the cotton wadding of his brain on painkillers, and a waitress from his homeworld had to ask him twice — "Same old thing?"

"Yeah." Hungry or not, he always ordered a cheeseburger with lettuce and tomato, a perfect food group, so his mother had said.

He recalled the first time Mom had led him to this place. That was the day following his release. During his confinement, she had sold their uptown condo and moved down here, closer to her place of work. That was the reason given then. Later he had discovered the truth. Mom had sold the condo to buy him an annuity that would take care of him after she was gone. She had taught him to negotiate the maze of West Village streets that so confused the tourists. And for that one year they had together, he had sat across this table from her every day, only seventeen years old when they had talked about his future — as if all his possibilities had not died in juvenile detention, where he had lost two teeth, his virginity and self-respect.

But he had gained a tolerance for pain and worse things. At thirteen he had cried for his mother; at fourteen he had learned to cadge drugs from doctors for the beatings he took, and when enough of his bones were broken, he had won a private room in solitary. And each visitors' day, he had taken his mother's hand and told her it was not so bad.

Today, he felt only a mild druggy buzz, and his mother was dead. All he had left of her was this old habit of lunchtime, his only reason to carry a watch. Without the ritual cheeseburger, his day would have no bones.

Phoebe watched Toby Wilder finish his burger.

Dead Ernest stared at her hands as she unconsciously rubbed the gold cigarette lighter. "If you keep doing that," he said, "you'll rub off the date. I can hardly read it anymore. It just looks like scratches."

She put the golden talisman back in her purse.

When Toby left the café, Phoebe went home to do penance — to read comic books aloud for the dead boy, who could never take his hands out of his pockets.

Comics had been the passion of the real Ernie Nadler, the living child. They had been his religion and his philosophy. One day, after school let out, Ernie had taken her into his father's den and opened a bookcase like a door to show her a walk-in safe. There were more comics in there than she had ever seen in her life, stacks of them, *walls* of them. This was his father's collection. Some issues dated back to the 1930s, and these had belonged to Ernie's grandfather.

That was the day Ernie had shared his

best-loved memories: bedtime story hours of his kindergarten days, when his father had turned the pages of these collector items and read aloud to his only child.

"Comic-book heroes are in the family genes," Ernie had said to her then.

And so, of course, she understood why he had to die.

TWENTY-SIX

Spider Girl is mutating. This morning in algebra, Willy Fallon shows me her new manicure, fingernails filed to sharp points, and she flexes them close to my eyes. I guess those claws are supposed to make her more like an animal — maybe a cat? Well, that would take social climbing for an insect like Willy. But I get the message, and when class is over, I run.

— ERNEST NADLER

As Charles put his key in the lock, Coco hugged their patrolman escort in farewell and gave a hello hug to the officer who guarded the front door.

Once inside the apartment, Charles laid down the envelope that contained pictures of Toby Wilder's walls. He opened a paper bag to show the child his recent purchase from a stationery store, a tablet with pages of blank lines where notes would go. "Music paper."

An hour later, they sat on opposite sides of the kitchen table. Between them was a bowl of popcorn and the score for a jazz symphony. He had no difficulty working out the order of the police photographs; music followed logical progressions, and he quickly transcribed pictured notes to paper. The child was still laboring over the first photo that he had discarded. He could see that her interest in drawing had waned. Charles waved one hand to get her attention, and she waved back, slow to smile, tired now.

"Coco, if you take a nap, you can stay up late. We're going out tonight." He did not want to call on Mrs. Ortega to mind the child this evening. The woman would take nothing from him in payment for anything connected to this little girl. "Do you like jazz?"

She nodded and bowed her head to the task of drawing music — so serious. Her attention span for this exercise was longer than he had expected, and he now realized that this was because it was a project for Mallory. Perhaps there was an upside to that relationship. The child delivered monologues to most people, but she held actual conversations with the detective she loved.

Charles stared at Coco's odd attempts at copying: flags without notes and notes without stems, numbers and symbols arranged in a mystifying order, some touching the lines for the musical scale only by accident — a completely alien pictorial language. Once more, the two lonely people waved to each other from different planets while seated at the same kitchen table.

Only one thing was painfully clear. She had a little dream. It would never come true.

Coco laid down her pencil and stared at the door, listening, waiting — for Mallory.

"Willy Fallon was casing Toby's place." Detective Janos laid down a fax record of wireless calls. "She went through all the Wilders in the phonebook to find him."

Lieutenant Coffey stared at the screen of his desktop computer, clicking on the images of the socialite downloaded from Janos's cell phone. "What happened to the guard on her hospital room? Where the hell was he?"

"I talked to his sergeant," said Janos. "Willy declined police protection. So he pulled off the guard."

"And when did that idiot plan to tell us our crime victim was running loose on the streets?" Jack Coffey held up one hand to say never mind, and he turned to the wide window on his squad room.

Seated at a desk by the staircase door was Arthur Chu, a plainclothes cop in the white-shield limbo between a uniform's silver badge and a detective's gold. During Mallory's absence, Chu had been borrowed from another precinct. He had done well on surveillance assignments — *very* well. And Coffey had neglected to return the young man to the squad that owned him.

"Put Arty Chu on shadow detail. Tell the kid he stays on Willy's tail until we wrap this case. Where's our girl now? Do we know?"

"I found her." Janos held up the data for a triangulation of pings off cell-phone towers. "Looks like Willy's heading back to the hospital."

The effect of her last pain pill had worn off. Sore and tired, Willy Fallon looked forward to lying down in her hospital bed and ordering more painkillers to ease the lingering aches of muscle and tendon. On the way to her room, she passed a clock in the corridor. She was right on time for her next massage from the physical therapist. Oh, and she wanted her special button, the one used to run the nursing staff ragged.

She opened the door to find an orderly stripping sheets from her bed. Well, this was better maid service than her hotel provided. Another staffer, the nurse called Hey You, was standing at the bedside table, scooping pill bottles into a box.

"Hey! I might need that stuff!"

"Not anymore," said the nurse. "You've been discharged, Miss Fallon."

"No way. I didn't check out. I just had some personal business to take care of." There had been people to stalk and people to threaten — a very busy day. But now she wanted her damn bed and her meds and the service of her handmaids. And that massage — oh, how she needed that. "So now I'm back. Get my doctor in here. Tell him I need more meds. *Move!*"

Something had changed while she was away. This nurse no longer had the look of a beaten dog. The woman actually seemed cheerful, and Willy planned to fix that. "Are you listening to me?"

The nurse placed the last bottle in her collection box. "Your bill's been paid. You've been discharged. We need the bed."

"My parents paid the bill?"

"Their lawyer did."

"But they called, right? They asked for me?" Did that sound too needy?

The nurse hated her, but the woman dropped her smile, and her eyes conveyed something approaching pity.

"Did my parents leave me a message?"

The response to this question was so terribly important, and the nurse must have intuited this. Her voice softened when she said, "Well . . . *reporters* have been calling all day." The woman was taking no satisfaction here, only leaving Willy to draw the obvious conclusion: Mummy and Daddy had *not* called. And they never would. They were done with her.

Willy sank down on the bare mattress, sore, tired and hungry. Her hotel only offered a bed, nothing more. Who would take care of her now? Subdued, she opened her purse to pull out her magic paper bag, and she held up a wad of cash as an offering. "Let me stay?"

"We need the bed."

They loved her. They *adored* her.

Cameras, cameras everywhere, flashes and strobe lights.

A reborn Willy Fallon, jazzed on four lines of cocaine, stood before a stretch limousine parked outside her hotel. She lowered her sunglasses to accommodate the paparazzi and followed their camera directions of

"Hey, Willy, give us a smile," and "Willy, baby, turn this way." Reporters in this mix were holding out microphones and asking *not* where she had been all this time or how long had she been back in town, but did she know the Hunger Artist's victim, Humphrey Bledsoe? And what about the other one? "Miss Fallon, who was the third victim in the Ramble?"

Willy ignored the questions. She had a better story, and when she had told it, she ducked inside the limo and handed the driver Detective Mallory's card. "That's the address." When the car was under way, she turned to look out the rear window. *Good.* The reporters were in pursuit.

"No, there's no truth to it! . . . Yeah, that's right. She *lied!*"

Jack Coffey hung up on the fact-checker for a network news show, the third one to call and ask him to name the detective who had attacked Willy Fallon on her sickbed. *Oh, God.* Why did this have to happen now? If the chief of D's did not take Mallory's badge today, the mayor would — not for the bogus assault charge, but for the bad press.

The lieutenant stood by the street-side window and looked up to the sky, where

God might be, and he splayed his hands to ask, "So what did Mallory do to *you?*"

Down below, reporters were gathering on the sidewalk outside the station house. Damn lynch mob. He opened the blinds for the window on the squad room. With a wave, he signaled Detective Gonzales to bring in the visitor earlier announced as Bitch of the Western World. Miss Fallon had been kept waiting, steaming and complaining for the past half hour.

Before the woman could open her mouth, the lieutenant said, "I'm sorry, the matter is out of my hands. It's a civil case now — or it will be if you give those reporters the detective's name. Her personal attorney will be handling the lawsuit against you."

"What do you —"

"I'll get you her lawyer's name and number." The lieutenant flipped through his Rolodex. "Robin Duffy? Yeah, that's it." He looked up at Detective Gonzales. "You know — the guy who sued the feds a while back — and beat the crap out of 'em."

Willy Fallon smiled, so unimpressed with this fairy tale. "I came here to file charges against Detective Mallory."

"Police brutality," said Coffey. "That's what the reporters tell me. Those charges have to be filed with Internal Affairs. But

362

that can wait till you make bail. Detective Gonzales will handle your booking."

Gonzales had taken most of her abuse, and now the man wore a wide grin as he handed his boss a copy of Riker's assault report, typed up minutes ago and back-dated.

"Your attorney should read this," said Coffey, "before you're arraigned on the criminal charge." He leaned back in his chair, feigning nonchalance. "I hear you had Detective Mallory's partner by the balls — so to speak." He pretended to read the report. "Oh. *Literally.* You had the poor guy by the balls. That makes you a sex offender. Detective Riker was willing to let it slide because of what you'd been through. But now I guess we'll have to jail your ass, lady."

"Suppose I call off the reporters?"

"I could live with that — if you tell them you made a mistake. Let's say you were swacked on pain medication, maybe hal-lucinating." Jack Coffey pushed a yellow pad across his desk. "And put it in writing."

She did. And when she had left his office, he turned to the street window and looked down at the foot traffic on the sidewalk below. It took him a while to locate Officer Chu among the locals. The young shadow cop was that good at blending in. The lieutenant kept watch until Willy Fallon left the building — and Chu followed her down the street.

The assistant district attorney with the yellow bowtie had no secretary of his own, no gatekeeper to turn away stoned socialites. But Cedrick Carlyle had no fear. Mr. and Mrs. Fallon, the power couple of Fallon Industries, had retired from public life to hide behind the walls of the family compound in Connecticut, a safe haven where their daughter was persona non grata.

Willy Fallon leaned over his desk, clicking through pictures on her cell phone to show him shots of a man who was giant size in proportion to a redheaded child. "Who *is* this guy?"

"That's Charles Butler, a psychologist. Sometimes we use him as an expert witness." ADA Carlyle looked up to see her eyes, manic and angry. *Crazy bitch.* "You don't want to fool with him, Miss Fallon. Dr. Butler comes from old money — bluer blood than yours — and some of his best friends carry guns."

But who was the child on the small screen? Butler had no offspring.

In the next shot on Willy's cell-phone screen, the little girl held hands with a menacing brute. Janos? Yes, that was the name of this detective from Special Crimes Unit. And then Carlyle noticed the large decorative numbers on a building's front door. He shook his head. *No!* This was the address on the search warrant. Bimbo socialites could be dangerously stupid. What the hell had she been doing at Toby Wilder's place? *Now* he was afraid. He snatched the phone from her hand for a better look at the picture. Who was this child? Why would a detective watch over her? And then the answer came to him. Oh, *Christ.* Another little girl with red hair.

Willy broke into his reverie, yelling, "Hey!" And when she had his attention, she banged on the desk. "You told the cops about us, didn't you?"

"I never did."

"Make it all go away! That's what you do, isn't it?"

While his visitor ranted on, he transferred the child's pictures from her phone to his own.

The two detectives watched from their parked car on Hogan Place as Willy Fallon left the massive gray building that housed the District Attorney's Office and an army of more than five hundred lawyers.

Riker answered a ringtone, listened a moment and then said to his partner, "It's Janos. He says Carlyle just called Rocket Mann."

"There's our guy." Mallory pointed to the officer in blue jeans and shades.

Arthur Chu was the perfect surveillance cop for a multi-ethnic town. He had his mother's curly brown hair, his father's Asian eyes and a Bronx accent. With only a few accessories, a cap or sunglasses to wear or discard, he could blend in anywhere, and his baby face was a bonus. No one would ever peg him for a cop. At twenty-six, Mallory's age, Chu looked years younger, more like a high-school kid.

In the rearview mirror, Riker watched the shadow cop follow Willy down the sidewalk and disappear around a corner. Since Mallory's return to town four weeks ago, she had never taken any notice of this youngster. And now that she was aware of him, Riker could only hope that the boy would not screw up.

"Is Chu any good?"

"Yeah," said Riker. "Arty worked one of my cases while you were gone. I don't think the kid slept for three days. He's real eager to please." Oh, poor choice of words. In Malloryspeak, that translated as a weakness.

Her cell phone rang, and Riker held up a ten-dollar bill. "I bet that's him now."

"No bet." Mallory showed him Chu's name on her cell screen, and then, with a click, she was connected to the young cop and demanding to know, "What happened?" She turned to Riker, shaking her head to tell him that nothing had happened — and she was not happy. Her voice was testy when she spoke to the cop on the phone. "You don't have to call in your position every six seconds."

Riker took the cell phone from her hand, and his tone was friendly when he said to Officer Chu, "Arty? If Willy kills somebody, you can call that in. Otherwise — just take notes."

Rolland Mann stepped off the elevator and walked down the hall to his apartment. His workday was far from over, but he had to know — would Annie still be there? Every phone call had gone to the answering machine. And though it was not uncommon for his wife to let the calls ring through, his anxiety had been ratcheting up all day. He opened his front door and found her huddled on the floor beside a packed suitcase, weeping again — frightened again.

Kneeling down beside his wife, he said to

her, so gently, "It's okay, Annie. I'm not mad."

Annie was slow to gain her legs, and then she was unsteady. He picked her up in his arms and carried her into the bedroom, where he laid her down and covered her with a quilt. After a search of the nightstand drawer, he selected a bottle from her stash of pharmaceuticals. When she had taken the dose he gave her and chased it with water, he sat down on the bed, watching over her until the sleeping pill did its work. Her eyes closed.

He needed her — and feared her. Did she know how much power she had over him?

Rolland fetched her suitcase from the front room and unpacked it. While folding her clothes into dresser drawers, he whispered, so as not to wake her, "Better luck next time, Annie."

Turning on his cell phone, he checked the calls that had gone to voice mail. One message from ADA Carlyle was brief — "Call me." But more was said by the whining tone of the recorded voice and by the companion photographs that appeared on Rolland's screen. The first one was a snapshot of a little girl standing outside of Toby Wilder's apartment building with Charles Butler, a police consultant. In the next shot, she was holding the hand of Detective Janos from Special Crimes.

Unusual child — and familiar. He could place her now. On the day of the funeral, while he stood in line with the other mourners, this little girl had walked past him, hand in hand with Detective Mallory.

Was she one of Humphrey Bledsoe's victims? That freak always had a penchant for very young redheads. Another thought occurred to him as he pocketed his phone and collected his keys and ran for the front door.

The child was a witness.

TWENTY-SEVEN

While I'm getting dressed for school, my father walks into my room. He sees the bites and bruises all over my body. My mother would've screamed. Dad only gives me a slow nod. I think he's commending me for not ratting out the kids who beat me senseless every day. And then he leaves without a word. No help. I'm on my own. I can take a beating without tears, but my father — who never raised a hand to me — he makes me cry.

— ERNEST NADLER

The visitor had not been announced, and the police officer who guarded the door was gone.

"He'll be back in a few minutes, Dr. Butler." Rolland Mann held out a business card that identified him as a deputy police commissioner. "Mind if I come in?"

In fact, Charles *did* mind. "I hear Commissioner Beale is in the hospital. How's he doing?"

"He's back in surgery." The acting commissioner, a person of merely average height, craned his neck to look up at the tall psychologist. "There was a complication."

"Sorry to hear it." Charles was doubly sorry, lacking a good impression of this man next in line for Beale's job. He had been repulsed by the filmed interrogation of the schoolboy Toby Wilder. And now he was also put off by the visitor's furtive movements and darting glances into the apartment. "What can I do for you?"

"I've come to see our star witness." By the flicker of eyes and a pursed mouth, Rolland Mann gave himself away. He was clearly fishing, testing waters.

Charles knew he could not lie to this man — or anyone else for that matter. By telltale blush, he had been genetically programmed to be truthful. However, by another accident of birth, he could play the fool without even trying. He smiled, realizing that this somewhat goofy expression always made him the clown in the room. Tilting his head to one side, he was the very portrait of a clueless simpleton. And it was unnecessary to add, *Witness? What witness?*

The politician flashed him a condescend-

371

ing smile. "The little red-haired girl, where is she?"

"My ward? She's taking a nap."

"Dr. Butler, this is police business. I need a few words with the girl — alone."

"No, I don't think that's going to happen."

Rolland Mann stepped forward to enter the apartment. So obviously accustomed by rank to having people move out of his way, now he was confronted by the immovable object of Coco's guardian, who leaned down and said, so politely, "It's not going to happen."

"I've known Toby Wilder for most of his life. I can tell you that much." The white-haired man looked at each detective in turn, though he never looked either one of them in the eye. This was a common enough quirk in New York City, and all too common was the evasiveness of his entire breed. "And now that you know the boy is represented by counsel, all your questions must go through me."

Damn all lawyers.

The private office of Anthony Queen was not tidy, but it did show signs of a recent and suspicious cleanup. A blank space on the attorney's wall outlined the typical shape of a calendar recently taken down.

372

His desk was clear of all paperwork, and there was no appointment book, no Rolodex, only a tumbler of pens and pencils. This bit of housekeeping had probably been done in a hurry upon hearing that cops were at the door.

Mallory shot a glance at the secretary, a plump, motherly soul lurking on the threshold. And now, judging by the expression of *Oh, dear,* this woman correctly deduced that the game was up.

Maybe this had been the lawyer's idea of a joke, and he was good at it. The performance showed longtime practice almost to perfection. *Almost.* But now — the police critique. Mallory picked up a sharp pencil and sailed it point-first past the old man's head. By quick birdlike turns, Anthony Queen first reacted to the noise of the little missile hitting the wall behind him — and then to his secretary's sudden intake of breath.

"So I'm guessing," said Riker, "all the papers with those funny little Braille dots got shoved in a drawer before we walked in. Am I right?"

"Stone blind," said Mallory. "No wonder his client wound up in jail."

"Juvenile detention," said the blind man, correcting her, but smiling to say that he took no offense. As Mallory had taken his measure, he had taken hers and apparently pronounced her worthy, for now he inclined his white head a bare inch, courtly as a bow, and waved one hand toward the chairs in front of his desk. "Please sit down."

The detectives remained standing, and Queen must have guessed this by the lack of the scraping noise that chair legs would make on a bare wood floor. He continued to look up at them, turning his sightless eyes on Riker and then to the place where Mallory should be. But she had moved around the desk to stand by the lawyer's side, so stealthy that she startled him when leaning down to say, "Toby Wilder doesn't have a job, and he didn't have a rap sheet after his release."

"No petty theft," said Riker, "no breaking-and-entering charges. So we wondered where the kid got the money to support his drug habit."

The old man shook his head to tell them that this was the first he had heard of any drug use. The secretary was also surprised. Their reactions might be genuine. With ready cash to feed a habit and stave off withdrawal symptoms, a junkie could pass for clean and sober seven days a week. Even addicted surgeons managed their habits with steady hands.

So Toby Wilder was a maintenance addict. What more could she do to trip the blind man? "We *know* you're supporting his drug habit. All his money comes from you."

The lawyer shook his head again. "I can't discuss his —"

Mallory pressed folded sheets of paper into his hand. "Those are your client's bank records. All his deposit checks are signed by you." But she knew little more than that. This attorney had no computer that she could plunder. She turned to the row of file cabinets that would contain his hard-copy records. Luddites would always pose obstacles.

"Of course I sign the boy's checks. I'm the executor of his mother's estate. And Toby's taxes are done by my own CPA. Everything is in order."

"You're not a criminal lawyer," said Riker. "Not a trial lawyer. You only handle wills and trusts, but you were at Toby Wilder's arraignment fifteen years ago."

Too subtle.

Mallory leaned in close. "Whose idea was it to hobble that kid with a blind attorney?"

The old man's eyebrows arched. His smile was sporting, and his voice was maddeningly pleasant when he said, "I went to court that day as a favor to Toby's mother. The judge had already appointed a criminal lawyer, but I didn't know that — not at the time — and neither did Mrs. Wilder." He turned his sightless eyes from one detective to the other. "I knew you'd find that interesting."

"You were the one who entered the plea of not guilty," said Mallory.

"True," said the lawyer. "That's when the prosecutor — I think his name was Carlyle — he pulled me aside and informed me about a plea bargain . . . and a *confession*. You see, when the police brought the child in for questioning, apparently a detective had Susan Wilder sign a waiver of parental rights. And that was *another* surprise. She had no idea what she'd signed away. Did I mention that Toby's mother was blind? That's how we met. Susan was a teacher. She taught me to read Braille when I lost my sight."

Mallory and her partner exchanged glances. Rocket Mann had tricked a blind woman.

Rolland Mann pressed one hand flat against the door, deluded that he could keep it open that way. "Dr. Butler, I'm giving you a lawful police order. Stand aside. I *will* talk to that little girl."

"Oh, no. I've seen the way you talk to children. That old interrogation tape of Toby Wilder? That was brutal."

Mann was looking past him and, with more urgency now, renewed his efforts to gain entry. "Let me in!"

Charles turned his head to see Coco standing behind him and clearly disturbed by the angry voice from the hall. Her hands were spinning, and her body was weaving from side to side.

Rolland Mann put all his weight against the door and yelled, "Don't make me call that cop back up here!"

And now, as if the smaller man weighed no more than a bothersome fly, Charles easily pushed him into the hall by simply closing the door. Rolland Mann beat on the wood, and the pounding grew louder as each of three dead-bolt locks was secured.

Coco put her hands to her ears and ran down the hall.

Charles caught up to her in the guest room. She sat on the bed, tailor-fashion — rocking, rocking, as her little world tilted, all at sea. She held the one-button cell phone in both hands and held on tight, as if it were her lifeboat. And it was.

He gently took it from her hands. "Good

idea. Let's call Mallory, shall we?"

"I've never heard of Ernest Nadler," said the lawyer. "Toby was charged in the death of an unidentified wino."

Riker stepped closer to the blind man's desk. "Where was Toby's father while this was going on?"

"Long gone," said Anthony Queen. "Mr. Wilder abandoned his family when Toby was ten. I only know that much because I had the man declared legally dead. Susan wanted to sell her condo, and the absent husband was a cloud on the title."

"Let's get back to that bogus waiver," said Mallory, "the one that signed away the mother's parental rights. Did you even bother to challenge it?"

"Of *course* I did. And the judge was ready to hit the prosecutor with his gavel. Toby was a minor, a child. So I insisted that his confession be tossed. But *then* the court-appointed lawyer showed up. He was hired by the Driscol School. Very pricey legal talent — way out of *my* league. I can't disclose the conversation in chambers, but when court resumed, Toby pled guilty to a charge of manslaughter. The plea-bargain arrangement killed the boy's right of appeal, but his mother and I filed a complaint against

Detective Mann. Two angry blind people. I always wondered if they were laughing at us, those policemen at Internal Affairs. I imagine they made a paper airplane out of Susan's statement. It took me four years to get Toby out on early release. His mother was dying. I bought them a year to say goodbye."

Behind him, Riker heard Mallory's cell phone ring. A moment later, he turned around, and she was gone.

Rolland Mann's secretary did not look up from the screen of her computer. Miss Scott wore a secretive, joyful little smile, and he assumed that she had found another job. No doubt he would find her letter of resignation on his desk. But that was not the surprise that awaited him when he opened the door to his private office.

A detective was seated at his desk — leaning back in *his* chair — just begging to be fired for gross insubordination. "Mallory, are you *insane?*"

"Oh, yeah. Ask anybody." She lifted a newspaper from the desk blotter to expose a weapon lying there, and it was not a police-issue semi-automatic. It was a revolver — a big one.

Rolland observed the traditional body

language for dealing with a whack-job cop: the missed beat of the heart, the tension of every muscle, the gaping dry mouth.

The detective's face was a mask, and neither was there any expression in her voice when she said, "Charles Butler tells me you have an interest in a little girl. . . . He called it an unhealthy interest." She picked up the revolver and studied its muzzle. *Now* she showed emotion — she *loved* the gun.

He felt a cold wetness spreading on his crotch. Rolling down his legs. The smell of piss was in the air.

Point taken.

Mallory holstered her weapon and left the office.

Twenty-Eight

We're better trackers now, Phoebe and me. Today we keep Toby in our sights for a long time before losing him in the Ramble. Then we hear the scream, a grown-up's voice, lots of anger. We can't tell where the sound comes from. Though we don't mean to, we run toward it, crashing through bushes and ferns and into a clearing. The place has the stink of an outdoor toilet. And other smells, beer and vomit. A buzz of black flies. A thousand gnats.

And there's Toby standing on a path up ahead. Next to him is a wild man — hair matted and stringy, clothes dirty, teeth missing — fists waving. Toby holds one hand to a bright red patch of skin on his face, and we know that crazy bum hit him. Then the man slaps something out of Toby's hand. It falls on the ground. Golden. Shiny. Toby leaves it there, turns his back and walks away. The crazy man lurches into the clearing. Sobbing, he falls to his knees on the grass.

Phoebe picks up the shiny thing, a gold cigarette lighter. And I say, "So Toby smokes cigarettes? How cool is that?" Phoebe says no, it must be a keepsake. Toby never smells of smoke; he smells like soap. Only Phoebe would know his scent. She would taste him if she only could.

And then we hear the laughter from above. We look up to the high ground of a boulder, and there they are, Humphrey, Willy and Aggy. While we followed Toby, they had followed us.

They jump down from the rock. It's raining monsters.

— ERNEST NADLER

Lieutenant Coffey's destination was only a short walk from the station house, but he had made a detour along the way. After parking his personal car, he stood on the sidewalk, looking up at an apartment window above the SoHo cop bar. He entered the saloon, an alcoholic's dream come true, only a short stumble up the stairs to Riker's apartment.

And now Jack Coffey climbed those steps to knock on the detective's door.

Riker had his six-pack smile in place when

he greeted his commanding officer. "Hey, Lieutenant."

Coffey entered the front room, a dumping ground for take-out cartons, crushed beer cans and unwashed glasses that had done double duty as ashtrays. A tower of dirty socks, junk mail and newspapers was precariously stacked on a straight-back chair. The stack moved. He could not look away. Any second now —

Surprise. A walkway had been cleared from the front door to the kitchen, where dirty dishes were stacked up in the sink and along the countertop. But a small table had been swiped clean of debris. Whatever liquid had been spilled on the linoleum, it stuck to the soles of the lieutenant's shoes and made a tacky sound as he crossed the small room. "Well, this is touching. You cleaned up for me."

Riker, the quintessential host, put a cold beer in the lieutenant's hand. "Pull up a chair."

Coffey sat down at the table and tipped back his bottle for a long, cold swallow on a warm summer night. "Where's your partner?"

"Probably following the money."

"She ditched you, right?" The lieutenant could hear the rattle of the air conditioner in the next room, but it was doing little to cool this apartment. He wondered if Riker had ever cleaned the AC filter. *Stupid idea.* "I went back to my place to go over Mallory's credit-card charges for the time she was gone."

"You ran her card trace from your home computer?"

"Yeah. I couldn't put her in the department goldfish bowl. But I did it by the book. I guess she backtracked the search with my badge number. It's not like I was hiding anything. I figured that was her reason for driving me nuts for the past month."

"Naw," said Riker. "That was just payback for all that desk duty."

"Maybe — maybe not." The lieutenant tipped his chair backwards on two legs and looked up at the ceiling, a haven for spider-webs and trapped flies.

"God knows she's not normal," said Riker. "But nobody working homicide is all that well-adjusted." He held up a cigarette to ask his commanding officer if he minded the smoke — *Riker,* who deferred to nobody — and this was evidence of a worried man.

"The chief of D's called again. He ran his own trace on Mallory's cards — for the lost time on the road."

"Then he's got nothing," said Riker. "So

the kid likes to drive. So what? Beats the hell out of booze and drugs to forget the last body count. You know her car?"

"I've seen it," said Coffey. "A Volkswagen convertible."

"Naw, it only looks like one. You lift up the hood, roll back the top, and what've you got? A damn Porsche with a roll bar."

"Disguised as a VW. . . . Oh, yeah, that's normal." But that would explain how she had traveled from place to place so fast, wandering aimlessly at breakneck speeds. "She was gone for three months, Riker."

"I've lost more time than that in drunk tanks. Every cop needs a hobby. I drink — she drives."

Jack Coffey found a clean deli napkin on the floor at his feet, and he used it to draw a crude map of the lower forty-eight states. "The charges she racked up are mostly gas stations, food, hotels." The lieutenant drew a row of dashes running out of New York. "For a few hundred miles, it almost looks like she's got someplace to go." And then the westward line disintegrated into weaves and jogs and doubling-back circles as the lieutenant's pen traveled across the paper-napkin country. "But she's got no plan, no destination. The kid's got nothing." Paradoxical Mallory, a girl with a full tank of gas — running on empty and covering lots of ground to go nowhere. His pen pressed down on the West Coast. "This is where she ran out of land." The pen moved along the edge of America, hugging the barrier ocean as it traveled north on the ragged paper coastline and stopped again. "Here's where she decides to come back home." The pen described wide spirals — a cartoon of a clockwork spring, months long from coast to coast. "Not your typical tourist route. Circling, circling . . . the way people travel when they're lost."

"But she's fine now," said Riker.

The lieutenant waited until the man met his eyes, and then his words were carefully meted out. "She was never fine."

And she never would be. Life could only beat a little kid half to death so many times and still expect her to grow up normal. But Mallory *was* a highly functional cop, and the best he had ever known, even better than her old man. It was a tribute he could not afford to pay to her face because — she was *not* fine. At best, he could say she was back in form, smart and edgy and totally —

"She isn't nuts," said Riker.

Jack Coffey nodded in agreement. "Crazy is just a game she plays." It was like a new toy she had found out there on the road.

"And Mallory's been playing *me* — playing crazy — in front of a squad of witnesses."

Hubris. It had never occurred to her that she could fail a psych evaluation. And then she had counted too much on Charles Butler's rebuttal exam to save her.

"Every time Chief Goddard calls me," said Coffey, "it's like a threat to take her badge. Even if she gets a new evaluation, he can still drag her into a formal hearing anytime he likes. Let's say the whole squad has to testify to her behavior — like hogtying a CSI. If just one of those bastards slips up and forgets to lie like crazy — under *oath* — that's the end of her."

Riker could only stare at the napkin. There was no need to remind this man that some of those detectives might not care to risk their own careers — not for her sake.

Jack Coffey finished the beer and pushed back his chair. "Much as I'd like to tell Mallory she shot herself in the foot, it could only make things so much worse. You got a picture of that in your head, Riker? Mallory going to war on Joe Goddard?"

The detective nodded. "I won't tell her."

This time, Jack Coffey believed him. They were done.

The lieutenant gathered up his car keys. "I don't need to know the details. But

387

whatever Goddard wants from you guys —
bring it home real fast."

Riker was across the street from Sardi's
restaurant when he saw the red neon light
of Lou Markowitz's favorite nightclub in
the distance. He held a cell phone to his ear
and talked as he walked, saying to the
shadow cop who followed Willy Fallon,
"Stay on her till she goes back to her hotel.
Then go home, Arty. Tomorrow you can
sleep late. Party girls don't wake up till
noon." He folded his phone into his pocket
and strolled down the sidewalk, mingling
with the theater crowd as the shows were
letting out, and then he put on some speed
to beat these people to a seat in Birdland, a
place of low lights, booze and live music.

The detective was late to pull up a stool
at the bar, and he made his apologies to
Charles Butler. Coco sat between them on
a cushion of two telephone books so she
could reach her drink, a pink concoction
with three cherries. Riker smiled and flashed
his badge at the bartender. "Tell me you
carded the little girl."

"The kid's legal. She's a performer. Isn't
that right, Coco?" The bartender had obviously fallen deeply in love with the short
piano player. Turning back to Riker, he said,

"She did a solo between sets."

"And she got a standing ovation," said Charles Butler. "But it's way past her bedtime, and she's a little tired."

Coco smiled like a world-weary trouper. She took a long, noisy sip on her straw and drained her pink drink dry.

Now the bartender recognized Riker and called him by his name, "Lou's Friend." A shot of whiskey and a water back was ordered, and then the detective listened to Coco's diatribe on the cannibalism of hungry rats, accompanied by a sax-and-strings rendition of "Summertime." The combo ended its last number, and now he spotted a familiar piano man whose day job was writing orchestra arrangements for classical music and Broadway show tunes. Chick Dolan's nights belonged to jazz. The man had to be pushing seventy, but he had aged with unnatural grace. He moved toward the bar with glides and slides.

Damn. *So* cool.

And now a flash of the pearly whites. "Hey, Riker. How long's it been, man?"

"A few years." In the company of Lou Markowitz, who loved everything from bebop to rhythm and blues, Riker had once been a regular patron of Birdland. Though his first love would always be rock 'n' roll, over time, he had been forced to admit that jazz rocked, too.

"I'd love to know where this came from." Chick Dolan laid a short stack of sheet music on the bar. "Your friend here won't say." He nodded in Charles's direction. "So the cops got a sudden interest in jazz?"

"Yeah. Lou's kid and me. We're working a case, and that's part of it." He glanced at the musical score transcribed from Toby Wilder's bedroom walls. "What can you tell me?"

"It's good," said Chick, "and it's a real tease. There's a signature in the sax riffs and piano rolls, but I can't think who it belongs to. Well, I can see the guy's face. I just can't put a name to him." Pointing to his head, where the last white hair had fallen out at least five years ago, he said, "I think every time I learn something new, something old falls out of my brain."

"Can you play it?"

Chick grinned. "All I got is a three-man combo. You'd have to bring me — oh, about fifty more musicians."

"You can't just noodle the melody?"

The other man's expression was clear: *No, you idiot.* Some translation was obviously required, and fortunately Chick knew Riker's first language. "Mick Jagger had the world's greatest rock 'n' roll band. Suppose those boys had just come out onstage and whistled a few bars for the audience?"

Riker had to admit that it would not be quite the same experience as the blowout concerts of his younger days.

"Your friend tells me a kid wrote this score fifteen years ago," said Chick. "The melody *is* original. If I've never heard it, no one has. But then there's style — something older than the boy's melody. The riff's the thing — like fingerprints." The man rolled up the score of sheet music. "Leave this with me. I'll get back to you." Tomorrow, he explained, there would be a rehearsal for the series of free park concerts. "It's a symphony orchestra, but it's got lots of switch-hitters, classical and jazz, and a few old-timers like me." And one of those musicians would recall the signature in the music.

Across the street from the Midtown hotel, an officer in blue jeans sat in the back of a cruiser, courtesy of two patrol cops who were taking a late dinner break in a nearby restaurant. Arthur Chu had been told to go home once Willy Fallon returned to her room. Her tenth-floor window was lit, but he would not trust the socialite to stay tucked in.

If Detective Riker was right about party girls sleeping till noon, it was because they never went to bed this early.

As a white shield, not yet a detective, Arty knew his perch in Special Crimes was tenuous. Every member of that squad was an elite gold shield. He was only hanging on to his desk moment to moment. With the first screwup, they would send him packing back to his old precinct. And so, tonight, he worked off the clock. He would give up sleep. He would also sacrifice fingers and toes — if they would only let him stay.

The light went out in the woman's hotel window, but Arty was not deceived. No way she was going to sleep. He counted off the minutes for her elevator ride down to the lobby. The uniforms, back from dinner, slid into the front seat just as Willy Fallon appeared on the sidewalk, one hand outstretched to fish a passing taxi from the stream of traffic.

"My girl's on the move," said Arthur Chu. "Follow that cab!"

And though surveillance detail was not their job tonight, the patrolmen obliged him, trailing the yellow taxi from a distance of two car lengths, heading uptown, rounding the monument of Columbus Circle, straight up Central Park West and past the

Museum of Natural History. A few blocks later, Willy got out of her vehicle, and Officer Chu left his.

He followed her over a crosswalk and down a side street of brownstones, but hung back as she stopped in front of a large building decorated with gargoyles. The name of the Driscol School was engraved in large letters above the doors.

Arthur Chu crossed over to the other side of the street and played the role of a bum, descending three steps to a well of concrete sunk below the level of the sidewalk, a place where trash was stored. As he riffled through plastic receptacles and bags, he watched her move toward a tall wrought-iron gate that barred an alley between the school and a building next door. Willy Fallon dipped a hand into her purse and pulled out something he could not see.

A key? It must be. A moment later, the gate swung open.

Twenty-Nine

Losing them is easy in the Ramble. We know where to hide so no one can find us. Hell, even we can't find us. We hold our breath, Phoebe and me. They pass us by, and then they double back — double-fisted. Hunting. They call out our names — so angry because they can't find us, hurt us. Then Humphrey and the girls gang up on another target. From the first scream to the last, we can't move. We can only listen to what they do to that poor crazy bum. They do it forever, dragging out the pain. The wino screams. Phoebe cries. I'm scared out of my mind — still scared even as I write this line.

— ERNEST NADLER

Phoebe Bledsoe ran down the alley and across the garden to her cottage. Only time enough to dress, and then she would have to hurry, run all the way if she must. She

394

dare not be late to the gathering at her mother's mansion.

The gleam of a garden lantern shone through the crack as she opened her front door, and there on the floor was a note that had been slid under the sill.

Another threat?

"Don't turn on the light!" Dead Ernest stood by the window, looking through a slit in the curtain. "Light attracts bugs like Willy."

Phoebe's hand hesitated on the wall switch and then dropped to her side. She made her way across the dark room by touch of chair and couch and table to find the drawer with the flashlight. She clicked it on and trained a yellow beam on the notepaper. Willy Fallon's handwriting was almost illegible. Phoebe had to labor over every obscenity.

"Murder makes people crazy," said Dead Ernest.

No, none of them had been crazy — only cruel.

A shadow passed by the curtain of the front window. Then came a knock at the door, and Willy Fallon yelled, "I know you're in there!" Rapping knuckles escalated to banging fists. "Tell your mother she has to talk to me!"

Willy slammed her body into the door. Screaming and kicking at the wood, she finally got the attention of the night watchman. On the other side of the garden, old Mr. Polanski opened the school's back door. Armed with his own flashlight, he aimed it at the intruder.

Willy fled.

They were driving home from Birdland in Midtown traffic. Riker had always loved the city best by night with the car windows all rolled down. He stared at the windshield, a panorama of neon colors and diamond-bright headlights. A duel of Latin music versus rap blasted from car lanes up ahead, but the detective hardly noticed. He had trouble on his mind.

The child sleeping in his arms was lightly snoring. He turned to the man behind the wheel, who had just ended the story of a surprise visit from Rolland Mann. "When Mallory said she took care of it, did she say how?"

Charles Butler shook his head. "She only told me he wouldn't be back — ever."

"Well, I know she didn't kill him. Word gets out when you shoot the top cop." Riker slumped low in the passenger seat. What had she done to that man? Could things get any worse? The tallest buildings were behind them now as the car traveled south through Greenwich Village, a neighborhood built on a more human scale. He looked down at the sleeping child. "So when were you planning to tell the kid that her granny's dead?"

"I thought I'd deal with one trauma at a time," said Charles. "Perhaps we'll talk about the death tomorrow."

"Mallory told her yesterday."

Charles's hands tightened around the wheel, the only sign that he was angry. His voice was calm as he turned east on Houston. "Coco took it in stride, didn't she? No crying, right?"

"Yeah. How'd you know?"

"She always knew Granny was dead. Coco never asked me any questions about her — never talked about going home. She knew she had no one to go back to. That's why she fastened all her hopes on Mallory. From the moment they met, Coco was angling for a new home and someone to love her." They shifted across the lanes of wide Houston in silence, and then, as Charles made the turn down to SoHo, he said, "This would be a good time for Mallory to back off — just walk away. There has to be a breach that a real parent can step into. That has to happen very soon."

"You're probably right, but Mallory thinks the kid knows more than she's telling. It's gonna take us a while to crack the fairy-tale code."

"I say it ends now. I have the strongest legal claim on Coco. Thanks to Robin Duffy, I'm the recognized guardian in both New York and Illinois. The law says —"

"Mallory *is* the law." The Mercedes pulled up to the curb in front of the saloon that Riker called home. "You got no shot. You never did."

Charles cut the engine. "I'm very close to placing Coco in a permanent home. That's what she needs right now. She's in crisis. The child can't go on this way. But Mallory won't sign the papers to let her go. . . . This is *heartless.*"

Riker did not want to end the night like this. "Heartless? Yeah, that's my partner. But you know she'd take a bullet for Coco . . . and maybe she already did. You never asked her how she solved your problem with Rolland Mann. She just told you the kid was safe, and you believed her. Absolute faith, right? I guess it never occurred to you that she could ever go into a fight — and lose everything. Charles, you know — you *know* she went after that bastard and scared him shitless. That's her style. . . . That's her *romantic* side," he said to the sorry man who loved Mallory — heart or no heart.

The salon at the mansion was in full swing when Phoebe Bledsoe arrived with sweat stains under her arms from racing two blocks on this muggy night.

The caterer's people, all more formally dressed, carried trays laden with glasses of red wine and white, moving through a babble of voices from every quarter of the wide room. Most of her mother's guests stood in conspiracies of two and gangs of four or more. Others sat on chairs, divans and sofas positioned in conversational clusters. In this social hierarchy of furniture, there could only be one throne. High above her mother's favorite chair, the chandelier burned bright with electric candles and a thousand pieces of reflecting crystal. Another chair, a smaller one, had been placed beside her mother's, allowing only one person at a time to curry favor. It was the most coveted seat in the house, and people made wide circles around it, waiting for a chance at the ear of Grace Driscol-Bledsoe, a maker and breaker of careers and fortunes.

Phoebe's late father had called this weekly affair the Night of the Toadies. As a child, she had taken this term to mean a squishiness of character, slimy souls — and a stink. "Yes," he had said to her then, "that's exactly right."

She walked about the room as her mother's feeble apprentice, accepting kisses from familiar CEOs and politicos, but only handshakes from the up-and-comers. Every fifteen minutes, the drab companion, Hoffman, popped into the room to see that all was well with her employer, and then, after a moment or two, popped out — a clock's broken cuckoo silently announcing the quarter hour. And finally, *finally,* at the end of the evening, when the room had been cleared of every toad, and coffee was served for two, Phoebe sat in the petitioner's chair beside her mother.

"Seriously? That's what this says?" Grace Driscol-Bledsoe stared at the note of scrawled lines. "Willy's pushed a few of these through my mail slot, but I never actually tried to *read* one." Nor this one — she crumpled it into a ball and set it on the small table that held her coffee cup.

"Did you really throw Willy out of the house?"

"Hoffman did — with the help of those lovely detectives who interrogated you. I rather hoped they'd shoot her, but they only loaded her into an ambulette."

"If you'd just talk to Willy, she'd leave me alone."

"Scary little beast, isn't she? Well, you could move back into the mansion with me. It's very safe here, and your old room is always waiting for you."

Of course it was. This was an old conversation. It had gone on for years. She was still regarded as her mother's runaway child. And this was not the first bribe to bring her home — only the most callous one.

"So that's what it's going to cost me to get rid of Willy?" Phoebe stood up, preparing to leave now that she understood her true place — a bit of a shock. She was one of the toads.

"Send him up," Mallory said to the doorman at the other end of the intercom. Minutes later, when she heard the soft knock, the detective was ready with a bottle of wine under her arm and two glasses in hand. She opened the door to Rabbi David Kaplan, a slender, middle-aged man with a neatly trimmed beard, a sweet smile and a penchant for poker.

"Kathy." He was among that close circle of men who had loved her foster father, and the rabbi was fearless in the use of her first name. He kissed her cheek, already forgiving her for not returning his calls. "It's been a long time — too long." He spread his open hands, and slowly shook his head. What was he to do with her? "Are you coming to the poker game this week?"

In lieu of an answer, she handed him the wine bottle, and he read the label of his favorite vintner. Now suspicion would begin. The rabbi would wonder if she could have known that he would drop by tonight unannounced.

Mallory smiled to say, *Oh, yeah.*

After failing with Riker, of course Charles Butler would send another diplomat to plead the case for moving Coco beyond the reach of the police. Also, she had noticed the rabbi standing on the sidewalk below and looking up at her dark street-side windows, awaiting an opportunity to catch her off guard with no excuse for refusing to see him. She had only to flip a light switch in the front room. Then, following a count to ten, the doorman had announced him.

"So," she said to the man who lived on the other side of the Brooklyn Bridge, "you just happened to be passing by?" The detective stepped out into the hall. "Let's go to the roof."

They entered the elevator. As the doors

closed, Mallory said, "I know you called my boss while I was away — quite a few times."

"Kathy, you were gone so long, months and months." He raised his eyebrows in a gentle reprimand. "No goodbye, no postcards."

Following elevator etiquette, they both turned their eyes to the lighted numbers for the rising floors.

"So you hounded the lieutenant."

"Hounded? No." The rabbi shrugged. "Well, it could've been worse. I wanted to file a missing-person report, but Edward stopped me. He said you wouldn't want that kind of thing on your record. So *then* I went to Lieutenant Coffey. A nice man, very sympathetic. He told me he'd know if you were in trouble. He said he was always the *last* to know, but eventually . . . if anything bad should happen . . . he would know."

"And what about your poker cronies? How many times did *they* call Jack Coffey?"

"I rat on no one." David Kaplan was devoted to his friends, though he would take their money at cards every chance he got. In a penny-ante poker game, that might be a ten-dollar win. *What a player.* The rabbi, the gentlest man in creation, so loved this little fantasy that he could be ruthless.

The elevator doors opened onto a narrow

stairwell, and they climbed these steps to a well-lit roof with a wooden deck and chairs in clusters around metal tables. The summer wind was warm. Above them, the moon and a poor show of stars could not compete with this view of a million city lights. She sat down with Rabbi Kaplan and poured the wine. "So you badgered Lieutenant Coffey every day."

"A *few* times. He told me nothing. Well, he did say that no news was good news."

"I bet you spent a lot of time talking about me on poker nights."

"Oh, Edward and Robin always talk about you behind your back. They've been doing that since you were a little girl. They *love* you." The rabbi sadly shook his head. "Those *bastards*." Now he graced her with his most innocent smile, the one he used for killer poker hands. And yet this man probably still wondered how she had managed to fleece him at cards all through her childhood.

He laid a folded sheaf of papers on the table. "More legal work for Coco."

"From Robin Duffy?"

Now why was that a hard question?

The first document was a court order for Coco's travel to the state of Illinois. It was subject to the qualification of adoptive parents. Buried in the fine print of legalese was the second condition: the child's release from material-witness protection. The next sheet was the companion form that required Mallory's signature to bind the deal. Robin Duffy had already given her copies of this paperwork, but those had been left undated pending the wrap of her case. She turned back to the court order. It bore today's date. And it was already signed by a judge. "This wasn't Robin Duffy's idea."

That was only a guess, but a good one.

David Kaplan widened his sweet smile, inadvertently confirming that this was Charles Butler's plot. The man picked up his wineglass for another taste — a stall. And now, in classic rabbi evasion, he said, "I know you want what's best for the child. You want her to have every good thing that Louis and Helen gave to you."

In the cold tone of a machine that could talk, she said, "How well you know me."

The rabbi's smile faltered, perhaps with a suspicion that he knew her not at all.

She laid the papers on the table. "I have to wonder why you thought this was a good idea. It *isn't* — not if you want me to keep that kid alive."

Only moments ago, everything had been clear to this man, but when he looked down at the document once more, he regarded it with some confusion.

Good. It was Mallory's turn to smile. She was certain that Robin Duffy had not obtained the signature on this court order, though the old lawyer knew the signing judge quite well — and so did the rabbi. Judge Cartland was sometimes a guest player in the Louis Markowitz Floating Poker Game. The detective lifted her glass and drank deeply. "Charles sent you. You forgot to mention that." She tapped the document's signature line. "When did the judge sign this — like an *hour* ago?"

Maybe right after Charles Butler got home from Birdland?

David Kaplan raised both hands to say, *You got me.* "That little girl is in very deep trouble, trauma layered over trauma. Charles has a list of likely parents in Illinois. And he's lined her up with a therapist in Chicago, a very good doctor. This poor fragile child needs a —"

"That kid's not going anywhere. She's a material witness in a murder investigation."

"Charles says she's not good witness material. When I spoke to the —"

"You *told* that to the judge?" She read her answer in his face, his quizzical eyes with no trace of denial, only wondering what he had done wrong. "You *did!*" Mallory slammed one hand down on the table. "Behind my *back!*"

Had she ever yelled at him before? No, never. They stared at each other with equal surprise.

Angry still, she said, "You trust Charles Butler's judgment more than mine." She leaned toward him. "In a *homicide* investigation?"

How upside down was that? How would it square with this man's flawless rabbinical logic? It would not. He simply had no faith in her. There was no other way to spin this night.

"Rabbi, it was a mistake to mess with my case." She crushed the court order into a ball. "So you chose up sides." Not *her* side. "And then you gave that judge a reason to screw with me." She rolled the paper ball between her hands, making it smaller, harder. With the flick of a finger, she sent it spinning across the table, and it came to rest by his wineglass. "Keep it. . . . Something to remember me by."

The rabbi's eyes were sad, for this was a death of sorts, an end to things. She had stabbed him with words, and the win was clearly hers.

Or not.

"Kathy, when you only *figuratively* cut out someone's heart — that won't necessarily get rid of your problem. . . . I will *always* love you." David Kaplan leaned back in his chair and emptied his glass. "I'll always be here for you." The rabbi rose from the table and kissed her cheek in farewell. "But I'm guessing you won't be sitting in on the poker game this week." He shrugged and smiled. "Well, maybe next week."

When he had left her alone on the roof, she smashed her wineglass into the brick parapet. Unconditional love could be infuriating.

The den in Mallory's condo had one wall lined in cork. She had stolen it from Lou Markowitz's office after the old man's death. As far as Riker knew, it was her only theft of sentiment.

To accommodate her electronics, the temperature of this back room was always on the chilly side, but it was ice cold by the looks of it — decorated with metal furnishings, wires and cables, steel shelves of manuals and gadgets. Even the damn carpet was gunmetal gray.

And baby had a brand-new toy.

The four computer monitors on workstations no longer had pride of place. They had been upstaged by a gigantic flat screen, and Riker gawked at it. A television set this size was every guy's wet dream on Super Bowl Sunday. But he did not salivate; it was just another computer. No need of a keyboard or mouse — she only pointed to the picture of a file holder and pages tumbled out in animation. With two fingers, she caught them in midair and juggled them into positions across the wide field of electric blue. It was not bad enough that his partner's only stable relationships were with machines — now she had found one that responded to her touch, one that could feel her body heat, and this vaguely creeped him out — possibly because he was drunk.

Riker had moved on to the good stuff, Mallory's single-malt whiskey, as he watched glowing boxes of text enlarge their type for the benefit of his middle-aged eyes. Standing up as straight as the liquor would allow, he gave his best impression of actually listening to her lecture on a tired old theme: How to Buy a Politician.

Elected officials loved to see their names plastered on charities, so said Mallory. But all the worthy causes listed on her screen were funded by the Driscol Institute, and the Institute was funded by moguls in search of political whores to bed down with.

"Good works get votes."

When she turned around to see if he was paying attention, Riker recited what came to all New Yorkers with their mothers' milk. "The politicians wow the voters and then screw 'em over after the election." He said this in the tone of *Yeah, yeah, what else is new?*

She rewarded him by refilling his glass. How many times had she done that? He had lost count of his shots tonight.

Mallory capped the bottle. "The mayor doesn't run this town. Grace Driscol-Bledsoe does." She faced her giant screen and pointed to one of her lists. "These council members were bought with small stuff, their names on scholarship funds and after-school programs." Her pointing finger moved to the next column of more impressive charities. "The Driscol Institute funded a civic center with the mayor's name engraved in stone. That bought him votes in a district that hated his guts. Coincidentally, that's when he dropped his opposition to a building site for a high-rise on the West Side. The land was owned by a real-estate broker, one of the major donors to Grace's family charity — and he made a fifteen-million-dollar profit overnight. I figure Grace's cut was ten percent."

And now Riker *was* paying attention. "Why didn't the feds pick up on that? I thought they were tracking this stuff."

"They are. Corporations have to declare every donation to charity, but that has no effect on a money-laundering racket like this one. There's nothing on paper that ties a charity donor to a politician. The trustees of the Driscol Institute are the middlemen."

"The money cleaners — and Grace is their leader." Riker looked down to see Mallory topping off his glass — a small bonus for staying awake. And so, just to prove that he was somewhat sober, he asked, "How does Grace collect her cut? Wouldn't that show up in an audit?"

"No. She gets paid by the donors." With a touch of the screen, Mallory opened another folder. "And here they are." This was an old client list for the late John Bledsoe's consulting firm. "Grace used to channel the payoffs into her husband's company. It looked good on paper — like legitimate earnings for a lobbyist. And the taxes got paid. No red flags for the IRS."

"So all that money her husband left to Humphrey — that really belonged to Grace? Well, that explains why the portrait of hubby and the kid was hung over a toilet." And now he could clearly see a pissed-off Grace

Driscol-Bledsoe out in the woods, stringing up bodies, one of them her own son. "But can the lady climb a tree?" He raised his glass for a deep swallow. "For a hundred million bucks, I say she can. That broad's in better shape than I am."

His partner smiled — she was smiling at his empty glass. And then she turned back to the screen. "After the husband sold his company, Grace had no holding pen for the next batch of money-laundering fees, and her personal finances had to jibe with legal earnings." Mallory touched another folder, and a slew of facsimile checks spilled out across the blue screen, all of them made out to the woman's personal companion. "Here's the weak spot, a stupid mistake. Hoffman is underpaid. I'm guessing Grace gives out weekly cash bonuses."

"I bet she does a lot of things with cash," said Riker. "She'd never trust another partner to launder her own money — not after what her husband did to her."

"Right. And the feds have been tracking large cash flows for years. I know she's got big money squirreled away — but she's been selling off her jewelry." With one finger, Mallory dragged a parade of photographs across the screen. "These were taken after her husband sold the company and walked out on her. Count the jewels."

Riker stepped up to the screen and looked at the first photo of the society diva all decked out in shiny gemstones. Years later, in the final shot, she was almost modest. "So the lady's down to her last strand of pearls — and that silver medallion."

"Grace really *needs* Humphrey's millions," said Mallory. "It's the only money she can spend in the open. Every cash transaction is a risk."

"Are we gonna share this with the rest of the squad?"

"If we do, it'll get back to Joe Goddard." One hand waved over her list of top politicians on the charity circuit — and on the take. "You want him to *run* this town?"

"Oh, God, no." Crazy bastard — the chief of detectives was on a twisted mission, collecting dirty secrets for the good of the force, an extortionist on the side of the angels and the NYPD. It would be insane to give him the entire city. Yet Riker's next thought was for a day down the road, when he might need to use all of this, trade the whole town to that lunatic to save his partner's badge — and to keep her from waging a war she could not win.

"It's all about power with him," said Mallory, "but the chief's just another version of

413

Grace — just as dangerous."

Amen to that.

"So . . . if the bad guys don't get us, the good guys will?"

"Now you've got it." Mallory tilted the whiskey bottle, and when she had filled his glass to the brim, she looked deep into his eyes, as if she could extract his soul this way. "That day — when Goddard told us he planned to get rid of Rocket Mann — he put his own job on the line. So he already knew he could control us . . . but how? A blackmailer has to put his leverage on the table. There's no other way to get what he wants."

Through one clear spot in a fog of alcohol, he saw the true purpose of tonight's civics lesson. *Civics my ass.* It worried him how often Mallory's paranoia panned out. She knew the leverage *had* been laid out — for her partner.

Riker shook his head to plead clueless. He waited for the accusation of betrayal, but all that came back on him was heartache. She only stood there so quietly — waiting for the truth.

Standoff.

He set down his glass and showed himself out.

The alarm on the bedside monitor woke Grace Driscol-Bledsoe. The loud noise was enough to terrify her even before the door opened and the apparition flew into the room. By the poor light of a bedside lamp, she saw a disembodied head with balls of fire for eyes. *Oh* — only the nurse wrapped in a black robe. The lenses of Hoffman's eyeglasses reflected the opaque globe of the lamp on the night table as she leaned over her employer to fuss with the tangle of sheets.

"You slipped off the finger cuff, ma'am. Here it is." Hoffman had found the small device that was attached to the monitor by a cord, and she replaced it on Grace's index finger.

So this was not a stroke — more like a rehearsal.

When the nurse had returned to her own room, Grace lay back on the pillows, but sleep would not come. After switching off the monitor and removing its connecting finger cuff, she rose from her bed with only the security of her emergency-alert medallion. With one press of the button at its center, a voice would boom from a box,

415

seeking her out wherever she might be, increasing its volume and sound sensitivity until it found her and assessed her needs. During all her waking hours, this level of security would do. It was the nights that frightened her. She was most vulnerable in sleep.

Barefooted, she padded down the hall to the room where her father had died. It was much the same as it had been all those years ago when Papa had been crippled by a stroke.

As a girl, Grace had seldom visited the sickroom, so repulsed was she by the sight of that drooling man rolling his eyes and making pathetic attempts to form words, half her father's face gone slack and the other half crying. In recent years, Grace came here all the time. Taking inventory soothed her. The closet had been restocked with supplies, and now she counted the bottles of medicines not yet invented in the days of Papa's drawn-out death. Prized above all of them were doses of tbs, not legally obtainable outside of a hospital. This precious contraband was also kept in Hoffman's black bag — kept close at hand every hour of the day and night.

Moonlight gleamed on the chrome rails of the mechanized bed — her inheritance. It was still serviceable, though a new mattress had been purchased against a day when Grace might suffer another stroke of her own, a trauma more debilitating than the other two. It ran in the family — this *other* legacy from her late father. Papa, thank you *so* much.

She inspected the red lights on a march of bedside machines, assurance that they were operational. Last, she opened a door to a linen closet, making certain that the stacks of sheets had not become musty while awaiting the worst day of her life.

And the checklist was done.

There were clinics in this country that were not so wonderfully equipped. This room guaranteed that she would not end her days in a nursing home, however feeble she might become. Hopefully, by the time she could no longer fend for herself, Hoffman would have been replaced by another nurse, one with greater incentive to keep her alive. And Phoebe would sleep at the foot of the bed, much like a good and loyal dog.

Phoebe Bledsoe's friend, Mr. Polanski, was a skinny twin to Santa Claus and a kindred soul, another one who walked with the dead. The night watchman could not part with his late wife, and so he took her with him on his solitary rounds. But not tonight. "I talk to her more as I get older," he said, accepting a thermos of ice tea from Phoebe's hand.

"But your wife never talks."

"No," he said, "not like your Dead Ernest. I missed that little boy when he left us."

Years ago, Mr. Polanski had been the Driscol School's man of odd jobs, a janitor and a fixer of leaks, a mender of cracks in the plaster and sometimes a roofer. In later life, physical labor had been too hard on him, and so he had become the protector of priceless furnishings and artwork. With a change of title from handyman to watchman, he had been kept on in this place of tradition — just another antique to the board of directors.

And Phoebe, a former student, had been recycled as the school nurse.

She accompanied the old man on his rounds, and they strolled through the gallery of alumni portraits dating back to the 1800s. Most of the people pictured here were renowned in the seas of politics and commerce. These lying walls advertised respectability beyond reproach.

The gallery opened onto the dining hall, a vast space lit by streetlight slanting down

418

from a bank of tall windows. The long mahogany tables and their chairs wore ghosty dust covers. Long ago, this had been a place of sanctuary. The table in the far corner was where she had sat with Ernie, two children catching their breath and licking wounds in the no-cruelty zone of lunch hour.

Mr. Polanski and Phoebe retraced their steps to the grand staircase and climbed to the next floor, where classroom doors stood open in a hallway lined with wood paneling and freestanding lockers that clanged when hit with the soft body of a child. Ernie had once asked her why he was the only one singled out for physical violence in a school that offered so many variations on torture. Phoebe had theorized then that it was because he was two years younger and ten years smarter than his tormentors.

When Mr. Polanski had completed his rounds on every floor, they descended the back stairs to the garden door and went outside into a warm night scented by flowers. The watchman shined his torch on shrubs that hid a portion of the rear wall from the rooftop security lights.

Phoebe stared into a patch of absolute darkness where it was daylight in an old memory. This was where Humphrey and the

419

girls had Ernie pinned down, his back to the wall. And here he had disappointed them. All his fear had been spent that day. The boy had given himself up for dead and faced them down with a calm resolve.

A mistake.

Nothing could have angered them more. Before they tired of him, one of them — was it her brother? No, that time it was Willy Fallon. She had grabbed Ernie by the ears and knocked his head into the gray stone wall. The little boy had slumped to the ground, leaving a slick of his blood to mark the spot. It was still there on the following day. And all that day long, other students had streamed into the garden to gawk at a child's blood. Eleven-year-old Phoebe knew the teachers had seen it, too, but they kept walking past it.

Mr. Polanski saw the train of her gaze, peeked into her mind and said, "It took me a long time to get rid of that stain."

No. Phoebe shook her head. *It's still there.* And it was on her hands. It was everywhere.

THIRTY

Phoebe wants no part of this. Okay with me. But she won't come back to school. She won't even come to the phone when I call her house.

I need to talk to somebody.

I think about that dead wino all the time. Twenty times a day, I can hear him screaming. It took that poor crazy man a long time to die. I remember counting off the minutes from the hiding place in the Ramble. That's what I tell the police. But Detective Mann doesn't believe me.

— ERNEST NADLER

By early-morning light, Detective Mallory scrutinized the alley gate for the Driscol School. "A ten-year-old kid could pick that lock. It's an antique."

"I'm sure Miss Fallon used a key," said the white shield, Arthur Chu. "She got something out of her purse, and then it only

421

took her a few seconds to open this gate."

Riker finished reading the prowler report filed by Mr. Polanski, the night watchman. "No mention of Willy's name, no description." He pocketed his bifocals and turned to his partner. "But the time works with Arty's sighting of Willy Fallon on the run. Mr. Polanski thought Phoebe must've left the gate open. Maybe that's how Willy got in so fast."

Officer Chu shook his head. "She pulled something from her purse to —"

"But you didn't see a key," said Mallory. "You were across the street. It was dark." She reached into the back pocket of her jeans and pulled out a velvet pouch that contained her kit of picks for breaking and entering. Inspector Louis Markowitz had confiscated it on the night of her arrest at age ten — *nearly* ten. She had lied her age up to twelve years old, and, failing at that, they had later agreed that she *might* be eleven. After his death, she had found the pouch among the contents of her foster father's safe-deposit box. Sentimental old bastard, he had been unable to part with baby's first lock picks. She showed them to Arthur Chu. "Maybe this is what Willy got from her purse." She restored the pouch to her back pocket and then held up a pair of bobby pins. "Or these." The detective turned her back on the white shield for a few seconds' work — and the gate swung open. "A kid could do it."

The somewhat dejected Officer Chu was dispatched to Willy Fallon's hotel to continue his shadow detail. And when the young cop was out of sight, Riker said, "Poor guy. If he'd been right about that key —"

"I think he was." Mallory faced the narrow alley beyond the gate. She could go no farther. The police had been barred from getting within two hundred feet of Phoebe Bledsoe's residence behind the school. "This lock is at least a hundred years old. Who knows how many keys are floating around?" She looked up at the lintel above the school's door, where the Driscol name was engraved. "I bet Phoebe's mother has a key to this gate — or *had* one."

Chief Medical Examiner Edward Slope was a man of ramrod posture — but not this morning. He slouched in the chair behind his desk, one hand covering his tired eyes. His sleep had been fitful, and the caffeine jolt from his coffee had not yet kicked in when his secretary announced that there were detectives on the other side of his office door. Had Kathy come to gloat?

Last night's affair had been his first visit to Grace Driscol-Bledsoe's mansion, and he would never go back there again. A party invitation extended on the occasion of identifying her dead son — well, that should have given him pause.

He had left the mansion within ten minutes of his arrival. That was all the time needed to identify a number of politicians and other nefarious characters who belonged in jail, men and women he would never shake hands with in public or in private. It would sully a pope's reputation just to be seen with such people. But a chief medical examiner, like Caesar's wife, must take even more care with appearances. If not, his reputation and his word would be worthless in or out of court.

Kathy Mallory was the first one to enter, followed by Riker.

"Let's make this quick." Edward Slope was not up for another round of her war games. "I've got a busy day ahead. Contrary to the mayor's last press conference, violent death appears to be an ongoing thing in New York City. I'm stacking up bodies as we speak."

Both detectives sat down in the chairs facing his desk to let him know that this might take a while, and the doctor sipped another dose of coffee.

"One got past you, Doc." Riker slapped a death certificate down on the desk. "You've been robbed. This kid's autopsy was done in a hospital."

Edward Slope read the old hospital-issued certificate for Ernest Nadler, age eleven. "Cardiac arrest? I gather it wasn't a congenital defect, or you two wouldn't be here." He leaned back in his chair. "So . . . you have the boy's medical history, hospital records, some kind of evidence?"

"No," said Riker. "We were hoping you could help with that."

Dr. Slope trained his gaze on the other detective, the computer witch. She had certainly hacked her way into the hospital files. And so, on a sarcastic note, he asked, "Seriously, Kathy? You have no clue?"

She glared at him, not appreciating the innuendo, but she did not correct his use of her given name. And that could only mean that she wanted something. "Let's assume the boy was never treated for a heart defect the whole time he was in the hospital."

The doctor smiled. "Yes, let's *assume* that." He held up the death certificate. "So you think this is a major screwup by the —"

"A cover-up," she said. "The boy was a

425

crime victim. He died a month after an assault. That means his body should've come here, right?"

The doctor nodded. "Every time. I don't even care what ultimately killed him. It's still a suspicious death."

"So the hospital conspired to bury a murder," said Riker.

"Not necessarily." Dr. Slope folded the certificate into his breast pocket. "When a hospital is involved, I always begin with the presumption of gross incompetence. But we'll see."

The detectives' badges were on display, shining brightly from breast pockets.

"I know this man." Edward Slope paused in the hospital corridor to inspect his little gang of two. "If you want to scare him, we'll do this *my* way. Don't speak. You're only here for window dressing." He marched his troops into the reception room, passing by a secretary, deaf to her attempt to stop them.

They entered the private office of the hospital administrator, a man with a very large desk and a small moustache, a man who amazed one and all by the act of walking upright in the absence of a spine. Dr. Kemper was stunned and quick to stand.

"Dr. Slope, what a surprise." His worried eyes darted to the badges of the police escorts. Voice lost, Dr. Kemper reached out to shake hands with the more important visitor, who had celebrity status in the world of medicine.

Edward Slope ignored the proffered hand. He crossed over to the far side of the room, where chairs were gathered around a small table. When he sat down, he forced the administrator to leave the safety of his desk — to be exposed. The detectives took up their posts, standing behind the chief medical examiner. They were silent but watchful, clearly distrustful of Dr. Kemper, who came toward them with mincing steps.

Dr. Slope laid the death certificate on the table. "Ernest Nadler. It was a long time ago, but I know you'll remember the boy. After being assaulted, he lingered for a month and died in your hospital. With only those details, I'd make a call of murder. But then I was told that the boy was dehydrated when he was admitted — and *starved* — for *three* days. Oh, and then there were bondage wounds on both wrists. *That* was a clue. So you can imagine how surprised I was when the police informed me that the autopsy was done here. Every crime victim's body comes to me. That's the law."

"Quite right." Dr. Kemper wormed one hand around the other in a rather good impression of Dickens's Uriah Heap. "I do apologize if one of my people bungled a protocol."

"I also have a problem with the cause of death."

Dr. Kemper picked up the certificate, and when he had read it, he raised his eyes, mystified. "Cardiac arrest. I don't see the problem. It's signed by the attending physician."

"Who's conveniently dead of old age," said Slope. "I'm going to exhume the body."

"Oh, I'm sorry, sir. The remains were cremated."

"Interesting that you would know that detail off the top of your head. You still have the same pathologist on staff. I'll talk to her. And I want to see the boy's records, all of them. No computer spit-outs." That would be a waste of his time; he had that much faith in Kathy Mallory's hacking skills. She had, no doubt, found the electronic files sketchy and useless. "I want the actual charts, the patient's medical history, autopsy findings and photographs . . . *everything.*"

"Sir, this boy died fifteen years ago." And now the administrator turned his lame smile on the detectives — the law — while he explained the law to them. "We're only required to keep the original records for four years."

"But you kept *these* records." Dr. Slope folded his arms and smiled at Kemper's guilty reaction, the swipe of clammy hands on pant legs. "You put the originals in permanent storage. I'm guessing the hospital's legal counsel didn't give you any choice. That lawyer wouldn't risk his license by allowing the destruction of evidence . . . just on the off chance that I might drop by. And now I want all that paperwork in my hands so fast it takes my breath away."

The meeting was moved to a hospital conference room. This larger space was needed to spread out the records on the short life and long death of Ernest Nadler. When the chief medical examiner stepped back from the table, Riker and Mallory began to work their way through the manila envelopes and file holders, beginning with the emergency-room procedures on the day the child was admitted. The detectives had yet to speak a word to anyone.

It was Edward Slope who conducted the interrogation of Dr. Emily Woods, a thin, graying woman in her late fifties — too old to be looking for a new job as a hospital pathologist. She looked down the length of the table, seeking out the eyes of the hospital administrator, desperate for reassurance.

"Don't look at him," said the chief medical examiner. "*I* make the call on what happens to you." He held up the death certificate of the eleven-year-old boy. "Cardiac arrest? Not likely. There was no congenital defect." The wave of his hand included all the records spread along the tabletop. "Not one mention of a pre-existing heart condition. But you went along with this — this *nonsense* about heart failure." He sat on the edge of the table and leaned down to her. "Tell me if I've got this right. The boy's heart was simply the last organ to fail him. Ultimately that's how we all die, isn't it? The heart . . . stops."

"I didn't want to do the autopsy." Dr. Woods would not meet his eyes. "I refused. But then I was told that the police had no problem with it."

"And who told you that? Oh — shot in the dark — your boss, Dr. Kemper?" Edward Slope picked up the pathologist's photographs of a dead child, and he sifted through them. "The boy's eyes are closed in every shot. Did you even bother to pull back the lids and check for —"

430

"Oh, *Christ!*" Midway down the long table, Riker looked up from his reading. "You guys chopped off the kid's hands? *Doctors* did this?"

"I can explain that," said the hospital administrator.

"I bet you can." Mallory bent Dr. Kemper over the table and handcuffed him while her partner did the honors for Dr. Woods. "We're all going *down*town."

In the watchers' room, the rows of raised seats held five detectives and their commander. Lieutenant Coffey was flanked by the chief medical examiner and an assistant district attorney with a yellow bowtie. In the lighted room on the other side of the one-way glass, Mallory and Riker sat at the table with Dr. Emily Woods, and the detectives were playing a brand-new game: Bad Cop, Bad Cop — Abandon All Hope.

"Kiss your medical license goodbye," said Mallory to the hospital pathologist. "The best you can do is turn state's evidence. That might keep you out of jail."

Jack Coffey stared at the glass as he spoke to ADA Cedrick Carlyle. "Dr. Woods told us you gave her a green light to do the autopsy at the hospital."

"Well, I didn't." The man straightened his

bowtie and then fussed with imaginary lint on his suit. "I never —"

"Oh, yeah?" All heads turned to Detective Gonzales, the dubious voice in the dark at the back of the room. "I sat in on Dr. Kemper's interview. He backs up the lady doc. He says the word came down from you."

"Clearly a misunderstanding." Ignoring the minion in the back row, ADA Carlyle addressed the lieutenant beside him. "But no real harm done. I told the hospital administrator there wouldn't be a homicide investigation for Ernest Nadler. The case was solved — closed. As you know, the prime suspect confessed."

"For killing the wino," said Coffey, "not the kid."

"We only needed one charge to put Toby Wilder away. His plea agreement stipulated that the assault on the child would be dropped, and he wouldn't be charged with a second murder if the Nadler boy died. The judge had no problem with it."

"Well, I got problems with it," said Coffey. "I got ten autopsy pictures of a kid with no hands — but no crime-scene photos. Whose call was that?"

"When the police found the boy, he was all in one piece. I believe the assault was originally written up as some sort of prank."

"A prank?" Incredulous Detective Janos sat directly behind the ADA, and now he leaned forward to breathe in Carlyle's ear. "The kid was left hanging in a tree for three goddamn days — no food, no water."

In the back row, another detective said, "Ernie was strung up with wire around his wrists. No circulation. We know his hands were already turning black when they cut him down."

"Necrotic tissue," said Dr. Slope. "The boy's hands were amputated in the hospital. So even if Dr. Woods was dead drunk on the job — and that's probably true — she had to notice that Ernie Nadler was a crime victim. Her idiot boss couldn't have missed that detail, either. Apparently it was your idea to do the autopsy in the hospital."

"Looking back," said ADA Carlyle, "I can see where they might've gotten the wrong idea from our conversation. Of course the boy's body should've gone to the Medical Examiner's Office. No question. That was a huge screwup by the hospital. But Dr. Kemper and Dr. Woods hardly fit the description of criminal conspirators. It's just an act of gross stupidity."

"Well, thank you for clearing that up," said Jack Coffey.

Chief Medical Examiner Edward Slope leaned back in his front-row seat. "That won't get Woods and Kemper off the hook. The little boy was showing signs of improvement in the week before he died. He was on the mend. The prognosis was good . . . and his heart was sound. According to the bloodwork, he managed to beat off the infection from the necrotic tissue. So that didn't kill him, either."

The lieutenant reached out to knock on the glass, alerting his detectives to get on with the good part. On cue, in that other room under the bright fluorescent lights, Mallory made a rolling motion with one hand, a signal for Dr. Emily Woods to repeat the highlights of her earlier rehearsal interview.

"There was another autopsy report," said the pathologist. "What you read — that was the amended version. I found hemorrhaging in the boy's eyes. The attending physician told me it was caused by medication. Dr. Kemper agreed. He made me redact that line. Why complicate things, he said."

"And you just went along with that?"

"No. I knew medication didn't cause the hemorrhaging. Sometimes these clowns forget that I'm a doctor, too. A *doctor* — not a lawyer. That assistant DA — I forget his name — a little jerk with a yellow tie. He said the case was settled." She splayed her hands. "Settled? Well, I knew that was wrong. This wasn't a damn traffic violation."

"You thought it was murder — but not from the injuries," said Riker. "The kid's eyes were bloodshot."

"Hemorrhaging," said Mallory. "A sign of suffocation. Any pillow would do the job, right? So you were ordered to cover up a murder. And that didn't bother you?"

This was pure theater. In real life, this pathologist was a drunk and a hack who lacked even the store of forensic details that might have been gleaned by watching television. When Jack Coffey had sat in on the woman's earlier, uncoached interview, Dr. Woods had only found it odd that the administrator would ask her to redact the words *petechial hemorrhaging*. Unfortunately, she had not found the requested alterations odd enough to save her original report.

"Lucky she kept the original report," said Lieutenant Coffey. On any other day, it would be worth his job to deceive an assistant district attorney, but he was allowed to lie to a suspect all day long. "Kemper and Woods are looking at conspiracy charges. The kid was definitely killed in the hospital." He unfolded a sheet of paper. "We're gonna exhume the body."

A neat trick, since the boy's corpse had been cremated.

Carlyle's hands tightened on the armrests of his chair. Apparently he had not been privy to this detail. And that was predictable. The disposal of victim remains would not even make a footnote in a prosecutor's records. By the dim lights of the watchers' room, the lawyer strained to read the exhumation order signed by the chief medical examiner. It was all there in black and white — so it must be true.

Coffey smiled. *Oh, yeah.* This man was a believer. The ADA had that *Oh-shit* look on his face. Perhaps it had finally dawned on the lawyer that *he* was the real interrogation subject, but the lieutenant would not leave this to chance. He leaned closer, lowering his voice. "Carlyle? Is there something you'd like to tell me?"

The lawyer looked up. On the other side of the glass, the interrogation room was empty. The show was over. He did not argue when the lieutenant took him by the arm and led him to a chair in that room. Four detectives leaned against the walls. And then they were joined by the rest of the squad. Riker and Mallory were the last to walk in the door. The detectives all moved in unison to surround the lieutenant and the lawyer. The shoe shuffling ended abruptly, and all that could be heard was the tick of an old-fashioned pocket watch borrowed from Mallory.

Ten seconds. Twelve. Thirteen, fourteen.

Interrogator and suspect faced one another across the table in a contest. Jack Coffey would not be the first one to speak.

"Things seem to have gotten out of hand," said the lawyer.

"Somebody got away with murdering Ernest Nadler," said Coffey. "And you helped with the cover-up."

"Nobody got away with anything. The killer was locked up in Spofford."

"For killing a wino, not a little boy."

"It *started* with the wino! Don't you get it? It was *always* about the wino. You should talk to Rocket —" Carlyle shook his head and waved one hand to erase that nickname from the air. "Rolland Mann will back me on this. The Nadler boy was strung up and left to die because he saw Toby Wilder murder that wino. There's no chance he identified the wrong kid. They went to the same school. And there were three other witnesses. They all named Toby as the wino's killer — and fifteen years later, all three of 'em get strung up in the Ramble. Toby is the Hunger Artist. He was getting even for —"

"Screw the Hunger Artist," said Jack Coffey. "We're not working that case today. Toby was locked up when the Nadler kid was murdered in his hospital bed. Care to spin that one for us, Counselor?"

"All right," said Carlyle, as if this might be a reasonable invitation. "What if those other witnesses lied about Toby and the wino? My theory works even better that way. Suppose Ernest Nadler *knew* they lied? Maybe he threatened to lay the blame on those three kids. Now let's say Ernie's little classmates came to visit him in the hospital."

Coffey pushed back from the table. "So you're telling us *kids* murdered Ernie Nadler?"

"The police guard at the door wouldn't find children suspicious," said the ADA. "Maybe *that* was the cover-up."

"But not the cover-up you bargained for," said Coffey.

"Not the one you got paid for," said Mallory from the back of the room.

Good shot. Carlyle was frozen for a moment. And then one stiff hand tugged at his tie, as if it might be a tight fit today.

Mallory stepped up to the table with her

first lie. "We *know* what you said to the parents." She leaned down to the ADA's ear to bring this bluff home. "You told the Nadlers a student from the Driscol School was arrested for Ernie's assault. But you never said it was Toby Wilder. That wouldn't have made any sense to them. They *knew* their son never blamed that kid for the wino's murder. . . . And you knew it, too."

Every little twitch of Carlyle's mouth was a confession. "I couldn't give the Nadlers any details," said Carlyle. "Juvenile records are sealed."

"And they bought that?" Jack Coffey smiled. He could still be surprised when Mallory's lies came true. "Well, I guess the parents were a little distracted at the time. Maybe they were wondering what to do when their little boy woke up — how to explain his amputated hands."

"But then," said Mallory, "after Ernie was murdered in the hospital — that solved all your problems with the bogus case against Toby Wilder."

"I want a lawyer," said the lawyer.

THIRTY-ONE

I know the headmaster believes me. He goes a little pale while I tell my story in his office. I sit there between my parents. My mother seems embarrassed by murder, and I'm sure my father is disappointed in me for ratting out the wino's killers. The smirking detective stands by the window, hardly listening.

The headmaster knows I'm telling the truth, but he was once a teacher, one of the deaf-and-blind people. I guess that's why he tries not to hear me, shaking his head, shaking out my words. And when I'm gone, he'll probably forget that he ever saw me while I was alive.

— ERNEST NADLER

"Hey, man, you're early." Chick Dolan smiled and waved the detective into his Chelsea loft.

"Nice digs." Riker had no idea that writing musical arrangements paid so well. The price of New York living space was measured in light, and the street side was almost solid glass. No interior walls — only furnishings to define the spaces for sleeping and lounging, shooting a game of pool — and work. Riker admired the grand piano. He was about to ask what came of Toby Wilder's musical score for a jazz symphony.

"This is it." Chick handed him a CD. "Nothing fancy, not like a studio cut. Just a crummy pocket recording from the rehearsal session. But that's your music, and now I know who those riffs belong to. I should've remembered the other night in Birdland. I'm gettin' old. Listen here." He played a ripple of piano keys. "This kid — well, he wouldn't be a kid anymore, maybe in his fifties now. I didn't know him well, and I sure didn't know him long — just his style. He was a studio musician when he wasn't playing clubs. He's got credit lines on at least ten of those albums." Chick pointed to the large freestanding bookcase behind them.

Riker whistled. There were enough CDs, vintage cassettes and old vinyl records to open a small music library.

"You won't find any written scores for the best of them," said Chick. "This guy

441

couldn't even read sheet music. He was all tunes in freefall, improvisations on a theme. Finest kind. So his style comes shining through every time. Jess left the scene twenty years ago. Back in the day, he played the sax better than any man on the planet. Now, on piano, I'd have to say he was merely fucking marvelous."

Riker hefted the CD in his hand. "So he's in the wind."

"On the run? I wish. No, Jess was still young when he flamed out, and then he drank himself away. Last I heard, he was panhandling on the street, but that was ages ago. Sorry, man. You got this dead-end look in your eye."

Charles Butler opened the door of his apartment to greet his second guest of the day, the detective who did *not* hold a grudge against him.

When Riker entered the front room, Mallory flashed a look of irritation. *Always late.* Her partner held up a CD as a peace offering. "Chick Dolan's buddies recorded the music, and it's not a total loss." He smiled, possibly waiting for some sign of interest from her. Giving up on this idea, he handed Charles the sheet music transcribed from Toby Wilder's walls. "Chick underlined all

the signature passages. And he gave me a
—"

"You're interrupting," said Coco.

"Sorry, kid." Riker gave the disk to Charles
and then joined his partner on the couch,
where he patiently listened as Coco explained how a cat-size rat could fit through
a hole the size of a quarter.

Charles opened the doors of an
eighteenth-century armoire that hid a
twenty-first-century stereo, a stack of state-
of-the-art components, and one of them
would even play his collection of archaic
vinyl records. This was the only electronic
gift from Mallory that he actually liked and
used. She had wired his entire apartment to
surround him in sound so that he could
walk around inside of sonatas and sympho-
nies. He slipped in Riker's CD, but hesitated
on the play button until Coco had concluded her lecture on the compression factor of rat bones.

"Sorry I'm late," said Riker. "I made a
stop at the Hall of Records." He leaned
across Coco to hand his partner a sheet of
paper. "That's a birth certificate for Toby.
The kid's father was Jess Wilder, a *great* sax
player." He turned to Charles. "Chick says
the style is pure Jess, but the guy couldn't
read or write sheet music. And he only

played other people's tunes."

Charles pressed the play button. "Then this score belongs to Toby." He riffled the pages of sheet music to see all the highlighted passages. "But the father's influence is everywhere." Literally. He saw it everywhere on all the pages.

And now he could hear it as well — all around him.

A rippling passage from a saxophone began the overture, and other instruments dropped in notes with a perfect balance of sound from speakers on every wall, drums to the right of him, strings to the left. Piano keys, soft as shadows, followed the saxophone through the music that wound throughout the room.

"I don't care how gifted the father was." Charles paused for a wilding of notes, an auditory landscape of windblown strings and horns. "A man who can't write sheet music can't do an orchestration for fifty instruments. This is the son's creation."

Charles lost his train of thought, as did they all. And they heard out the rest of the work, waiting for a crescendo. The tension was exquisite — any moment — soon, *soon*. Every chin was lifted, waiting to catch the high notes when they crashed to earth. But then the music wandered off, tapering down to the sax playing solo notes that ended mid-sentence, and a piano finished the saxophone's song.

This departure from the logical progression of music was akin to defying gravity. "Beautiful — and *original.*"

Charles riffled a drawer to find the police photographs of music writ on walls, and he laid them out on the coffee table in front of the detectives, pointing to places in every picture where notes had been whited out and written over. "Toby altered the very structure of the bones — his underlying melody. You can actually see the creative process at work."

Ah, but now he could also see that Mallory wanted the short version. After years of training him, she had only to raise one spread hand, a signal for him to cut to the best part — something useful.

"It's not derivative work," said Charles. "It's a virtual fusion of father and son. I think Jess Wilder was still in Toby's life when the boy was locked up in Spofford."

"If the father is the saxophone," said Coco, "he's dead." In unison, every pair of eyes turned to the little girl, and she picked up on this as a cue to perform. "It's a story." She pointed to the stereo. "Play the last part again."

Mallory walked to the stereo and cued up the last few cuts of the disk. Now the symphony played once more, and Coco stood center stage in the middle of the room. Her eyes closed, and she lifted her face, hands cupped as if to catch rain. Charles fancied that he could actually see music washing over her.

"You hear it?" Coco opened her eyes. "There's something wrong with the saxophone."

"That's a stylistic effect," said Charles.

The child shook her head in both denial and a warning. "*No*, the saxophone is *sick*."

Now Charles realized this was not a conversation. He had interrupted her performance. "Sorry." He sat down on the couch beside the other two members of the child's audience.

"This is a story about the saxophone." The symphony was nearing its end, and Coco pointed at thin air, here and there, as if she could see the notes winging by. "This is the place where the saxophone dies." And then they were down to the last instrument, a velvet piano solo. "And this is loneliness. The piano loved the saxophone, and now it's crying."

"Flowers," said Mallory. "Toby's flowers."

"What?" Charles turned to see the back

of the detective as she slipped into the foyer, heading for the door. Coco ran to hug Mallory goodbye, delaying the escape but not by long. And Riker followed close behind his partner.

The detectives sat at their facing desks, sifting through the recent fruits of search warrants for ADA Carlyle's home and office. They were looking for flowers.

Riker found the original booking sheet for Toby Wilder, age thirteen. "Here's a note under tattoos and identifying marks. 'Left arm. Numerals.' Everything after that is crossed out." He stared at the scribbled-over line. "What do you bet that's when the booking cop figured out that the kid drew it with a pen? Say Toby's got a pen but no paper, so he writes stuff on his arm. We all do that."

"I don't," said Mallory.

Riker studied the crossed-out numerals mistaken for a child's tattoo. Some of the printed figures were still partially visible. "Hey, this ends with letters." He handed her the booking sheet. "Can you make 'em out?"

She held the paper up to the bare bulb of her desk lamp. "Looks like an old toe-tag number. I can't work out the whole date, but the letters — that's a designation for Potter's Field."

"Where they would've buried the wino," said Riker. "So Toby paid a visit to the morgue. And he got up close and personal with the wino's corpse — close enough to read a toe tag."

Mallory flipped through pages of Carlyle's confiscated files. "If the kid saw the wino's body, he never made a formal ID. The morgue would've sent the form to the ADA on that case, and it's not here."

"Okay," said Riker, "but the kid *was* at the morgue. That's the only way he could've seen a toe-tag number. It's too long to memorize — so Toby writes it on his arm when nobody's looking." He said this on the possibility that his partner *might* be listening to him. "That could only happen *before* Toby was questioned on the Nadler kid's assault. He was in custody after —"

"It all comes down to the flowers." Mallory stared at a document from the files. "And here they are again. Toby brought flowers into the Ramble. The way it's written up here, he laid them down in the place where they found the dead wino. If this is true, it looks like Toby witnessed that murder. That's how he knew where to lay his flowers."

"Or Toby did the killing," said Riker. "And maybe he strung up the Nadler kid, too. Did you believe Carlyle when he said Ernest Nadler was a witness to the wino's murder?"

"Who knows? If there ever was a witness statement, you know it got shredded fifteen years ago."

"Yeah." Elbows planted on his desk, Riker rested his head in his hands. "And we still got nothing solid on Rocket Mann. Chief Goddard's gonna shit a brick if that bastard comes up clean. We're screwed."

"Maybe not." Mallory turned her laptop around to show him a screen from the NYPD archives. "Ernest Nadler was strung up for at least three days . . . but there's no report on file with Missing Persons — or any other department." She smiled. "The kid doesn't come home from school one day. After a few hours, his parents get worried. Dinnertime comes and goes. Then it gets dark outside. There's no record that they ever called the police. But most parents really like their kids. And that's how I know they ran all the way to the nearest police station — on the Upper West Side."

"Rocket Mann's old precinct when he was a detective. Bastard — he probably shined off the paperwork."

"But the parents keep coming at him,"

said Mallory. "Days go by. Maybe Mann sends out the uniforms to knock on some doors in the neighborhood. The Nadlers are half crazy. Eventually, just to shut them up, Detective Mann does a little work, checks out the kid's hangouts and his friends. Then somebody put him on to the Ramble."

"Okay, that explains why he was on the spot when Ernie was found hanging in a tree." Riker lifted one hand in a gesture of *So?*

"Now back up," said Mallory. "What if there's a reason why Mann wound up with the parents of a missing kid? Maybe it wasn't just luck of the draw when the Nadlers walked into the station house. What if the parents already knew Detective Mann?"

"*Before* their kid went missing? You figure Mann was the cop who took down Ernie's statement on the wino murder?"

"I know he was." Mallory pointed to highlighted text on her screen. The old entry named Rolland Mann as the detective assigned to the murder of a nameless derelict. "If Ernie came forward, he would've given his witness statement to the cop who owned that case. The parents would've been there with their son . . . and that was the first time they met Rocket Mann."

"Then later, when their kid goes missing,

the Nadlers ask for help from the only cop they know."

Rolland Mann's wife sat up in the dark. She rose from their bed and left the room. Lately, Annie seemed to have an internal clock for the scary hours when she was afraid to sleep — afraid of him. When morning came, he would find her lying on the couch, where she felt safe — safer. This pattern had begun with the first morning paper to carry a new piece of a very old puzzle. Perhaps Annie already knew what he had done.

But fifteen years had passed, and she was still alive. What more proof of love did Annie require?

No sleep tonight.

Rolland reached out to the nightstand, picked up his cell phone and turned it on to check his messages. Ten of them were from ADA Carlyle. And a new one was ringing through. He held the phone to his ear. "Yes? . . . What witness statement? . . . You *moron.* They scammed you. How much did you tell them?" He glanced at the lighted dial of the alarm clock. Right about now, the detectives of Special Crimes Unit would be pulling records for the final phone call of a terrified ADA reaching out to him — in

451

the scary hour.

Phoebe Bledsoe lay in her bed — listening — eyes moving from window to window.

Click, click. What was that? Bedcovers fell away as she sat bolt upright. Was someone trying the lock on the door? No. She recognized the hum of the refrigerator's automatic ice-cube maker. More cubes clicked into their plastic container. Phoebe lay back on the pillow. So — only imagining things — she was too good at that. And still she could not lose the fear that someone was out there.

And in here, Dead Ernest was with her, a little corpse lying beside her in the dark.

"I counted on you," he said. "I thought you'd come for me. . . . I waited. I held on, because of *you*." Dead Ernest moved closer to whisper in her ear. "You were a witness, too. And now Willy's out there somewhere." He nodded toward the window. "I hear footsteps. She's coming for you. Now you know how it feels."

The greatest flaw in her homemade wraith was the lack of a heart. This little doppelgänger only bore a physical resemblance to her old friend. Even the way it smiled lacked Ernie's personality. But what of the real boy, the living child — what if he *had* counted on her to come for him — to save him?

She had never been allowed to visit Ernie during his monthlong coma. Humphrey had told her why: "Mom and Dad don't want you to know his hands were hacked off." Taking this for no more than routine torture by her brother, she had not believed it then. Not then. But, because she was an invisible child, ignored by everyone, she had found her way into Ernie's hospital room.

To this day, she would not allow Dead Ernest to pull his phantom hands from his pockets — to discover what had been done to him during the long sleep.

There was a rap, tap, tap on a window-pane. In a small, still rational compartment of her brain, she knew this was only a tree branch knocking around in the wind. She rose from her bed and hesitated before parting the curtain, only intending to peek through a slit.

She sucked in her breath and lost her balance, falling to the floor and dragging down the curtain with its rod. Willy Fallon's face was pressed up against the glass, fleshy features smeared in monstrous distortions.

Phoebe screamed.

Willy laughed.

THIRTY-TWO

Aggy the Biter pulls back the collar of my shirt. Maybe she wants to admire her handiwork, but the last bite mark has faded since class picture day.

This time, when they threaten to kill me, I point out that they've been trying to do that all year. I even know this will make the beating worse. I just can't help it — sarcasm is my best superpower. But Humphrey just giggles and walks away with the girls.

All day long, I wait for them to come at me. Anticipation is a killer.

— ERNEST NADLER

On her knees, Phoebe Bledsoe scrubbed the marking-pen letters from her cottage door. Only two words — and *still* Willy had managed an error in grammar. The scrawled message YOUR NEXT was faint now, but only a coat of paint would make it disappear.

Phoebe dropped her sponge, startled by the sound of footsteps coming up behind her.

"It's only me." Mr. Polanski came to the end of the flagstone path. Keys jingled on his belt loop as he hunkered down by her side. "I called the headmaster at his summer home. He won't let me change the gate lock. He says it's an antique. Well, you know how the school feels about every really old thing. So I didn't even ask if I could put a chain and a padlock on that gate. . . . I thought the headmaster might say no." The old watchman smiled and held up a small key. "This goes to your new padlock, Miss Phoebe." And now he handed her another one. "That's the spare. You're the only one with keys. Do you feel safe now?"

Did she? Would she ever?

Dr. Slope was not available, but a more agreeable pathologist was on call this morning. Mallory stood before him, hands on hips, her way of saying, *Give up.* And the man responded well to intimidation — less work for the detectives.

"It's not here." The young doctor faced his computer monitor. "No death certificate

455

on file, not under that name."

"Okay, pal," said Riker. "Let's say we're just shopping for a dead wino. We'll take anything you had in stock that day." The date they had given him corresponded to the death of a homeless man in the Ramble, the unidentified murder victim of Toby Wilder's plea bargain.

The man in the lab coat scrolled down the screen and then stopped. "Got it. There's only one body that fits. No name, just a number. It was found in Central Park." He tapped the keys to call up autopsy photographs. "Well, two odd things. There's a big gap between the time this John Doe came in and when the paperwork was finished. And see here? These pictures show damage from a beating, but the body was never cracked open."

"You gotta be kidding me." Riker leaned down to the screen image of a savagely beaten corpse. "This guy's a mess. He was a murder victim."

"Yes, sir, he was. And that's noted right here."

Mallory motioned for the pathologist to get up and get out of her way. She slid into his chair to click through the photographs one by one. "No good head shots. The beating really bloodied up his face. We'll never get an ID from these pictures. Wait. Look at this one."

Riker stared at a close-up shot of an injury to the flesh. A scalpel lay next to the body, and this was the only guide to scale. "A bite mark."

Mallory nodded. "*Little teeth.* Kids killed the wino."

Riker turned to the pathologist. "Why the third-rate autopsy? A homeless bum wasn't worth the time?" He pointed to the screen. "Nobody thought that was weird enough for a closer look?"

"We want an exhumation," said Mallory. "We want it *now.*"

"I understand you two are slandering the reputation of my department?" The chief medical examiner had suddenly become available to the police.

Kathy Mallory stood next to the computer in Edward Slope's private office. "I need your password to bring up the autopsy photos."

"Of course you do," said the doctor, sardonic to the bone.

His young assistant sat down at the keyboard with the impression that the detective might actually need help.

When the file was retrieved, copied and

laid on Slope's desk, he scanned the top sheet. "This autopsy was done by Dr. Costello, not the best pathologist I ever had. He didn't last long." And this file was brief. A few minutes later, he looked up from his reading. "I don't have a problem with the findings in the bloodwork. A call of alcoholism works nicely with a notation that the victim smelled like a brewery. The blood-alcohol level is the highest possible for a man in an upright position." Next, he glanced at pictures of the corpse. "The cause of death was obviously a beating. It's quite well documented here."

He rose from his desk to stand behind the younger pathologist at the computer. "Raymond, bring up our social calendar for the same date." Slope leaned down to scrutinize the text on-screen. "When this body was examined, we had four corpses stacked up from a nightclub shootout. Now, *those* victims got full autopsies. But we also had three upstanding taxpayers killed in a traffic accident. The one with the severed head was driving a BMW convertible. Could there be a more obvious cause of death? No, I think not. And the well-heeled, headless guy didn't get any more attention than your favorite wino." Edward Slope smiled as another conspiracy theory turned to ashes.

Mallory leaned over his desk and spread out the autopsy photographs until she found the picture that she liked best. "So . . . if you'd done this one yourself . . . if you'd seen those little teeth marks." She let the rest of her question dangle.

Slope snatched up the photo and stared at it. "Very *small* teeth marks — a child's teeth." And now he went through each shot, taking more time, looking closer. "Didn't I say that Dr. Costello was not a shining star in this department?" He laid the pictures down. "To answer your question — I would've done a full autopsy and pulled out all the stops." He had clearly underestimated the incompetence of his erstwhile pathologist. How could the man have missed this extraordinary evidence of a very uncommon murder? And the answer? It was in the notation, *'smells like a brewery,'* and the John Doe designation of a homeless man — as if this might justify a three-minute autopsy on a busy day with more reputable corpses stacking up on the tables. "This doesn't change the fact that your wino was beaten to death. And you know bite-mark identification is wildly overrated."

Kathy Mallory laid down the photograph of a smiling schoolboy wearing blazer and tie — and a partial bite mark on his neck.

"I say it's a match. If your man had bothered to write up a kid's bite marks on the wino's body, that case would never have been fobbed off on a probie detective like —"

Edward Slope held up one hand, a signal that there was no need to finish that accusation. Smiling, he picked up the school photograph. "And now, of course, it's clearly *my* fault the Nadler boy was murdered."

As if in agreement, she said, "It's not too late for a better autopsy on the wino."

"Yes, it is." The younger doctor sat at the computer, reading text on the screen. "The wino's body was claimed ten years ago for private burial, but that's the only mention of a second internment. No details, no idea where the body was buried the second time."

Riker pulled out a notebook. "What's the name on the exhumation order?"

"There isn't one," said the assistant. "There's no record of the city paying to dig him up. And the body wouldn't come back here unless there was a question about cause of death. So — if there's no police interest — we don't need to sign off on it. Any judge could've approved the exhumation."

"Somebody had to identify that body

while it was still fresh," said Mallory, "still here."

"We keep scrupulous logs on visitors," said Slope. "But the computer will only show you a list of people who made positive IDs. And no one did — not in this case. We still don't have a name for your dead wino."

"What about the sign-in sheets for visitors?" said Riker.

"Fortunately, we never throw anything away," said Edward Slope. "Now, if you give me a year, I *might* find those sheets in a storage facility in one of the outer boroughs — assuming the paper isn't *completely* rotted away — or covered with mold — maybe eaten by mice." He said this last part purely for the entertainment of his assistant.

The detectives were gone.

Mallory held a fax sheet of names and dates close to the blind attorney's ear. And Anthony Queen could hear her crumple it into a tight ball. "The funeral home gave you up, old man." She bounced the paper ball off his desk to make him flinch.

"According to Graves Registration," said Riker, "Toby's mother was buried upstate in a family plot. There were *two* burials that day — Susan Wilder and that wino Toby killed."

"He never killed anyone. He was innocent."

"Spoken like a true ambulance chaser," said Mallory. "A year after the kid's release, he gave you a coffin number to claim the body for burial. Toby got that number from a toe tag when the wino's corpse was still in the morgue. There's no other way he could've picked the right pine box in Potter's Field. And he brought flowers into the Ramble — to the exact spot where the man's body was found. How did that kid know where to put the flowers if he didn't kill the wino?"

The old man made no denial. Though Riker could come up with alternate explanations, the lawyer could not. Now, *that* was interesting. "So you always knew."

"No. I didn't," said Anthony Queen. "I gave the coffin number to a funeral home. They claimed the body, not me."

"I stand corrected," said Riker. "You didn't *want* to know."

"Toby waited until his mother died," said Mallory. "That's when the wino's body was claimed. Toby didn't want her to know the murdered man was Jess Wilder. That's the name he had engraved on the wino's tombstone. You let that kid plead guilty to murdering his own father."

Anthony Queen appeared to be in shock — if the blank stare could be believed. He seemed not to notice that the detectives had walked out of his office. They were standing in the reception room when Riker looked back to see the lawyer lay his head on the desk. Was this an act of sorrow — or just an act? He made a mental note to ask Coco if rats could feel remorse.

Mallory and Riker stood before a cork wall in the incident room, pinning up the evidence that flowed from Toby Wilder's flowers.

Other detectives wandered in after no success in canvasing Ernest Nadler's old neighborhood. They had been following up on the death certificates for the boy's parents, who had died soon after losing their son. Fifteen years later, the building super had changed, and so had many of the tenants. The last man through the door, Janos, had struck gold, and now he tacked a yellow sheet of lined paper to the wall.

Riker donned his bifocals to read the small, neat handwriting. It was a witness statement, written and signed by a resident of the murdered boy's apartment building. "Mallory, listen to this. It's about Ernie's parents. The neighbor, Irene Walters, says, 'I never knew Ernie was missing. I did know he was seriously ill, but not the details. His parents were never home. Always at the hospital with Ernie, days, nights, all the time. I tried to see the boy once, but the policeman who guarded the door would only allow immediate family. Well, I guess a month went by.

" 'I came outside one morning, and there were people gathered on the other side of the street. They were all looking up at my building. I remember hearing sirens when I crossed the street. I turned back, and there they were. Ernie's parents stood on the ledge outside their window. They were holding hands. They were always holding hands whenever I saw them out walking. And there was no fear at all when they stepped off the ledge — like they were just out for a stroll in the sky. It seemed to take forever before they hit the sidewalk. And that's when I knew their little boy had died.' "

Coco took on the scale of a doll as she sat on Detective Janos's massive lap and recited the list of poisons favored for killing vermin. Charles Butler walked down the hall to the incident room, where he was wanted. He looked back once to see Janos, that most excellent playmate, extending his hands to illustrate a measure, no doubt describing the biggest rat he had ever seen.

The tall psychologist entered the room lined with cork. One wall was decked with photographs of autopsied bodies and Toby Wilder's musical score — blood and song. The rest of the space was dedicated to pages of text, maps and diagrams. Detectives in shirtsleeves stood in clusters, examining a wall of documents.

Charles walked toward the only woman. His relationship with Mallory was so at odds these days. He approached her now like an awkward teenager bent on asking a pretty girl if she might like to dance with him — or spit on him — one of those two things. In lieu of hello, the young detective tapped a sheet of paper pinned to the cork, and he turned his head to read an eyewitness account of two people stepping off a ledge to their deaths.

"Somebody's going to pay for that," she said. "We need a psychological autopsy."

"As court evidence? But Edward's staff does that sort of thing, and probably with much more —"

"Naw," said Riker, coming up behind him. "It would take weeks to get the final report from Slope's people. You can do it faster."

Mallory led him to the place where hospital records papered the wall. And he knew this was her work, this neat precision that other people could only manage with a ruler and a carpenter's level. This section was devoted to medical charts, bills and accounting sheets for the care of a child, age eleven. "We can't even find the boy's ashes," she said. "This is all that's left of the Nadlers' son."

Charles strolled down the wall, trying not to be too obvious about reading at light speed with all these eyes on him. To the casual observer, he might be only browsing as he took in every word, the whole grim hospital history of a little boy who had lost his hands and then his life. Upon reaching the end of the papers, the end of the boy, he turned to the two detectives.

"I'll tell you what's not here. According to the neighbor's statement, the parents spent all their days and nights at the hospital. So I'm sure they were given a room and a bed near the intensive care unit — a common practice. The Nadlers probably slept in shifts so one of them could be with their son all the time."

He backed up to the sheet that transferred Ernest Nadler from intensive care to a private room. "The boy was out of danger for the last week of his life, but I know the parents still stayed with him, day and night. This is a suite — very expensive — a second room and a bed for the mother and father. They didn't want Ernest to be alone when — *if* — he should come out of the coma. I'm certain of that. The amputated hands — no parent would want a child to face that horror without them."

He walked to the end of the wall and tapped three papers. "These statements didn't come from the hospital. They're from a private nurse — a freelancer."

"Huh?" Riker checked the exhibit numbers against the list on his clipboard. "You're right. That paperwork came from a storage locker with the Nadlers' personal effects — and their unopened mail."

"Well, this is the saddest part of the story," said Charles. "By the time the boy was stabilized and on the mend, the parents must've been exhausted. They hired a private nurse to sit by the bed — just a few hours here and there. By this time, the parents were in desperate need of a break — some fresh air, a quiet dinner outside of the hospital — something *normal.* And during one of these rare absences — while the nurse was on duty — their little boy died."

Riker stepped closer to read the time sheet for the nurse's last shift. "Nobody caught that. We're still plowing through all this stuff."

Charles walked back to the beginning of his tour and stood before the witness account of the double suicide. "These two people were drained by an emotional rollercoaster ride. According to the patient charts, their child was improving. They were looking forward to bringing him home. And then, with no warning, their son died. I know they blamed themselves. Guilt always follows a death in the family. But there's more to it than that. You see, they didn't just leave the boy to a common sitter from a temp service. They hired a registered nurse, the best watcher that money could buy. And why? Because they'd spent a solid month in that place. They would've heard all the stories, all the things that might befall a helpless child left to the vagaries of the hospital staff. But they left him — dropped their vigilance for an hour — and he died. Exhaustion, grief . . . guilt. They stepped off the ledge to stop the pain." He turned to face the detectives. "There's no mystery here."

"So whoever murdered their son — he killed the parents, too," said Mallory. "Can you put that in writing?"

"Complicity in the suicide, yes. You'll have

468

my finding by the end of the day." Charles turned back to the wall. "Wouldn't there be a policeman guarding a crime victim's room?"

"Twenty-four seven," said Riker. "But the cop's only there for protection. We got no record of who went in and out of the kid's room. Fifteen years ago, nobody knew Ernie Nadler was murdered in his bed. So nobody interviewed the only witness — the cop on duty when it happened."

"But *you* did?"

"He's a drunk," said Riker. "Soup for brains. The guy can't remember squat."

"What about the nurse?"

"We'll look for her." Mallory pulled the nurse's time sheet from the wall. "But what are the odds she'll admit to stepping out of the room while somebody offed her patient?"

"The parents only used that woman three times," said Charles. "Those are very rare windows of opportunity."

"I see where you're going," said Riker. "We still got the cop who did guard duty on the kid. He's in an interview room. But I don't think he'll remember making any phone calls to our killer."

Now Mallory was taking a new interest in the nurse's time sheet. "There's a pattern of three dinner hours, the same time three nights in a row." She smiled. "Rolland Mann would've known about that. If the kid was improving, he'd want to know when his star witness woke up. He'd keep close tabs on everything — including this nurse. So he wouldn't need a heads-up from the cop on guard duty."

Eyes closed in sleep, Police Commissioner Beale lay on the hospital bed of the intensive care unit. The old man's security detail had been stripped down to a single officer, who sat by the door on the other side of the busy ward — out of sight, out of earshot, the next best thing to not being there. Beale was so frail, half dead by the look of him. He could not last much longer.

Sooner was better.

Rolland Mann could have done without the old man's job, but now absolute power was a prerequisite to contain the chaos of his unraveling life. He stared at the tubes running in and out of the patient's every orifice. Beeping monitors of colored lights recorded the beats of a badly damaged heart and every breath.

So fragile — vulnerable.

THIRTY-THREE

I can see the pastor at my funeral one day.
I can hear him say, "Little Ernie was a
good boy, a fine boy. He didn't have an
enemy in the world." Then the old twit nat-
ters on about the mysterious ways in
which God works to murder little children
on their way home from school. And a
ghost of me screams, "You jerk, there's no
mystery! I told EVERYBODY!"
— ERNEST NADLER

Hours into a second shift, the nurse remained at the bedside of the heart patient,
Police Commissioner Beale. The woman
showed the wear of a long night into day,
yet she continued to smooth the sheets each
time the old man stirred.

"You can leave," said Rolland Mann. "Get
a cup of coffee. I'll stay with him till you
—" His words broke off at the shake of her
head.

She was not going anywhere. This point was made by her white shoes firmly planted and by her boxer's stance. Had this woman sized him up? Had some intuition informed her that he was not to be trusted? No, it was more than that. The nurse glanced at her watch and then turned to a gap in the privacy curtain.

Waiting for reinforcements?

Beyond the curtain, he could see the police officer he had handpicked for this security detail. Nothing out of the ordinary there. The doors to the ward swung open, and another man in uniform entered the ward. The regular guard then walked out the door, leaving his post.

On whose authority?

The nurse raised her hand, hailing the new arrival, "Officer Wycoff?"

"Yes, ma'am." The young policeman stepped inside the confines of the privacy curtain and faced down Rolland Mann. "I'll need to see some ID, sir."

"What? I'm your *boss.*"

"No, sir, that would be my sergeant. And he gets his orders from —"

"Never mind." Rolland waved one hand to spare himself the litany of command ranks. He doubted that this idiot could tell him who had dared to countermand the orders of an acting police commissioner. The chief of police would never cross him; he was certain of that. His anxiety was climbing as he considered the mayor and wondered who had that little man's ear today. Rolland pushed through the doors of the ward and walked down the corridor. He felt a constriction in his chest, the kind that came with fear. This linked to thoughts of Mallory, the whack-job cop. And, along her chain of command, he was led to the most likely adversary, Chief of Detectives Joe Goddard.

Rolland pressed the button to summon the elevator. Before the doors could open, he had formed a plan to transfer Goddard to the Criminal Justice Bureau, a place where out-of-favor chiefs were sent to be buried alive.

The unofficial investigation of Rolland Mann required a meeting in neutral territory. Riker had chosen a comfort zone for the chief of detectives, and now he waited for the man in the southwest corner of Washington Square Park.

Riker had loved this place in the summers of his younger days when it was open twenty-four hours, an all-night, all-day circus of jugglers and fire eaters and all kinds of freaks, boys and girls with guitars, loud boom boxes and mellow horns. Oh, and the smells — pastrami and hot dogs, women's perfume walking by, cigarette smoke and marijuana. But years ago, a curfew had been imposed by a previous mayor, whose friends had complained that their little darlings were scoring drugs in the park. Teenagers smoking dope — who knew? Fences had gone up, and one more of life's charms had been lost to nights in Greenwich Village. Now, on hot summer days, the vendors hawked odorless ice cream and sodas from look-alike carts with white-and-green umbrellas — so clean, so sterile.

This city was going to hell.

The sun beat down on the center of a small plaza defined by curved blocks of stone, tall trees and a circle of small tables footed in cement. Benches were bolted into the asphalt floor, but these seats were not for the weary. This corner of the park was a haven for chess hustlers. Riker moseyed over to a game in progress and flashed his badge. "Sorry, guys, I need your table."

Both men obliged him too eagerly, rising to leave with wide smiles, a good clue that they were carrying drugs and maybe dealing, too.

"Not so fast," he said.

They dropped their smiles, correctly guessing that their escape had been entirely too easy. But all the detective wanted was conversation. He showed them a cell-phone picture of Joe Goddard, and they gave up the chief of detectives as a regular in this corner of the park.

"Yeah, he plays every Sunday," said the older man.

And his young friend said, "That mother-fucker's a real *bad*ass player."

In the parlance of New York City, there could be no higher praise.

"Well, this is my first game with the guy," said Riker. "Any tips on strategy?"

"Hey, man, you got a gun, right? I guess that's all you need."

Enough said.

The detective cut them loose and settled down at the small table. The players and dealers at neighboring tables had already slipped away. He watched people strolling through this plaza entry to the park. It was no longer easy to tell the Village residents from the tourists and the NYU students. They were all wearing clothes from the same summer catalogue, and every head of hair was a color found in nature — no more neon highlights or rainbow Mohawks. The oddball madness was long gone — and he missed it.

Riker opened a paper sack and pulled out his recent purchase from a toy store. This chess set was a cheap one, cheesy as they come, with plastic pieces and a board of stiff paper. He had not played this game since Kathy Mallory's puppy days. After he had taught her enough to finally beat him, the little thief had stolen one of his chessmen as a souvenir, and he had never thought to replace it.

He leaned back. No clouds today. The sun was —

A massive bulk blocked out the light. The detective raised his eyes to see the chief of D's casing the plaza, looking for faces out of place, an old habit of the fine cop he used to be — back in the days when he was dangerous in a good way.

Joe Goddard looked down at the detective's sorry plastic chessmen with disdain. "You better have something for me."

"I do," said Riker. "I got solid proof that a high-ranking cop buried evidence of murder. Actually, he was just sitting on it. But that's a firing offense, right? And maybe some jail time for obstruction."

"It took you guys long enough." The chief sat down on the other side of the small table. "Let's see it."

Riker took his time fumbling in his pockets for a match. He lit a cigarette and killed a few more seconds exhaling a blue cloud of smoke. Then he tapped the board in an invitation to play. "White or black?"

"What?" The chief's eyes narrowed with the understanding that there was another kind of game in the works. "You don't wanna screw with me, Riker." And never mind the rule of white goes first. The chief picked up a black pawn and slammed it down on an adjoining square. The other pieces rattled. "Time's running out for you and your partner — *especially* your partner."

The detective nudged a white pawn two squares down the board. Next, he borrowed a leaf from the Mallory Manual for Survival in Copland: *When in trouble with the boss, shoot first.* "You lied to us." Riker slipped sheets of paper off his lap and laid them down on the edge of the table. This was Goddard's own evidence, copies of Patrolman Kayhill's old notes, written fifteen years ago on the night a child was cut down from a tree.

Silence. Then came the slam of another black pawn. "Explain yourself, or kiss your badge goodbye."

Riker's move. "That doesn't scare me."

He launched another white pawn. "But I'm so good at my job, sometimes I scare myself." His eyes were on the chessboard, and, for all he knew, the chief was pointing a gun at his head. "You were right about Officer Kayhill. Alzheimer's fried his brain." He looked up to see a flicker of surprise cross the chief's face — just a flicker. "The nursing home tells me his wife died a while back. These days, Kayhill only has one visitor — and it's not you. So I had to wonder how you got the old guy's personal notes. I looked up his daughter. Nice lady. She lives on Staten Island. That's where Kayhill was transferred the day after he found the Nadler kid strung up in the Ramble."

In quick succession, more pawns were moved to open the backfield for the power pieces, and one of Riker's captured chessmen went flying off the board to clatter on the asphalt. "Kayhill's daughter remembers you coming out to the island to see her old man. You were a captain then — like visiting royalty. She's not sure exactly when you showed up, but she says they were still unpacking boxes from the move. I figure that's when you collected her father's personal notes on the Ramble assault. I bet I can pin that date down to Rocket Mann's first big promotion. Did that get your attention? Him going from a baby dick to a gold shield?"

Goddard's bishop was rushing down the board in a play of sudden death, when Riker said, "Fifteen years ago, Officer Kayhill had no ID for the park victim. So . . . it took me a while to figure out how you made the jump to Ernest Nadler."

The chief flung a captured pawn at the low stone wall with enough force to crack the plastic man. "I *told* you . . . *and* your partner. The Nadler kid was missing three days before —"

"His death certificate was issued a month later," said Riker. "If he died from his injuries, it was murder. No other way to read it. But you couldn't find any record of an investigation. You *knew* Rocket Mann buried that case. You've known it for fifteen years. Oh, and thanks for giving us your old copy of the Nadler kid's death certificate. Funny thing about that. I mean the date — but not the day the boy died. You picked up your copy the *next* day — when it was filed at the Hall of Records."

This time, a white pawn landed quietly in the grass — ten yards away. The chief turned back to the detective. "You don't know *when* I —"

"Yeah, I do." Riker pushed a chessman to

479

another square, and it hung out there alone in a dangerous neighborhood of the board. "So I know you kept tabs on Ernest Nadler for a solid month. It's like you were just . . . *waiting* for that little kid to die."

One move of the black bishop and a swipe of the chief's hand cleared the white pawn from the table. This one bounced twice. "You're fired."

"I'm so fucking good at my job, I don't think I'll ever get fired." The detective countered with his white rook and watched the chief's bishop retreat — though the piece was not in peril. Riker's queen was. Goddard could have taken it, but now he was dragging out the kill. It was the kind of play that said, *You wanna dance? Okay, we'll dance . . . for a while.* The chief laced his fingers together and waited on the detective's next move.

"Your copy of the death certificate has an *issue* date," said Riker. "It's hand-stamped — real light. It could've passed for a smudge. Not surprising you missed that detail." He laid a different copy of the document on the table. "Here, see? It showed up better on this Xerox — after I jumped up the toner in the machine. The heavy ink brings out the numbers. That's a trick I learned from an old buddy in Documents.

480

Fifteen years ago, you had solid proof that Rocket Mann buried the kid's murder — and you sat on it — 'cause you *knew* it would come in handy one day. So now you're wondering who else knows? . . . Nobody. I put your copy in an evidence bag. Then I went down to the Hall of Records and got me a new one."

With the swipe of one hand, the chief wiped the board clean. The detective never broke eye contact as he listened to the chinks of plastic chessmen raining on the ground.

"What do you want, Riker?"

And what *did* he want? Well, job security for his partner. But what he said was, "Names and numbers. The ones you pulled from Mann's phone. You remember — that throwaway you found in the trash?" Riker pulled out his own cell and clicked through pictures till he came to one of Rolland Mann tossing his phone. "I took that shot the day we interviewed him. You wanted us to flush him out. We did. And then we tailed him. I counted three calls while we were following Rocket Mann — and you." Riker called up another picture.

Chief Goddard looked down at the tiny screen to see a photograph of himself rutting around in a city trashcan for Rolland

Mann's thrown-away cell phone.

"There was no time for a connection on his first two calls," said Riker, "but the guy had a conversation on the third try." When the chief hesitated, Riker folded his arms. "Why would you even *wanna* hold out on us? You plan to keep that weasel for a pet? Or do you want him gone?" The detective opened his notebook to a clean page, and he pulled out a pen. "Who did Rocket Mann call that day?"

"Three calls," said the chief, "but two of them went to the same number."

The detective scribbled Goddard's next words in a quick line ending with a question mark. Then he folded his notebook and rose from the table. "Oh, while I was down at the Hall of Records? I noticed your name was still on file — and the date you picked up your copy of Ernest Nadler's death certificate . . . but I don't think anybody's gonna go looking through those old records." He shrugged. "Why would they?" Ah, but now — an afterthought. "Well, *Mallory* might — if she knew about this." He held up an evidence bag with the chief's own copy of the document, and he left it on the chessboard as a gesture of goodwill — and checkmate.

Riker had arrested cops before, but he had

never extorted one. In mere proximity to Mallory, people's better angels were always dropping like dead houseflies.

Rolland Mann returned home in the middle of the day. His wife dropped a glass from her shaky hand, and it shattered on the kitchen floor. She was terrified. Did he reprimand her? No, he never did that. Long ago, he had become accustomed to her panic attacks, though they had always been occasioned by a fear of public places.

In their early years together, she had preferred to remain indoors, so afraid of being recognized. And now she was housebound. At home, she always felt safe — until now.

He led her into the living room, and they sat down together on the couch. He glanced at the suitcase she had packed and left by the door — as if she could ever leave. On the coffee table, a newspaper was opened to the continuing story of the Hunger Artist and three victims strung up in the Ramble. Though they had never spoken of it, perhaps they should. Annie was clearly making connections. Tomorrow's newspaper might hint at a new development in the case, a tie to a little boy who died long ago — and the double suicide of Mr. and Mrs. Nadler. That would send his nervous wife right over the screaming edge.

He had never told her how the boy's parents had died.

Mallory unbagged lunch for two, spreading cartons of noodles and pork fried rice across the joined desks. She looked up at her partner, suspicious when she said, "Really — how did you get Chief Goddard to give up the numbers?"

"I *told* you. I traded my cell-phone picture of him with his head in that trashcan." *Brat.* She never liked his stories. Riker flipped through his notebook. "Rocket Mann's first call was to Grace Driscol-Bledsoe. Just time enough to go to voice mail, no time for a message. The second call was to his home number. Three seconds. Then he calls home again. That one lasted three minutes. Who's he talking to — an answering machine? He's got no kids, no wife."

THIRTY-FOUR

The hall is crowded when a hand comes over my shoulder and into my shirt pocket. Then I feel another hand in the back pocket of my pants — and another one. Later, in the school garden, behind a tree, I pull out the three notes. They all say the same thing, "Soon!"

— ERNEST NADLER

Their ears would lift up if they were only dogs. That was Jack Coffey's thought when every man in the squad room turned toward the sound of clicking high heels. But this was no sweet young thing coming their way, and the detectives returned to their work — all except Riker. Like a gawker watching a slow train wreck in the making, the detective's eyes followed the society matron as she walked down the aisle of desks. A boxcar line of lawyers and the companion Hoffman trailed behind her.

Lieutenant Coffey could have predicted this visit within an hour of the motion filed to freeze the probate of Humphrey Bledsoe's estate. With a slight nod of acknowledgment, Grace Driscol-Bledsoe sailed past him and through the door to his private office, where her followers filled the space to standing room only. Coffey signaled for Riker to join the party.

The detective took his own time, gathering papers from his desk, and he made a call to Mallory, letting her know that all the lawyers had turned out in force. Silence prevailed in Coffey's office until Riker walked in and announced, "My partner loves money motives." He handed the lady a transcript of her son's school records. "Your kid wasn't too bright. Mallory thinks busting the trust fund wasn't Humphrey's own idea. Did you give him a hand with that?"

"As you already know, Detective, I detested my son. Why would I help him?"

Good point. As mother material, this woman rivaled Medea.

Riker grinned. "Humphrey's millions — that's a motive. You had no way to get at it, not while your kid was locked up in that asylum. And we gotta wonder where all that money came from."

"I *told* you. My late husband funded Humphrey's —"

"Yeah, yeah. He was a political consultant. A lobbyist, right? There's a lot of cash in peddling influence. We think his racket was tied to the Driscol Institute. And that's where you come in, lady."

The lawyers spoke over one another's threats until Coffey yelled, "Hey! You're in *my* house now! Shut the hell up!" He turned a smile on Mrs. Driscol-Bledsoe. In a more civil tone, he asked, "So . . . how dirty *was* your husband's money?"

The lady smiled, enjoying this. "Is it relevant to my son's murder?"

"You bet," said Riker. "If your husband saw an audit coming his way, the kid's trust fund was a great holding pen for the whole fortune. But the guy didn't count on dying young — or his son busting that trust. Then Humphrey gets murdered, and all those millions come back to you — washed clean. Killing your own kid is an original method of laundering money. We've never seen it done that way before."

Still smiling, she said, "And you think I'm capable of that."

"Oh, yeah," said Riker, "but it's not my job to flatter you. So you don't wanna help us close this case? Fine by me. If nobody stands trial for your son's murder, we can freeze Humphrey's millions for the next hundred years. Or not. It's our call."

Jack Coffey was watching the expressions of the attorneys. They all worried in silence. And now he knew the bluff was going to pan out. The lady's face was not so easy to read.

But then she asked, "How may I help you?"

Dead Ernest was only the flotsam of scattered thoughts today. Phoebe Bledsoe sat alone at the table — so very thirsty — waiting for a waitress to notice her, but they kept passing her by — a typical day at the top of the lunch-hour rush, though she went unnoticed in every crowd at any hour.

When Toby Wilder walked into the restaurant, he did not see her, either — except as an appendage of her usual table. If she were not here, he might only notice that a piece of the furniture was missing. But now, as the young man settled in a chair by the window, his eyes fixed on a new arrival, and he could not look away.

Phoebe turned to see the detective, the insane one, standing just inside the open door. The heads of other diners were also turning to look at this tall, pretty blonde.

Invisible Phoebe held her breath as Mallory's searching gaze settled on Toby Wilder, and the woman showed a flash of recognition.

Oh, no, not him.

And then Detective Mallory's green eyes moved on — *slowly* — like gun sights, seeking, seeking. *Gotcha.*

Phoebe flinched.

The detective stepped up to the table and pulled out a chair. "Mind if I sit with you for a few minutes?" Her voice seemed so normal today, words rising and falling with human inflections.

"I'm not supposed to talk to you, Detective — not without an attorney present."

"Right now, the lawyers are all tied up with your mother. Call me Mallory." She remained standing as she looked around the room, then zeroed in on a passing waitress and, with only one raised hand, stopped that frazzled woman in her tracks. Apparently, Mallory had superpowers, for now the waitress came to her, smiling, eagerly offering up a menu — only *one* menu — because Phoebe was invisible.

A hand went to Mallory's hip, and the waitress was at a loss to understand what had displeased her. The detective pointed to Phoebe and said, "I'm with *her.*"

The invisible woman was promptly promoted to a very important person. Now Phoebe listened to a recital of the day's specials and was asked for her preference in salad dressings. A busboy was flagged down, and his tray was raided for a basket of breadsticks and buns, silverware — and an icy glass of water.

So thirsty. *Thank you, thank you.*

When the waitress had departed with the luncheon order, Mallory settled into a chair on the other side of the table. Her face was not unfriendly, and there was nothing crazy about her eyes today; they were merely unsettling. "I'm curious about the family finances. When your father set up Humphrey's trust fund, was that like a bribe so your brother wouldn't leave the asylum?"

"A bribe? No, that trust couldn't be revoked. So it's not like Daddy could threaten to take the money back. And the trust income wasn't paid to Humphrey. It went to his custodian, the asylum."

"So your brother was a cash cow . . . and the doctors were never going to let him go."

"Ironically, that was the argument his lawyers used to break the trust fund and get him released."

"And what about you, Phoebe? You got nothing when your father died. He didn't care about you at all. Did that make you angry?"

"He loved me." There was no defensiveness in Phoebe's tone. This was more like a schoolgirl delivery of incontrovertible fact. *The earth revolves around the sun, and Daddy loved me.*

Nodding, the detective appeared to have no quarrel with this. There was only curiosity in her voice when she said, "But he didn't leave you a dime."

"Daddy didn't *have* a dime. He died broke." Phoebe offered up more factoids. "After he left my mother, he lived in hotels for ten years. That costs a lot of money. And he spent the time drinking himself to death. It surprised him that it took so long to die that way. He worked very hard at it." And now, with great pride, she said, "I paid Daddy's last bar bill."

In the child's fashion of measuring things, she might describe her own smile as six feet wide. And this made Charles Butler smile, too.

"He could've been a lady," said Coco, uncertain as she spoke to Mallory on the one-button cell phone. "I wasn't wearing my glasses."

The little girl gave up one more remembered thing. "A baseball cap pulled down low. . . . No, he didn't say anything. . . . Well, he did, but he talked with his hands." The fingers of her free hand curled to hold an imaginary pencil, and she made a scribbling motion on the air. "Like he wanted something to write with. . . . And then? . . . Uncle Red turned around. . . . I don't know." Her legs drew up. Her smile was gone. Anxious now, Coco raised one arm, as if to ward off a blow. The detective on the other end of this conversation was obviously breaking the rules again with leading questions.

"I don't *know!*"

Charles took the phone from her hand and killed the connection to Mallory with no word of goodbye.

When Riker walked in, the geek room was humming with electronics, and every monitor was aglow.

Mallory laid down her cell phone. "Coco's remembering more details. Our perp wore sunglasses — at *night.*"

"Well, that explains the holes." Previously, the little girl had alluded to great dark holes in the blurry face of Uncle Red's killer.

"There's more," said Mallory. "Before Humphrey's skull was cracked, the killer got him to turn around by asking for a pen — in *sign* language. The Hunger Artist played mute so his voice wouldn't be recognized."

Riker nodded. With these elements of disguise, they could rule out murder for hire. "And how goes the search for the Nadlers' private nurse?"

"She might be dead. She hasn't paid income tax in fifteen years."

"We've got a visitor," said Riker. "Dr. Slope sent her."

The two detectives walked down the hall to the smallest interview room, the one used for private conversations that were neither taped nor covertly watched. One of the three chairs was occupied by Detective Janos, who dunked teabags with a gray-haired woman he introduced as "Dr. Sills — a retired pathologist." Janos rose from the table. "She used to work in the Medical Examiner's Office." He walked toward the door, saying, "She remembers our dead wino."

Riker's smile was broad as he pulled up a chair beside the woman. "Thanks for coming in, ma'am."

"Anything for Edward Slope. He said you were interested in people who came in to view the body of a derelict."

Mallory sat down across the table from the doctor. "You brought paperwork on the wino's ID?"

"There's no paperwork, dear. I brought my memory. Edward had to jog it a bit. He said that corpse was autopsied the same day a traffic fatality came in with a severed head. An unforgettable day. That's when we found the derelict's body. Someone had stored it in a locker that was supposed to be empty. No idea how long it was in there. But I'm sure Edward told you that."

"No," said Riker. "That must've slipped his mind." He would bet that a morgue attendant had pocketed a bribe for *misplacing* that body, another black mark for the Medical Examiner's Office.

"Well, that was odd," said Dr. Sills. "And the paperwork was missing, too. I remember that because we had to call every precinct in Manhattan."

Now the wino was so much more interesting.

"But it doesn't surprise me that Edward forgot the paperwork problems for *that* day."

Riker nodded. Of course not. Why would Dr. Slope give Mallory more ammunition for their next war? Sending in Dr. Sills was probably the ME's idea of remorse for not coming clean. Even a lie of omission would cost that dead-honest man a night's sleep.

"It was total chaos," said the retired pathologist. "A full house between a gang shoot-out and a ten-car pileup — so many corpses, all those poor family members coming in to identify remains. But only one was a child, maybe twelve or thirteen years old. A beautiful boy. He came in all by himself, looking for his father. He broke my heart."

"You remember his name?"

"No, I'm sorry. This was so long ago."

"Does Toby Wilder sound familiar?"

She shook her head. "I did ask for his school ID. It was a private school, I remember that much. I had to call them for the mother's home phone number. Then I had the boy fill out forms to keep him busy until she could get there. It upset him when his mother walked in. I gather he wanted to spare her the ordeal. And then I saw the white cane."

"His mother was blind," said Riker.

"Yes. That's the only reason I allowed her son to view the body. When I pulled back the sheet, the boy began to cry — so quietly, not a sound, only tears. Well, I thought this *must* be his father, but he said no. Then the blind woman said she wanted to *see* the body. She ran her fingertips over the dead

495

man's face, tracing all his features. And then she was crying, too — quietly, like the boy. She wiped her tears with a sleeve — hiding them from her son. That was my impression. Then the mother said it wasn't her husband."

"We read the autopsy report," said Mallory. "The wino's body was skin and bones. Malnutrition. He also had a broken nose, old damage, and a lot of teeth were missing."

"I understand what you're saying, Detective. Yes, that would change a man's features radically. But I assumed there had been some recent family contact — or how would the boy have known to go looking for his father in the morgue?"

"Their reactions bothered you," said Mallory. "You knew there was something wrong. Who cries over a stranger?"

"Yes, that was disturbing."

THIRTY-FIVE

In civics class, I read aloud from my essay on the rules of comportment during a homicide investigation. It's the only class I share with all of them, Humphrey, Willy and Aggy the Biter. While I talk, they never move a hair. They forget how to breathe. I scare them shitless.

It's my best day ever.

— ERNEST NADLER

Riker entered the tony restaurant of the Wall Street crowd. It was all done up in velvet curtains and wood paneling, real silver on the tables and money on the hoof. He pegged the maître d' for an ex-convict. There were no visible prison tats, but the man gave himself away when he did not immediately sneer at the detective's bad suit and scuffed shoes, foreplay to hustling an unwanted customer out the door. Instead, the maître d' saw *cop* in those hooded eyes.

497

Even as a child, Riker had always seemed on the verge of arresting everyone he met. "The deputy police commissioner is expecting me."

With great relief on the part of the man in the better suit, the detective was shown to a table, where a solitary dinner was in progress.

Rolland Mann had found a new way to establish his dominance: divide and humiliate. Riker had been told to come by himself, and now he was commanded, by an offhand gesture, to sit down and watch his superior eat a juicy steak.

The acting police commissioner noticed the turning heads of nearby diners, one man nudging another, and appreciative smiles. He looked up to see Riker's partner framed in a window close to his table. Fortunately, covert surveillance was not Mallory's job tonight. From the other side of the glass, she stared at Rolland Mann in the same way that he had regarded his steak. Laying down his knife and fork, he deigned to speak to the other cop, the silent one at his table. "You were told to come alone."

Ignoring this, Riker fished in his pockets for a notebook. "We opened a new homicide case for Ernie Nadler. Turns out he was murdered in his hospital bed. We interviewed the cop posted outside the kid's room. He remembers you hanging around."

"I was a detective in those days. I had a —"

"So we got parents, doctors, nurses." Riker flipped a notebook page. "And *you*. The cop on guard duty says you visited the kid's room a *lot* in that last week."

And that was a lie. When interviewed, that guard had recalled nothing of the kind. His month of hospital duty had blended into a single memory of boredom only broken by the wail of Mrs. Nadler when she found her son dead. But there was no contradiction from Rolland Mann.

"We've been over this, Riker. You saw the damn tape. You *know* why I had an interest in that little boy."

The detective closed his notebook, a signal to his partner out on the sidewalk. "If you got anything useful on the kid's murder, now's the time to tell me. When did you get to the hospital that night? Was it before or after the kid was murdered?"

"When I left Ernie Nadler's room that *morning,* he was still alive."

Riker jotted down a few words. So Mann *had* been present on the day of the boy's death. "The cop on duty remembers you dropping by in the evening," he lied,

499

"around dinnertime."

"Well, he's wrong! Or maybe he's —"

The conversation stopped abruptly when the maître d' stepped up to the table and laid down a pad of lined yellow paper, the kind favored for witness statements. "Compliments of the lady," he said.

Rolland Mann turned to the window, but the lady was gone.

Riker pointed to the half-eaten steak. "Take that away." The maître d' almost saluted before he hastily cleared the plate from the table — without even a nod to the high-ranking politician who was paying the tab.

The detective pushed the yellow pad in front of the deputy police commissioner. "You know the drill. Just write it all down, everything you remember about the kid's last day." Riker held out the pen, and Rolland Mann took it — automatic reflex. When this move was done right, when the timing was perfect, the interview subject would always take the pen, and then there was nothing left to do but use it.

When the page was filled by half, only two short paragraphs, the acting commissioner laid down the pen and reread his words. He had not yet noticed Mallory quietly standing behind his chair. This was her gift. No one ever heard her coming. Now she bent down close to his ear and said, *"Sign it!"*

The wine went flying as the glass was knocked to the floor by the unwitting hand of a rattled Rocket Mann, but he would not acknowledge the young woman behind him. After a moment for fist-clenched composure, he picked up the pen — as if it were his own idea — and signed his name.

The detectives took their leave with no farewell. Their hit-and-run victim continued to sit at the table, looking down at the place where his steak had been, and then, blindly reaching for the glass that was no longer there, clutching air.

Chief Medical Examiner Edward Slope entered the squad room bearing a gift. At this late hour, only one desk lamp was lit, and Kathy Mallory sat facing her laptop screen. He paused for a rare opportunity to watch her while she was unaware. He felt pangs of regret for every recent argument, though she was always clearly in the wrong.

But she had such a genius for shifting guilt — or creating it from scratch — like now. She turned around in her chair to catch him standing there, holding his peace offering, his present, sans ribbons and wrapping paper.

The doctor crossed the room to lay his heavy brown envelope on her desk. "My people put this together for you. It's everything you need to nail the hospital administrator and his pathologist. And, as you know, I make an excellent witness in court."

Never even glancing at his present, she turned back to her computer. "I had to cut them loose."

"What? Those two conspired to cover up the murder of a child." He slapped his envelope. "It's all there. I *proved* it. There's no way in hell they bungled that autopsy by negligence or ignorance. They had to know what they were doing."

"The administrator took directions from that assistant DA. And Carlyle's done worse, but I had to let him go, too."

Slope folded his arms. "Well, I won't go along with it."

"Yes, you will." This was not couched as an order. She said it softly with resignation. "Your old buddy Grace set you up. The day the hospital did that bogus autopsy on the Nadler kid, the Driscol Institute made its first donation to your rehab clinic — it was huge. And every year after that —"

"Grace is hardly my *buddy.* And I met her *after* my clinic got that donation."

"I believe you. But on paper it looks bad.

Let's say I can prove Grace had a reason to want the boy's murder kept quiet. The donation makes it look like you helped her bury that autopsy — like she paid you to look the other way. If Grace and her pet ADA go down for this — so do you." Mallory turned her screen around so that the doctor could see it. "You're not the only one. I'm still following the money, but so far I've got a slew of politicians in key positions. They all had pet projects funded by the Driscol Institute. Some of them did favors for Grace's friends — tax breaks, city contracts, political appointments. They're sitting in traps like yours. It's a kind of extortion that never ends. It's all in the public record — where anyone can find it. I'm sure Grace will be happy to explain how it works if you make any trouble."

"You can't let her get away with this — not because of me. I *want* this to come out. We'll drag the whole mess into open court. I *insist!* I can't fight these insinuations if you're doing dark little backroom deals."

Mallory's voice was calmer than his when she said, "Rules of New York City. You can get away with murder here. Or you can live your whole life without putting one foot wrong . . . and lose everything. So the dirt stays buried. I'll find another way to bring that woman down. Count on it."

In a minute more, he would regret speaking without his wits about him, but he was angry when he said, "And I'm supposed to be grateful that you're covering this up for me? You figure I'll owe you for this?"

Kathy was so rarely startled.

She had given him the pure gift of her protection. And he had stepped on it. Of course she was right. There could be no insinuation of wrongdoing in the Chief Medical Examiner's Office. Even if it were only a campaign of whispers, he would step down. He would lose everything, though he had done nothing wrong. She was saving him from a fight he could only lose — and how he had thanked her for that.

The young detective dropped his envelope of evidence into a deep desk drawer. He anticipated a slam, but she only closed the drawer and locked it. After turning out the lights of computer and lamp, she sat very still, her face in shadow, a silent invitation for him to leave her now.

He would have preferred that she had shot him. The doctor rose from his chair. "Kathy?" His voice was hoarse, and what more could he say? He leaned down and kissed her hair, and then he took himself away.

Tonight Officer Chu carried field glasses on a strap around his neck. Key or no key? The big question was about to be answered as he followed Willy Fallon in her march toward the Driscol School's iron gate, passing garbage bags and stacks of newspapers on the sidewalk. A sofa had also been put out for curbside pickup, and he trained his binoculars on it — no signs of wear. Trash night in New York City was a free flea market of amazing finds. In a pile for recycled metal was a bundle of perfectly good window blinds. Did rich people throw them away when the slats got dusty?

Willy Fallon stopped before the tall alley gate. Arthur Chu's high-powered lenses could make out the clasp and even the stitches in the leather of her open purse. Would she pull out a key or lock picks? *Oh, no.* She stepped away from the gate. Something had spooked her. The woman flattened up against the wall of the building.

The shadow cop turned his lenses back to the gate, and now he noticed the padlock and chain. That was new. Two plump, white hands reached through the bars. The padlock was undone, the gate swung open, and a woman stood at the mouth of the alley. He recognized Phoebe Bledsoe from her picture on the wall of the incident room. She carried a plastic trash bag out to the curb.

Willy Fallon stepped away from the wall, hands outstretched and fingers curling into claws as she stole up behind the other woman.

Arthur Chu wanted to shout out a warning, but Detective Mallory would kill him for breaking cover. And so every civilized thing his mother had ever taught him was suppressed.

Phoebe Bledsoe was bending down with her bag of trash when Willy Fallon knocked her off balance with a shove. The falling woman crashed into the cans and knocked them over like dominoes, one hitting the other, and she let out a cry of surprise just before hitting the sidewalk. And there she lay sprawled in garbage.

The last can to fall was filled with metal window blinds. The clatter on the sidewalk was so like the clang of being slammed into lockers at school. Phoebe saw the back of a skinny woman and knew it was Willy before her assailant said, "You were there, too.

You're next." And the X was dragged out in a hiss.

Her old schoolmate walked away, transforming in comic-book fashion as she passed in and out of the lights of street lamps. Ernie's world of monster mutants was more real than Phoebe knew — and now, in mind's eye, she watched Willy quick-scrabble down the pavement on eight spider legs.

Limping on one sore ankle, Phoebe shut the gate behind her and secured it with the padlock. She made her way to the end of the alley just as the telephone rang in her cottage across the garden. The answering machine had been turned off after the last message from Willy, and the ringing continued. Upon entering the cottage, she stared at the telephone, as if waiting for it to explode. So many rings. Did the caller *know* she was home, just standing there — afraid? She picked up the receiver, but her mouth had gone dry, and she said nothing.

After a while, a man's voice said, "Phoebe?"

It was Rolland Mann.

"What do you want?"

"I'm still concerned about your safety," he said, "and your . . . *involvement.* Did the detectives ask you about Ernie Nadler's death? Do you think they know?"

"Know what?"

"Don't you remember?" he asked in his talking-to-idiots voice. "When that little boy was strung up and left to die in the woods, you waited three days before you told me where to find him."

THIRTY-SIX

Tonight, I listen from the hallway while my parents sit at the kitchen table with Detective Mann. He tells them I made the whole thing up, and the autopsy proves it — kids didn't murder the wino. He says I only ratted out my classmates to get even with them for bullying me at school.

My father nods. He's seen the evidence of bullies — the marks they left on my body. He believes the detective. Mom cries. She believes him, too.

I have lost everything.

— ERNEST NADLER

Elderly Mrs. Buford bent down to fetch her morning *Times,* eager to read the next episode of the Ramble murders. The saga of the Hunger Artist had become her new soap opera.

The door across the hall opened, and she braced herself. The neighbor woman's

509

husband had done morning paper duty for the past few days. Such a creepy fellow, he had interfered with the digestion of her breakfast. But now — oh, thank God — she saw Annie standing on the threshold.

What a relief. Rolland Mann had apparently not done away with his wife after all.

Well, now they could resume their old morning ritual, cordial exchanges of hellos and comments on the weather. Or maybe not. Mrs. Buford noticed the suitcase. "Going somewhere?"

Escaping, perhaps?

Annie nodded.

"Have a lovely time." The old woman closed the door only to open it a minute later at the sound of weeping. Annie Mann had traveled only a few steps from her own door before she crumpled to the floor beside her luggage. She sat huddled against the wall.

Mrs. Buford belted her robe and bustled across the hallway with the shush of fuzzy pink slippers. Bending creaky knees, she knelt down beside her fallen neighbor and took the woman's hands in hers, rubbing the cold, clammy flesh till it warmed, till Annie's breathing was less of a struggle, and the sweat of her brow ceased to roll into her eyes. The younger woman fumbled with the catch on her purse and spilled a dozen pharmacy bottles across the carpet.

"I'll get you some water so you can take a pill." Mrs. Buford had no sooner entered her own apartment than she heard the ping that announced the arrival of the elevator. When she looked out the door, it was a great surprise to see two uniformed policemen in the hall — a greater surprise for Annie Mann, who slumped over in a dead faint. And perhaps that was for the best. Poor woman. She never could have left the building fully conscious. One officer picked up Annie's wallet from the spilled contents of her purse. He nodded to the second man, who carried her limp body to the elevator, leaving the suitcase behind. A young blonde knelt on the carpet, scooping the pill bottles back into the fallen purse. How odd.

Well, in any case, Annie had made her escape.

Of course, Mrs. Buford had imagined this scene a hundred times, but she had always envisioned the husband in police custody — not the *wife.* She was about to close her door when a voice called out, "Wait!" She poked her head into the hall once more and saw the long-legged blonde coming toward her — closer, closer. *Oh, my, what strange green eyes.*

The young woman showed her a gold badge and a police identification card that made her a detective. A *detective!* How exciting. As the blonde restored the badge to a back pocket of her jeans, her blazer fell open on one side, and now a very large gun was on display in a shoulder holster.

Oh, this was simply *marvelous.* Mrs. Buford was fairly giddy when she said, "Tell me it's *murder.*"

"Yes. Yes, it is."

The old woman rose up on her toes, all atingle with anticipation, and when the young woman asked, "Wanna play?" Mrs. Buford replied, "*Could* I?"

Coco perched on a desk near the stairwell door and lectured Detective Gonzales on the terrible importance of toilet-seat locks. "The rats can get in that way. They swim up through the water in the toilet bowl. But if the seats are locked down, they just swim round and round till they drown."

The lieutenant stood with Mallory and Riker on the squad-room side of the window, watching the action in the next room through the blinds. Via an open intercom, the three of them eavesdropped on a conversation between the people inside the not-so-private office, where the two civilians were on a first-name basis now, Annie and Charles.

The lady was not what Jack Coffey had expected, not the pretty trophy wife of a political up-and-comer. She looked so ordinary — if he discounted the fact that she was terrified.

Annie Mann held tight to the arms of her chair, so afraid that she might lift off into space. Despite the fear, she smiled when Charles Butler did. This new expression transformed her. No longer plain, she was all warmth and charm personified. Magnetic. It was almost a magic act. But the illusion was short-lived, and she shifted back into panic mode, eyes darting everywhere, on the lookout for danger in the corners of the room. And now she panted like a dog.

Charles perused the pharmacy stash from the woman's purse, then selected a bottle and handed her a single pill. She popped it in her mouth and chomped it like a candy. When she was calm, he left her alone to join the covert observers on the other side of the office window.

Mallory looked through the blinds, staring at the woman as she spoke to the psychologist. "Is she crazy?"

"No," said Charles. "Not at all."

"So she's faking," said Riker.

"Oh, no. I agree with Mrs. Buford's diagnosis. Annie's genuinely phobic. She tells me she's always been prone to panic attacks in social situations."

The lieutenant and his detectives feigned interest in this, as if they had not been privy to every word. And now, with the mistaken idea that they were *actually* interested, Charles continued. "Well, that's how agoraphobia begins. In the early stages, Annie was quite functional. Hospitals were her primary safety zones — areas of competence and confidence for a nurse."

"She hasn't worked for fifteen years," said Jack Coffey, in a game attempt to speed this along.

"And during that time," said the man with no short answers, "the rest of her safety zones also dwindled. She's afraid of having panic attacks in public areas. Over the years, she's avoided a growing list of such places. And finally, she had nowhere to go. Then there's the additional reinforcement of long-term confinement. She hasn't left her apartment since they moved in."

"We saw you give her that pill." Mallory said this as if accusing him of drug trafficking.

"A very mild sedative," said Charles. "She was badly frightened — about a minute away from meltdown. I assume you want her coherent?"

"*Legally* coherent," said Coffey. "Is that woman stoned?"

"No, I'd say she's more clearheaded now."

"That's all we need to know." The lieutenant signaled Detective Janos, who entered the office and led Annie Mann outside to the squad room and down the hall to a place for less genteel conversation.

"Rats have agoraphobia, too," said a small voice closer to the floor.

Four people looked down to see that Coco had ditched her babysitting detective, and she was not smiling anymore.

"Rats don't feel safe in open spaces." Coco's solemn eyes followed the woman being led away. "That's why they keep close to the walls."

And now all of them watched Annie Mann's body grazing the wall as she was escorted down the hallway.

Her shoulders hunched. Her eyes were wide.

The interrogation room with its puke-green walls and blood-leaching fluorescent lights was too alien for this agoraphobic — but not scary *enough*. Riker wondered how edgy the woman might have been without the damn sedative.

"You changed your name," said Mallory.

"I got married," said Annie Mann.

"She means your *first* name," said Riker. "You used to be Margaret — now it's Annie."

There was no hesitation when the woman said, "I was always Annie to my friends."

"You gave us the wrong Social Security number," said Mallory.

"I changed it. I was worried about identity theft."

This was the first stumble. Thus far, Mrs. Mann's responses had been too quick, and they had the tone of a memorized script, but now the detectives had what they were waiting for. This was the hook, the first bungled lie.

"Fifteen years ago," said Riker, "nobody worried about identity theft. I don't think we even had a name for it."

"My wallet was stolen — my license, credit cards —"

"You never filed a police report, never checked your credit report." Mallory tapped keys on her laptop computer. "And you didn't replace the driver's license. It says here, your license expired. So did your charge cards. I can't find any paper on you for the past fifteen years." She turned the computer around so that Annie Mann could see the document on-screen. "Look at this. Your name isn't even on the deed for your condo."

Annie leaned closer to the screen, as if that might clarify the line of type that declared her husband the solitary owner. "This can't be right."

"You didn't know? Your neighbor, Mrs. Buford, thinks you're married, but she's the only one in the building who's ever seen you."

"I'm *married!*"

Riker leaned forward. "We pulled all the phone records. You never called your husband at the office — not once. His secretary tells us he's single."

Mallory raised more documents on the screen. "You're not a beneficiary on his pension plan. You're not even listed as a dependent on his health insurance."

"But, hey," said Riker, "you don't need health insurance. You're low risk. According to the neighbor, you never leave that apartment."

"Rolland Mann files as a single taxpayer," said Mallory. "No dependents. So you lied when you said you were —"

"We're *married.* We were married in Canada."

Riker smiled. "I'd like to believe you. But there's no record of a marriage registered in *this* country. There's no trace of you anywhere, Annie. It's like he wiped you out of existence fifteen years ago. You know how we found you? My partner stopped by to find out why Rolland made a three-minute phone call to his empty apartment."

"If he killed you today," said Mallory, "the only one who'd miss you is the old lady across the hall."

"We're trying to help you, Annie." Riker reached across the table and covered her cold hands with his. "So . . . you and Rolland, you met at the hospital — when you were watching the Nadlers' kid. Nurses and cops, that's a natural combination."

"No. Rolland was my boyfriend *before* that. He's the one who got me the job with the —" Annie Mann pulled her hands back and covered her mouth. And now in the posture of *I give up,* her shoulders slumped and she bowed her head. "It was just a few hours a night, but the Nadlers paid me for whole shifts. Real nice people. They'd been cooped up in that hospital for a solid month. They only wanted to step outside for a regular meal together . . . like *normal* people . . . just a few hours. Their kid was *supposed* to be stable."

"You were on duty when Ernie Nadler died," said Mallory. "You were the last person to see him alive. And that looks bad for you, Annie. The parents did everything they could to keep Ernie safe, but their little boy was murdered on your watch."

"No. He died from the injuries — or maybe infection from —"

"You *know* it was murder," said Mallory. "You were in that hospital room when he was killed, smothered to death with a pillow."

"Oh, my *God.* It wasn't me. I wasn't even there when he died. I went out for a smoke on the fire escape. I swear I was only gone a few minutes. When I came back, the boy was dead. Rolland — he was a detective then — he was in the room. He can tell you."

"You should worry about what he *already* told us." Mallory pushed a sheet of paper across the table. "That's his witness statement. You recognize the handwriting? He says he was at the hospital in the morning, *not* the evening — not when the kid was murdered."

"I'd like to help you, Annie," said Riker. "But I need to hear your side of it."

"He was *there!* When I got back to the kid's room, Rolland was standing by the bed. He asked me where I'd been. I was *so* freaked out. 'Don't worry,' he says. He won't tell anybody I wasn't there when the kid died. He told me to wait fifteen minutes and then call a doctor. He saved me from a negligence charge. And then Rolland *married* me to save my ass. He said a husband can't testify against his wife."

"He lied," said Mallory. "A husband can't testify to spousal conversation, but he can testify to events. That's why he kept you around for fifteen years. You're a bone he can throw to the cops if everything goes sour. When the doctor came in to pronounce the boy dead, you told him you were there the whole time. Isn't that what happened? Isn't that what Rolland told you to say?"

"Rolland *loves* me."

"The guy really planned ahead," said Mallory. "So he was the last one to see the kid alive. But guess who's getting hung out to dry, *Annie.* It's all on you now. You — the crazy lady who can't even leave her apartment. The nutcase with a pharmacy of drugs in her purse and a —"

"*No!* I'd never —"

"A nurse who kills her patients," said Mallory. "That's how it'll play out in court. You felt bad for a little kid with amputated hands. You wanted to spare Ernie all that horror — when he woke up from the coma. So you took a pillow, and you —"

"*No!* I wasn't even *there* when the Nadlers' son died!"

"It's gonna be okay, Annie." Riker pushed a yellow pad across the table. "I'll help you. Just write down what happened that night. *Your* side of the story." He handed her the pen.

She took it.

There were only two watchers in the dark on the other side of the glass, and they remained there while the woman in the interview room wrote out her statement. Lieutenant Coffey locked the door. Now that privacy and secrecy were assured, he turned to the chief of detectives. "We're still building the case. I don't wanna rush it."

"What've you got for motive, Jack?"

"We think the Nadler kid was a witness to a wino's murder. If he ever came out of the coma, the boy could've blown up Mann's case against Toby Wilder. Mann would've done jail time for witness tampering, withholding evidence, obstruction." Coffey held back on Mallory's alternate theory. Not everyone shared her love of profit motives, and she had given him no solid proof for that idea — nothing beyond a series of promotions for a mediocre cop's rise to the top of the NYPD food chain.

"Okay," said Chief Goddard. "So far, so good. Rocket Mann marries the nurse for insurance. If things go sour, she takes the fall. I call that long-range planning — like the Hunger Artist. But first you gotta nail him for killing the Nadler kid."

"Yeah," said Jack Coffey. "Just one problem. Why smother the boy? Mann was a detective. He had to know the forensics would point to murder. Even a drunken hospital pathologist noticed hemorrhaging in the kid's eyes."

"Petechial hemorrhaging wasn't in Rocket Mann's vocabulary back then. I remember him in those days. He didn't know shit about forensics, and he couldn't bother to learn a damn thing. Never attended an autopsy, never cracked a book. And the guy couldn't keep a partner for more than a week. Nobody wants to work with the screwup cop. That's why he was riding solo when he was still a probie. I was the captain who assigned him to the wino murder."

"I know that," said Coffey. "My detectives are very thorough. They also tell me you started your vacation that same day . . . sir."

"And you wondered why I never volunteered that information." Joe Goddard waved one hand toward the window on the next room, where Annie Mann was still writing out her statement. "So this was staged for my benefit. I heard you guys do suspect interviews on both sides of the glass." He laughed, not a scoff — a belly laugh.

Jack Coffey would never have predicted that response. "Why did you assign a homicide to a white shield with no partner, no oversight?"

"The wino murder was busywork, a case nobody cared about. If Mann screwed up — and I knew he would — no harm done. Then I could bust him back to a beat cop. I was on a fishing trip in Oregon when he pinned that murder on the Wilder kid. I could smell the stink all the way across the country. By the time I got back, strings had been pulled to get Mann transferred out of my precinct. And that little fuckup was sporting a gold shield. That's when I knew he was dirty."

"How much did you know about Ernest Nadler? When he went missing, the parents —"

"When I got back, I only knew a kid got lost, and he was found alive. That bastard Mann worked the assault off the books. *No* paperwork. I always knew he didn't have the makings of a cop, and I was right about that . . . but I didn't give him credit for brains. That was my mistake. I never knew what happened to that little boy, not until your detectives dug up the old ViCAP questionnaire. Satisfied, Jack?"

"Yes, sir." No, *sir.* Lieutenant Coffey knew this was a lie, but his only proof was the chief's relief when this story went unchallenged.

"Your guys better make a strong case, Jack. I don't want Rocket Mann getting off 'cause the public watches too many cops shows on TV. If you had a problem with the forensics, so will the damn jury. And I don't want your case blowing up on a technicality of spousal privilege. Find out if he's legally married to the nurse."

"He is. The marriage was registered in Toronto, Canada. My detectives knew that before they walked into the interview. And Mallory's right about spousal privilege. It won't apply to what Annie Mann saw, and she saw Rolland Mann in that hospital room with the dead boy."

"Then it's his word against hers. You need more to charge him on the kid's murder. And I wanna see some evidence for the murders of Humphrey Bledsoe and Aggy Sutton."

"We've got no connection between Mann and the Hunger Artist."

"Make one. Dump the wife in Witness Protection. I don't want word getting out she was ever here. Don't let her go home to pack a bag. Take her straight to a safe house."

Coffey nodded to say he was following this. "So Rocket Mann goes home tonight. No wife, no missing suitcase. All her clothes are still in the closet."

Goddard grinned. "What's he gonna do? Everybody thinks he's single. He let that game go on too long. And now he can't even file a report on a missing wife, not without explaining why he erased her on paper. He'll wonder where she is — and who's she talking to? He'll come unglued."

Jack Coffey's detectives were already busy rattling Rolland Mann, and they needed no help from Joe Goddard. But it would be impolitic to tell the chief of D's that his plan was already in the works. Mallory and Riker had unpacked Annie Mann's suitcase and then enlisted the aid of the neighbor across the hall. Mrs. Buford was thrilled by the whole idea of becoming an agent for the police, and her silence was guaranteed, should Rolland Mann come to her door.

Joe Goddard had never been inclined to

micromanage any homicide investigation. So why the change of style? Did Goddard miss the chase of a street-level cop? No, not likely. Jack Coffey decided that the chief of D's had something to hide — and keep hidden.

The two detectives sat at their facing desks, doing paperwork on the most recent interview. Riker pushed aside the conflicting statements of Rolland and Annie Mann. "Are we missing something here? When Rocket Mann took Annie to Canada — you think he had a plan to kill her and dump the body up there? Maybe he chickened out? Killing isn't his best thing. He bungled the forensics on Ernie's murder."

"I think Annie was right," said Mallory. "He wanted to save her."

"So . . . you don't think he smothered Ernie?"

"Oh, yeah. He did it, all right. The bastard's a stone killer. He's just not real good at it. *That's* what bothers you."

"I have a headache," said Riker.

THIRTY-SEVEN

The dead man in the Ramble is the last thing I think about when I go to bed — but not to sleep. I lay awake and wonder — did somebody close the wino's eyes before he was buried? Or do bugs get into his coffin and crawl on his eyeballs? I wake up my parents to ask them.

— ERNEST NADLER

Hoffman lingered in the drawing room, not liking the looks of the visitor, and who could blame her?

Grace Driscol-Bledsoe rose from her chair to tower over her son's former — schoolmate, co-killer — oh, what was the word she was searching for? No matter. "Don't worry, Hoffman, I'm sure I can take Miss Fallon two falls out of three."

When the door had closed behind the departing nurse, another brown bag full of cash was passed from Grace's hand to her

527

guest's. "That should tide you over."

"Thanks." Willy Fallon tossed the paper bag on a chair, so dismissive of money. She stood before the front window and pulled back a white gauze curtain. "I think I'm being followed. It's just a creepy feeling."

"I wouldn't be surprised, my dear. Do you think the police know what you did — you and your little friends?"

"You still worry about that, don't you?" Willy turned on her, smiling just a bit too wide, telegraphing that she was here to make more demands.

Grace, an old campaigner, launched the first salvo. "Obviously *someone* knows. While you were hanging in that tree — surely you must've formed an idea of who would benefit by your death. Perhaps someone regarded the three of you as loose ends? Maybe someone who needs to put all that unpleasantness behind him?"

Well, Willy Fallon had never been the brightest student at the Driscol School. The older woman leaned toward the younger one, willing her to work it out. *Think! You psychopathic moron!* Ah, a light shone in Willy's eyes, evidence of a brain at work, albeit a tiny one. "You had a thought, my dear." Grace said this with absolutely no sarcasm.

"When we were kids, Humphrey told me you were making payoffs — to keep it quiet."

This came as no surprise. Children were the best of spies in every household. She often wondered how much her daughter had pieced together from those bad old days. Oh, and now she could see that Willy was having another thought. Two in one day — how taxing.

"I think we can help each other, Grace. Just give me a name. I'll take care of it. I'll get rid of him for you." Smiling, she bent down to pick up her bag of cash. "Say we double this . . . once a month?"

"I'm truly shocked." And did Willy believe that? Well, of course she did. The girl was an idiot. All that remained to Grace was to sit back, assume a worried look and perhaps profess a sudden onset of palpitations in that place where common people kept their hearts. Eventually, after much prodding by the idiot, a name would escape Grace's lips.

Rolland Mann had gone out in search of a disposable cell phone, but he would not throw this one away. There were reporters around every corner, waiting for crumbs from One Police Plaza, and some might be waiting in ambush. In any case, he was not

529

done calling home, hoping that Annie would answer the phone. He wanted the privacy of his office, where the news media could not hound him for updates on the Hunger Artist. He tightened his hold on the cell phone hidden in his pocket, so badly in need of this tether to his wife.

He was within yards of the courtyard gatehouse when a young woman crossed his path on the plaza. Such a cruel smile. The newspaper photos on the front pages of late had never captured that quality, only the practiced grin of a professional party girl, who had fallen off the scandal sheets years ago. Today, she planted herself in his way and folded her arms to announce that Willy Fallon was back. Badder than ever. Bigger news.

No lie.

Down the sidewalk, he saw snouts lifting to catch a scent in the air, and the first of the paparazzi was running toward them. Then another and another. The photographers caught him in the act of running away from Willy.

While the socialite preened for pictures, Officer Chu kept the distance of a good shadow, and he scribbled in his notebook — just a few lines about Miss Fallon's odd run-in with the acting police commissioner and his sudden flight, hands flailing.

Rolland Mann ran like a girl.

Willy Fallon was on the move again, waving goodbye to the gang of photographers. How they loved her. One of them blew her a kiss. And Arthur Chu followed her.

The woman spoke on a cell phone as she walked westward, and the young officer dutifully noted the exact times for three calls in a row. After the phone was returned to her purse, she absently glanced at her wristwatch. Now there was an attitude of urgency as she looked around her, up and down the street.

Hunting a cab? Lots of luck at this hour. Even if she found one, a car could only crawl in this traffic.

The surveillance officer followed her to the subway station on Warren Street, and watched her step down below the sidewalk. He was impressed that this rich bimbo might know how to operate a turnstile. Then it occurred to him that she had probably used mass transit more than once to elude reporters on a bad-hair day. Yes, he was right. No need to stop at the cashier's booth to buy a ticket to ride. She pulled a yellow transit card from her purse.

Was that purse a good deal fatter now?

Had he missed something?

Rolland Mann looked up when his pouting
secretary walked in. She had resented him
from the moment he had moved his belongings into Commissioner Beale's office,
perhaps finding it ghoulish that he was so
confident of the old man's impending
demise. "Any calls, Miss Scott?"

"Yes. She didn't leave a name this time,
either, but it's the same woman."

Not the woman he most wanted to hear
from, not Annie. She knew better than to
call him on his office phone. He still
doubted that his wife could have made her
way through the door to the street. On those
rare occasions, when he had taken her out
for dinner, she had been nervous and
jumpy, only calming down when they were
home again. That was years ago. Today, she
would not, could not, leave the apartment.
But she *could* overmedicate. *Yes.* She was
probably deep in a barbiturate haze, unable
to hear the phone ringing.

Miss Scott broke into his thoughts. "The
woman said you better call her back or else."

"Or else what?"

"She didn't say, and I don't read minds."
The secretary slapped a piece of paper on
the desk. It was only a telephone number

and the brief threat.

It could only be Willy Fallon.

"And I'm not paid to listen to your friend's obscenities." Miss Scott slammed the door on her way out.

Now he knew that his secretary had finally been successful in finding another position. Another runaway woman.

He pulled the throwaway cell from his pocket and called his residence. One ring, two rings — three. *Annie, my Annie, come to the phone.*

Willy Fallon climbed out of the subway near the Greenwich Village movie theater. She turned a corner and walked westward into that patch of New York City where grid logic broke down, where Fourth Street ran north and south of West Tenth. When she was within half a block of Toby Wilder's apartment building, she saw him step out on the sidewalk.

Lunchtime.

She knew her quarry was a creature of habit, thanks to a tip paid to a local shopkeeper, a man who bragged that he could set his watch by Toby Wilder. Willy followed her old classmate on a trek across the Village to a Mexican restaurant on Bleecker Street. She saw him pass through the door to reappear at a table by the window. He never noticed her standing there on the sidewalk, watching him. When he did happen to look out on the street, he paid her no more attention than the fire hydrant.

He was still beautiful.

After all these years, it rankled her that he would never know what she had done to him. While she stood by the window, another patron rushed in the door to find a table on the far side of the room and close to the kitchen. Why would Humphrey's sister pick the worst seat in the house while better ones went begging?

Phoebe Bledsoe was taller now, but she still lugged around all the baby fat of childhood. And apparently she had not outgrown her crush on the boy by the window. The girl settled into the chair with the worst possible lighting to watch Toby Wilder from a shy distance.

Pathetic.

Willy entered the café and walked up to the far table to see her favorite expression — naked fear — on Phoebe's face. Willy sat down, liking this power over the other woman — hardly a woman — a lump of a schoolgirl who would never grow up. "What's that?"

Before Phoebe could close her hand over

the gold cigarette lighter, Willy grabbed it, saying, "You never smoked. You wouldn't dare. Neither would I, not if Grace was *my* mother."

"Give it back!" Humphrey's sister was anxious, reaching for the lighter that was evidently precious to her.

Willy played a schoolyard game of keep-away, holding it high, tossing it from hand to hand, and then she took a closer look at her prize. It was heavy — solid gold. The scratches in the metal appeared to be damage at first glance. At second glance, she remembered where she had seen this lighter before. The surface scratches had been deeper then, and it had been easier to read them as a clear date — the year of her birth — though not the same month and day.

Smiling, Willy cadged a glance at Toby Wilder. It had to be his birth date scratched into the metal. Turning back to Phoebe, she held the gold lighter just out of reach. "I know where you got this. You found it in the Ramble. You went *back* for it."

It was supposed to be found beside the wino's dead body — this cigarette lighter dropped on the path by Toby Wilder — with his fingerprints on it. Planting the lighter had been Humphrey Bledsoe's idea — that moron. He thought the police kept everyone's fingerprints on file, even those of schoolboys.

"I *know* who this belongs to." Oh, that look of sick fear was priceless — almost orgasmic, and Willy hungered for more. She rose from the table and turned around to face her old classmate on the other side of the room. "Hey, Toby!" He looked in her direction. Behind her, she could hear the scrape of an edged-back chair and then Phoebe's heavy footsteps running toward the door.

But Willy was the one who commanded Toby Wilder's attention — at last — though he seemed only mildly curious. She flung the cigarette lighter across the room. He snatched it from the air, and stared at it. And now a closer look, head shaking, not believing his eyes. He held it up to the light of the window, the better to read the faint date scratched in gold. He turned back to her, rising from his table, but Willy was already at the door and passing through it, laughing, *laughing.* The chase was on.

Officer Chu was in a quandary. Willy Fallon's protection might not be his chief concern today, but it *was* a cop's job. However, she did not look like a woman in any danger. Every few running steps, she turned back to smile at the long-haired young man who chased her up MacDougal Street. Savvy Village residents hugged brick walls and storefront windows, but a few tourists went down like bowling pins. Arthur Chu followed the pair on the run into Washington Square Park, where they played a fast kids' game of *catch me if you can.*

Grinning like a maniac, Willy ran around the fountain, and her pursuer cut across its wide basin, slogging through the pool and getting drenched by arcs of water from the rim and the bubbling tower at the center. On the other side, he was within grabbing distance of Willy. But now a helpful, though misguided, park visitor tripped the running man to end the chase, and the poor bastard went down on one knee, wincing as bone met concrete. Willy, the clear winner, and Officer Chu were gone before the loser of the race could get to his feet.

Rolland Mann waited on the sidewalk at the corner of Columbus Avenue and West Eighty-sixth Street, hardly a neighborhood that attracted paparazzi in search of celebrities, not that his own face was all that well known around town. Four southbound buses had passed by since his arrival at this meeting place.

Willy Fallon was *that* late.

Two other people stood beside him, both of them tourists. They gave themselves away by waiting on the sidewalk for their chance to legally walk across the intersection. Their sheep's eyes were glued to the glowing red sign in the shape of a hand that commanded them not to move.

The real New Yorkers were standing in the street — *screw* the traffic light — waiting for the next break in the flow of passing cars. Poised three steps from the sidewalk, the locals liked this competitive edge on timid curbhuggers from out of town. And, in the ongoing war of pedestrian and driver, there were points to be scored if one could terrify the other with a near miss.

A teenage girl approached the corner, oblivious to her environs, hooked into music by earphones, and she stepped off the curb. She was pretty, else Rolland would not have noticed her. And now the southbound bus was also in his line of sight as it barreled down Columbus Avenue, ramming its way across the lanes of the intersection — as it had done every ten minutes or so during the long wait for Willy Fallon.

The teenager stepped in time to the music from her earphones and never saw the bus — as she walked into its path. A stunning moment. He *knew* she was going to die. The bus was bearing down on her. A millisecond more, and she would be smashed like bug soup on a windshield.

The bus was gigantic, filling out his field of vision. Closer, closer.

A middle-aged man in greasy coveralls reached out, grabbed the girl's collar and yanked her back a step. The metal behemoth, brakes screaming, came within inches — *inches* — of the girl, and it failed to stop for six more yards beyond the point where she really should have died. A stench of burning rubber was in the air. There was time enough for the driver's quick look in a rearview mirror, a sigh of relief, and then the bus rolled on. Three pedestrians stopped to applaud, as they would for any near-death experience; it was a theater town.

The show was over, and the audience dispersed. The teenage girl could only stand there, staring at the departing bus, eyes glazing over as shock set in. And now her savior, the man in coveralls, released his handful of her blouse, saying, "Jeese, I'm so sorry, kid. What was I thinking?"

The girl turned to face her rescuer. Huh?

The hero smacked his head in a mime of *Dummy me.* "If that bus had hit you, you'd be set for life." The girl, head shaking, uncomprehending, was still surprised to be there, upright and *alive,* when the man started across the street, waving goodbye to her, saying, "Sorry, kid."

The Good Samaritan's guilt was understandable. A lawsuit involving a city bus would have paid off in millions. But that girl would never have survived a direct hit by tons of rolling steel.

Though he had been instructed to wait on the corner, Rolland stepped off the curb, moved three more steps into the street, and there he waited for Willy Fallon.

THIRTY-EIGHT

The headmaster doesn't know whether or not the bums of Potter's Field are embalmed. I tell him this is important stuff, and I've already asked my teacher. She doesn't know, either, and that's why she sent me to him. Well, I tell him, the dead wino's body will turn to soup without embalming. So this is my problem, I say. How can I picture this man in my head, day after day, if I don't know how fast his body is decomposing?

The headmaster gets up and leaves his office. Hours later, at the end of the school day, his secretary finds me still sitting in there alone. She tells me to go home. I tell her I don't think I can get there from here. The secretary calls my mother to come and get me.

As we walk home, I take Mom's hand the way I did when I was six.

— ERNEST NADLER

When Willy Fallon arrived at the designated corner, Rolland Mann appeared to have given up on her. He was standing in the street, waiting for a chance to cross or looking to hail a cab. She called to him from the sidewalk. "Hey!" He glanced at her over one shoulder and then turned back to face the oncoming traffic.

"Where are you going?" She stepped off the curb to join him in the street. He smiled and placed an avuncular hand on her shoulder. And that set off the first alarm.

Creepy bastard.

She shook off his hand, squared her shoulders and faced him down, but his eyes were turned toward the approach of an oncoming bus — not a city bus, but a huge double-decker tour bus. Her first instinct was to step back before it could flatten both of them, and now Mann's hand was lightly pressed to the small of her back.

Oh, shit! You prick! No way!

In the spirit of self-preservation, she reached down to squeeze his testicles, though she had planned to do that anyway. He doubled over in agony. They all did that. And now, with no trouble, only a kick in the pants, she guided the hunched-over man into the bus lane.

Then a screech, a whack, and he was gone.

■ ■ ■ ■

Before Willy Fallon vanished from the scene of the traffic fatality, one of the witnesses heard her mutter, "Fucking *amateur.*"

However, the tourist's first language was Danish, and Officer Chu thought the woman might have heard this wrong. Nevertheless, the plainclothes policeman wrote the words down in his notebook. Two uniformed cops collected cameras from the other tour-bus passengers, and a citywide search was under way for the apprehension of a killer socialite.

So ended Arthur Chu's surveillance detail and his best shot of advancement in the NYPD. After this fiasco, the department would not trust him to polish the shoes of detectives from Special Crimes Unit.

He had already given his own witness statement to the local police, and now he repeated it on his cell phone for the benefit of Detective Mallory. With a glance at the bloody smear on the front of the vehicle, he said to her, "Oh, yeah. *Really* dead." He explained that the acting police commissioner had made a pass at Miss Fallon. The lady had taken offense and retaliated — New York style — by the balls. Oh, and then, of course . . . by the bus.

Toby Wilder opened his door, and there she was, the skinny brunette who had tossed him the gold cigarette lighter. Her eyes were too bright, and her skin was flushed. The lady was in a fever when she said, "Let me in."

Why not?

He stepped aside, and she walked into his front room, asking, "Where do you keep the booze?"

When he had rinsed out two glasses and returned from the kitchen with the wine, the kind that came with a cap instead of a cork, his visitor had appropriated the couch, arms sprawled across the back cushions, both feet up on the coffee table.

He handed her one of the glasses. "Who the hell are you, and where did you get my lighter?"

"You don't remember me?" Her tone was asking, How could he *not* know who she was?

Toby shook his head to say he had no idea. He could see that she did not believe him. "No, thanks," he said, when she offered him pills from the stash in her purse. And this also surprised her.

He was still feeling a buzz from his last

round of oxycodone, neither jonesing for another rush nor stoned. All his heavy doses were for the nighttime hours, and then only pills that guaranteed sleep without dreams. Come morning came the painkillers he favored over every other drug to chase away the sweaty shakes and nausea. Lunch at one o'clock, and then there were more pills to pop. He had his routine. It never varied. Every day was the same day relived — until now.

She swallowed the wine in one long draught and handed him her empty glass. "Get me another one."

Why not?

He brought in the bottle to fill her glass again. When they were seated facing one another, she dropped names into the conversation: the Driscol School, Humphrey, Aggy — each one ending with the lilt of a question to prompt his recall or maybe to catch him in a lie.

Finally, she came back to his cigarette lighter. He sipped his wine and answered her questions, though she responded to none of his. "Yeah," he said, "you could call it an heirloom." He pulled the lighter from his shirt pocket, and looked down at the etching in the metal, so faint now, he could barely read the numbers. "My father scratched in this date on the day I was born. Dad *loved* this lighter." It had been left to Jess Wilder by his own father, another drunk who had abandoned his family. "He left this with my mother."

Dad had been afraid that he might pawn it. He had hocked everything else he owned to pay for booze, but not this lighter. Never this. Toby's mother had given it to her son when he was old enough to understand the family tradition: Leave your kid a gold cigarette lighter before you run out on him.

His visitor's voice seemed far away when she said, "I remember when you lost that lighter. The crazy bum in the Ramble, the one who hit you — did he try to take it away from you?"

"No. I was trying to give it back to him." Toby slurred his words. Odd. He stared at his glass. "So you were there that day." And this should have been a more exciting revelation, but he was *stoned*. Not drunk on wine — he could drink all day and never feel it. His breathing was slow and shallow, then — full stop. For ten seconds of panic, he fought for air. When he could breathe again, his heart was racing at the pace of a heart attack.

"You *bitch*, you *drugged* me!"

The oxycodone bottle lay open on the coffee table. He grabbed it up and emptied the remaining two pills into his hand. How many had gone into his wine? When he reached out for the woman, she sprang up from the couch and danced away, laughing. The dregs of his knocked-over glass were splashed across the carpet like spilt blood.

The squad room down the hall was a chaos of phones ringing, detectives hollering, chasing down leads on Willy Fallon. But here in the incident room, it was quiet. "The news is carrying the story as a traffic accident," said Jack Coffey.

"Good," said the chief of detectives. "Let's hope our guys collected all the civilian cameras." Joe Goddard walked beside the lieutenant, eyeing the latest exhibits on the cork wall. Many of these tourist photos contradicted any possibility of accidental death. Alongside them were the pinned-up phone messages faxed over by Rolland Mann's secretary.

"This is where it begins." Mallory tapped one of the shadow cop's cell-phone shots taken earlier in the day, when Willy had visited Grace Driscol-Bledsoe. She was pictured here, emerging from the mansion with a bulging purse. "Grace claims she can't stand the sight of Willy Fallon."

"So I called the lady," said Riker. "Asked her if they kissed and made up." He talked with pins in his mouth as he affixed more pictures to the cork. "According to Mrs. Driscol-Bledsoe, Willy just stopped by to pay condolences on the death of her beloved pervert son. But we figure Grace sicked her on Rocket Mann." The next exhibit was another one of Officer Chu's pictures. "A fast cab ride later, here's Willy standing in front of Police Plaza with the deputy commissioner. Arty Chu says Rocket Mann ran away when the reporters closed in on them. And here's Willy with her cell phone out."

"She made three calls to Rocket Mann's office." Mallory strolled down the wall to stand before the fax from the secretary, Miss Scott. "Willy didn't feel the need to leave her name. Her last message was *Call or else.*"

"The secretary says the messages rattled him," said Riker. "Then Willy gets a call on a phone that was reported stolen. Had to be one of Mann's throwaway cells. So they meet on the Upper West Side." The detective tapped the last photograph from Officer Chu. It was a rear view of Rolland Mann and Willy Fallon standing in the street. "Here he's got one hand on her back." The next shot was a frontal view taken by a

Nebraska tourist, who had mistaken the bland neighborhood as a point of interest worthy of a photograph. "In this one, Rocket Mann's watching the oncoming bus, picking his moment." The next shot was the local precinct's photo of a badly smashed body. "But Willy got him first."

"And she skates on self-defense," said Joe Goddard.

"Murder," said Mallory. "Grace Driscol-Bledsoe set him up for the kill. She aimed Willy like a gun."

"But you'll never prove it." The chief of D's was reading Officer Chu's witness statement forwarded from the Upper West Side precinct. "Your surveillance cop thinks Rocket Mann made a pass at Willy. And then the little bitch went psycho. You know that's the way her lawyer's gonna play it."

"Willy did a murder," said Riker. "And we don't think it's her first time out."

"The West Side cops will handle the bus *accident.*" And now that the detective stood corrected, Chief Goddard turned to the lieutenant, suddenly remembering the chain of command for issuing orders. "Jack, your guys need to focus. They're gonna sidestep Mrs. Driscol-Bledsoe. All I care about right now are the Ramble murders. You got a nice revenge motive for Toby Wilder. Nail him for the Hunger Artist murders — and *we* are *done*."

We?

This did not go over well with Riker. His feet planted solidly in a showdown stance, he faced off against the chief of D's.

Lieutenant Coffey failed to catch his detective's eye. He could only will the man to be careful.

Mallory moved between her partner and Goddard, saying, "Works for me, Chief. Except for sidestepping *anybody* on our shortlist — and the part about railroading Toby Wilder."

The lieutenant stood frozen, waiting for the chief to knock her down the ranks or fire her. It was like watching Mallory take a bullet in slow motion. Jack Coffey had always known this moment would come. Was she crazy? Absolutely. And she was also in the right. He kissed his pension goodbye and stepped forward.

But his fine adrenaline rush was all for naught.

Joe Goddard was blind to Mallory. She did not exist for him. He had locked eyes with the man behind her, saying to Riker, "It's your call — your case." And then, so calmly, hands in his pockets, the chief of detectives strolled toward the door.

Jack Coffey had a curious feeling of letdown. Next came suspicion.

And Mallory shared it. She spoke to her partner as she stared at the chief's retreating back. "What've you got on that bastard?"

It did not occur to Willy Fallon that she might be a fugitive from the law, that any trace of herself had been left behind for the police to find. *Dumb cops.* And so, with no sense of urgency, she watched Toby Wilder weaving, stumbling around with his overdose eyes, pupils gone to tiny pinpricks on a field of spooky blue irises. He crashlanded in an armchair.

She leisurely prowled through all his drawers and cabinets, but found no more street drugs, only empty bottles. Toby was definitely an addict, but his drugs were painkillers and sleeping pills, nothing purely recreational, nothing *fun.* She sat down on the couch once more and glanced at the broken television screen. She tapped the power button. The volume still worked. "So this is what you do all day? You *listen* to TV and get stoned?"

He was high, *flying,* but not deaf, and neither was he up to another chase around the furniture. He could only stretch out one accusing hand as he lurched forward in the chair. "What were you doing in the Ramble that day?"

Willy smiled, pleased to see him more docile now, though he was far from dead. Apparently she had misjudged his overdose. Oh, of *course.* She slapped her forehead. *Stupid. Stupid.* She had failed to factor in the tolerance level of an addict.

She took one more slow stroll around the apartment, checking the inventory of lethal things. There were knives in the kitchen. No — too messy. Ah, but out in the hall were steep stairs. A broken neck? Yes, that would do nicely. And many thanks were due to Rolland Mann. She had the hang of murder by accident now. Willy opened the door to the hallway, only a short walk to the staircase. All that remained was the problem of getting Toby Wilder from in here to out there.

"So that dead wino was your father? Well, I guess we're almost even now."

Grace had been so wrong. Rolland Mann could not have been the Hunger Artist. The bus had been a clumsy attempt to kill her, an opportunistic fumble. The Ramble murders of Humphrey and Aggy — that was clearly a different kind of kill. "I *know* it was you."

Toby Wilder shook his head, uncomprehending — stoned.

She reached out to take the gold cigarette lighter from his hand, an easy theft. His reaction time was crippled. Willy held it out as bait, a shiny lure. As she backed up to the open door of his apartment, Toby slowly rose to a stand.

"Good boy." She slipped into the hallway, calling out to him, "Humphrey Bledsoe hit your father with a rock to drop him. Then he used that rock to break the guy's kneecaps so he couldn't get up again." Toby was moving toward her, but he was *so* slow. This was going to take all damn day. "Humphrey liked the sound of breaking bones . . . so he broke your daddy's arms. I'm the one who kicked in the bum's teeth."

He was out the door and standing in the hall close to the stairs. She moved down a few steps below him. It was going to be so easy, dodging round him, and then a gentle shove — but Toby fell all by himself. She flattened up against the wall as he rolled past her. Down on the next landing, he lay on his back and moaned.

Not dead yet? No problem. She had stairs to spare.

Willy danced past the stunned boy and on down to the next floor, stopping, calling out to him, "You remind me of your father after Humphrey broke his bones. All he could do is lie there . . . and *scream*."

Toby crawled along the landing to the next flight of stairs, and he managed a bent-over stand. Still as a statue now — still trying to absorb it all? This time, it would be necessary to give him a push in the right direction — toward a broken neck. She climbed the steps and circled round him. The shove was not gentle, and she delighted in the sound of his skull knocking into wooden stairs.

Oh, dear.

Not only was he still alive, but he seemed to feel no pain this time. Well, junkies — they had rubber bones. She could probably bounce him down stairs all day long with no real damage.

Willy descended to the floor below and stepped over his body. His hand reached out to grab her leg. Too slow, too late. She skipped past him to the street door. And now she was inspired — death lessons from an amateur — but a bus would not do for Toby Wilder. The boy with the rubber bones might bounce.

How next to entice him and get his ass in gear? "*God,* how that wino screamed when I kicked out his teeth. Broken knees and broken arms — all he could do is lie there and take it. His blood was all over my shoes."

Was Toby crying? Yes, and he was moving, finally standing. *Good job.* She backed up through the door and into the street. "Let me tell you what Aggy Sutton did to him — Aggy the Biter."

Thirty-Nine

It's a war of whispers now, no more bruises or bite marks. When I talk about the death threats at the dinner table, it makes me sound like the crazy one. Mom chugalugs her wine tonight. I've never seen her do that before. And Dad says, "Kid stuff. Words can't hurt you."

"They killed the wino in the Ramble," I say, "and they *will* kill me."

Disgusted, my father folds his napkin and drops it on the table. Then he leaves the room — leaves me.

— ERNEST NADLER

The whole squad was manning phones and fielding tips from cops in every precinct where a Willy Fallon look-alike had been spotted.

"Did she try to neuter you?" Riker asked of one officer on the phone. "No? Then it's probably not our girl." He listened more closely when another cop read him a report that included the screams of a teenager who had been caught with his hand in a woman's purse. According to witnesses, the boy had clutched his crotch as he fled the subway.

The subway was the only snag in this story. Riker saw Willy as a taxi-and-limo type. But the ball-buster MO could not be ignored.

Detective Janos consulted the latest numbers pulled from the cell-phone company and then bent down to watch Mallory run a trace for pings off cell-phone towers to triangulate a location. "Nothing? You think she might've gone underground — like the subway?"

"Yeah!" Riker returned to his conversation on the subway neutering — Willy's trademark.

Mallory looked up from her computer. "The phone's out in the open again. It's on the move near a subway line in the Bronx."

Janos called the station house closest to the location on Mallory's screen and fed the coordinates to a sergeant in that borough. He cuffed the mouthpiece and said, "It's a schoolyard. There's a patrol car thirty seconds away."

Mallory shook her head. "I'm not sure Willy could even *find* the Bronx. I say she lost her phone or ditched it."

Riker yelled, "No, it's her! A skinny brunette got robbed on the subway!" Riker held up his phone, still connected. "And this cop tells me the robber will never have children. That's Willy."

"We're screwed." Janos hung up on his connection to the Bronx precinct. "They just collared a teenager on the playground. He's got Willy's phone. He stole it."

Toby Wilder was flagging again at the top of the subway stairs, but this place was too public for a helping shove to get him all the way down any faster.

Willy danced up to him, just out of reach. She held the lighter in one outstretched hand. "Aggy bit him everywhere. She took a chunk of flesh from his face and spit it out. I couldn't believe she did that. Your daddy smelled so bad — like booze and piss and turds. How he *screamed* when Aggy bit off pieces of him."

Toby lurched forward and grabbed the rail to stop himself from falling down stone stairs. He needed more encouragement.

Willy complied. "It took him so long to die. Humphrey punches like a little girl. He didn't do that much damage with his fists. So he used the rock again — and *again.* And your daddy just *scre-e-e-eamed.* His mouth was full of blood, and there was more blood from Aggy's bites. It just went on and *on.*"

He was moving faster now, down the stairs, unbalanced in his mind and blind with tears.

Gonzales hollered out, "Arty Chu redeemed himself!" The detective shrugged into the sleeves of his blazer, and the others followed suit even before he sang out, "Road trip!"

While men pulled guns from desk drawers and holstered them, Gonzales shouted the rest of his report to the lieutenant on the other side of the squad room. "Arty back-tracked his steps to a restaurant in Greenwich Village. A waitress ID'd Toby Wilder as the guy who chased Willy outta there. So Arty finds the kid's apartment, and the door's wide open. Nobody home. Then he talks to the neighbors, shows them pictures on his cell phone. Willy's been there and gone. They left together, her and Toby, moving east. Our boy Arty's heading that way now."

The rest of the squad was moving in tandem, through the door and down, feet slapping stairs. Riker was on the phone to Arthur Chu before he landed on the ground floor of the station house. "Did you ask the neighbors if they looked cozy? . . . Yeah, like a couple." He covered the phone and said to the running woman beside him, "A neighbor said Willy was leading the way. Toby was moving real slow and weaving. She thinks the kid was falling-down drunk or stoned."

Willy Fallon wondered how he kept his balance. They still had a ways to go before they reached the edge of the train platform. She walked backwards, facing him, talking to him in a tone of normal conversation, saying hideous things so he would not lose momentum. "We saw you leave your daddy in the Ramble. You think he wondered why you didn't come back to help him? You were long gone when we brought him down — but do you think he knew that? Your daddy's brains were really scrambled. He kept screaming for help through his broken teeth and the blood. And Aggy kept biting him. He must've thought he was being eaten alive."

Riker was in the lead car, one of the perks of riding with a vehicular maniac at the wheel. Mallory killed the engine at West Eighth, where Officer Chu was doing a canvas of the sidewalk, showing people pictures on his camera phone. And now they had a lead, a pedestrian pointing toward the entrance of the subway.

Mallory issued orders to Chu on the fly. "Run down to Fourth Street and cover that entrance. The rest of the squad is on the way."

Riker yelled at the running shadow cop's back. "Call 'em, Arty! Bring 'em all up to speed!" And down underground he went with his partner. He took the upper level, and she plunged down the stairs to the lower one.

Willy had given this subway station some thought. There were trains running here on single tracks that offered a fallen rider no way to escape — no room between a train and the platform. Anyone pressed up against the tiled wall on the other side would be electrocuted by the third rail. This was more certain than death by bus — if the timing was right.

Toby teetered on the edge of the platform. Riders were sparse at this time of day, spread out all the way down the track, standing between thick metal support girders painted green. Here and there, one straphanger nudged another, pointing into the dark tunnel. And there was the tiny burning light of an oncoming train. No one was watching the boy balancing near the edge, weaving in and out of the flimsy cover offered by widely spaced pillars of steel. But someone might notice Willy walking backwards just out of Toby's reach. Well, so what? Walking backwards wasn't a crime.

"Don't fall," she said to him, and she meant it. "Steady now." *Not yet — not quite yet.*

The light in the tunnel was still too small, too far away. If he fell right now, there would be time enough for some do-gooder to pull him back up from the tracks below.

Toby stopped to slump against a support post, his eyes rolling up to stare at the low ceiling, not stoned enough to die, not sober enough to stay alive. She had no fear of him fighting back or doing her any damage, not anymore. He was that wasted. Willy walked up to him and took him by the arm. She leaned out over the lip of the platform to see into the tunnel. The light was brighter now, and she could make out the form of the train, huge and streaming toward them. Toby was only two steps away from falling onto the tracks.

She pushed him and backed off. "Don't miss your train."

He was falling forward, one foot on the

platform and one foot over the rails. Any second now. A blown kiss would send him over the side.

What the hell? The boy flew backwards! *What the mother-fucking hell?*

Far down the platform, the train was filling out the mouth of the tunnel.

And only steps away, Mallory held the limp junkie by the arms and dragged him back from the edge. The detective dropped her heavy load — and not gently. Willy was in her sights. Mallory was coming for her, and more cops were pouring down the stairs. No way to run, nowhere to hide. Across the platform, another train was pulling in.

What were the odds of —

Fortuitously, a mommy with a baby in a stroller wheeled up to the edge of the platform. Willy bent down and snatched up the sleeping child.

Riker hit the floor of the lower level in time to see Mallory jump off the platform. *Christ!* The train was almost on top of her.

The breaks were screaming, but the tons of metal kept rolling, no time to stop, sparks flying, people yelling. And now he saw a baby flying through the air and out of harm's way to be caught by the outstretched hands of civilians. There was no time for a second rescue. And there was no room between the train and the wall to keep her alive.

"Mallory!" Riker's legs would not hold him. He sank to the ground. Before the train stopped, two cars had passed over the place where she had gone down. Farther along the track, he heard Detective Janos, a gentle soul by nature, screaming at the window of the lead car, his voice so loud and in such pain. "Back up this train or I'll shoot you fucking dead!" A conductor exited the car to tell him it was not that easy, but help was underway.

Gonzales squatted down beside Riker. "I saw it from the stairs. Willy tossed a kid on the tracks to get away from Mallory, but she didn't get past any of us. The detective glanced at the empty track on the other side of the platform. "Maybe Willy caught a getaway train." His attention turned back to his friend on the ground. Riker's face went slack, his eyes were blanks, and he made no response to shaking by Gonzales. "Hey! Can you hear me, buddy? You okay?"

No, he was far from okay; his partner was dead, and he was sliding into shock. How could any of this be real? How could she be ripped out of her life this way? *Impossible.*

And the situation was *so* unreal, for a moment there, he thought he heard Mallory screaming, "Get me *out* of here!"

A cheer went up, and all around him cops and civilians embraced. And *that* never happened in real life, either. Riker lowered his head — a bow to the absurd. He wept and he laughed, and his hands raised up in clenched fists of victory and a prayer for booze. *God,* how he needed a drink.

When technicians had cut the power to the high-voltage third rail, the tracks were flooded with uniforms and detectives, Riker among them. His partner had survived by laying her body down in the path of the oncoming train. The whole squad buzzed with questions. How could she *do* that when every human instinct screamed *run?* And how she could just lie there while a damn train ran over her? The general consensus was that she might not be human, but she *was* alive, so what the hell.

Mallory was pulled from the trough between the rails, her clothes smoked and scorched by sparks from brake shoes and wheels. Her hair and face were coated with dust and smeared with oil from the undercarriage, and the back of her was covered with caked dirt and debris from the ground. Oh, how the neat freak must hate that. She was lifted high in the air by a whistling, hollering, real happy crowd and handed up to the waiting arms of more brother and sister cops.

When at last she stood on solid ground, Riker grabbed her and held on tight. He was probably crushing the life out of her, but he could not stop himself. He hugged her and cried and yelled, "My God, you're *filthy!*"

And Mallory said, "So . . . you lost Willy."

"Hey, get outta the way! We got an OD here!" Two paramedics made their way through the welcome-back-from-the-dead party, and an unconscious Toby Wilder lay on the stretcher they carried between them. Mallory left her tight family of cops to walk alongside the stretcher as Toby's personal escort to the world up the stairs and the light of day.

FORTY

Normally I don't suck at math. Today my father sees the failing grade on my test paper. He works his butt off for this family, he says, and I only have this one little job — school. How, he asks, can a kid be so smart and screw up this bad? I wanted to say, "Well, I'm a little distracted, Dad. I'm waiting for them to kill me." But what's the point? He thinks I lied about the wino's murder.

"Be a man," he says. I tell him I can't. I won't live that long. And he smacks me. This is the first time he's ever done that. But I don't cry. I don't even flinch. I've taken worse, and I tell him so. My father just stands there. So surprised. It's like he's the one who got hit.

And he's the one who cries.

— ERNEST NADLER

Toby Wilder had been hospitalized for his

overdose, and his prognosis was good. The white shield, Arthur Chu, had earned his pay for the day by following Willy Fallon onto her getaway train to arrest her. And then the young cop had dragged his trophy prisoner into the squad room of Special Crimes Unit, where Willy had promptly lawyered up.

Mallory was pronounced fit for duty — only in need of some soap and a change of clothes. This was not the medical opinion of the emergency-room doctor, but Lieutenant Coffey had bought that lie. And it had been Riker's privilege to see the lady home. Chagrined, he realized that she could have done without his help, his game of blackmail chess with the chief of D's. As a hero cop, she could fail ten more psych evaluations and still keep her badge.

Riker wondered what a department shrink would make of Mallory's apartment, where everything was black or white, all sharp corners and hard edges. There were no personal elements, nothing to say that a human being lived here — except for the sound of a shower running in the bathroom. On the glass coffee table, Mallory's cell played rock-a-bye music to identify her caller, and Riker picked up the phone to have a conversation with Coco.

"Naw, she's fine," he said to the worried child. "You can't believe what you hear on the news. Mallory can only be killed by a silver bullet."

There was no sign of media interest in the grand-scale event going on at One Police Plaza, even though a gang of reporters had permanent roosts in the building's press-room.

Willy Fallon had been caught on a tourist's camera while throwing a baby into the path of an oncoming train, and that televised video had upstaged a coup at the Puzzle Palace, where a press secretary was madly spinning today's demonstration as a silent tribute to Rolland Mann, recently whacked by a bus, thus ensuring that it would be buried on the obituary pages of tomorrow's newspapers. None of the reporters — with police-issued press credentials — thought to ask why all of the demonstrators were women.

Outside on the plaza, the afternoon sun was hot enough to melt lipstick.

Jack Coffey stood by the red sculpture near the street. The promenade was impassable. He had been summoned here by the chief of detectives. Both men watched the crowd of uniformed officers filling the plaza and much of the courtyard beyond the gate-house to NYPD Headquarters. There were hundreds of them, tall and short, pretty cops and ugly ones, all packing guns — all of them policewomen. It was stunning and threatening and illegal as hell, but who could be called in to disburse them — the police? Male officers, who worked in the building, stood idly by the entrance, complacent prisoners.

"This is why you don't see any broads on patrol," said Joe Goddard. "They're all here — except for the seven cops upstairs at Dr. Kane's hearing."

Lieutenant Coffey had not been invited to the competency hearing, and neither had the chief of D's. The orchestration of this event had bypassed the Detective Bureau. Failed psych reports had been leaked only to affected patrol cops — every female in uniform ever evaluated by Dr. Kane — all seven of them labeled as sociopaths unfit for duty.

"Go figure," said Joe Goddard. "A police psychologist who's afraid of women with guns."

Not so long ago, Jack Coffey had heard these same words from Riker. He should have listened then. And now? He fancied that he could hear that detective laughing at him. The lieutenant's eyes traveled over the legion of cops awaiting the reinstatement of sister officers. Inside the building, every high-ranking official had a captive's view from the upper floors. "I bet it'll be the shortest hearing on record."

"You got that right," said Goddard. "But the hearing's just a formality. Dr. Kane was toast *before* these women showed up. That twit's psych reports were shredded hours ago. *All* of them. . . . Detective Mallory's, too." The chief looked up to the high windows. "I talked to the computer whiz kids on the top floor. They can't figure out who leaked those evaluations and organized this demonstration. All these cops think the orders came from their union. They *didn't*. But the instructions were routed through a union computer."

And now Jack Coffey learned that a hacker had used that computer to generate an automated mailing to every precinct. All of these women had received printed invitations to this party. And the sealed envelopes had been handed out this morning — by their own sergeants.

Joe Goddard rocked back on his heels. "We only know this was planned by a hacker with world-class skills . . . and she doesn't leave tracks." The chief was not a man to waste words on rhetorical questions, and yet he asked, "You got any theories, Jack?"

"Nope." Well, *yeah*. If he had to guess — at gunpoint — he might think that Mallory had ransacked the department data bank, looking for Charles Butler's rebuttal evaluation — the one never filed. It had probably taken her all of three minutes to figure out why the chief of D's was sitting on her failed psych evaluation. She had a natural gift for recognizing extortion potential. Lieutenant Coffey stared at his shoes. He had underestimated her so badly. And now she was gunning for Joe Goddard.

The chief of detectives was still waiting for a better answer — one that would probably come as a three-o'clock-in-the-morning epiphany: Mallory *wanted* Goddard to know that she had done this. Contrary to what the computer techs believed, there were footprints everywhere. This massive show of force, this overkill, was all Mallory, summoning hundreds of guns into play for one warning shot. Joe Goddard should not mess with her one more time — or there would be war in Copland. But that understanding would come later. Just now the man was tapping his foot — waiting.

"No idea." Jack Coffey folded his arms. "Not a clue." And then, since they both knew this was a lie, he told the truth. "No one's gonna look at one of *my* people for this — sure as hell not Mallory. She wouldn't be caught dead at an all-girl turnout. There's not one feminist bone in her body." She had no need of one. Only a rare and suicidal man might suggest that his detective was of better use barefoot and pregnant.

His point was made. His boss was nodding. And Mallory was going to get clean away with this.

The lieutenant's thoughts turned back to his pathetic paper-napkin map as evidence of her lost-soul state of mind. Riker had tried to tell him that he was wrong about the road trip, her unauthorized vacation from the job. And the proof? Mallory was getting away with that, too.

Yeah, her partner was definitely laughing his ass off right about now.

In a building across the street from One Police Plaza, the two detectives stood before a fourth-floor window that overlooked the demonstration. Riker had been braced for trouble all the way downtown, and now his partner broke her long, frosty silence.

"That'll be the day," said Mallory, "when *I* can't pass a psych evaluation."

Riker bowed his head, an act of contrition. He should have known better. It should have been obvious that Dr. Kane's finding of sociopathy was bogus — even if that twisted, frightened shrink had accidentally gotten this one thing right.

"Here they come." Mallory handed him her field glasses.

He focused the lenses on the entrance as a small gang of suits, union reps and lawyers, exited the building with seven female officers in dress blues. They all raised their fists in victory. Riker expected cheers, but the demonstrators remained silent and standing at attention. The now unemployed Dr. Kane was the next one through the door. He saw the barrier of uniforms, so many of them. The man clutched his breast and paused long enough to lose his mind before he ran back inside. And *now* Riker got the joke. The female officers broke ranks, standing at ease and then laughing as they peeled away from Dr. Kane's wide-awake nightmare, a mob of mighty women with guns.

And people said Mallory had no sense of humor. *Hah.*

All that worry for nothing. Riker looked down at his watch. They had a suspect in custody and awaiting interrogation. "We

574

gotta get moving."

Mallory idly jingled the car keys. "I *know* what you did." Her head did not turn his way. It swiveled. Like a cannon. And she said, "But I don't know *how* you did it."

Riker sensed that this was no prelude to a warm, fuzzy moment. He held up both hands in a don't-shoot-me posture. "I get it, okay? You never needed any help." Did this mollify her? Well, no, of course not. He knew why she had dragged him down here, why he had to see her handiwork up close, a damn army in the service of the ultimate control freak.

"I know what Goddard was using for leverage on us — on *me,*" she said. "Now tell me what kind of dirt you used on *him.*"

Tough one.

Extortion or no, a deal was a deal, and he was honor-bound to keep it. If he ratted out the chief of D's, he would lose her respect. And if he didn't? Well, the lady carried a gun. And so he said, "Shoot me."

Willy Fallon sat in the interrogation room with her cut-rate attorney, a baby-faced man in a cheap suit. According to Mallory's background check, he had graduated near the bottom of his law-school class.

Counselor and client had been kept wait-

ing for an hour before the detectives saun-
tered in. Riker held up a sheet of paper and
began to read a list of the state's grievances.

In response to the first charge of murdering Rolland Mann, Willy shouted, "He tried
to kill me *first!*"

Well, that was predictable, and so Riker
said his scripted lines, and his delivery was
rough. "That's gonna be a hard sell to a
jury. This is what they'll see." He showed
her a picture on the small screen of a
tourist's cell phone. "Here you are squeez-
ing the poor bastard's balls." Now he clicked
to his favorite shot. "And here you are
again, kicking his ass in front of the bus.
Don't tell us you didn't see that bus coming. It's a double-decker."

The attorney chimed in, "That's not
murder. At best you've got an assault with
mitigating circumstances."

The detectives stared at this man, as if he
might be speaking some off-planet language.

"I'm trying to work with you guys," said
the lawyer. "Okay? Now my client's a first-
time offender."

"No," said Riker, "she's not. And we got a
few more charges. One of her victims was
only ten months old. Willy threw the kid on
the subway tracks. So, Counselor — what
are we calling *attempted murder* today? You

576

got mitigating circumstances for that one? Did the baby say something rude to Willy?"

After an exchange of whispers with his client, the lawyer smiled. "I'm still willing to work with you."

Riker pulled a ten-dollar bill from his wallet and showed it to his partner. "I say he's gonna tell us the joke about sending her to drug rehab instead of jail."

Mallory shook her head — no bet. She laid out an evidence bag filled with capsules and pills. And then she said, so politely, almost apologetically, "Your client's stash is evidence for another charge."

"Willy drugged a guy," said Riker. "Not the one she pushed in front of a bus. This was a completely different guy — the one she tried to push in front of a *train.*"

"That's related to the drug charge." Mallory's comment was low-key, as if she had no stake in this game. She was the soul of sanity and clarity — and no hard feelings, by the way. "Toby Wilder was given a lethal dose of narcotics."

Riker grabbed the evidence bag and held it up to the attorney as he squeezed the stash of pills in a fist. "Toby says she drugged his wine."

"That was only fair!" yelled Willy, all but confessing before the attorney could lean over and say, "Shut the hell up."

"I won't!" she said. "Toby was the one who strung me up in the Ramble. He tried to kill me."

"You're lying," said Riker. "You couldn't identify your kidnapper. And that's backed up by the ER doc who examined you."

Mallory, in the spirit of being helpful, pushed the doctor's statement across the table. "He said the blow to the back of your head wiped out ten or fifteen minutes of memory. So you couldn't —"

"It *had* to be Toby!" Willy's voice was climbing into a high whine. "I know it wasn't that creep Rolland Mann. He was a fucking *amateur* at killing. He's *dead*, isn't he? So it *had* to be Toby."

The detectives looked at each other in mutual understanding of Willy logic: Their suspect had deduced this by process of *lethal* elimination.

"So let's recap," said Riker, addressing the only grown-up on the other side of the table. "Your client pushes one victim in front of a bus, and then she drugs another one. Tries to push *that* guy in front of a moving train. And the charge of resisting arrest brings us back to tossing the baby on the tracks. Maybe you saw the baby-tossing video? It's on every TV channel."

"I do watch the news," said the lawyer. "So I know Detective Mallory here survived being run over by a train. I'm told there's two feet of clearance between the rail bed and the —"

"Don't." Riker, with only this one syllable, promised the lawyer that it was worth his life to continue that thought. "When you toss a baby on the tracks, you can count on injury from the fall. And then there's an expectation of *sudden death!*" He pounded his fist on the table to punctuate those last two words and then turned his angry face to Willy. "The kid's gonna be okay, but the mother's suing you for every dime you'll ever own." And now back to the lawyer once more. "So I hope you got paid up front, pal. We talked to Willy's parents. They're not laying out one dime for legal expenses. Her credit cards are maxed out, but she's got about five grand in a paper sack. Will that do you?"

This was clearly a surprise to the lawyer. His smile of confidence faltered and failed. It was easy to read his face when he brightened up a little. Hey — *five thousand dollars.* The man stole a glance at his wristwatch, probably counting the money flying by per minute. "I propose a reasonable plea agreement for lesser charges."

"What?" Riker was on his feet and leaning over the table, as though he meant to throttle the lawyer. His partner rested one light hand on his arm, and he settled back into his chair.

Mallory smiled pleasantly, as if the lawyer had said something sane. "I think we can work out a deal."

On the other side of the looking glass, Jack Coffey shook his head in wonder. He had previously supposed that only in hell could Mallory play good cop to Riker's bad cop.

A visiting VIP, District Attorney Walter Hamlin, was also seated in the front row of the watchers' room. This distinguished man — in pop-eyed shock — leaned toward the one-way window. He listened to the intercom with rapt attention — while Mallory magnanimously offered to write off the murder of a deputy police commissioner as a traffic accident.

Score one for the smiling chief of detectives, who sat in the chair on Coffey's right. The problem of Rolland Mann was neatly disposed of, and the department would escape the worst police corruption scandal in twenty years.

In the next room, Riker was throwing up his hands in a show of disgust. And when

580

he quit the interrogation, he slammed the door behind him.

Now Coffey heard his remaining detective agree to throw in the attempted murder of Toby Wilder. "We'll call it a misunderstanding," said Mallory. "Why not? The guy was stoned. He won't remember anything."

Willy's lawyer nodded and smiled.

The district attorney in the watchers' room turned to Jack Coffey. "Does Detective Mallory know I'm here — *listening* to this?"

"Hell, yes," Chief Goddard answered for the lieutenant. "Walt, you know an ADA would never have the balls to sign off on this deal. That's why I invited *you.*"

In the next room, Mallory was making it very clear that Willy would have to plead guilty to the unfortunate baby-tossing *incident.* "But we can knock that down to a misdemeanor."

The defense lawyer leaned toward the *nice* detective to ask what she wanted in return.

Mallory proposed a trade of new murders for old. "Willy was only a kid when that wino died in the Ramble. I'm also interested in an assault on a boy from her school. If she tells me everything she knows, those old cases go to a judge in Family Court. She'll get the same sentence as a juvenile offender."

Riker entered the watchers' room and stepped up to the glass. "Can you believe that lawyer? Willy got him out of the yellow pages. I'm guessing his biggest case was in traffic court. Zero experience in criminal law."

This was the defense attorney every cop prayed for.

"Detective," said DA Hamlin, calling for Riker's attention. "Even if I put Mallory's deal in writing, it'll never stand up in court. Eight million New Yorkers are watching the baby-tossing film on television — right *now*. There isn't a judge in town who won't set aside the deal and hit Miss Fallon with the maximum sentence."

Riker grinned. "Yeah, we're counting on that."

DA Hamlin was not done yet. "About that wino. If Miss Fallon confesses to a murder done as a juvenile, she'll still do time in an adult facility — most likely the maximum time allowed by law. Do you think she fully understands this?"

"No," said Riker. "But I'm only required to read Willy her rights. She's a moron, and the lawyer isn't much smarter. Look at that smile on the guy's face. He thinks this is a *good* deal."

■ ■ ■ ■

When an hour had passed, the signed plea agreement was put on the table in the interrogation room. Mallory also laid out morgue photographs of the wino's dead body savaged by three children in the Ramble. "I already know most of the details. I can even tell you how many times Agatha Sutton bit the victim. Aggy the Biter — isn't that what you called her?"

Willy Fallon stared at the pictures. She was frozen, holding her breath — *big* eyes — as good as a guilty plea.

"If you lie to me, Willy, just *one* lie, the deal is off, and I can't help you anymore. You'll rot in jail for the rest of your life."

The lawyer nudged his client, prodding her into a nod.

And so it began, halting at first — and then with gusto.

The watchers in the next room sat in the dark — the only proper way to listen to a scary story. They heard the secondhand screams of a homeless man broken by rocks and torn by little teeth, bleeding and dying on the grass. And then came the long travail of Ernest Nadler. On days following the cruelty of stringing up the little boy by his wrists, his three torturers had returned to climb the hanging tree, to poke him with sticks — and other things — and the pain went on and on. Willy would not shut up. She was reliving all the torture, reveling in it — she *crazy* loved it.

FORTY-ONE

I sit in the garden and tell my story to Mr. Polanski, the school handyman. "I think the dead wino is being erased," I say. "Like Poor Allison, the jumper."

I look down at that place on the flagstones where the chalk girl appears on the first day of spring, and I ask him, "After I'm dead, do you think one day you'll hose me away, too?"

The handyman shakes his head and puts up both hands. He doesn't want to hear anymore. But I need to talk to somebody. I tell him, "I love my mom and dad. How do you say goodbye to people when they don't believe you're going anywhere?"

Mr. Polanski doesn't walk away from me. He runs.

— ERNEST NADLER

Chief of Detectives Goddard stood by the mayor's side during the televised press conference. The split-screen image also showed the baby-tossing video, now the most popular film clip with audiences everywhere. And though the town's top politician had just announced the capture and confession of the offending baby-tosser, one reporter had the temerity to bring up the Hunger Artist's unsolved murders. When the mayor's tongue tangled, Joe Goddard leaned into the microphone to say, "You bastards know the drill. That's an ongoing investigation."

The mayor cringed at the chief's wording, but he gamely went on to announce the death of Rolland Mann in an unfortunate traffic accident.

With a flick of the remote, Jack Coffey turned off the television set in his office and faced the flesh-and-blood version of the chief of D's, who had appropriated his desk. The lieutenant did not sit down in one of the vacant chairs. He preferred to stand alongside his detectives, Mallory and Riker.

"Now," said Joe Goddard, "about the funeral arrangements for Rocket Mann. Either he gets the twenty-one-gun salute with bagpipes — or we shove him in a pine box as an embarrassment to the department. The widow's leaving it up to us. Annie Mann really doesn't care, as long as she never has to leave her apartment again. My concern is blowback. What are the odds?"

"He murdered Ernie Nadler," said Riker.

"Then the bastard got what was coming to him," said the chief. "Case closed."

"No, it's not," said Riker. "What if we can prove that Mann was *hired* to kill that kid? How's that for blowback?"

The chief swiveled the desk chair left and right as he considered the intractable detective. He turned to the man's commander. "Jack, concentrate on the Hunger Artist. I want that case wrapped up fast. So maybe somebody pays and somebody skates. Don't get too precious, okay? And please tell me Rocket Mann wasn't on the shortlist for that one."

"No," said Mallory, "not his style. He favored crimes of opportunity, like trying to push Willy in front of a bus . . . like smothering a little boy in his hospital bed."

Was she baiting Goddard?

"Mallory?" Coffey tapped her shoulder. "Shut up!" And to the chief of D's he said, "We don't see Rocket Mann spending years collecting a murder kit. And we don't see him out in the woods with a winch and a drill. He'd never put that much effort into a murder . . . but he *was* a killer. A real cold —"

"I guess we got three votes for the pine box," said the chief. "But this ain't a democracy. So Rocket Mann gets the fallen hero's funeral. *Nothing* comes back to bite the department." This was couched as an order to leave that mess buried. "Now back to the Hunger Artist. Where'd you stash that junkie, Toby Wilder?"

"He's in the hospital," said Mallory, "getting his stomach pumped."

"He stays there under guard till I say otherwise." Onto the next order of business, the chief held up the detectives' request for a search warrant. "The DA squashed it. Heller and Slope won't sign off on the chloroform angle. The CSU test was inconclusive, and the ME's tissue samples got backed up in the lab. All the rest of the stuff on your list is too vague. Any old winch and drill won't do. The DA says you need to be more specific to get in the door."

"I guess nobody wants to piss off the wrong people," said Mallory.

She was the city's hero cop today, the golden girl of the NYPD, and, following her coup at One Police Plaza — *Hubris, thy name is Mallory* — she believed she could get away with mouthing off to the chief of D's in front of witnesses. She could not. Coffey could tell that much by the change in the atmosphere — the dead silence of a room with too many guns in it.

"I know how to make the warrant less vague." Riker now commanded the chief's attention. And once more, Lieutenant Coffey had to wonder what kind of power this detective had over Goddard.

"We got an expert witness," said Riker. "She's like a little catalogue of sounds. Coco can identify the brand of a vacuum cleaner if she only hears the motor. I've seen her do that trick. And she was in the Ramble the night Humphrey Bledsoe was strung up. Suppose we let her listen to the sample winches and drills CSU collected?"

Jack Coffey shot a glance at Mallory, who seemed to share his own surprise. Either Riker was lying to distract the chief from demolishing his partner — or he had been holding out on her.

Joe Goddard was not impressed. "Your expert witness is an eight-year-old kid?"

"A kid genius," said Riker. "She's got a gift for this stuff. And it gets better. We can document it. We got Charles Butler, an authority on gifted people. He'll sign off on this."

At the door to the station house, the two detectives parted company with a plan to

589

meet up later at Charles Butler's apartment. Riker had winches and drills to collect, but a little old lady was blocking his way.

"So it *was* murder," said Rolland Mann's elderly neighbor. "I saw it on TV." Mrs. Buford turned her head from side to side, cagey now and mindful of officers passing by. She dropped her voice to a hoarse whisper. "I'm sure he had it coming to him."

Oh, no — a snag, a little gray-haired loose end.

If just one reporter had the brains to canvas Rocket Mann's building — if this neighbor was questioned — everything could come unraveled. Riker gave her his widest smile. "Naw, it was a traffic accident."

"Detective Mallory said *murder.* She said that the first time we met. And that was *before* Rolland Mann got hit by the bus. Very prescient, wouldn't you say?"

Damn.

"My partner was talking about a different murder," said Riker, "an old one. And we appreciate your —"

"The TV reporter interviewed a Danish tourist who saw the whole thing. He said Rolland Mann was struggling with a woman when that bus came along. Was it Detective Mallory? I do hope she's not in any trouble."

In Mrs. Buford's mind, his partner was either clairvoyant or a killer cop. Fortunately, the old woman actually liked Mallory. Twenty minutes later, over a cup of coffee in the lunchroom, Riker had convinced her that the sudden death of her neighbor was not a conspiracy of cops — or that was his thought, based upon much nodding and smiling on her part.

But then she winked, and with that slow, sly drop of an eyelid, she put a lie to everything. "I understand," she said. "I'm as silent as the Sphinx. I would never say anything that might get Detective Mallory in trouble. Such a *sweet* girl. So *kind*."

"Yeah, that's my partner." Riker glanced at his watch. Right about now, his little angel would be busy torturing a blind man.

Anthony Queen was posturing, railing against the storm-trooper tactics of law enforcement.

On the other side of his desk sat Mallory — the law — quietly, calmly planning to cut the blind man at the knees to keep him away from reporters.

"There's a guard posted outside of Toby's hospital room. The police are denying me access to my client. I have a *right* to —"

"Toby has rights," said Mallory. "You

don't. And he's better off without any more help from you. When he was a kid, you stood by while the Driscol School's pricey lawyer bargained him right into Spofford. You always believed that boy was guilty."

"I never did."

"You *still* do. That day you showed up in court with Toby's mother — that's when the ADA told you where Toby laid down his flowers — the exact spot where the wino died. That's when you knew the boy was a killer."

"No. I never —"

"Liar. That's why you let Carlyle lock him away in that hellhole. You could've stopped the plea bargain, but you *knew* Toby was guilty. You thought a four-year sentence was a good deal . . . for a *killer.*"

"I *always* believed in him."

"Yeah, *right.* Here's the kicker, old man. Toby didn't do it. If the case had gone to trial, the defense would've been entitled to exculpatory evidence — a witness statement that would've cleared him. But that never came out because of the plea bargain. So Carlyle put an innocent kid away, and you helped him do it — as a *favor* to Toby's mother."

When he had fully absorbed his own part in the damage to Toby Wilder, the lawyer's face was a study in pain. However, because he *was* a lawyer, Mallory waited for the light to go on behind his blind eyes — that telling spark, the evidence of machinations, plots and schemes.

And now he smiled — so sly when he said, "Then Carlyle *knew* the boy was innocent."

"Forget it, old man. There won't be any lawsuit for wrongful imprisonment. If you try that, Toby gets put away for life. Fifteen years ago, all three of the Hunger Artist's victims blamed Toby for the wino's death. . . . Does that sound like a revenge motive for anyone we know?"

Queen's mouth opened wide — and closed. His store of words had failed him.

Shock was good, but Mallory toyed with the idea that she could make a lawyer cry. "I know what you did to Toby's mother — your very good friend. I talked to people who worked with Susan Wilder. They tell me she was a one-man woman, and she loved Jess Wilder till the day she died. But she loved her son even more. So I wondered why she'd go along with the plea bargain. That bothered me. That was *your* work, wasn't it? That woman trusted you. Toby was a minor child. Before a judge would let him plead out to murder — first you'd have to convince the mother that her son was guilty — that he murdered his own father."

"But Susan never knew who the wino was."

"She *knew*," said Mallory, "even before Toby's arrest. And I can prove it."

Anthony Queen's expression could only be read as *Please stop.*

Not yet, but soon. Just now she was on a get-even roll. "Susan Wilder went to the morgue to view the wino's body . . . with her fingertips. Stone blind, she *knew* that was her husband. I have a witness who tells me she cried. . . . She *loved* that man. And thanks to you, Susan died believing that her son beat him to death. . . . It's like you poisoned all the time she had left."

Tears. *Perfect.*

"You think you're sorry *now?* Don't make me come back here, old man." She rose from her chair and walked toward the office door. "Stay the hell away from Toby Wilder."

FORTY-TWO

My mother smiles at me all the time now.
Sad smiles. I think I'm driving her bug-shit
crazy. I'm sorry, Mom.
— ERNEST NADLER

"Maybe it's a bad idea. Loud noises drive
the kid up the wall." Riker used a small
hand truck to roll the heavy carton down
the hallway in Charles Butler's building.
The cardboard box was filled with every
winch and drill that would fit the Hunger
Artist's murder kit. "Charles is never gonna
go along with this."

"He's in Chicago," said Mallory. "Robin
Duffy's babysitting."

Well, problem solved. That particular
lawyer would let his partner set fire to a bus-
load of orphans just to see her smile.

When the door opened, Mallory suffered
through another bear hug of warmth and
affection. Fingers to his lips, Duffy whis-

pered, "Coco's taking a nap." He ushered them into the kitchen, where documents were laid out on the table. "Charles found these wonderful people in Chicago — the Harveys. They were pre-qualified for adoption a year ago, and they're both teachers in a charter school. This is *so* great. She'll have parental supervision all day long. Charles says the best part is that Coco can go to school like every other kid. She can have a normal life." He sat down at the table and sifted through the paperwork. "Oh, here it is." He handed one sheet to Mallory.

Reading over her shoulder, Riker scanned another copy of the release form that would allow their material witness to leave the state of New York.

"Just sign there, Kathy." Duffy pointed to the signature line at the bottom of the page. "The Harveys are flying back with Charles today. If everything goes well, they'll take Coco to Illinois for a probationary period."

"No way." Mallory folded the form. "The kid's not going anywhere until we wrap this case."

And when she laid the form down on the table, the old man said, "Charles wants you to know that the Harveys have a big backyard full of bugs. He thought that might be meaningful to you."

"She stays until —"

"Fine." Duffy put up both hands in surrender. "Whenever you're ready, Kathy. The Harveys will be in town for a while."

"You can go now," said Mallory. "I'll stay with Coco."

"Yeah," said Riker. "I'll walk you out."

Robin Duffy hesitated, stalling, his eyes rising to the clock on the wall. "Charles told me to stay — just until Mrs. Ortega gets back. She's out running errands." The old man had a worried look about him.

Riker was confused.

Mallory was not. "What else did Charles tell you? Did he tell you not to leave me alone with Coco? Did he tell you not to trust me anymore?"

Riker left the apartment with a very contrite Robin Duffy, and though the door was closed gently, the sound woke Coco from her nap. She ran out of the guest room and shot down the hall to wrap her arms around Mallory, so happy was she, her smile so wide. And, yes, she would love to help solve a murder. *Great* fun.

The detective wheeled the carton into Charles Butler's kitchen, and the child watched her open it to pull out the first winch. Mallory connected it to an adapter to make it run on household current. "Riker says you have a good memory for motors."

Coco rattled off a catalogue of motor-driven things, old ones and their replacements over the years: her grandmother's blenders and washing machines, vacuums, electric brooms and carving knives. And then there were the neighbors' motors, more brand names and models. And all the while, the child watched the detective cover the countertop with elements of a murder kit.

The little girl's words broke off as her eyes turned toward the kitchen door. "Mrs. Ortega's coming. Those are her shoes in the hall. You hear them?"

No, Mallory heard nothing. A moment later came the clicks of a key working the lock to the front door. She left the child in the kitchen and entered the living room to see the cleaning lady flop down in an armchair. Shopping bags lay on the floor at her feet.

"Hey, Mallory." Mrs. Ortega bent down to one of her bags. "Wait'll you see what I got for the kid." She pulled out a shoebox and opened it to display a small pair of pink sneakers. "A going-away present. Real shoelaces instead of that Velcro crap."

"But she can't tie the laces," said Mallory.

"If she can learn buttons, she can learn laces," said Mrs. Ortega. "No more damn Velcro. That's like buying a wheelchair for a kid who only limps a little. It'll cripple her."

"But she can't —"

"She *has* to!" Exasperated, the cleaning lady threw up her hands. "How's that kid gonna make it in life if she can't even tie her shoes?"

Indeed. Mallory, in her feral days, had survived by packing razor blades in the pockets of her child-size jeans; and by stealing only the best running shoes, and running like crazy to escape kiddy rapists; and she had learned to make her bed only places where she was most likely to live through the night. She had stolen wallets and wheedled money from whores and acquired so many other skills that Coco could never learn for lack of guile.

The little girl stood in the doorway, and her face had a worried look. Of course, she had overheard everything, and now her steps were timid as she stole up beside the detective and shyly took her hand. Those blue eyes were full of hope — and thus alien to Mallory, who saw all hope as pointless.

The cleaning lady went downstairs to ready an apartment for Charles Butler's guests, the Harveys of Illinois. And the detective sat on the floor, teaching Coco to tie shoelaces so that this tiny child could survive in the wide world. Their fingers intertwined for hours as they worked the laces together. The child so loved Mallory that, though she tired, she would not stop until she had done this one thing right. And so the final triumphal knot was a gift that each of them gave to the other.

When Charles Butler entered his apartment, he heard the sound of a motor running, and Coco was yelling, "Stop! That's *it!*"

He raced to the kitchen, and there he found the child seated at the table, both hands pressed to her ears. Her mouth formed a silent scream — while Mallory powered down a mechanical device. His kitchen counter was lined up with motorized things. This was torture for a child with hyperacuity.

"Hi." Mallory turned to Charles, smiling as if this might be a perfectly normal way to occupy a little girl's time. "Coco identified the motors she heard in the Ramble. I need a letter from you to back up how good she is with sounds."

Coco was rocking back and forth, hugging herself — calming herself.

Charles's face was grim. "A moment, Mallory? Out in the hall?" This was not an invitation. He took her by the arm and propelled her from the kitchen, through the apartment and into the outer hallway, shutting doors behind him so the child would not hear him ask the detective, "Are you *insane?* I can't believe you put her through that. Don't you *ever* go near that child again."

The detective was squaring off, gearing up for a fight. "I need —"

"Who cares? The prospective parents are downstairs right now. Don't make that little girl choose between you and them. Even *you* couldn't be that cruel."

Did she flinch? She did.

He pressed on. "Those two people are all prepared to love that child on sight. You have only the most *superficial* interest in Coco. Get out, Mallory! Just go!"

Mallory turned away from him, and she was striding toward the elevator when Coco came running out the door, screaming, "Wait for me!" She wriggled free from Charles's grasp and flung herself down the hall, lurching, crying, "Mallory! Mallory!"

The detective never even turned her head to acknowledge the little girl. She only put up the flat of her hand and commanded,

"Stop." Obedient as any dog, the child did stop. "Stay," said Mallory as she stepped into the elevator and vanished.

"No! *No-o-o!*" Coco ran to the end of the hall and banged the metal doors. She sank to the floor, a puddle of a child. Charles was at her side, reaching down to her. She waved her arms to ward him off, and then her interest wandered to a shoelace that had come undone.

Laces?

Her face was anguished. Lost again, anchorless. Her arms flung wide, small hands curling into fists. This was the breach he had wanted; the precise moment to replace one bond for another was now. He knelt down beside her. "There are two very nice people downstairs. They've come all the way from Illinois to meet you."

"I want Mallory."

"She won't be back."

Coco shook her head. "Mallory loves me. She *loves* me."

And now he watched her bow her head to — *tie — her — shoelace.* And when she was done, she looked up at him, so defiant. She stuck out her foot to show him this accomplishment of an awkward child-tied knot. "Is *that* superficial?"

Oh, God — her remarkable hearing. Every

word said in the hall had been overheard.

Coco leaned toward him, eyes glittering and wet, and there was anger when she said with great dignity, "Mallory *loved* me."

Past tense.

Stripped of all hope, the floundering child wrapped her arms around his neck. Her tiny body was shaking with sobs, her voice cracking as she recited a litany of deep pain. They sat there in the hallway for a very long time, Charles dying, Coco crying, grieving over every unfair loss, lost home, lost love.

The Harveys of Illinois had finished unpacking their bags in the downstairs apartment, and now they were surprised when the elevator doors opened upon the sight of a tiny child with swollen red eyes. Mrs. Harvey picked up the little girl to carry her down the hall and through the open door to Charles's apartment, saying all the while in tones of motherlove, "Everything's going to be all right." In charge now, Mrs. Harvey pulled a tissue from her purse and wiped Coco's face clean of tears.

Charles was unprepared for the child's reaction to this small kindness, and it killed him to watch it play out.

Coco's fabulous smile was instant and wide — if not genuine — as she informed the Harveys that rats were carriers of bubonic plague. Next, she ran to the piano in the music room. She played them a song and sang for them, then danced back into the parlor and began a monologue of vermin trivia. How hard she worked, auditioning for a new home and negotiating for love to replace what was so recently ripped away. And the Harveys were blindly enchanted by a child's ruthless pitch for survival.

Excusing himself, Charles retired to Coco's bedroom, where he sat alone with his pain. The drapes were drawn, and the only light was the glow of fireflies. How bright. How odd. They should have begun to die off long before now, but there was not one dead insect in the jar.

Oh, fool. Would that he could die of foolishness.

It was so obvious. Mallory had been entering by stealth, by night — every night — to replenish the lightning bugs so that Coco would not wake up in a dark place.

The sorry man reached beneath the pillow and found Coco's one-button cell phone. He pressed the button, and the connection was instant. "Mallory?"

And she said, "I signed Coco's release form. You'll find it on the kitchen table. Are you happy now?"

"No," he said.

This summer afternoon would remain in his memory forever, a bookmark to a sad and curious passage that he must return to again and again. Well into his nineties and long after the death of Kathy Mallory, on every fine, warm day, he would sit in a garden where he would only suffer daisies to be planted. Sometimes his great-grandchildren would find him there, tearing petals from flowers. They would smile to see the old man playing a children's game of *loves me, loves me not,* never suspecting that he grappled with an old problem of bugs in a jar.

He, who was whole and sane and fully human — he would never have thought to light a child's way through the night with fireflies. And so he plucked the daisies bald, alternating Mallory's possibilities, saying with one torn petal, "She had no heart," and with the next petal, "She did."

Riker walked down a row of cages made of wood and chicken wire, flimsy protection for the artifacts of those who had died without leaving wills, all their goods condemned to probate limbo. He paused by the only storage space that burned with interior lights. His partner had been busy rewiring. Extension cords trailed down from a ceiling fixture and hooked up with table lamps to illuminate rooms of furnishings crowded into the space of an oversized closet.

The largest item was the Nadlers' walk-in safe, and it was wide open. Evidently, Mallory had tired of following their boss's instruction to wait for a proper work order to get the lock bored out. A huge drill lay on the floor, and the safe now had a gaping hole in its door — and a cop inside.

"Find anything useful?" He leaned into the safe and whistled at the walls of stacked-up comic books. On top of one of the shorter piles was a pristine Batman issue that was older than he was.

Mallory sat on the metal floor, reading handwritten lines in a small book. "The city would've found the Nadlers' will if they'd bored out the damn lock fifteen years ago."

"Lucky thing they didn't." Riker flipped through the comics in archival covers. "The mice would've chewed all of this to bits. This is no kid's collection. It's worth a fortune."

"Those belonged to the boy's father. They're mentioned in the will. But I found Ernie's comics, too — what's left of them." She pointed to the floor outside the safe and a box with mouse-chewed holes.

He hunkered down beside it and lifted the cardboard lid. The top layer had been shredded for a nest to bed down a litter of blind, newborn vermin. They wiggled and squeaked. But Riker, a good New Yorker, did not find them cute. He snapped on a latex glove and burrowed underneath them to pull out two comic books that were still intact. "Another Batman — like father, like son. And here's a Superman."

And now he realized that Mallory had been moving the furniture. All the effects of Ernie's life were gathered in this corner around a boy-size bed, a matching nightstand and a cracked lamp in the shape of a ceramic surperhero.

"I found the Nadlers' suicide note." Mallory walked out of the safe, holding the small leather-bound book that she had been reading. "This is Ernie's diary." She pulled a folded sheet of paper from between the pages and handed it to him.

Riker opened the note and read the simple line written by one of the parents before they died, a goodbye of five words: *For those who wonder why.*

Mallory sat down on a wooden chair that matched the boy's bedroom suite. "The pages of Ernie's diary are dusted with glass fragments from a broken lightbulb." She opened the top drawer of the nightstand. "Look. More fragments in here. This is probably where he kept it. That's why the drawer was open. So this is what happened. After Ernie died, the Nadlers got home from the hospital that night. They came into his room and sat down on that bed — and they read his diary. And when they were done, one of them threw it at the wall, and it cracked the lamp."

"And broke the lightbulb." Riker could see Ernie's parents holding each other in the dark.

FORTY-THREE

They stand over me at the Losers' Table — watching me eat a bite of my lunch. It won't stay down, and Humphrey giggles when I throw up in my napkin.

I pick up my tray and carry it across the dining hall to sit down beside Toby Wilder, though I know he likes to eat his meals alone, and every other kid in school gives him the space of half a table. But he doesn't even notice me. His eyes are closed to slits, and his fork conducts an orchestra inside his head.

I look up and there they are, settling down on the other side of the table, three stealthy crows come to peck me to death. Screw them. I eat my lunch, fearless. Humphrey wouldn't dare pull any shit, not here, and Willy only stares at me with spider eyes. But Aggy just can't help herself. She clicks her teeth nonstop, promising me another bite. I never rat her out for biting me — murdering a bum, sure — but not for something personal. Those clicking teeth get Toby's attention. He opens his eyes, and the three of them sit up real straight. And then he says, "Get the fuck out of here, you freaks!" And they leave the table, knocking over chairs to do it in a hurry. I will worship Toby Wilder until I die.

— ERNEST NADLER

The detectives stepped out of the car and walked up Central Park West. As they turned the corner onto a quiet side street, Mallory made a cell-phone call to CSU and tortured Heller with the news that a little girl had done what his team could not do: Coco had identified makes and models for the winch and drill used by the Hunger Artist. And then she suggested that he take his botched chloroform test and farm it out to a lab with better equipment, adding that she was fresh out of children to develop more evidence.

Riker could easily fill in the gaps of this conversation with obscenities, and when her call had ended, he asked, "Did Heller make any death threats?"

"No, he's in a good mood today. He says we're even now."

What? Had Heller forgiven Mallory for hog-tying and bagging his new CSI? *Naw — not a chance.* However, she *had* trained CSI Pollard to pay attention to details, and Heller might see that as a win. But why share this thought with her? Why spoil her day?

The next call was made to District Attorney Hamlin. The man had received Charles Butler's hastily written affidavit, and then he had found a judge to sign off on a child's genius for identifying motors. Pocketing her phone, Mallory said, "Our warrant's on the way."

It was a thousand-to-one shot that anything from the murder kit would be found, but they were not searching for any of those items today.

Their stroll ended halfway down the block when they paused to case a private home guarded by stone lions at the top of a short flight of stairs. It was twice the width of the surrounding brownstones but no taller. Looking upward, they could see only tips of rooftop foliage. The detectives crossed the street and pressed all the buzzers for an apartment building next door. The first tenant to answer the intercom was drafted into service, and she led them up — and *up* — to the fifth floor of a century-old building with nothing as fancy as an elevator. And yet Riker, though short of breath, made no vows to quit smoking.

At the top of the last flight of stairs, they dismissed their guide and stepped out onto a roof of chimneys and cable lines, weathered deck chairs and tar paper pocked with pigeon droppings. It was a grim far cry from the lush garden atop the adjoining roof. They climbed over the low parapet and onto a soft carpet of grass. All around them were the trees, ferns and flowers of a smallish park in the sky. At the center of this fairyland, they found a small structure for the door leading down into the house, its walls hidden by ivy. Near the street side, a patio had been carved out with flagstones and decorated with a table and padded wrought-iron chairs.

And an *ashtray!*

Riker was a happy man when he sat down and lit up a cigarette. "It just doesn't get any better than this."

"It will." His partner settled a heavy knapsack on the table, pulled out her phone and placed a call. When she had worked through the responding Hoffman, and when the lady of the house was at last on the line, Mallory said, "You've got cops on the roof."

■ ■ ■ ■

The three of them were gathered on the rooftop patio, and Grace Driscol-Bledsoe had selected Riker as the pushover cop. Her small talk was directed toward him, and then she won his heart by lighting up a proffered cigarette.

Mallory quietly endured the bonding ritual of smokers. And when the older woman finally looked her way, the detective flashed her a *Gotcha* smile and laid the old ViCAP questionnaire on the table. "I think you've seen this before."

The society matron's upper lip curled back with this unexpected and nasty surprise, but she was a quick-recovery artist. Turning to Riker, fellow smoker, one of *her* people, she insisted that he must call her Grace. "And what should I call you?"

"*Detective.* Me and my partner, we got the same first name." He stubbed out his cigarette. "We were hoping you'd clear something up for us — *Grace.*" He picked up the ViCAP questionnaire. "Rolland Mann was blackmailing you with this. So we figure it wasn't his own idea to murder the Nadler kid."

Mrs. Driscol-Bledsoe never glanced at the

613

sheets in his hand. Her smile was still in place when she said, "You suspect Rolland of extortion *and* murder? Poor *dead* Rolland. Well then, as I see it, your job is done. Good work."

Riker feigned incredulity, and Mallory knew he had to fake it because nothing surprised him anymore. "Are you trying out your defense strategy on us? We don't like Rolland for the Hunger Artist murders. And Willy Fallon didn't string herself up in the Ramble."

"So we need another stone killer," said Mallory. "Somebody with the patience of a long-range planner." She turned an admiring glance on the environs. "That was smart — *Grace* — planting the trees back from the street — no sidewalk advertising for unreported income."

"Seven years ago," said Riker, "the Driscol Institute paid to reinforce this roof."

"The Institute is responsible for maintaining my house. Perfectly legal."

"Not quite," he said. "You needed the extra support for this damn park. How many tons of soil —"

"A legitimate business expense," said Grace. "The Driscol Institute *owns* my house, and I host the charity's fund-raisers."

"Not up here," said Mallory. "We talked

to your caterer, the one who bills the Institute for your weekly fund-raisers. He's never even seen the roof." The detective opened her knapsack and pulled out a heavy paperbound volume. She slammed it down on the table, and the glass ashtray danced close to the edge. "That's the Institute's charter. It covers bare maintenance on the mansion . . . no rooftop landscaping." The wave of Mallory's hand encompassed all the trees and shrubs. "So the Driscol Institute paid a contractor to shore up the roof. I've seen the canceled check and a legitimate work order. But you're the one who paid for the landscaping — in *cash* — lots of it. Where did all that money come from?"

Riker reached down behind his chair to pluck a brilliant pink flower, and Grace gasped. He twirled the stem in his fingers. "I've never seen one like this before. Real expensive, huh?" He tossed the flower over one shoulder. "Did your landscaper pitch a fit when his dolly got stolen?" And when her silence dragged out too long, he said, "A dolly — maybe you call it a hand truck. You know, two wheels, long handle. This one had a car battery attached. Your landscaper used it to power a joist. That's how he lifted those trees up here — and tons of soil."

"Cheaper than a crane," said Mallory. "Easier to hide what you were doing — with unreported, *untaxed* income. Crane operators require city permits — a paper trail you couldn't afford."

"But a joist is overkill," said Riker. "If you only wanna string up a few bodies, a light winch will do just fine — three times in a row." He laid down his notebook. It was open to a page that listed the brand names of items from the murder kit. "This particular dolly had a wider platform than most. You'd need something like that to transport an unconscious victim to the Ramble."

The woman was slow to respond. When she finally spoke, her tone was condescending. "Is that how I did it?"

"Yeah," said Riker. "You covered the theft of the dolly with cash and a sweet tip for the landscaper. No police report. What were the odds that the cops would ever trace it back to you seven years later?"

"Indeed." The socialite seemed to agree with him — smiling, nodding, much too calm, even if she did have the best lawyers that dirty money could buy.

Mallory stared at Grace's cigarette. The ash at the end had gone dark and smokeless. "You don't inhale. That's probably wise." She leaned forward and lightly touched the silver pendant chained to the older woman's neck. "Will that gizmo work up here?"

Grace's hand instinctively went to her breast to cover the medic-alert medallion that dangled there. "Yes, there's an electronic responder in that little building over there." She nodded toward the small structure for the roof door. "Would you like a demonstration, Detective Mallory?"

"I know how panic buttons work. It's a service for old people — a lot older than you — and people with medical problems, the ones who live alone. But you've got Hoffman."

"You got a live-in nurse," said Riker. "And you're still so freaked out, you wear that medallion. Don't you trust Hoffman to call the ambulance? Afraid she might not like you that much?"

"She can't be *too* paranoid," said Mallory. "She's already had a stroke."

Riker made a show of consulting his notebook for the plunder of Mallory's raid on insurance-company files. "She's had *two* strokes."

Grace Driscol-Bledsoe had the look of a woman stripped naked in public. She turned to the sound of the roof door opening. Hoffman was running toward them, yelling, hands waving. There were cops in the house. They were everywhere. Everywhere!

On every landing, doors stood open to reveal the search in progress, men and women in uniforms upending drawers and turning out closets. Two flights away from the ground floor, an officer handed Grace Driscol-Bledsoe the search warrant. She read the text as she spoke to the detectives standing beside her on the stairs. "I gather this only pertains to the Hunger Artist?"

"No," said Mallory. Once they were assured of getting in the door, she had tacked on a few other charges and more items, like trees and plants. "We're also looking for any loose cash you have lying around."

"Whoa," said Riker. "Looks like they found it." He backed up against the wall, and the others did the same to make room for uniforms coming down the stairs, carrying clear plastic bags filled with currency.

Mallory watched the money walk past them. "Grace, I don't think your income will account for all that cash. Large bills, maybe three hundred thousand a bag? Does that sound about right?" More officers with bags paraded past them. "So we're looking at millions here."

The older woman resumed her reading of

the warrant. "The Driscol Institute owns this house — furnishings, paintings, even the silverware. My lawyers won't have a problem extending that ownership to cover money, too."

As they passed the first door on the next landing, Mallory looked into a room outfitted like a small clinic. "You do plan ahead." A pantry stood open to reveal an impressive larder of medical supplies. Detective Janos was pointing to shelves of pharmacy bottles as he questioned Hoffman.

"What's up?" Riker turned to his partner. "She's got a phobia about hospitals?"

"No, that's not it," said Mallory. "If Grace has another stroke, she can't afford a long hospital stay. There's a residence clause in the charter — her great-grandfather's idea to force every heir into keeping his family name. If there isn't a Driscol in residence for a continuous year, the board of trustees has to sell the mansion."

"But she's got a kid," said Riker.

"Phoebe's only a Bledsoe. Blood doesn't count. Neither one of Grace's kids had a claim on family income or property. Their mother neglected to add a hyphenated Driscol to their birth certificates. That's all they needed. It's spelled out on page five of the charter. I'm sure the family lawyers reminded Grace before the first child was born. I guess she just *forgot*."

"Twice." Riker turned on the last Driscol. "Lady, you're a piece of work."

"Grace was only thinking ahead. Strokes run in the family. She wanted to give her kids a reason to keep Mom alive — but not in a nursing home." Mallory faced the society matron. "And you thought of that when they were only babies — a true long-range planner."

"You think I'm a —"

"The first time we met," said Mallory, "you told me what you were. You said monsters are begot by monsters."

Bravado held sway. The lady smiled. "Will a jury believe that I strung up three people to cover the murder of my own son? Or will they find a grieving mother sympathetic? Seriously, Mallory, monster to monster, what do you think of my chances?"

Mallory was not listening. Detective Janos was coming toward her, carrying a bottle of chloroform. It should not be here — *still* here — but there it was.

"This is comfier than a police lockup." Riker opened the door and stepped back. "Ladies first."

His prisoner entered the chicken-wire

cage at the end of a long row of such enclosures. She stared at the furniture and tall stacks of cartons. "You're planning to keep me in a warehouse?"

"Oh, not just any warehouse, Grace. When people die intestate, all their stuff comes here — just till the city can legally steal all the money they leave behind. These things belonged to Ernest Nadler's parents." But now, with the discovery of the will, it might only take another fifteen years to release the little family's personal effects. The detective opened the small Gladstone bag that Grace had taken from Hoffman on the way out the door. Now he was staring at a pharmacy bottle of liquid and its companion syringe. "So you *are* shooting up."

"Give that back! If I have a stroke, there's only a small window of time to take that shot. It prevents permanent damage." One hand closed around her medic-alert medallion, though it was useless in this place so far out of signal range.

"No problem. When I go, there'll be a cop posted right here. I'll leave the needle with him, okay?" No, he could see that was not okay with her, but she would not give him the satisfaction of begging. Riker rested one hand on the back of an overstuffed armchair. "Mallory says this is the best seat."

He clicked on a floor lamp. "A reading light — you'll need it. My partner spent a lot of time down here, reading Ernie Nadler's diary. She made a copy just for you." He pointed to a stack of Xeroxes on the floor. "You'll wanna get a jump on the evidence before the arrest."

"*Before* the arrest? I'm already —"

"No, you're being detained as a person of interest. Until we charge you, there won't be any phone calls to the lawyers. Not what you expected, huh? Let's see if I can guess the plan. Halfway through your trial, your lawyer lets it slip that Phoebe's nuts — hears voices — maybe kills people." And now he echoed the words of Aggy Sutton's brother. "Crazy is good. That's reasonable doubt for a jury." He hunkered down to open a carton of Ernie Nadler's favorite things, his comics — and a nest of baby mice.

Grace Driscol-Bledsoe stared at the mewling, pink vermin with a moue of distaste. "Where's your partner? Why didn't she come with us?"

"Mallory thinks I'm wrong." Riker pulled out a slightly chewed comic book and leafed through the pages. "She bet me twenty bucks you'd never drag your kid into this mess. She says you've got other plans for

Phoebe. If you have another stroke, you won't wanna spend the next thirty years in a state nursing home."

"You forget. I inherited millions from my son. More than enough to —"

"Naw, that'll stay frozen in probate." He set down the comic book and pulled out another one. "And the cash we found in your house was impounded. If Phoebe's in jail when you stroke out, the trustees will get you certified incompetent. They'll dump you in a cheap nursing home and sell the house out from under you. What's that place worth? Maybe ten million? I bet the trustees sell it for twenty. They're a greedy bunch, really ruthless. Even Mallory was impressed."

He laid down the comic book to answer his cell phone. "Yeah? . . . It's a done deal? . . . Good." He ended the call and smiled at his prisoner. "That was Walt Hamlin, the DA. He says you just lost your job, lady."

And now he explained what had been going on elsewhere during the long ride to this warehouse. The district attorney had convened a meeting of the Driscol Institute's board of trustees. All the bags of cash taken from the mansion had been laid out on the boardroom table.

"I collected that money as cash donations to charity."

"Yeah, sure you did. It was the landscaping that nailed you. The DA showed them pictures of your private park on the roof." With only these visual suggestions of criminal acts, the trustees had unanimously elected not to go to jail with Grace. "It took them six minutes to enforce a morals clause. They voted you out of the director's chair."

"My compliments," she said. "However, you must know I'll never do a day in prison."

"Maybe not." Riker held up the Gladstone bag. "But you'll have a problem paying Hoffman's salary." He opened the bag and took out the syringe. "What if she's not around when you really need this shot?"

"Where *is* your partner?"

"I guess Mallory's right. You'd never let Phoebe take the fall for you. You need a relative to keep you out of nursing-home hell. You need somebody who gives a crap if your adult diapers get changed now and then. And Phoebe can never leave you. She's too damaged to make it on her own . . . thanks to good old Mom. That's the payoff for years of standing by, doing nothing, just watching your kid go nuts."

"My daughter's not insane. She's a school

nurse, a functional, productive —"

"Crazy Phoebe won't keep that job much longer. She's getting wiggier by the day. But she's still functional enough to spoon-feed you when you can't even remember her name anymore. . . . But what if she finds out why you paid Willy Fallon all that cash?"

Now she was frightened. And so half the job was done. The detective stepped outside the cage and locked the door. As he walked down the corridor, the woman found her voice, and he heard her call out to him.

"Riker, where is Mallory? What is she doing right now?"

FORTY-FOUR

Tonight, I get a phone call from Phoebe. Just the sound of her voice makes me happy. I'm not alone anymore. But then she tells me I have to take back my story about the wino's murder. Standing by my statement is "sheer folly," and she's crying when she says this, but she won't tell me why. Or she can't. "Sheer folly" is not a Phoebe-like thing to say. I take this as code for "My mother is listening." I stretch these very unPhoebe words to mean that she is and always will be on my side.

— ERNEST NADLER

When Phoebe Bledsoe had read this bookmarked passage, she closed the diary and pushed it back across the table. "Thank you. Yes, my mother was listening. That was the last time I ever spoke to Ernie."

Under the fluorescent lights of the interrogation room, Mallory opened the small volume to an entry that followed the assault on a wino. "After that man was murdered, your parents kept you home from school?"

"My mother's idea. Daddy had nothing to do with it. She was better at cleaning up Humphrey's messes. That's what my father said to her — *yelled* at her."

"You were there when your parents had that fight?"

"No, I was locked in my bedroom, but I could hear their voices — the slam of the front door. After my father left the house, my mother screamed at Humphrey. She told him he'd better get on Daddy's good side or else. Aggy Sutton was there that day. Willy Fallon, too. When they were all yelling all at once, I could barely understand the words. But I heard Ernie's name, over and over. That was before he went missing."

"And *after* Ernie disappeared?"

"His parents came to the house with the police. I heard Mrs. Nadler crying, Mr. Nadler hollering. They wanted to talk to me. I banged on the door of my room. I screamed, I *howled* until my mother let me out. I told the Nadlers that Ernie was scared, and he might be hiding out in the Ramble. Detective Mann didn't believe me. Mr. Nadler said he'd search the whole park by himself. Then the detective agreed to do it, and that was the night they found Ernie hanging in a tree. Later . . . when Ernie died . . . I fell apart. That's when Daddy took me to the first psychiatrist. My mother didn't like any of them. She was always pulling me out of therapy."

Of course. Better to let a little girl suffer in silence than risk her giving up family secrets to a therapist. The detective looked down at her notebook of empty lines. "Did your father ever talk to you about what Humphrey did?"

"No, not in those days. Later he did — the year my brother turned sixteen. When Humphrey was in prep school, he was accused of raping a six-year-old girl. She wasn't the first one. But Daddy told me she'd be the last. That's when he dissolved his company and set up Humphrey's trust. It drove my mother crazy. She was so angry with my father. Daddy lived in hotels all the time after that."

"Your mother told us Humphrey was your father's favorite." Mallory laid down two circles of canvas cut from a portrait of father and son.

Phoebe smiled. "That painting was my mother's idea when Humphrey was ten years old. She thought spending time together would bring them closer. But Daddy never loved him. No one could."

Well, Grace must have loved him — when he was ten.

"He was a monster," said Phoebe.

Like mother, like son.

"I'm not sorry my brother's dead."

Of course not.

And Mallory's only regret was that Phoebe had no witness potential to hang her mother.

After dismissing the officer on guard duty, Mallory entered the chicken-wire cage that held the Nadlers' household goods and one prisoner. Grace Driscol-Bledsoe had finished reading the copied diary pages. The loose papers were neatly stacked in her lap.

"I know you have questions," said Mallory. "You're wondering if I told Phoebe why you gave Willy Fallon bags full of cash."

"I can only imagine what you've been telling my daughter — not that she'd believe you."

"I could show her Willy's statement." The detective circled around to the back of the woman's chair. "Willy says you paid her to terrorize your own daughter." Mallory leaned down close to Grace's ear. "You wanted Phoebe scared out of her mind. You thought she'd come back home . . . to you."

"So you haven't told her anything. I smell a negotiation. You don't even have enough to charge me." Grace had the smile of a true carnivore. "Weakness, my dear, I can smell that, too."

Mallory could only smell the pollution of mice and roaches. She sank down on the bare mattress of the Nadler boy's bed. "You know what happened to Ernie's parents?"

"A double suicide, I'm told."

"No, the way I see it, *you* killed them. When you sent Rolland Mann to murder their son, you might as well have pushed those people off that ledge."

"Old history." Grace waved one hand to dismiss these insignificant deaths.

Mallory absently stroked the mattress. "Phoebe really upstaged you." In sidelong vision, she saw the other woman's head slowly turning. "Your daughter went out and did her own damn killing. Hands-on — no hit-man cop, no gang of twisted kids."

"What did you —" The Xeroxed diary pages cascaded from Grace's hands in a slow slide and wafted to the floor.

"You knew she was the Hunger Artist. You knew it the minute we told you about the landscaper's dolly. Poor Phoebe," Mallory shook her head. "She was a wreck when I brought her in. Nerves all shot to hell. But after she put her confession in writing . . . she stopped biting her fingernails."

"That confession is worthless!" Grace's voice carried a single note of hysteria, but it was gone all too quickly. "My daughter is easily intimidated. Obviously, she wasn't in a rational state of mind when —"

"Well, crazy is a relative thing in New York City." Mallory leaned down to pick up the fallen diary pages. "Does Phoebe know what you did to Ernie? I mean — *before* you had him murdered. She wasn't in school when your little thugs changed their style of torture — when you made them stop beating on him. No more incriminating bruises or bite marks. Pure terror was better. You told them to scare Ernie into recanting." Mallory took her time gathering up the last of the Xerox sheets. "It's all here." She rippled the pages. "The stalking, the psychological torture — by three stupid kids? No, Grace, that was all you. Willy Fallon says you told them exactly what —"

"Willy?" The society matron's eyes turned gleeful. "Willy the *baby* tosser? Hardly a stellar witness. And the boy's diary proves nothing."

"Your little gang of morons went too far. The kids couldn't follow simple instructions. They couldn't help themselves. They just *had* to hurt that little boy. If Ernie Nadler ever came out of his coma, Humphrey would've been arrested along with his friends — and you, too. Kid confessions are easy. You *know* your own son would've ratted you out in a heartbeat. So you bought a cop to kill Ernie before he could wake up and talk."

"Oh, back to *that* again. So tedious."

"Did Rolland Mann ever tell you how badly he botched that murder? Did he tell you a nurse could place him in the hospital room when the boy died?"

No, apparently not. The woman was tensing up, physically bracing.

"I didn't think so," said Mallory, "only because that nurse is still alive — and talking. Rolland Mann was a mediocre cop in those days, never worked a major case, never met a stone killer . . . no one like you, Grace. Rich, powerful . . . not quite human. So he married that nurse and hid her away. He was afraid you'd have *her* murdered. And just in case you found out about the witness — his *wife* — he showed you a ViCAP questionnaire, his documentation of the Ramble assault on a little boy — evidence buried in a government computer. You couldn't buy it or destroy it. Did that scare you? That wasn't blackmail. It was *insurance* so you wouldn't hurt Annie, his wife. But Rolland Mann couldn't spell that out for you. He didn't want you to know she existed. So you bribed and extorted politicians to move his career along — all for nothing. He would've settled for keeping Annie safe."

"Very romantic, Mallory. I didn't think you had it in you." And now the diva impressed the detective by calmly bending down to flick a cockroach off the toe of her shoe. "But you'll never get a conviction based on that *theory.*" She plucked a small handkerchief from her dress pocket. The embroidered linen was so fine it was almost transparent. She wiped the fingernail that had come in contact with the insect.

So the woman of steel was . . . squeamish.

"You're a realist, Mallory. You know I'll never see the inside of a courtroom."

True enough. This woman had too many hostages in high office, too much extortion evidence banked away to suffer one day in jail.

"But what've you got left, Grace? I took away your control of the Driscol Institute. No more power. I took all your cash, too. And then there's Humphrey's millions. I can keep *that* money frozen in probate till you die. . . . For my last trick, I can take

Phoebe away from you."

Grace crushed the handkerchief in her hand, her only sign of anxiety. "We both know my daughter will never stand trial for murder. Not if she's —"

"Crazy? Well, Grace, that might be a stretch. Phoebe has great organizational skills. You know why she moved into that cottage behind the school? She needed privacy to assemble her murder kit — starting with the dolly she stole from your landscaper. And that was seven years ago. She's the queen of long-range planners. Impressed the hell out of everybody. We've never *seen* this kind of premeditation."

Grace feigned interest in a twitchy roach that sat on a cardboard carton at her eye level, and they watched one another, the socialite and the bug. This duo never noticed the detective unholstering her weapon. And then — BAM — the roach was smashed under the butt of the gun. Grace jumped in her skin, and the handkerchief fluttered to the floor.

So satisfying.

"Now, what was I saying?" Mallory leaned down to pick up the delicate square of fine linen, and she used it to clean bug guts from her revolver. "Oh, right — premeditation. Your daughter found the lawyers to get

Humphrey out of that asylum. She needed all three victims in town at the same time. Phoebe was so patient — *years* of waiting and collecting things to kill them. Most of the stuff in her murder kit was stolen, but not the chloroform. She couldn't use yours. Phoebe says that bottle is almost as old as you are — a souvenir from your father's day. So she mixed up her own batch with an Internet recipe."

Done with cleaning her gun, Mallory waved the roach-stained handkerchief, scattering tiny body parts as she spoke. "And your daughter knows right from wrong. All of this makes her legally sane — but that doesn't mean she's not crazy. It's *my* call. I can do what I want with Phoebe. All those politicians you bought? . . . They belong to me now."

The two women stared at each other, both of them so very still. Taking them for furniture, a mouse crept between them and sat down to lick its front paws.

Mallory smiled.

The mouse ran for cover.

"What do you want, Detective?"

Lying came easily, and Mallory was believed when she said, "Restitution."

And so their deal was begun. Grace's daughter would be judged incompetent to stand trial by reason of mental defect. Within a year or so, when some incompetent psychiatrist could be found to pronounce Phoebe cured, Toby Wilder would become the richest drug addict in New York City — if he could stay alive long enough to collect — just long enough for the ultimate end-game, one that had nothing to do with money. A beautiful and terrible payback would come when Grace was not expecting it.

Lessons of Phoebe: Mallory had learned how to wait.

FORTY-FIVE

My father doesn't own a gun. I've looked everywhere, in every drawer and closet, all through the night.

— ERNEST NADLER

This week, the Louis Markowitz Floating Poker Game had assembled at Rabbi Kaplan's home in suburban Brooklyn, a borough where people were not stacked up in towers, but lived in proper houses with lawns front and back. He opened a window to an evening breeze, and the scent of mown grass came inside to mingle with odors of beer and cigar smoke. David Kaplan joined the small gathering around his favorite piece of furniture, an oak table with a green felt top, to indulge his love of cards and close friends.

Edward Slope, wielding a knife, presided over platters with all the makings for triple-decker sandwiches, and Robin Duffy exchanged Charles Butler's money for poker

637

chips. White chips were a nickel, and red cost a dime. But the blue ones were twenty-five cents — high stakes.

The foster child of the game's founder was rarely in attendance anymore. It was the rabbi's theory that Kathy Mallory had lost patience with rules that allowed deuces wild when the moon was full. Jacks, of course, were always wild when it rained, and treys whenever it snowed. The rabbi would concede that a hundred such rules were perhaps too many. Or maybe Kathy had simply grown tired of winning so easily. Nevertheless, he set out the traditional chair for her, though he knew she would certainly not come tonight.

Maybe next week.

David Kaplan was a patient man, and he had great faith in the power of enduring love to drive her to the screaming edge of crazy and wear her down. Eventually. But not tonight.

And so it was a great surprise to hear his doorbell ring.

Detective Riker followed the rabbi into the den, and he smiled to see familiar faces. All the men on Mallory's hit list were seated in club chairs around the poker table. "Lou always said I had a standing invitation. You guys got a problem with that?"

"Not at all." Dr. Slope used his cigar to point the detective to the empty chair. "You were always welcome, but Lou told us you hated the game."

"He meant I'd hate *this* game." And now that Riker had set the tone for his visit, he pulled up a chair, lit up a cigarette and accepted a cold beer from his host. "I hear you guys play like old ladies." He popped the bottle cap. "I heard that from Mallory. I think she was twelve years old at the time." The detective laid two papers down in front of the chief medical examiner. "Could you sign these?"

The top sheet was the standard form to admit a junkie to the doctor's private rehab clinic for treatment. Edward Slope scanned the second sheet, a voucher, the city's promise to pay. "No way this is legal. Willy Fallon pleaded out. Why would Toby Wilder be —"

"Maybe it's not *strictly* legal," said Riker, "but it's fair. That kid lost four years of his life — and more."

Slope pushed the papers to one side, unsigned. "Then Mr. Wilder can sue the city. And good luck to him."

The detective shrugged as he dropped a ten-dollar bill on the table. Robin Duffy exchanged it for chips that would have totaled a thousand dollars in a game for grown-ups. But long ago the stakes were fixed within the limits of a child's allowance money. Lou Markowitz had devised this ritual poker night around his Kathy, a cold little alien spawn who would have gone friendless without these players, these very decent men.

Riker had come here to slaughter them.

He had not expected Slope to sign off on a city voucher. The chief medical examiner was legendary for scrupulous honesty. "Okay, screw the voucher. What about all those charity beds?"

"Every bed has a long waiting list," said Edward Slope.

No sale.

As guest of honor, Riker was offered the deck. He dealt out cards with the skill and speed of a born hustler, and that got their attention. So it came as no surprise to the other players when he announced, "Tonight we play cutthroat. The name of the game is five-card stud." Mallory's favorite. Back in her puppy days, she had walked in on a game in the station-house lunchroom, and not Lou's kinder, gentler brand of poker. That day, Riker, with an eye for raw talent, had staked the child to a seat at the table with men who carried *real* cash and guns. Now he reiterated little Kathy's rule. "No stupid wild cards."

No mercy.

The first bets were made on the two cards dealt to each of them, one faceup and the hole card facedown. Nickel chips clicked into a pile at the center of the table. When the doctor's turn came round, he raised them all by a dime. *What a shark.* The detective finished off the deal with three more cards to every player, and they all wanted in, perhaps forgetting that weather conditions and moon cycles no longer improved their chances.

Riker liked his hand, and he was standing pat. "Cards? Anybody?" He dealt them to takers with discards all around the clockwise circle. The last one he dealt to the doctor, and he leaned toward the man, lowering his voice to say, "Just so you know — Mallory's the one who wants to keep Toby Wilder alive. But she won't ask you for help. I guess she figures you don't owe her any favors."

For a moment, it seemed as though even Dr. Slope's cigar smoke was frozen.

No one despised junkies more than Mallory did. The doctor must find it curious that she would want one for a pet. Riker had also wondered about that. He could not always follow the plays of his partner's old game with Slope, one that had begun in her childhood — scorched-earth warfare.

With the next raise of the bet, Robin Duffy folded his cards to bow out of this round, and he did it with a smile. "Is Kathy coming tonight?"

"No," said Riker, "she's pissed off at you guys. I'm just keeping her seat warm till she gets over it."

The retired lawyer was stunned. "Why would Kathy be mad at us?"

"Well, maybe not *you.*" Who could be mad at Duffy? Riker turned to Charles Butler. "But you did your best to sabotage her case." And when the man could make no sense of this, the detective gave him a hint. "Coco? Mallory's material witness?" With a nod to the rabbi, he said, "And I hear you did your part. Talking to a judge behind her back? That was —"

"I can't believe I'm hearing this." David Kaplan had a wounded look as he pressed one hand to his breast, his heart. "Kathy *ratted* on me?" And when the man smiled and raised the bet, that was Riker's clue that the rabbi would run the best bluff in the game. But that was not saying much — not in this crew.

"David's not to blame," said Charles

Butler. "It was all my doing. That child has special needs. She —"

"The kid needed protection, and she *got* it — from Mallory." This dropped bomb was a reminder that his partner had risked her badge to keep Rolland Mann away from Coco. And now for the kill shot, Riker reached out and flicked Charles's cards with one finger. "You got nothin'."

A deep blush confirmed this, and the psychologist laid down his cards, saying, "I'm out."

Two players down — two to go.

Riker looked at his own cards and grinned like a winner, the same grin he wore when aiming his gun, a fair warning for hardened felons to give up or else. And the rabbi folded.

Only the doctor would not back down. And that had been predictable. Edward Slope was known to be reckless and daring with nickels and dimes.

The bet was raised again as Riker pushed all his chips to the center of the table. "I can guess why Mallory's pissed off at you, Doc. You had to jerk her around on those autopsies." The detective stared at his cards, head shaking. "Naw, that's not it. Sniper shots across dead bodies — that's just business as usual with you two. Maybe I missed something?" He smiled at the doctor. "What did you *do* to her?"

Edward Slope was all in to the last nickel chip when the cards were called. He laid down a pair of tens — and lost everything. Riker turned up his hole card to show the man three of a kind. And now the detective finally understood what Lou had meant when the old man once said that he had to cheat to lose to these guys.

The doctor's cache was gone, and he could buy no more chips. This was the most sacred rule of the Louis Markowitz Floating Poker Game, and no man would break it. So now Dr. Slope must sit out the rest of an evening that had just begun.

"Doc?" Riker gathered up the deck and shuffled it. "How about a side bet? Fast game of high card." He tapped the admission form for Toby Wilder. "This against everything I got."

Slope, who saw himself as a reincarnated riverboat gambler — yeah, *right* — would not be able to resist a play like that one. He looked to his friends, and there were nods all around the table. The other players had no problem with this loophole in the old rule.

Riker cut the deck and palmed a queen so that he could play a lowly three of hearts, though he had been told he could draw a worse card and still win. When Slope cut the deck, the detective could see, by the tell of flickered eyes, that the doctor's card was way higher.

"You win," said Edward Slope to the detective who had surely lost. The doctor covered his unshown card with the rest of the deck and shuffled twice. After signing the junkie's admission form, he crumpled up the voucher. "No charge to the city. I have rules. The boy's on scholarship."

Charles Butler leaned toward his friend. "Edward, I could write a check to cover the —"

"No, you *couldn't*." The doctor, a gentleman who paid his own debts — whether he owed them or not — handed the admission form to Riker.

The detective had what he came for, and now he took his leave.

Well played.

Charles Butler could only speculate on Edward's reason for throwing the game of high card. The good doctor fancied that he was born with a poker face that gave away no tells, but Charles could tell. What had his friend done to Mallory to account for such a guilty present? He might wager that even Riker would have no idea.

Ah, but just now, Charles was feeling his own remorse in matters of fireflies and shoelaces. On the following evening, he would go to Mallory's apartment with flowers in hand, his tokens of regret, and she would not be at home to him. But one night, the tenth or a twelfth night, she would open the door, and they would begin again as strangers, for he would not presume to know her.

He stood by the window, watching Riker slouch down the Brooklyn sidewalk, no doubt heading for a subway station. In this modern world, what the detective had done tonight might be called quaint and courtly. The man had avenged fair lady and won her a prize, and he had done this in a way that Mallory never could have managed. For one thing, the event was bloodless. And *shame* was not a word in her lexicon, nor a weapon in her arsenal.

Riker came to the end of the rabbi's tree-lined block and turned a corner. He bowed down to the open window of his partner's personal car. "It worked — play for play." Climbing into the passenger seat, he handed over his winnings, the admission form for Toby Wilder's drug program. "So *now* will you tell me? Why did Dr. Slope have to win — so he could lose?"

Mallory lowered the silver convertible's ragtop and turned up the radio, killing the idea of more conversation as they rolled through the neighborhood of lighted windows and green lawns.

He had run a game on the doctor with absolute faith in Mallory's script, but he had no clue why it had to end with Edward Slope's own beau geste. The detective was forced to reach into his store of old Gary Cooper movie titles to find those foreign words for the handsome gesture that would not abide any thanks. Though the idea of blackmail worked much better. Did Mallory have something on the doctor? No. It was too hard to imagine the chief medical examiner making a single misstep. Maybe the man *did* owe her a favor.

There was no point in asking; she would never say. He only turned his head in her direction, and the volume of the radio was jacked up higher.

Blasting tunes of rock 'n' roll, they sailed across the Brooklyn Bridge decked out in strings of light running all the way to Manhattan. A beautiful night. Wasted on him. His thoughts were still on the game of high card. Blackmail or payback — why not call in her own damn chips? Had she sent in a proxy to save the doctor's face? No. Their whole game, Slope's and Mallory's, was one protracted round of dodging knives and bullets; any show of civility would cost her points. So what was tonight all about? Only one thing was certain: The junkie's welfare was incidental. Mallory cared nothing about Toby Wilder now that her case was wrapped. She placed all his kind just below the level of a bug's kneecaps.

He would never figure this one out. It would cost him a night's sleep, and it would drive him crazy for a *long* time. Of course, that was no concern to Mallory. She was still angry with him for not sharing his dirty leverage on the chief of D's. That crime of holding out on her would never be forgiven.

But there *would* be payback.

Riker grinned, and then he laughed. The woman behind the wheel was good at poker — better than him — but driving him nuts, *that* was Mallory's get-even game tonight.

After showing her badge at the gate, Mallory drove into the parking lot of a large Victorian country house that Edward Slope had converted into a rehab clinic. This place allowed the doctor to derail young addicts on their journey to an overdose and his dissection table. Rarely did any patients leave until their drug programs were finished. The surrounding pine trees hid a formidable security fence.

Her passenger, Toby Wilder, was skin-crawling edgy and more awake than he wanted to be — thanks to a hospital stomach pump. Given the chance, he would dig up his dead parents and sell the corpses for a couple of pills to end his withdrawal hell.

Well, *tough.*

Mallory stepped out of her car and opened the trunk to remove a suitcase she had packed for him. "I put the rest of your stuff in storage. The apartment's gone." He might have forgotten that part. The junkie had been barely conscious when she had him sign his name to surrender the lease. "You've got no place to go back to."

Toby climbed out of the passenger seat, nodding his understanding that she had cut his legs out from under him. He took the bag from her hand and carried it as he followed her up the steps — entirely too compliant. She knew he planned to run as soon as her car rolled out the gate, but that escape fantasy would end the first time he was dragged back from the electrified fence, a crude form of shock therapy.

Together, they crossed the verandah to

enter the clinic. Its large reception room would pass for an upscale hotel lobby if not for the nurse behind the front desk. Mallory handed this man an admission form and filled out paperwork to complete the drug addict's transfer from a city hospital.

Two orderlies appeared on either side of Toby Wilder. Before the new patient was led away, Mallory placed a small parcel into his hands. "You'll need this."

When she was outside in the parking lot once more, she sat behind the wheel of her car, going nowhere, only staring at the windshield, impervious to a starry night. She had a lot riding on the junkie's survival. Dr. Slope's program had high success rates, but it was not a sure thing. What of Toby's chances? He was so wasted in his body and his mind. She saw only desolation for him in the days ahead.

But tonight there would be music.

Toby carried Detective Mallory's gift into his room at the rehab clinic, and he laid himself down on the bed. After adjusting the earphones of the CD player, he powered it up to get at the music inside. The orchestration of notes from the walls back home came alive in the opening bars to the overture, welling up in a giant wave of sound, and then subsiding and sliding into his jazz symphony. In the background, a piano played out the story, and up-front drums beat with the rhythm of a banging heart.

Early in this musical score — in the springtime of his father's life — when life was still good for Jess Wilder, when the man was sane and young and beautiful, the saxophone was a charismatic dazzle of rippling melody and riffs, attracting a crowd of coronets and strings, trombones and other voices.

The boy on the bed bobbed his head, keeping time, keeping up with the daddy sax.

FORTY-SIX

These are my superpowers. I run like a rabbit. I shiver like a whippet. I can scream like a little girl. And I remain the dead wino's witness.

— ERNEST NADLER

More than a year had passed. Another summer was drawing to a close, and Coco was chasing lightning bugs in the far-off state of Illinois.

Following an anonymous tip, an assistant district attorney with a yellow bowtie was found to have a pattern of selling generous plea bargains to fund his futile election-year races. Cedrick Carlyle had recently left his office in handcuffs, and a messy loose end was tied up.

Mallory was a tidy detective.

Willy Fallon had lost an eye during a fight in the prison laundry, almost poetic in a biblical way — that forfeit eyeball in balance with the mutilation of a little boy.

In Mallory's own twisted take on scripture, vengeance was hers, and she was not quite done. The young detective sat in the drawing room of the Upper West Side mansion, holding pen to paper, and she signed as a witness to the transaction between Grace Driscol-Bledsoe and Toby Wilder's attorney, a blind man who had seen the light and learned to do as he was told.

By the terms of a probate agreement, restitution had come due following a sanity hearing held this afternoon. As promised, Mallory had not attended. She had done nothing to block the early release of Phoebe Bledsoe, a somewhat misguided murderess, now pronounced cured.

Yeah, *right.*

"What a waste of money," said the former doyenne of New York charities. "That boy will die of a drug overdose before he turns thirty."

"Maybe," said Mallory, who had no faith in happy endings, but she believed in getting even. Humphrey's millions now belonged to Toby Wilder, and the deal was done.

Almost done.

The lawyer left. The detective stayed.

■ ■ ■ ■

Now that her daughter had been ransomed, Grace Driscol-Bledsoe waited for Mallory to leave — and she *waited.* And then, as a pointed invitation to *get out,* she said, "Our business is concluded."

"Not quite." The detective held in her hands a small book encased in a plastic bag and a tin box the size of a brick. She seemed to be weighing them, one against the other.

"Hard feelings, my dear?" Oh, it must be irksome to stand this close to a killer — one that the law could not touch. But must the detective stand *so* close? Grace stared at the box and the book. The younger woman handled them carefully — like treasures — or bombs. "You should be gone before my daughter —"

"When Phoebe gets out, she'll come straight to you."

Grace tilted her head to one side. What now? Small talk was out of character for this unwanted guest. "You know damn well my supervision was a condition of her release." And Phoebe had nowhere else to go. Her little cottage had been rented out from under her during the yearlong absence in an asylum for the rich and criminally crazy. The rental income had been sorely needed in the wake of Mallory laying waste to a fortune.

The detective looked around the drawing room. "Where's Hoffman? Oh, right, you can't afford a full-time nurse anymore."

"No . . . I can't." Life had been a bit harsh since the tax men had come to the door, citing cash expenditures beyond her means, seeking their share of that unreported income, and then confiscating the monthly rents on the cottage that was once her daughter's home.

"But you don't need hired help . . . now that Phoebe's going to live here."

"And I have you to thank for that." This was said with acrimony. There was *much* to thank Mallory for, but now there were no funds to hire some unspeakable act that would properly show her gratitude. Grace also lacked the influence to have the detective fired. The only remaining power card had been played as the single threat of scandal on a grand scale: If she stood trial for any crime, a great many politicians would keep her company in prison.

Grace's eyes were drawn back to the detective's belongings. A tiny clasp was now visible on the book. Could this be another one of Ernest Nadler's diaries? And what was in the tin box?

"What a comfort," said Mallory, "a loving child to look after you in your golden years."

The younger woman's tone was disturbing; no one else could make that platitude sound like a threat. "Yes, I'm sure we'll be happy together, Phoebe and I." The socialite stalked out of the drawing room and into the entry hall, another hint that this visit was over. Behind her she heard no sound of following footsteps on the marble tiles. When she turned around, she sucked in her breath. There was Mallory. So close — striking distance. Grace's hand went to the medallion on her breast — her panic button, and she instantly regretted this show of weakness. "Was there something else, Detective?"

"You're a lot braver than Willy's and Aggy's parents. They didn't want anything to do with their killer kids. But those people aren't in your league, Grace."

"You mean they're not monsters . . . like *me*." Oh — was there too much pride in her voice? "My dear, if that's your best shot —"

"It isn't." The detective snapped on a pair of latex gloves and then removed the leatherbound volume from its plastic bag. "Phoebe kept a journal. I found it last year — the

656

day I brought her in." The tin box was lodged safely under one arm as Mallory opened the little book. One searching finger trailed along handwritten lines. "Here it is. . . . Poor Allison." The detective looked up from her reading. "You remember her — a little red-haired girl? She was pushed off the school roof two years before the Nadler boy died."

"Allison Porter jumped! It was —" Grace's mouth went dry, and her voice cracked on the word, "— *suicide.*"

"Murder," said Mallory. "I had a long talk with the school's night watchman. Maybe you know Mr. Polanski. He was the handyman in those days, and he saw Allison fall. Then he went to the roof to see if there were more kids up there. He found the little girl's panties and brought them to the headmaster, the one who retired. I tracked him down, too. He told me those panties were collected by someone from the DA's Office, a man with a yellow bowtie . . . and that's how I know your son murdered her — *that* and the little girl's red hair. Did Allison scream? Is that why Humphrey pushed her off the roof — to shut her up?"

"You don't know what you're —"

"Phoebe knows. . . . She's always known."

Impossible.

"Poor Allison," said Mallory. "I can't find a case file on her — not even a police report. Was that your practice run for cleaning up the mess of Ernest Nadler? Here's a creepy thought. Did you pay Cedrick Carlyle a little extra to put the underpants back on that little girl's dead body?"

"Old business, Detective. Don't even think of —"

"The chalk girl in the school garden." Mallory turned a page of the journal. "That's an old tradition, right? It always appears on the first day of spring — a chalk outline of a little girl to mark the spot where Allison fell and died." The detective closed the book. "That must've driven you wild. Poor Allison just wouldn't go away."

"Get out!"

"Phoebe's the one who drew the chalk girl on the garden flagstones — so no one could forget what happened, and she hardly knew Allison. But then you sicked those three brats on Ernie Nadler — Phoebe's friend, her *best* friend. She *loved* him — even tried to rebuild him — a dead boy that can walk and talk."

Grace turned away and retreated to the center of the great hall. "I won't listen to any more of your —" This time, she heard deliberate footsteps coming up behind her, coming for her, and now she could sense the younger woman's heat at her back, and she could feel Mallory's breath on her neck with every spoken word.

"When Phoebe strung up Humphrey and his friends, I don't think she cared if they lived or died. She was marking the Ramble, the place where they tortured Ernie . . . just another version of the chalk girl in the garden. Phoebe couldn't let you get away with erasing her best friend. . . . It was making her *crazy.*"

"Hoffman!"

"Hoffman's gone," said Mallory. "Did you forget? Maybe you had another stroke. Maybe you're having one now."

"Enough!" Grace whirled around to face the smiling detective. "You've already taken *everything.*"

"Not quite."

"What more could you possibly —"

"I want you to read this." Mallory held out the journal. "Just a few pages. The last entry was written the day of Phoebe's arrest." And when Grace was slow to accept the book, the young woman thrust it into her hands. "*Read* it . . . before Phoebe comes home."

Grace opened the journal, her eyes downcast to scan her daughter's neat lines of script, and she found herself mentioned in every passage. Page after page regurgitated Phoebe's past, a child's hell on earth, where monsters and Mommy were interchangeable evil, pages of hurt and pages of hate. The last lines framed a new and brutal, certainly fatal, scheme of a long-range planner, a madwoman whose whole heart was set on one more kill. *Matricide.*

Mallory reached out and snatched the journal. Book and metal box in hand, she crossed the hall in long-legged strides, heading for the door and never looking back when she asked, "So, Grace . . . how fast can you run?"

A rhetorical question.

The door slammed.

And shock set in.

Grace's legs would not carry her to a chair. Slowly she sank down to the cold marble floor. The medallion around her neck could summon help within minutes, policemen to defend her against her own child. And after they took Phoebe away, what then? Years might pass without a crippling stroke, solitary years of growing fear. Or her inheritance might come tomorrow, the massive stroke that awaited every Driscol, the one that would send her down a long passage of infirmity and drooling degradation — as a pauper in the hands of strangers — a hell that might last thirty years.

Canny Mallory had left her two grim options, though the detective would certainly have guessed the outcome, the least nightmarish choice.

Grace did not press the panic button, but her fingers curled around the medallion as if it were a crucifix, a conduit for prayer. "Let it be quick."

Hours passed by with no drag of time, more like a flight of minutes only. Night fell, and she was sitting in the dark when she heard a hand try the knob on the front door. Now came the metallic sound of a key in the lock — Phoebe's key.

Backlit by street lamps, her daughter was silhouetted in the open doorway, growing larger, moving closer. But Grace's last thought was not of impending death. No, she was picturing the tin box in Mallory's hands. Odd to be thinking of that. And now she would never know what was —

Mallory walked down the dimly lit corridor of wooden frames and chicken-wire walls to stop by the Nadlers' storage cage. As she unlocked the door, things began to stir inside, a scramble of bugs and vermin. A mouse ran across the bare mattress on the boy's bed, still running when it cleared the edge, its paws madly pedaling on the air.

The detective turned on a floor lamp.

In one hand, she held the remains of Ernest Nadler. It had taken a long time to find him, hunting through forged documents and the crematoriums of three states. Dr. Kemper, the hospital administrator, had paid from his own pocket to have the boy's body — the evidence — reduced to ashes, but no payment for an urn — only a nasty tin box with a child inside.

Mallory, in turn, had destroyed Dr. Kemper.

With only this box in her hand and the threat of a public trial for conspiracy in the murder of a little boy, he had elected to go quietly to jail on a lesser charge. As for his partner in evidence tampering, the pathologist, Dr. Woods, was dead of a drunk's failed liver.

Big fish, little fish — all accounted for — almost done.

Just tidying up.

And toward that end, Phoebe's journal — with her mother's fingerprints on the binding, the proof of fair warning — was placed in the drawer of a nightstand. There it kept company with a murdered boy's diary and the brief note his parents had left behind. Absent any mention of living heirs in the Nadlers' will, and given the slow plodding way of city bureaucracy, many years might go by before anyone visited here again, and then no probate clerk would ever figure out what the detective had done.

In the squad-room mythology of Mallory the Machine, she had no shred of sentiment, neither empathy nor sympathy, and the young woman showed no emotion as she sat down amid the detritus of a small family's life, her cold eyes passing over their belongings to focus on an orphan sock.

Mallory laid the box of ashes on the mattress. And now that she had put him to bed, she switched off the light. "Good night, Ernie."

A child had made a stand, he had suffered and died. And then, though long gone, the little boy had snagged his unsentimental paladin with a kindred lament scrawled in a diary: *I'm lost.*

ABOUT THE AUTHOR

Carol O'Connell is the author of eleven previous books, nine featuring Mallory, and the stand-alone novels *Judas Child* and *Bone by Bone.* She lives in New York City.